ALSO BY E. L. DOCTOROW

CITY OF
GOD

CITY OF GOD

A Novel

E. L. Doctorow

RANDOM HOUSE

NEW YORK

All rights reserved under International and Pan-American
Copyright Conventions. Published in the United States by
Random House, Inc., New York, and simultaneously in Canada by
Random House of Canada Limited, Toronto.

RANDOM HOUSE and colophon are registered trademarks
of Random House, Inc.

Owing to limitations of space, acknowledgments of permission to quote
from previously published material will be found at the back of the book.

Library of Congress Cataloging-in-Publication Data
Doctorow, E. L.
City of God : a novel / E. L. Doctorow. — 1st ed.
p.   cm.
ISBN 0-679-44783-0 (alk. paper)
1. City and town life—New York (State)—New York—Fiction.
2. New York (N.Y.)—Fiction.   3. Spiritual life—Fiction.   I. Title.
PS3554.O3 C57   2000
813'.54—dc21   99-053215

Random House website address: www.atrandom.com
Printed in the United States of America on acid-free paper
2 4 6 8 9 7 5 3
First Edition
Book design by Victoria Wong

to
Alison
Gabriel
Graylen
Annabel
and
TK

CITY OF
GOD

So the theory has it that the universe expanded exponentially from a point, a singular space/time point, a moment/thing, some original particulate event or quantum substantive happenstance, to an extent that the word *explosion* is inadequate, though the theory is known as the Big Bang. What we are supposed to keep in mind, in our mind, is that the universe didn't burst out into pre-existent available space, it was the space that blew out, taking everything with it in a great expansive flowering, a silent flash into being in a second or two of the entire outrushing universe of gas and matter and darkness-light, a cosmic floop of nothing into the volume and chronology of spacetime. Okay?

And universal history since has seen a kind of evolution of star matter, of elemental dust, nebulae, burning, glowing, pulsing, everything flying away from everything else for the last fifteen or so billion years.

But what does it mean that the original singularity, or the singular originality, which included in its submicroscopic being all space, all time, that was to voluminously suddenly and monumentally erupt into concepts that we can understand, or learn—what does it mean to say that . . . the universe did not blast into being through space but that space, itself a property of the universe, is what blasted out along with everything in it? What does it mean to say that space is what expanded, stretched, flowered? Into what? The universe expanding even now its galaxies of burning suns, dying stars, metallic monuments of stone, clouds of cosmic dust, must be filling . . . something. If it is expanding it has perimeters, at present far beyond any ability of ours to measure. What do things look like just at the instant's action at the edge of the universe? What is just beyond that rushing, overwhelming parametric edge before it is overwhelmed? What is being overcome, filled, enlivened, lit? Or is there no edge, no border, but an infinite series of universes expanding into one another, all at the same time? So that the expanding expands futilely into itself, an infinitely convoluting dark matter of ghastly insensate endlessness, with no properties, no volume, no transformative elemental energies of light or force or pulsing quanta, all these being inventions of our own consciousness, and our consciousness, lacking volume and physical quality in itself, a project as finally mindless, cold, and inhuman as the universe of our illusion.

I would like to find an astronomer to talk to. I think how people numbed themselves to survive the camps. So do astronomers deaden themselves to the starry universe? I mean, seeing the universe as a job? (Not to exonerate the rest of us, who are given these painful intimations of the universal vastness and then go about our lives as if it is no more than an exhibit at the Museum of Natural History.) Does the average astronomer doing his daily work understand that beyond the celestial phenomena given to his study, the calculations of his radiometry, to say nothing of the obligated awe of his professional life, lies a truth so monumentally horrifying—this ultimate context of our striving, this conclusion of our historical intellects so hideous to contemplate—that even one's turn to God cannot alleviate the misery of such profound, disastrous, hopeless infinitude? That's my question. In fact if God is involved in this matter, these elemental facts, these apparent concepts, He is so fearsome as to be beyond any human entreaty for our solace, or comfort, or the redemption that would come of our being brought into His secret.

—At dinner last night, code name Moira. After having seen her over the course of a year or two and having spoken to her only briefly, always with the same sign within myself, I have come to recognize some heightened degree of attention, or a momentary tightness in the chest, perhaps, or a kind of, oddly, nonsexual arousal, that usually gives way in a moment to a sense of loss, to a glimpse of my own probably thrown away life, or more likely of the resistant character of life itself in refusing to be realized as it should be . . . I understood as I found myself her dinner partner why, finally, it was worthwhile to endure a social life in this crowd.

She wears no makeup, goes unjeweled, and arrives habitually underdressed in the simplest of outfits for an evening, her hair almost too casually pinned or arranged, as if hastily done up at the last minute for whatever black-tie dinner she has been dragged to by her husband.

Her quiet mien is what I noticed the first time I met her—as if she were thinking of something else, as if she is somewhere else in all our distinguished surroundings. Because she did not demand attention and was apparently without a profession of her own, she could seem entirely ordinary among the knockout women around her. Yet she was always the object of their not quite disguisable admiration.

A slender, long-waisted figure. Fine cheekbones and dark brown eyes. The mouth is generous, the complexion an even ecru paleness that, unblemished by any variation, seems dispensed over her face as if by lighting. This Slavic evenness, particularly at her forehead under the pinned slant of hair, may account at least in part for the reigning calmness I have always felt from her.

She nodded, smiled, with a clear direct look into my eyes, and took her place at the table with that quietness of being, the settledness of her that I find so alluring.

Things went well. *Let me entertain you.* . . . I spoke my lines trippingly on the tongue. She was responsive, appreciative in her quiet way. On my third glass of Bordeaux, I thought, under cover of the surrounding conversations, I should take my chances. My confession drew from her an appreciative and noncommittal merriment. But then color rose to her cheeks and she stopped laughing and glanced for a moment at her husband, who sat at the next table. She picked up her fork and with lowered eyes attended to her dinner. Characteristically, her blouse had fallen open at the unsecured top button. It was apparent she wore nothing underneath. Yet I found it impossible to imagine her having an affair, and grew gloomy and even a bit ashamed of myself. I wondered bitterly if she elevated the moral nature of every man around her.

But then, when dessert was about to be served, the men were instructed to consult the verso of their name cards and move to a new table. I was seated next to a woman TV journalist who expressed strong political views at dinner though never on the screen, and I was not listening, and feeling sodden and miserable, when I looked back and found . . . Moira . . . staring at me with a solemn intensity that verged on anger.

She will meet me for lunch up near the museum and then we'll look at the Monets.

—And everything flying away from everything else for fifteen or so billion years, affinities are established, sidereal liaisons, and the stars slowly drift around one another into rotating star groups or galaxies, and in great monumental motions the galaxies even more slowly convene in clusters, which clusters in turn distribute themselves in linear fashion, a great chain or string of superclusters billions of light-years on end. And in all this stately vast rush of cosmosity, a small and obscure accident occurs, a chance array of carbon and nitrogen atoms that fuse into molecular existence as a single cell, a speck of organic corruption, and, *sacre bleu,* we have the first entity in the universe with a will of its own.

Message from the Father:
—Everett@earthlink.net

Hi, the answers to your questions, in order: the Book of Common Prayer; surplice; clerical collar with red shirt; in direct address, Father, in indirect, the Reverend Soandso (a bishop would be the Right Reverend); my man was Tillich, though some would stick me with Jim Pike. And the stolen cross was brass, eight feet high. You are making me nervous, Everett.

Godbless,
Pem

—**Heist**

This afternoon in Battery Park. Warm day, people out. Soft autumn breeze like a woman blowing in my ear.

Rock doves everywhere aswoop, the grit of the city in their wings.

Behind me the financial skyline of lower Manhattan sunlit into an island cathedral, a religioplex.

And I come upon this peddler of watches, fellow with dreadlocks, a big smile. Standing tall in his purple chorister's robe. His sacral presence not diminished by the new white Nikes on his feet.

"Don't need windin, take em in de showerbat, everyting proof, got diamuns 'n such, right time all de time."

A boat appears, phantomlike, from the glare of the oil-slicked bay: the Ellis Island ferry. I will always watch boats. She swings around, her three decks jammed to the rails. Sideswipes bulkhead for contemptuous New York landing. Oof. Pilings groan, crack like gunfire.

Man on the promenade thinks it's him they're after, breaks into a run.

Tourists down the gangplank thundering. Cameras, camcorders, and stupefied children slung from their shoulders.

Lord, there is something so exhausted about the NY waterfront, as if the smell of the sea were oil, as if boats were buses, as if all heaven were a garage hung with girlie calendars, the months to come already leafed and fingered in black grease.

But I went back to the peddler in the choir robe and said I liked the look. Told him I'd give him a dollar if he'd let me see the label. The smile dissolves. "You crazy, mon?"

Lifts his tray of watches out of reach: "Get away, you got no business wit me." Looking left and right as he says it.

I was in mufti—jeans, leather jacket over plaid shirt over T-shirt. Absent cruciform ID.

And then later on my walk, at Astor Place, where they put out their goods on the sidewalk: three of the purple choir robes neatly folded and stacked on a plastic shower curtain. I picked one and turned back the neck and there was the label, Churchpew Crafts, and the laundry mark from Mr. Chung.

The peddler, a solemn young mestizo with that bowl of black hair they have, wanted ten dollars each. I thought that was reasonable.

They come over from Senegal, or up from the Caribbean, or from Lima, San Salvador, Oaxaca, they find a piece of sidewalk and go to work. The world's poor lapping our shores, like the rising of the global warmed sea.

I remember how, on the way to Machu Picchu, I stopped in Cuzco and listened to the street bands. I was told when I found my camera missing that I could buy it back the next morning in the market street behind the cathedral. Merciful heavens, I was pissed. But the fences were these shyly smiling women of Cuzco in their woven ponchos of red and ocher. They wore black derbies and carried their babies wrapped to their backs . . . and with Anglos rummaging the stalls as if searching for their lost dead, how, my Lord Jesus, could I not accept the justice of the situation?

As I did at Astor Place in the shadow of the great mansarded brownstone voluminous Cooper Union people's college with the birds flying up from the square.

A block east, on St. Marks, a thrift shop had the altar candlesticks that were lifted along with the robes. Twenty-five dollars the pair. While I was at it, I bought half a dozen used paperback detective novels. To learn the trade.

I'm lying, Lord. I just read the damn things when I'm depressed. The paperback detective he speaks to me. His rod and his gaff they comfort me. And his world is circumscribed and dependable in its punishments, which is more than I can say for Yours.

I know You are on this screen with me. If Thomas Pemberton, B.D., is losing his life, he's losing it here, to his watchful God. Not just over my shoulder do I presumptively locate You, or in the Anglican starch of my collar, or in the rectory walls, or in the coolness of the chapel stone that frames the door, but in the blinking cursor . . .

—

—We made our plans standing in front of one of the big blue-green paintings of water lilies. It is a matter of when she can get away. She has two young children. There is a nanny, but everything is so scheduled. We had not touched, and still did not as we came out of the Met and walked down the steps and I hailed a cab for her. Her glance at me as she got in was almost mournful, a moment of declared trust that I felt as a blow to the heart. It was what I wanted and had applied myself to getting, but once given, was instantly transformed into her dependence, as if I had been sworn to someone in a secret marriage whose terms and responsibilities had not been defined. As the cab drove off I wanted to run after it and tell her it was all a mistake, that she had misunderstood me. Later, I could only think how lovely she was, what a powerful recognition there was between us, I couldn't remember having felt an attraction so strong, so clean, and rather than being on the brink of an affair, I imagined that I might at last find my salvation in an authentic life with this woman. She lives in some genuine state of integrity almost beyond belief, a woman of unstudied grace, with none of the coarse ideologies of the time adhered to her.

===

—Drifting around town picking locations like the art director of a movie. I place St. Timothy's in the East Village, off Second Avenue around the corner from the Ukrainian hall and restaurant. There had to have been at least one church's worth of WASPs down here in the old days. Before Manhattan moved north to the sunnier open spaces above Fourteenth Street . . . St. Timothy's, Episcopal, typical New York Brownstone Ecclesiastic, little brother of the grander Church of the Ascension on lower Fifth Avenue. So to please the good Father I've now changed the name and the locale. (There is an actual old ruin of a church on East Sixth, but the wrong color, Catholic gray granite, with a steeple more like a cupola and the stained-glass bull's-eye all blown out and pigeon shit like streaks of rain on the stone. Three young men on the steps, one in the middle eyeing me as I pass, the other two covering each end of the block.)

Here in the neighborhood of St. Tim's, lots of people just getting by. On the corner, young T-shirted girl, braless, tight cutoffs, she is running in place with her Walkman. Gray-haired over-the-hill bohemian, a rummy, he affects a ponytail. Squat, short Latina, steatopygous. Stooped old man in house slippers, Yankees cap, filthy pants held up by a rope. Young black man crossing against the traffic, glaring, imperious, making his statement.

East Village generally still the six-story height of the nineteenth century. The city is supposed to deconstruct and remake itself every five minutes. Maybe midtown, but except for the Verrazano Bridge, the infrastructure was in place by the late thirties. The last of the major subway lines was built in the twenties. All the bridges, tunnels, and most of the roads and parkways, improved or unimproved, were done by the Second World War. And everywhere you look the nineteenth is still here—the Village, East and West, the Lower East Side, Brooklyn Bridge, Central Park, the row houses in Harlem, the iron-fronts in Soho . . .

The city grid was laid out in the 1840s, so despite all we still live with the decisions of the dead. We walk the streets where generations have trod have trod have trod.

But, Jesus, you're out of town a couple of days and it's hypershock. Fire sirens. Police-car hoots. Ritual pneumatic drilling on the avenues. The runners in their running shorts, the Rollerblades, the messengers. Hissing bus doors. Sidewalk pileups for the stars at their screenings. All the restaurants booked. Babies tumbling out of the maternity wards. Building facades falling into the streets. Bursting water mains. Cop crime. Every day a cop shoots a black kid, chokeholds a perp, a bunch of them bust into the wrong apartment, wreck the place, cuff the women and children. Cover-ups by the Department, mayor making excuses.

New York New York, capital of literature, the arts, social pretension, subway tunnel condos. Napoleonic real estate mongers, grandiose rag merchants. Self-important sportswriters. Statesmen retired in Sutton Place to rewrite their lamentable achievements . . . New York, the capital of people who make immense amounts of money without working. The capital of people who work all their lives and end up broke and gray New York is the capital of boroughs of vast neighborhoods of nameless drab apartment houses where genius is born every day.

It is the capital of all music. It is the capital of exhausted trees.

The migrant wretched of the world, they think if they can just get here, they can get a foothold. Run a newsstand, a bodega, drive a cab, peddle. Janitor, security guard, run numbers, deal, whatever it takes. You want to tell them this is no place for poor people. The racial fault line going through the heartland goes through our heart. We're color-coded ethnic and social enclavists, multiculturally suspicious, and verbally aggressive, as if the city as an idea is too much to bear even by the people who live in it.

But I can stop on any corner at the intersection of two busy streets, and before me are thousands of lives headed in all four directions, uptown downtown east and west, on foot, on bikes, on in-line skates, in buses, strollers, cars, trucks, with the subway rumble underneath my feet . . . and how can I not know I am momentarily part of the most spectacular phenomenon in the unnatural world? There is a specie recognition we will never acknowledge. A primatial over-soul. For all the wariness or indifference with which we negotiate our public spaces, we rely on the masses around us to delineate ourselves. The city may begin from a marketplace, a trading post, the confluence of waters, but it secretly depends on the human need to walk among strangers.

And so each of the passersby on this corner, every scruffy, oversize, undersize, weird, fat, or bony or limping or muttering or foreign-looking, or green-haired punk-strutting, threatening, crazy, angry, inconsolable person I see . . . is a New Yorker, which is to say as native to this diaspora as I am, and part of our great sputtering experiment in a universalist society proposing a world without nations where anyone can be anything and the ID is planetary.

Not that you shouldn't watch your pocketbook, lady.

=

—Uncounted billions of years idle away as this single-cell organism, this speck of corruption, this submicroscopic breach of nonlife, evolves selectively through realms of slime and armor-plated brutishness, past experimental kingdoms of horses two feet tall and lizards that fly, into the triumphant dominions of the furry self-improving bipeds, those of the opposed thumb and forefinger, who will lope out of prehistory to sublime into a teenage nerd at the Bronx High School of Science.

Of the brilliant boys I knew at Science whose minds were made to solve mathematical problems and skip happily among the most abstruse concepts of physics, a large number were jerks. I've since run into a few of them in their adulthood and they are still jerks. It is possible that the scientific character of mind is by its nature childish, capable through life of a child's wonder and excitements, but lacking real discernment, lacking sadness, too easily delighted by its own intellect. There are exceptions, of course, the physicist Steven Weinberg, for example, whom I've read and who has the moral gravity you would want from a scientist. But I wonder why, for instance, the cosmologists and astronomers, as a whole, are so given to cute names for their universe. Not only that it began as the Big Bang. In the event it cannot overcome its own gravity, it will fly back into itself, and that will be the Big Crunch. In the event of a lack of density, it will continue to expand, and that will be the Big Chill. The inexplicable dark matter of the universe that must necessarily exist because of the behavior of galactic perimeters is comprised of either the neutrino or of weakly interacting massive particles, known as WIMPs. And the dark-mattered halos around the galaxies are massive compact halo objects, or MACHOs.

Are these clever fellows mocking themselves? Is it a kind of American trade humor they practice out of modesty, as the English practice self-denigration in their small talk? Or is it bravery under fire, that studied carelessness in the trenches while the metaphysical rounds come in?

I think they simply are lacking in holy apprehension. I think the mad illiterate priest of a prehistoric religion tearing the heart out of a living sacrifice and holding it still pulsing in his two bloodied hands . . . might have had more discernment.

=

—Heist

Tuesday evening

Up to Lenox Hill to see my terminal. Ambulances backing into the emergency bay with their beepings and blinding strobe lights. They used to have QUIET signs around hospitals. Doctors' cars double-parked, patients strapped on gurneys double-parked on the sidewalk, smart young Upper East Side workforce pouring out of the subway.

Lights coming on in the apartment buildings. If only I were elevating to a smart one-bedroom . . . a lithe young woman home from her interesting job awaiting my ring . . . uncorking the wine, humming, wearing no underwear.

In the fluorescent lobby, a stoic crowd primed for visiting hours with bags and bundles and infants squirming in laps. And that profession of the plague of our time, the security guard, in various indolent versions.

My terminal's room door slapped with a RESTRICTED AREA warning. I push in, all smiles.

You got medicine, Father? You gonna make me well? Then get the fuck outta here. The fuck out, I don't need your bullshit.

Enormous eyes all that's left of him. An arm bone aims the remote like a gun, and there in the hanging set the smiling girl spins the big wheel.

My healing pastoral visit concluded, I pass down the hall, where several neatly dressed black people wait outside a private room. They hold gifts in their arms. I smell nonhospital things . . . a whiff of fruit pie still hot from the oven, soups, a simmering roast. I stand on tiptoe. Who is that? Through the flowers, like a Gauguin, a handsome light-complected black woman sitting up in bed. Her bearing regal, her head turbaned. I don't hear the words, but her melodious, deep voice of prayer knows whereof it speaks. The men with their hats in their hands and their heads bowed. The women with white kerchiefs. On the way out I inquire of the floor nurse. SRO twice a day, she says. We get all of Zion up here. The only good thing, since Sister checked in I don't have to shop for supper. Yesterday I brought home some baked pork chops. You wouldn't believe how good they were.

—Another one having trouble with my bullshit is the widow Samantha. In her new duplex that looks across the river to the Pepsi-Cola sign, she's been reading Pagels on early Christianity.

It was all politics, wasn't it? she asks me.

Yes, I sez to her.

And so whoever won, that's why we have what we have now?

Well, with a nod at the Reformation, I suppose so, yes.

She lies back down. So it's all made up, it's an invention.

Yes, I sez, taking her in my arms. And you know for the longest time it actually worked.

Used to try to make her laugh at the dances at Brearley. Couldn't then, can't now. A gifted melancholic, Sammy. The dead husband an add-on.

But almost alone of the old crowd she didn't think I was throwing my life away.

Wavy thick brown hair parted in the middle. Glimmering dark eyes set a bit too wide. Figure not current, lacking tone, glory to God in the Highest.

From the corner of the full-lipped mouth her tongue emerges and licks away a teardrop.

And then, Jesus, the surprising condolence of her wet salted kiss.

-for the sermon

Open with that scene in the hospital, those good and righteous folk praying at the bedside of their minister. The humility of those people, their faith glowing like light around them, put me in such longing . . . to share their trustfulness.

But then I asked myself: Must faith be blind? Why must it come of people's *need* to believe?

We are all of us so pitiful in our desire to be unburdened, we will embrace Christianity or any other claim of God's authority for that matter. Look around. God's authority reduces us all, wherever we are in the world, whatever our tradition, to beggarly submission.

So where is the truth to be found? Ecumenism is politically correct, *but what is the case?* If faith is valid in all its forms, are we merely making an aesthetic choice when we choose Jesus? And if you say, No, of course not, then we must ask, Who are the elect blessedly walking the true path to salvation . . . and who are the misguided others? Can we tell? Do we know? We think we know—of course we think we know. But how do we distinguish our truth from another's falsity, we of the true faith, except by the story we cherish? Our story of God. But, my friends, I ask you: Is God a story? Can we, each of us examining our faith—I mean its pure center, not its consolations, not its habits, not its ritual sacraments—can we believe anymore in the heart of our faith that God is our story of Him? To presume to contain God in this

Christian story of ours, to hold Him, circumscribe Him, the author of everything we can conceive and everything we cannot conceive . . . in *our* story of *Him? Of Her? OF WHOM?* What in the name of Christ do we think we are talking about!

—*Wednesday lunch*

Well, Father, I hear you delivered yourself of another doozy.

How do you get your information, Charley? My little deacon, maybe, or my kapellmeister?

Be serious.

No, really, unless you've got St. Timothy bugged. Because, God knows, there's nobody but us chickens. Give me an uptown parish, why don't you, where the subway doesn't shake the rafters. Give me one of God's midtown showplaces of the pious rich and famous and I'll show you what doozy means.

Now listen, Pem, he says. This is unseemly. You are doing and saying things that are . . . worrying.

He frowns at his grilled fish as if wondering what it's doing there. His well-chosen Pinot Grigio shamelessly neglected as he sips ice water.

Tell me what I should be talking about, Charley, if not the test to our faith. My five parishioners are serious people, they can take it.

Lays the knife and fork down, composes his thoughts: You've always been your own man, Pem, and in the past I've had a sneaking admiration for the freedom you've found within church discipline. We all have. And in a sense you've paid for it, we both know that. In terms of talent and brains, the way you burned up Yale, you probably should have been my bishop. But in another sense it is harder to do what I do, be the authority that your kind is always testing.

My kind?

Please think about this. A tone has crept up, a pride of intellect, something is not right.

His blue eyes look disarmingly into my own. Boyish shock of hair, now gray, falling over the forehead. Then his famous smile flashes over his face and instantly fades, having been the grimace of distraction of an administrative mind.

What I know of such things, Pem, I know well. Self-destruction is not one act, or even one kind of act. It may start small and appear insignificant, but as it gathers momentum it is the whole man coming apart in every direction, all three hundred and sixty degrees.

Amen to that, Charley. You don't suppose there's time for a double espresso?

Oh, and his other line: We're absolutely at a loss to know what is going on inside you, Father. But I'm pretty sure you are not availing yourself of the strength to hand.

That may well be, Bishop, I should have said. But at least I don't do séances.

===

—This afternoon, two soft taps on the door. At the beginning it was awkward, looking at my books, the prints on the walls, my digs. She drank only water from the tap. In thrall to her quietness, I had not much to say. She went into the bedroom and closed the door. All was silence. Finally I went in. She was in bed with the covers up to her chin. She was skittish, balky, turned her head away from my kiss. She had to be dragged into it. She had to be held down to do what she had come to do.

Afterward it was as if I lay in the blue-green warmth of Monet's pond, feeling the wet lilies clinging to my skin.

===

—Heist

Friday

All right, that wise old dog Tillich, Paulus Tillichus—how did he construe the sermon? Picked a text and worried the hell out of it. Sniffed the words, pawed them: What, when you get right down to it, is a *demon*? You say you want to be *saved*? What does that mean? When you pray for *eternal life,* what do you think you're asking for? Paulus, God's philologist, that Merriam-Webster of the DDs, that German . . . shepherd. The suspense he held us in—bringing us to the edge of secularism, arms waving. Of course he saved us every time, pulled us back from the abyss and we were okay after all, we were back with Jesus. Until the next sermon, the next lesson. Because if God is to live, the words of our faith must live. The words must be reborn.

Oh did we flock to him. Enrollments soared.

But that was then and this is now.

We're back in Christendom, Paulus. People are born again, not words. You can see it on television.

Saturday morning

Following his intuition, Divinity Detective wandered over to the restaurant-supply district on the Bowery, below Houston, where the trade is brisk in used steam tables, walk-in freezers, grills, sinks, pots, woks, and bins of cutlery. Back behind the Taipei Trading Company, too recently acquired to have a sales tag, was the antique gas-operated fridge with the mark of my shoe sole still on the door where I kicked it when it wouldn't stay closed. And in one of the bins of the used dish department, the tea things from our pantry, white with a green trim, gift of the dear departed ladies' auxiliary.

Practically named my own price, Lord. With free delivery. A steal.

evening

I walk over to Tompkins Square, find my dealer friend on his bench.

This has got to stop, I say to him.

My, you riled up.

Wouldn't you be?

Not like the Pops I know.

I thought we had an understanding. I thought there was mutual respect.

They is. Have a seat.

Sparrows working the benches in the dusk.

Told you wastin your time, but I ast aroun like I said I would. No one here hittin on Tim's.

Not from here?

Thasit.

How can you be sure?

This regulated territory.

Regulated! That's funny.

Now who's not showin respeck. This my parish we talkin bout. Church of the Sweet Vision. They lean on me, see what I'm sayin? I am known for compassion. No one lies to me. You dealin with foreigners or some such, thas my word to you.

Ah hell. I suppose you're right.

No problem. Unsnaps attaché case: Here, my very own personal blend. No charge. Relax yoursel.

Thanks.

Toke of my affection.

Monday night

I waited in the balcony. If something stirred, I'd just press the button and my 6-volt Bearscare Superbeam would hit the altar at one hundred eighty-six thousand miles per second—same cruising speed as the finger of God.

The amber crime-prevention streetlights on the block making a perfect indoor crime-site of my church. Intimations of a kind of tarnished air substance in the vaulted spaces. The stained-glass figures yellowed into lurid obsolescence. For how many years has this church been home to me? But all I had to do was sit up in the back for a few hours to understand the truth of its stolid indifference. How an oak pew creaks. How a passing police siren in its two Doppler pitches is like a crisis being filed away in the stone walls.

And then, Lord, I confess, I dozed. Father Brown would never have done that. But there was this crash, as if someone had dropped a whole load of dishes. The pantry again—I had figured them for the altar. I raced my bulk down the stairs, my Superbeam held aloft like a club. I think I was shouting. As in "Cry God for Tommy, England, and St. Tim!" How long had I been asleep? I stood in the doorway, found the light switch, and when you do that, for an instant the only working sense is the sense of smell: hashish in that empty pantry. Male body odor. But also the pungent sanguinary scent of female pheromone. And something else, something else. Like lipstick, or lollipop.

The dish cabinets—some of the panes shattered, broken cups and saucers on the floor, a cup still rocking.

The alley door was open. My sense of a bulk of something moving out there. A deep metallic bong sounds up through my heels. Someone curses. It's me, fumbling with the damn searchlight. I swing the beam out and see a shadow rising with distinction, something with right angles in the vanished instant of the turned corner.

I ran back into the church and let my little light shine. Behind the altar, where the big brass cross should have been, was a shadow of Your crucifix, Lord, in the unfaded paint of my predecessor's poor taste.

What the real detective said: Take my word for it, Padre. I been in this precinct ten years. They'll hit a synagogue for the whatchamacallit, the Torah. Because it's handwritten? Not a mass-produced item? It'll bring, a minimum, five K. Whereas the book value for your cross has got to be zilch. Nada. No disrespect, we're related, I'm Catholic, go to mass, but on the street there is no way it is anything but scrap metal. Jesus! whata buncha sickos.

Tuesday

Mistake talking to the *Times*. Such a sympathetic young man. I didn't understand anything till they took the cross, I told him. I thought they were just crackheads looking for a few dollars. Maybe they didn't understand it themselves. Am I angry? No. I'm used to being robbed. When the diocese took away my food-for-the-homeless program and merged it with one across town, I lost most of my parish. That was a big-time heist. So now these people, whoever they are, have lifted our cross. It bothered me at first. But now I'm beginning to see it differently. That whoever stole the cross had to do it. And wouldn't that be blessed? Christ going where He is needed?

Wednesday

Phone ringing off the hook. One coldly furious bishop. But also pledges of support, checks rolling in. Including some of the old crowd, pals now of my dear wife, who had thought my diction quaint, like hearing Mozart on period instruments. Tommy will now play us a few pieties on his viola da gamba. I count nine hundred and change here. Have I stumbled on a new scam? I tell you, Lord, these people just don't get it. What am I supposed to do, put up a barbed wire fence? Wrap up my church like the Reichstag?

The TV news people swarming all over. Banging on my door.

Mayday Mayday! I will raise the sash behind this desk, drop nimbly to the rubbled lot, pass under the window of Ecstatic Reps where the lady with the big hocks is doing the treadmill, and I'm gone. Thanks heaps, Metro section.

=

—This just in . . . the elusive invisible heretofore only deduced neutrino has a detectable mass. How is this verified? There's this cult of neutrino physicists, and all over the world they're building great huge tanks to hold heavy water deep inside mountains, under the Aegean Sea, on the bottom of Lake Baikal in Siberia, in tunnels under the Alps, below the Antarctic ice cap . . . so they can watch the flying neutrinos that can slip so easily, effortlessly through the diameter of the earth, like bats at night flooping behind your ear and lifting your strands of hair with their wing wind—and detect with powerful light sensors the minuscule voltage emitted by the neutrinos plunging through the dark giant tanks of pure heavy water. . . . Some say Enrico Fermi figured out the neutrino had to exist. He may have given it its name, but unknown to all but me, the neutrino was discovered at the Bronx High School of Science, in the study hall one afternoon in 1948, when this fat jerk of a kid, Seligman, borrowed my algebra homework to copy and in return privileged me with the information that he'd proven the existence of a subatomic particle that had no physical properties whatsoever. So excited that he sprayed me with his words, very unpleasant. On the other hand we both got grades of 100 for our homework.

Well if the neutrino is, after all, something with mass and it is monumentally present throughout the universe, why . . . shouldn't that define dark matter? And doesn't it suggest that space is not empty, not merely the capacity of distance between objects, but itself a qualified substance . . . and so far beyond our sensing abilities, like dog whistles, like ghosts, that for all our science nerdwork, we are just beginning to understand we are only at the beginning? I mean, if the universe has such mass, will it inevitably cease to inflate? There'll be this moment of peace, a universe at neap tide, everything still, and then, with a little groan and creak, it will quietly shift into its shrink mode, slowly and then more quickly sucking itself back in the direction of itself again. And then what? Never mind the Big Crunch. What will it have left behind, vacated? Nothing? How can there be nothing! That was what Leibniz wanted to know: How, he said, can there be nothing? And what if neutrinos in their uncountable multitudinous dark-matteredness gravitationally directing the universe . . . are the souls of the dead? Has that ever been considered by the hotshots of the Bronx High School of Science?

Jesus, I think I am going crazy.

=

—The Midrash Jazz Quartet Plays the Standards

ME AND MY SHADOW

Me and My shadow,
Strolling down the avenue.
Me and my shadow
Not a soul to tell our troubles to . . .
And when it's twelve o'clock
We climb the stair
We never knock
For nobody's there
Just me and my shadow
All alone and feeling blue.

The song speaks of oneself shadowed by loneliness
The singer of the song may be a shadow of himself
He could be singing, "Me and the me that's a shadow
    of me,
We are here in this nameless avenue
We don't see anyone else in view,
Must be they're under the apple tree
Left the whole damn city to my shadow
    and me."
He is saying the Fall of Man is misery:

"I hear no footsteps but my own
And the avenue goes straight on down
    between the tall buildings
For miles and miles, and the lights turn green
And the lights turn red,
As if it mattered, as if there were metered
    taxis and trucks and cars and buses
Bumper to bumper, hellish ruckuses
Of horns blowing, cops blowing their whistles
A river of people, eddying souls
The avenue flowing as far as you can see
    with millions of folks none of them me.
But that's not what I see. I'm all alone
I'm casting my shadow on a sunny pavement
Scuttling along in the street of my enslavement
    chained to my shadow, bone by bone."
And then the singer hears the clock strike twelve—
    is it noon or the midnight hour?
Is it the end of time, the end of the time
    of His patience?
The singer's way to heaven is an open door in space.
He thinks, If there's no heaven
    beyond this door—
If there is nothing more for this poor mortal,
    why have I been brought here,
What is this life for?

                                        (*tentative applause*)

But think for a moment what a shadow portends
The sun is in its heaven,
    that's what that means,
This may not be the world that's on your string
But this is God's world, there is goodness there is sin
We have to learn the difference
    again and again
Your shadow is the Good Lord's light not passing
    through you,
You are dense, you're opaque

that ought to tell you
   something, for God's sake!
At twelve o'clock when my time comes to an end?
I know that I will climb the stairway to
   heaven!
I will hear them say, Don't bother knocking
   the gate is open!
I will feel His warm celestial light shine down upon me
And when I turn around my shadow will be gone!
Sent back down to bring another soul along!
O happy day, when the bell begins to toll
   for all the world's poor souls—
I can tell you they won't be feeling blue
When they find out it's His glory they've been
   strolling to!

                             (*enthusiastic applause*)

The singer is saying, "Of all the troubles I've seen
The last and worst is the trouble of never again
   having someone to tell my troubles to."
In fact he's saying, "I'd be trouble-free
If I had someone to listen other than me."
This is a mourning song of love lost
Remembering a time of past happiness
When he was one half of a fine-looking high-stepping
   couple enjoying a walk on the day of rest
Where now he has only his own pale shadow for company.
And it's not as if this isn't some festive scene
   everything in color, alive and humming
   with other fine-looking high-stepping couples
   on their Sabbath walk under the flags
   in the warmth of the morning sun
So that it might be an Easter parade of the city's
   population—
Not at all. The rest of this city is turned out in its
   best
Whereas for him, singing a dirge of his soul's lost
   romance

Alone, independent, he's atonal, he is
    dissonance.
And when he reaches the destination
    of all shadowed beings,
the most silent and mysterious of
    buildings,
Before he can knock the door swings open
And he steps into the darkness
    of the shadow cast by God.
And the singer has to acknowledge
    as he steps through the door,
"In His shadow I am nothing, don't even have my shadow
    anymore."

                                         (*a few hands clapping*)

Shadow me,
    shadow you,
    what's a shadow
    gonna do . . .
Up at dawn,
    hides at noon,
    evening comes
    does the moon
Go to ground,
    make no sound,
    mourners done,
    shadow's gone.

—What if there's no heaven, just a door?
—I don't even have my shadow anymore . . .
—We don't know the glory we are strolling toward . . .
—Gone, shadow's gone.

Me and My shadow,
Strolling down the avenue.
Me and my shadow
Not a soul to tell our troubles to . . .

                                       (*wild acclaim*)

—That the universe, including our consciousness of it, would come into being by some fluke happenstance, that this dark universe of incalculable magnitude has been accidentally self-generated . . . is even more absurd than the idea of a Creator.

Einstein was one physicist who lived quite easily with the concept of a Creator. He had a habit of calling God the Old One. That was his name for God, the Old One. He was not a stylish writer, Albert, but he chose words for their precision. One way or another God is very old . . . because archaeologists in the fifties discovered a sacred ossuary cave of the Neanderthals on the Tyrrhenian coast of the Pomptine Fields in western Italy. They found the skull of a male buried within a circle of stones. The cranium had been severed from the jaw and brow and used for a drinking bowl. That's how old God is. So Einstein is right about that. And *One* . . . because God is by definition not only unduplicable and all-encompassing but also without gender. So the phrase is really very exact: the Old One. Not much in the way of a revelation, of course. Albert thought of his work in physics as tracking God, as if God lived in gravity, or shuttled between the weak nuclear force and the strong nuclear force, or could be seen now and then indolently moving along at one hundred eighty-six thousand miles per second . . . not exactly the concerned God people pray to or petition, but, hell, it's a start, it's something, if not everything we have if we want to be true to ourselves.

—Heist

Wednesday

Trish giving a dinner when I got here. The caterer's man who let me in thought I was a latecomer. Now I think about it, I was looking straight ahead as I passed the dining room, a millisecond of time, right? Yet I saw everything: which silver, the floral centerpiece. She's doing the veal paillard dinner. Château Latour in the Steuben decanters. Oh what a waste. Two of the hopefuls present, the French UN diplomat, the boy-genius mutual fund manager. Odds on the

Frenchman. The others all extras. Amazing the noise ten people can make around a table. And in this same millisecond of candlelight, Trish's glance over the rim of the wine glass raised to her lips, those cheekbones, the amused blue eyes, the frosted coif. That fraction of an instant of my passage in the doorway was all she needed from the far end of the table to see what she had to see of me, to understand, to know why I'd slunk home. But isn't it terrible that after it's over between us the synapses continue firing coordinately? What do you have to say about that, Lord? All the problems we have with You, we haven't even gotten around to Your small-time perversities. I mean, when an instant is still the capacious, hoppingly alive carrier of all our intelligence? And it's the same damn dumb biology when, however moved I am by another woman, the tips of my fingers are recording that she isn't Trish.

But the dining room was the least of it. It's a long walk down the hall to the guest room when the girls are home for the weekend.

We are on battery pack, Lord, I forgot the AC gizmo. And I am exhausted—forgive me.

=

In the E-mail:

"dear father if u want to no where yor cross go to 2531 w 168 street apt 2A where the santeria oombalah father casts the sea shels an cuts the chickns troats."

"Dear Reverend, We are two missionaries of the Church of Jesus Christ of the Latter-day Saints (Mormon) assigned to the Lower East Side of New York . . ."

"Dear Father, I am one of a group of your neighbors in nearby New Jersey who have taken a Sacred Oath to defend this Republic and the name of Our Lord Jesus Christ from alien heathen interlopers wherever they may arise, even if from the federal government. And I mean defend—with skill, and organizational knowhow and the only thing these people understand, The Gun that is our porrogative to hold as free white Americans . . ."

===

—This afternoon as we lay side by side on our backs Moira told me about herself: She grew up in a working-class family in Pennsylvania. She went to Penn State for two years before dropping out and leaving for New York. She thought a job in publishing would be nice but in the meantime was working as a temp in a corporate headquarters when her future husband, the CEO, happened to notice her. I knew the rest of the story: He had her assigned to his own secretarial staff, took her out a few times, proposed, and set about terminating his twenty-year marriage. You find invariably among CEOs that life is business. There is an operative cruelty which is seen as an entitlement. In another era, spats and top hats, he might have gone to the theater and picked out a girl in the chorus line. We are not so flamboyant now, we have culture, real art hangs on the office walls, we sprinkle our dinner parties with novelists, filmmakers. We know who Wittgenstein was.

For her part, Moira severed the little connection she had with her family by not inviting them to her wedding.

And that is the genealogy of her serene certitude, and her charming air of being unimpressed to be among them, that the men and women of our set, myself included, found so intriguing.

I feel deceived not by her but by appearances: how real they can be in my America. I feel no animus for her husband, I hardly know him. He's a powerful figure in business often quoted in newspaper articles about the economy. She said he is a child who needs her unceasing admiration and praise. He worries constantly about his position in the business world, she has to listen to his anguished reports of matters she does not really understand and suffer his wild private swings from vanity and pride to whining self-doubt. He is afflicted with nameless fears, he has night sweats, and often expresses his dread that everything he's made for himself, everything he owns, will one day be taken away from him. Including me, she said by way of conclusion.

She turned on her side. She was smiling. Including me, she said again, whispering and then putting her tongue in my ear.

═

—When a song is a standard, it can reproduce itself from one of its constituent parts. If you recite the words you will hear the melody. Hum the melody and the words will form in your mind. That is an indication of an unusual self-referential power—the physical equivalent would be limb regeneration, or cloning the being from one cell. Standards from every period of our lives remain cross-indexed in our brains, to be called up in whole or in part, or to come to the mind unbidden. Nothing else can as suddenly and poignantly evoke the look, the feel, the smell of our times past. We use standards in the privacy of our minds as signifiers of our actions and relationships. They can be a cheap means of therapeutic self-discovery. If, for example, you are deeply in love and thinking about her and looking forward to seeing her, pay attention to the tune you're humming. Is it "Just One of Those Things"? You will soon end the affair.

═

—Heist

Yesterday, Monday,
voice mail from a Rabbi Joshua Gruen of the Synagogue of Evolutionary Judaism on West Ninety-eighth Street: It is in your interest that we meet as soon as possible. Clearly not one of the kooks. When I call back he is cordial but will answer no questions over the phone. So okay, this is what detectives do, Lord, they investigate. Sounded a serious young man, one religioso to another, mufti or collar? I go for the collar.

The synagogue a brownstone between West End and Riverside Drive, a steep flight of granite steps to the door. I deduce Evolutionary Judaism includes aerobics. Confirmed when I am admitted. Joshua (my new friend) a trim five-nine in sweatshirt, jeans, running shoes. Gives me a firm handshake. Maybe thirty-two, thirty-four, good chin, well-curved forehead. No yarmulke atop his wavy black hair.

A converted parlor cum living room with an Ark at one end, a platform table to read the Torah on, shelves with prayer books, and a few rows of bridge chairs, and that's it, that's the synagogue.

Second floor, introduces me to his wife, who puts her caller on hold, stands up from her desk to shake hands, she too a rabbi, Sarah Blumenthal, in blouse and slacks, pretty smile, high cheekbones, no cosmetics, needs none, light hair short au courant cut, granny glasses, Lord my heart. She is one of the assistant rabbis at Temple Emanuel. What if Trish wore the collar, celebrated the Eucharist with me? Okay laugh, but it's not funny when I think about it, not funny at all.

Third floor, I meet the children, boys two and four, in their native habitat of primary-color wall boxes filled with stuffed animals. They cling to the flanks of their dark Guatemalan nanny, who is also introduced like a member of the family . . .

On the back wall of the third-floor landing is an iron ladder. Joshua Green ascends, opens a trapdoor, climbs out. A moment later his head appears against the blue sky. He beckons me upward, poor winded Pem so stress-tested and entranced . . . so determined to make it look effortless, I could think of nothing else.

I stood finally on the flat roof, the old apartment houses of West End Avenue and Riverside Drive looming at either end of this block of chimneyed brownstone roofs, and tried to catch my breath while smiling at the same time. The autumn sun behind the apartment houses, the late afternoon river breeze on my face. I was feeling the exhilaration and slight vertigo of roof-standing . . . and did not begin to think, until snapped to attention by the rabbi's puzzled, frankly inquiring gaze that asked why did I think he'd brought me there, why he'd brought me there. His hands in his pockets, he pointed with his chin to the Ninety-eighth Street frontage, where, lying flat on the black tarred roof, its transverse exactly parallel to the front of the building, its upright pressed against the granite pediment, the eight-foot hollow brass cross of St. Timothy's, Episcopal, lay tarnished and shining in the autumn sun.

I suppose I'd known I'd found it from the moment I heard the rabbi's voice. I bent down for a closer look. The old nicks and dents.

Some new ones too. It was not all of a piece, which I hadn't known: The arms were bolted to the upright in a kind of mortise-and-tenon idea. I lifted it at the foot. It was not that heavy, but clearly too much cross to bear on the stations of the IRT.

How did Rabbi Joshua Gruen know it was there?

An anonymous phone call. A man's voice. Hello, Rabbi? Your roof is burning.

The roof was burning?

If the children had been in the house I would have gotten them out and called the Fire Department. As it was, I grabbed our kitchen extinguisher and up I came. Not the smartest thing. Of course, the roof was not burning. But modest as it is, this is a synagogue. A place for prayer and study. And as you see a Jewish family occupies the upper floors. So was he wrong, the caller?

He bites his lip, dark brown eyes averted from the cross. It is an execrable symbol to him. Burning its brand on his synagogue. Burning down, floor through floor, like the template of a Christian church. I want to tell him I'm on the Committee for Ecumenical Theology of the Trans-Religious Fellowship. A member of the National Council of Christians and Jews.

This is deplorable. I am really sorry about this.

It's hardly your fault.

I know, I say. But this city is getting weirder by the minute.

The rabbis offered me a cup of coffee. We sat in the kitchen. I felt quite close to them, both our houses of worship desecrated, the entire Judeo-Christian heritage trashed.

This gang's been preying on me for months. And for what they've gotten for their effort, I mean, one hit on a dry cleaner would have done as much. Listen, Rabbi—

—Joshua.

Joshua. Do you read detective stories?

He cleared his throat, blushed. Only all the time, Sarah Blumenthal said, smiling at him.

Well, let's put our minds together. We've got two mysteries going here.

Why two?

This gang. I can't believe their intent was, ultimately, to commit an anti-Semitic act. They have no intent. They're not of this world. And all the way from the Lower East Side to the Upper West Side? No, that's asking too much of them.

So this is someone else?

It must be. Somebody took the cross off their hands—if they didn't happen to find it in a dumpster. And then this second one or more persons had the intent. But how did they get it onto the roof? And nobody saw them, nobody heard them?

Angelina, whom I think you met with the children: She heard noises from the roof one morning. We were already gone. That was the day I went to see my father, Sarah said, looking to Joshua for confirmation. But the noise didn't last long and Angelina thought no more of it, that it was a repairman of some sort. We assume they came up through one of the houses on the block. The roofs abut.

Did you go down the block? Did you ring bells?

Joshua shook his head.

What about the cops?

They exchanged glances. Please, said Joshua. The congregation is new, not much more than a study group, just a beginning. A green shoot. The last thing we need is that kind of publicity. Besides, he says, that's what they want, whoever did this.

We don't accept the ID of victim, said Sarah Blumenthal, looking me in the eye.

And now I tell you, Lord, as I sit here back in my own study, in this bare ruined choir, I am exceptionally sorry for myself this evening, lacking as I do a companion like Sarah Blumenthal. This is not lust, and you know I would admit it if it were. No, but I think how quickly I took to her, how comfortable I was made, how naturally welcomed I was made to feel under these difficult circumstances. There is a freshness and honesty about these people, both of them I mean, they were so present in the moment, so self-possessed, a wonderful young couple with a quietly dedicated life, what a powerful family stronghold they make, and, oh Lord, he is one lucky rabbi, Joshua Gruen, to have that beautiful devout by his side.

It was Sarah, apparently, who made the connection. He was sitting there trying to figure out how to handle it and she had come in from a conference somewhere and when he told her what was on the roof she wondered if that was the missing crucifix she had read about in the newspaper.

I hadn't read the piece and I was skeptical.

You thought it was just too strange, a news story landing in your lap, Sarah said.

That's true. News is what happens somewhere else. And to realize that you know more than the reporter knew? But we found the article.

He won't let me throw out anything, Sarah says.

Fortunately in this case, says the husband to the wife.

It's like living in the Library of Congress.

So thanks to Sarah, we now have the rightful owner.

She glances at me, colors a bit. Removes her glasses, the scholar, and pinches the bridge of her nose. I see her eyes in the instant before the specs go back on. Nearsighted, like a little girl I loved in grade school.

I am extremely grateful, I say to my new friends. This is, in addition to everything else, a mitzvah you've performed. Can I use your phone? I'm going to get a van up here. We can take it apart, wrap it up, and carry it right out the front door and no one will be the wiser.

I'm prepared to share the cost.

Thank you, that won't be necessary. I don't need to tell you but my life has been hell lately. This is good coffee, but you don't happen to have something to drink, do you?

Sarah going to a wall cabinet. Will scotch do?

Joshua, sighing, leans back in his chair. I could use something myself.

The situation now: my cross dismantled and stacked like building materials behind the altar. It won't be put back together and hung in time for Sunday worship. That's fine, I can make a sermon out of that. The shadow is there, the shadow of the cross on the apse. We will offer our prayers to God in the name of His indelible Son, Jesus Christ. Not bad, Pem, you can still pull these things out of a hat when you want to.

I'd been just about convinced it really was a new sect of some kind. I thought, Well, I'll keep a vigil from across the street, watch them take St. Tim's apart brick by brick. Maybe help them. They'll reassemble it as a folk church somewhere. An expression of their simple faith. Maybe I'll drop in, listen to the sermon now and then. Learn something . . .

Then my other idea, admittedly paranoid: It would end up an installation in Soho. Let me wait a few months, a year, and I'd look in a gallery window and see it there, duly embellished, a statement. People standing there drinking white wine. So that was the secular version. I thought I had all bases covered. I am shaken. What am I to make of this strange night culture of stealth sickos . . . these mindless thieves of the valueless who go giggling through the streets, carrying what? whatever it is! through the watery precincts of urban nihilism . . . their wit their glimmering recognition of something that once had a significance they laughingly cannot remember. Jesus, there's not even sacrilege there. A dog stealing a bone knows more what he's up to.

———

—Moira turning into a story, a woman crossing class lines. He's a bit of a snob, isn't he? Not sure I like him if he can spend his afternoons at the Met. He was shocked when she stuck her tongue in his ear. Not only the vulgarity of it, but as the act of a different person from the one he'd imagined her to be.

Only way to go with this is to rev up their moral natures, put motors in them, but then all you have is a movie.

Movie: Guy begins an affair with this really elegant trophy wife of a business leader—they are all three in the loosely bordered swirl of NY society comprised of publishing, the arts, advertising, journalism, Wall Street.

After some encouragement she turns out to be an ardent lover without guilt or self-recrimination. He can't devise anything she is unwilling to try. He is creative. She honors his every perversion and does not sulk and cannot be driven to anger.

Largely from conditions he has laid down she trains herself to ask for nothing more of the relationship than he will give. He assumes uncontested control—when they will meet, how they will conduct themselves, what endeavors he will think up for her in her torrid state of self-abasement. She is content to meet him, indulge them both, and go to her home until the next time.

But the total surrender of her will, and consequent stability of the affair, begins to bore him. He extends his control over her life with her husband: when she should withhold sex, when she should not withhold it, what clothes she must wear, what perfume, the dinners she is to order from their cook, the restaurants she is to insist upon, the destinations of their trips, even to the sheets he sleeps upon, the soap in the soap dish. It revives him to be exercising, through her, remote control of the private circumstances of her husband's life.

I see now that he is a real shithead. Why should I have anything to do with him? Once, by means of his direction, the husband finds himself with his wife in Maui—and while he, the husband, suns himself on a private beach, the lover is in his suite peeling off the wife's swimsuit, pinching up the sand grains he finds in the groinal cleft of her thigh and presenting them with a dot of his finger to the tenderest part of her person. He leaves her short of breath, she is addicted to the danger he's become to her, the threat to her well-being, her self-respect, her life.

Someone as bad as this guy has to be a star. I mean, if he were a fat bald slob who sucked air through his teeth, the audience would be repelled, aroused to indignation. Want their money back. So he is lean, fit, he takes very good care of himself in that way of someone profoundly faithless. He runs, works out almost religiously, for the self-maintenance that is his due. Drinks sparingly, does nothing to excess except plot. Makes no effort to ingratiate himself with others, does not indulge in the small talk designed to demonstrate one's unthreatening nature. He never raises his voice. When he is funny he is contemptuous, when he is angry he is quietly menacing. His selfishness is so smoothly distributed over every aspect of his life that it is not visible to others except as a patina of snobbery, a degree of arrogance that, in a better light, would be a visible ruthlessness. This is what attracts women. This is what attracted her.

I realize now his casual upper-class grace of knowing the compensations in wine, horses, sailing, and so forth derives from his former profession, that of a CIA covert-action planner with a background in foreign postings. How could it be otherwise? He evinces the condescension of one who has been on the inside of the geopolitical adventures of the cold war toward ordinary people, who get their news from the newspaper.

He is as middle-class as she is, born in upstate New York, perhaps, though it is wrong to place him precisely in that his whole life has been a training away from the specific identity attaching to a region or a family. More precisely, his nihilist moral endowment, or perhaps only the necessity of bringing the movie in under two hours, has erased any secondary compensation of character that is conferred by a religious or ethnic qualification.

By now he has wired his mistress so that he can hear the husband's private conversations with her, learn the weaknesses, the inflections of voice that betray fear or guilt, lust or love. The husband has a softness about the underchin, a mama thing in his most private moments, a desire for his wife's praise and admiration. Living with him she has felt imprisoned. The drama of his business life is like a bludgeon. She understands that his prideful attention to her in public is a kind of self-congratulation, in the same way that he will not go anywhere or accept any invitation that does not by its auspices bring honor or status to himself.

Why she has responded to the dark-hearted lover is not clearly thought out by her but is in fact what she responded to when her executive husband courted her, with the sense in both instances of rising on a tide that would lift her with immense power beyond any possibilities of freedom she could have realized for herself. But she has become as indentured to her lover and to his ways as she had been to her husband according to his, and freedom for her is realized as subjection, as an idea attainable only in its wreckage.

And so we have in these three roles three lives more or less unattached to reality, and vivified by that fact. The lover, for his part, envisions a grand finale to his enterprise that is so dangerous, so extreme, that he decides his life, heretofore adrift in boredom and alienation and the absence of serious conviction, may now be redemptively reconceived as an art form.

—This is my laboratory, here, in my skull. I can assure you that it is barely furnished. In fact, in a matter of speaking, my work has been to empty my laboratory of the furniture there, the beakers, measuring scales, cabinets, old books. While I have succeeded to some extent, there are still some things here that I can't seem to part with: the idea that the universe is designed, that there are a few simple rules, or laws, physical laws, from which all the manifold processes of life and nonlife can be derived. So you see I am hardly the undermining subversive revolutionary the Nazis of Hitler made me out to be.

Of course, the universe we have all known and seen since our childhoods is only apparently explained by the great, esteemed Sir Isaac Newton. That universe, with all the stars in the heavens and the planets turning in their orbits and night following day, and actions having reactions and objects in their gravity falling—all of it seems quite sound except to a mind like mine, nor is it the only one. Because my revered Sir Isaac's mechanical model of the universe makes one or two assumptions that cannot be proven. The idea of absolute motion and absolute rest, for example, the idea that something can move in an absolute sense without reference to anything else. This is clearly impossible, a concept that cannot be proven empirically, by reference to experience. The ship that moves on the sea does so with reference to the land. Or if you prefer with reference to another ship, moving at a greater speed or a slower speed. Or by reference to a dirigible overhead. Or to a whale beneath the sea. Or to the currents of the sea itself. Always to something. And this is true of a planet as well. There is nothing in the universe that can be proven to move absolutely without reference to something else in the universe, or for that matter without reference to the universe in its entirety.

Now, that is a very simple insistence upon which all my further thought is based. That absolute motion and absolute rest are false concepts that cannot be demonstrated. But you see the implications are enormous of this picky stubborn insistence of mine that we deal with these things only insofar as they can be proven. I'll show you, it's very simple. We will do a little thought experiment . . .

If I am in a rocket ship flying through space at millions of miles an hour . . . and you catch up to me in your rocket ship and decelerate your engines so that we are flying at the same speed side by side . . .

and a person asleep in each of our rocket ships wakes up and looks from his window into the other's window . . . without seeing the meteorites and bits of star material whizzing or drifting by . . . but seeing only into each other's cabin . . . they will not be able to say if the rocket ships are moving uniformly together or not moving at all. Because in either case the experience is the same.

You see how simple that is? I am really a simple man and I begin with the questions that a child would ask. For example, I was not much more than a child when I wondered what would happen if I traveled at the speed of light. Nothing in the universe can move faster than the speed of light. You know what that means? That means there are no instantaneous processes in our universe, because nothing can occur faster than light can move and light takes time to get from one place to another. That means for example that a person cannot be in two places at the same time. Also for example that there cannot be the ghosts which are cherished by so many people, because ghosts no more than anyone else can appear and disappear as if having taken no time to travel from one place to another. So what I realized when I was a child was that if I were traveling as fast as light while holding a mirror before me, I would not see my image in the mirror, because as fast as the image of my face in light moved toward the mirror, why, just as fast would the mirror be moving away. And there would be nothing I could see in the mirror I was holding up to my face. Yet that does not seem right. It doesn't feel that this would be the case, does it? It is a rather frightening idea, in fact, that if I moved at the speed of light, I could get no confirmation of my existence from an objective source of reflected light such as a mirror. I would be like a ghost in the universe, materially unverifiable in the stream of time.

So from this simple thought experiment I deduced the following: No object, neither mirror nor person, even a thinner person than myself, one who did not indulge in the Sacher torte or tea with raspberry jam or a scone with butter, no, not even the thinnest person alive can move through the universe with the speed of light. Because we are always visible to ourselves in our mirrors and to each other, we must move more slowly than that, though light itself is moving from the surface of our dear faces and from our mirrors at the same constant ultimate speed. We ourselves are slower than that. Even in our fastest rocket ships. Do you know what would happen if we moved toward or closer to the speed of light, going faster and faster, from zero miles an hour to one hundred and eighty-three million miles a second? Do you know what would happen to us? My goodness, we would get so leaden, heavier and heavier the faster we went, until our immense weight or density would be so great that the space around us would curve toward us and we would suck space into such density around us that . . . as fast as we might go, the less we would have the chance of attaining the speed of light . . . because the faster we moved, the more mass we would have and the more mass, the greater the resistance to our progress . . . until the celestial heaven around us would curl and bend and warp itself and us out of all recognition.

And from these few simple thoughts, perhaps simpleminded thoughts, I have discovered laws, physical laws, that alarm people to such a degree that they have decided the man in the street cannot be made to realize what I'm talking about, the revolution I have supposedly made. That I am some sort of genius to respect or even venerate while you scratch your head and say, God bless him. Look how funny, his hair is sticking up in every direction, perhaps from his having tried to fly into his mirror at the speed of light. Look at his sweatshirt, his unpressed trousers, not that this is practical for work but that forgetting to wear a coat and tie, he must be a genius. The chalk with which he writes his secret formulas on the blackboard, the chalk breaks in his hand! All this is the way the press and the radio people have relieved you of thinking about what I have to say. It is an insult not only to me but to you, because of course the human mind can always find out the truth, because however hidden it may be, eventually it will emerge. And nothing I have discovered is revolutionary, because I am seeing only what has always been as it is now and as far as I can tell always will be. It is only that our perception has become more . . . perceptive.

So: after all, we may with assurance say only the following about the Old One's universe: that nothing is constant other than the speed of light.

Of space all we may say with assurance is that it is something you measure with a ruler.

And of time all we may say is that it is something you measure with a clock.

But for the theological visions and screams and terrors this produces in our brains, I beg you do not hold me responsible.

===

—There are no science songs to speak of. No song tells you the force of gravity is a product of the masses of two objects divided by the ratio of the distance between them. Yet science teaches us something about song: Scientific formulas describe the laws by which the universe operates and suggest in equations that a balance is possible even when things are in apparent imbalance. So do songs. Songs are compensatory. When a singer asks, Why did you do this to me, why did you break my heart . . . the inhering formula is that the degree of betrayal is equivalent to the eloquence of the cry of pain. Feelings transmute as quickly and perversely as subatomic events, and when there is critical mass a song erupts, but the overall amount of pure energy is constant. And when a song is good, a standard, we recognize it as expressing a truth. Like a formula, it can apply to everyone, not just the singer.

===

—An odd sighting on the dock, a great blue heron looking out one way, almost back to back with a snowy-white egret peering in the opposite direction. This is why everyone should sometimes leave the city.

With the same food sources, I wonder that they get along, but there they stand with that mutual disregard. *I'm not looking, but I know you're there.* The egret breaks first, the neck outstretched, the yellow bayonet beak extended, a beautiful bird in flight, sleek, like a Pre-Raphaelite seaplane, but with merciless eyes . . . and the heron, looking rumpled with its round black shoulder patch, the feathered body more gray than blue, the long legs, feet, and beak black. It is a less comely bird, a less spiffy bird than the egret, although with its huge wingspan as it takes off low over the water it does achieve an airliner's stateliness. But there is a degree of sorrow in its gaze, and it is clearly a loner, a bachelor sort of bird who could use some female attention, some sprucing up, like me.

———

—**Heist**

A phone call from Rabbi Joshua:

If we're going to be detectives about this . . . we start with what we know, isn't that what you did? What I know, what I start with, is that no Jewish person would have stolen your crucifix. It would not occur to him. Even in the depths of some drug-induced confusion.

I shouldn't think so, I say, thinking, Why does Joshua feel he has to rule this out?

The police told you your cross had no value on the street. But if someone wants it, then it has value.

To an already-in-place, raging anti-Semite, for example.

Yes, that's the likelihood. This is a mixed, multicultural neighborhood. There may be people who don't like a synagogue on their block. I've not been made aware of this, but it's always possible.

Right.

But it's also possible . . . placing that cross on my roof, well, that is something that could have been arranged by an ultra-Orthodox fanatic. That's possible too.

Good God!

I'm not saying this is so. I'm just trying to consider all the possibilities. There are some for whom what Sarah and I are doing, struggling to redesign, revalidate our tradition—well, in their eyes it is tantamount to apostasy.

I don't buy it, I said. I mean, I can't think it's likely. Why would it be?

The voice that told me my roof was burning? That was a Jewish thing to say. Of course I don't know for sure, I may be all wrong. But it's something to think about. Tell me, Father—

Tom—

Tom. You're a bit older, you've seen more, perhaps you've given more thought to these things. Wherever you look in the world now, God belongs to the atavists. And they're so fierce, these people, so sure of themselves, as if all human knowledge since Scripture is not also God's revelation! I mean, is time a loop? Do you have the same feeling I have—that everything seems to be running backwards? That civilization is in reverse?

Oh my dear rabbi. Joshua. What can I tell you? If it's true and God truly does belong to the atavists, then that's what faith is and what faith does. And we are stranded, you and I.

-Monday

The front doors are padlocked. In the rectory kitchen, leaning back on the two hind legs of his chair and reading *People* magazine, is St. Timothy's newly hired, classically indolent private security guard.

I am comforted too by the woman at Ecstatic Reps. She is there, as usual, walking in place, earphones clamped on her head, her large hocks in their black tights shifting up and dropping back down like Sisyphean boulders. As the afternoon darkens she'll be broken up and splashed in the greens and pale lavenders of the light refractions on the window.

So everything is as it should be, the world's in its place. The wall clock ticks. I have nothing to worry about except what I'm going to say to the bishop's examiners that will determine the course of the rest of my life.

This is what I will say for starters: "My dear colleagues, what you are here to examine today is not a spiritual crisis. Let's get that clear. I have not broken down, cracked up, burned out, or caved in. True, my personal life is a shambles, my church is like a war ruin, and since I am not one to seek counsel or join support groups, and God, as usual has ignored my communications (no offense, Lord), I do feel some-what isolated. I will even admit that for the past few years, no, the past several years, I have not found anything better to do for my chronic despair than walk the streets of Manhattan. Nevertheless the ideas I'm going to present to you have real substance and while you may find some of them alarming I would entreat—would suggest, would recommend, would advise—I would advise you to confront them on their merits and not as evidence of the psychological decline of a mind you once had some respect for—I mean for which you once had some respect."

That's okay so far, isn't it, Lord? Sort of taking it to them? Maybe a bit touchy. After all what could they have in mind? In order of probability, one, a warning, two, a formal reprimand, three, censure, four, a month or so in therapeutic retreat followed by a brilliantly remote reassignment wherein I'm never to be heard from again, five, forced early retirement with full benefits, six, de-ordination, seven, ex-com. Whatthehell!

By the way, Lord, what are my "ideas of real substance"? The phrase came trippingly off the tongue. So, a little help here. What with today's shortened attention span I don't need ninety-five, I can get by with two or three. The point is whatever I say will alarm them. Nothing shakier in a church than its doctrine. That's why they guard it with their lives, isn't it? I mean, just to lay the *H* word on the table, it, heresy, is a legal concept, that's all. I mean the shock is supposed to be Yours, but a heretic can be of no more concern to You than someone kicked out of a co-op building for playing the piano after ten. So I pray, Lord, don't let me come up with something only worth a reprimand. Let me have the good stuff. Speak to me. Send me an E-mail.

> You were once heard to speak,
> You Yourself are a word, though deemed by some to
>   be unutterable,
> You are said to be the Word, and I don't doubt
>   You are the Last Word.
> You're the Lord our Narrator, who made a text
>   from nothing, at least that is our story
>   of You.

So here is your servant the Reverend Dr. Thomas Pemberton, the almost no longer rector of St. Timothy's, Episcopal, addressing You in one of Your own inventions, one of Your intonative systems of clicks and grunts, glottal stops and trills.

Will You show him no mercy, this poor soul tormented in his nostalgia for Your Only Begotten Son? He has failed his training as a detective, having solved nothing.

May he nevertheless pursue You? God? The Mystery?

—To assure you further that I am no genius whose ideas are too abstruse for the majority of mankind, let me give you some personal information. You will see how ordinary were my beginnings and how I was swept along like everyone else by the dreadful history of my time. I was without speech for the first three or four years of my life and after that, tongue-tied. Even into my ninth year I spoke slowly, as if dealing with a foreign language, which, as it turned out, I was. What does it matter—all language is a translation from something else and I have lived in that something else for seventy-three years.

My first memory is of the paving stones of Ulm, the ones I toddled on while I hung and sometimes swung about wildly on the axis of my wrist, in the firm grip of my papa. Each rounded stone I scuffed gave back to me its ineluctable mass. And how was it, I wondered, that the stones fit so nicely, like breadloaves in the baker's oven? Then I discovered the workmen's chisel marks which made each stone different though the same as the others. Every stone recorded its own shaping, it had the mark of its history of human work, and all the stones together represented an infinity of decisions under one plan, an intent to make a passable street. As they had—a street that went up the hill and spread suddenly in every direction into the great square of the cathedral, which was also of stone. The whole world was stone. Horse-drawn drays and carriages rolled through my vision with a great thunderous clattering that nevertheless did not end in any harm to me, and boots strode past my eyes, and swirls of ladies' skirts, and the dogged commerce of the whole city happened upon these separately sculpted stones placed one next to another long ago. And in the shadow of the great black stone cathedral, I experienced the child's revelation that he walks on the thoughts of dead men. And so the paving stones of Ulm, my medieval birthplace, are my first memory— not my mother's breast, not my bed, not a desperately loved toy, but a street, a way of passage from here to there.

My father's little engineering shop was located on the cathedral square. Here, with my uncle Jakob, he manufactured electricity motors. A wonderful whirring sound was to be heard, a soft sound with tone to it, a language of total elision, with inseparable words, the meaning instantaneous and at the same time incomplete.

The only thing like it came from the culvert that ran behind our house to carry one of the smaller tributaries of the river Blau. My mother was made very nervous by the children who played on the stone escarpment, tossing their twigs and paper boats into the stream and running along then to see the current take them. But I was a stolid, silent child. It was as if I didn't like to move too rapidly under the weight of my large head, I just stood and listened as the water flowed through its channel, laying its black slick along the stones, hissing and lapping in its passage like the busy burghers of another universe in urgent conversation.

You may think from these remarks that I attribute too much perception to my infancy. Of course I do, we all do. We go back and forth, revising our minds continuously. The entire problem of mind is of enormous interest, and yet it demands a superhuman courage to dwell on. The mind considering itself—I shudder; it is too vast, a space without dimension, filled with cosmic events that are silent and immaterial. For one's sanity it is preferable to track God in the external world.

Ulm was of course destroyed in the Second World War. Well before that war, my father and uncle took their little business to Munich, where they proposed to manufacture dynamos, arc lamps, transformers, and other electrical devices for use by municipalities. And for a while everything went well. We lived in a suburb in a big house behind a wall, where there was a garden with trees. Spring evenings were filled with the perfume of apple blossoms, here where the Nazis would be born. And now I had my little sister Maria with me, two years younger, Maja, my constant companion, whose enormous brown eyes made me laugh and for whom I captured crickets in a jar and made necklaces of dandelions.

In this house, at my mother's insistence, I began my violin studies. My mother was a musician, a pianist of resolute seriousness. For her, music was central to the education of a human being. I dutifully applied myself under the tutelage of Herr Schmied, a morose man who wore his thin hair long in homage to Paganini and whose fingers were yellowed with tobacco stain. How many years passed before I understood that notes were intervals, relationships of number, and that sound was a property of these relationships? But finally the system of music made itself clear to me and I trembled for the beauty of it, each piece the proposal of a self-contained and logical construction. I began to study in earnest. I wanted to bring precision to my bowing; I searched for the purest resonance of each note as an intellectual necessity, and the joy of making music, especially together with others, I felt as a form of mental travel within a totally reliable cosmos. Bach, Mozart, Schubert—they will never fail you. When you perform their work properly it will have the character of the inevitable, as in great mathematics, which seems always to be made of pre-existing truths.

I'll tell you by contrast the kinds of things I learned in school. I had a teacher in the Luitpold Gymnasium. When he came into the room we stood, and when he held the velvet lapels of his gown and nodded his head, we sat. This was quite normal. But I'd always thought discipline was their means of imposing intellectual rigor and maintaining alertness for the reception of ideas. And that is why in this ridiculous school we did not walk but marched, and stood and sat in unison and chanted our Latin declensions as if they were tribal oaths. It was altogether insulting, in my opinion, perhaps even deadly. After a term or two these boys lost all sparks of mind, curiosity was bludgeoned out of them, their personalities were sealed, and in recess I would sit with my back to the building and watch them running about or wrestling or kicking the football, but, whatever the game, trying undeniably to kill each other. In their recklessness, with their uniform jackets laid aside in neat piles so as not to suffer damage, was the rage of their smoldering beings dispersed helplessly among their comrades. So I saw this and kept myself apart, doing my work, which was undemanding enough, and not testing the ambiguities of possible friendship with any of them, for it was all ruination, in my view, and all from this clearly flawed Germanic principle of education through tyranny. I sat in the classroom and my mind wandered. I had been given a book by my mother's brother Casar on the subject of Euclidean geometry. I had read it as people read novels. To me it was an exciting, newsworthy book. And now on this one morning I was smiling to myself remembering the marvelous theorem of Pythagoras and the teacher was all at once standing in front of me and he slapped his map pointer across my desk to regain my attention. When the class was over, as I was on my way out with the others, he called me to the front of the room. He looked down at me from his lectern. He had a round red shiny face, this teacher, that reminded me of a caramel apple. One could bite into a face like this and expect to crack through the hard glaze to the pulp. You are a bad influence in my class, Albert, he said. I am going to have you transferred. I didn't understand. I asked what I had done wrong. You sit back there smiling and dreaming away, he said. If I don't have the attention of each and every student, how can I maintain my self-respect? With that remark I learned in a flash the secret of all despotism.

This same teacher, or perhaps it was another, it could as easily have been any of them, but no matter: He one day in class held up a rusty nail between his thumb and forefinger. A spike like this was driven through Christ's hands and feet, he said, looking directly at me.

I will say here of poor Jesus, that Jew, and the system in his name, what a monstrous trick history has played on him.

$$=$$

—Walt Whitman assures us of the transcendence of the bustle and din of New York, the sublimity, the exuberant arrogance, of the living moment. But do pictures lie? Those old silver gelatin prints . . . The drays and carriages, streetcars, els, and sailing vessels at their docks . . . A busy city, great construction pits framed out in wood, streets laid out with string. Men on their knees setting paving stones, great dimly lit lofts of women at sewing machines, men in derbies and shirtsleeves posing in the doorways of their dry-goods stores, endless ranks of clerks at their high desks, women in long skirts and shirtwaists instructing classrooms of children, couples greeting couples on Fifth Avenue, muffled-up ice skaters on the lake in Central Park . . . This is our constructed city, without question the geography of our souls, but these people are not us, they inhabit our city as if they belonged here, the presumption of their right to it is in every gesture, every glance, but they are not us, they're strangers inhabiting our city, though vaguely familiar, like the strangers in our dreams.

I feel such stillness, the stillness of listening to a story whose end I know. I am looking at times when people had a story to enact and the streets they walked upon were narrative passages. What kind of word is *infrastructure?* It is a word that proves we have lost our city. Our streets are for transit. Our stories are disassembled, the skyscrapers crowding us scoff at the idea of a credible culture.

Christ, how wrong to point out the Brooklyn Bridge or Soho or the row houses of Harlem as examples of our continuity. Something dire has happened. As if these photographs are not silent instances of the past but admonitory, like ghosts, to be of then and of now simultaneously, so as to prophesy hauntingly our forfeiture of their world, given such time only for our illusions to flourish before we're chastened into our own places in the photographs, to stand with them, these strangers of our dreams, but less distinctly, with faces and figures difficult to make out, if not altogether invisible.

═

—So I hear from Tom Pemberton and we meet for a drink at Knickerbocker's, Ninth and University Place.

He doesn't wear the collar these days, he's not defrocked but more or less permanently unassigned. Works at a cancer hospice on Roosevelt Island. He's grown heavier, the big face is more lined than I remember, but still open, candid, floridly handsome, the light, wide-set eyes moving restlessly over the room as if looking for someone to gladden his heart.

You write well enough, he says, but no writer can reproduce the actual texture of living life.

Not even Joyce?

I should look at him again. But now that I see the dissimilarity from the inside, so to speak, I think I'll be wary of literature from here on.

Good move.

You're offended. But I'm telling you you're exemplary. It's a compliment. After all, I might have chalked you off as just a lousy writer. It's unsettling reading about me from inside my mind. Another shock to another faith.

Well, maybe I should drop the whole thing.

You don't need my approval, for God's sake. I agreed to this—that's it, there are no strings. I wouldn't even ask you to keep that mention of my girls out of it. They're older now, of course. Apartments of their own.

Consider it done.

Trish is remarried. . . . Why didn't you say who her father is?

That's to come.

I still hear from him. The usual smirk from on high, though I have to say he enjoyed having a peacenik priest in the family.

Good for the image.

I suppose. But now, listen, you're using the real names. You told me—

I know. I'll change them. Just now they're still the best names. On the other hand they used to be the only possible names. So that's progress.

And it wasn't the *Times* that picked up the story of my stolen crucifix. It was only one of the free papers.

Well, Father, when you compose something, that's what you do, you make the composition. Bend time, change things, put things in, leave things out. You're not sworn to include everything. Or to make something happen the way it did. Facts can be inhibiting. Actuality is beside the point. Irrelevant.

Irrelevant actuality?

You do what the clock needs to tick.

Well there are some things just plain wrong.

Oh boy. Like what, Pem?

I'm not telling you what to write, you understand. It's hands-off. But it wasn't a sermon at St. Tim's that got the bishop on my back. And what you have me saying is not really the cause. Really it was a bunch of things.

You told me a particular sermon—

Well yes and no—I've thought about this—and I think it could have been a guest stint I did over in Newark that he felt was the last straw. But I'm not sure. By the way, it's different in that diocese, they are broad church over there. Bring in the women, the gays . . . the liberal side of the argument. My side. You don't want to oversimplify. The Anglicans are all over the lot. There's actually more leeway for people like me than you give the church credit for.

What did you say?

What?

Your bishop's last straw.

Oh—it was simple enough. I merely asked the congregation what they thought the engineered slaughter of the Jews in Europe had done to Christianity. To our story of Christ Jesus. I mean, given the meager response of our guys, is the Holocaust a problem only for Jewish theologians? But beyond that I asked them—it was a big crowd that morning, and they were with me, I could feel it, after the empty pews of St. Tim's it seemed to me like Radio City—I asked them to imagine . . . what mortification, what ritual, what practice might have been a commensurate Christian response to the disaster. Something to assure us our faith wasn't some sort of self-deluding complacency. Something to assure us of the holy truth of our story. Something as earthshaking in its way as Auschwitz and Dachau. So what would that be? I went into some possibilities. A mass exile? A lifelong commitment of millions of Christians to wandering, derelict, over the world? A clearing out of the lands and cities a thousand miles in every direction from each and every death camp? I said to them I didn't know what the proper response would be . . . but I was sure I'd recognize it if I saw it.

That's what you said?

For starters.

I see.

Yeah. That was the doozy.

—The simplest digital invasive techniques deliver the husband's brokerage and bank accounts, insurance policies and medical records, mortgage payments, school and service records, credit ratings, political contributions. All available for study and eventual confiscation. His support services, legal, accounting, investment counseling. Who and where they are. Means of communication with. Handwriting analysis. Voice analysis—an easily rendered Philadelphia twang. Analysis of a typical month's credit card and phone bills for the secrets in his life, a girlfriend, a dependent mother. Nothing. No undue trade with jewelers, florists; the husband is a squeaky-clean narcissist, the only affair, though all-consuming, is with himself.

Some ten or fifteen years older than either of them, the husband is something of a corporate wonder, the CEO of a computer manufacturing corporation, who is being courted by a Japanese conglomerate with international holdings in satellite communications, electronics, and the soft drink industry. The lover understands that at this level, effective management does not require any special knowledge of the nature of a business. He instructs his mistress to persuade her husband to accept the challenge—life in another city, regular trips to Japan, new fields to conquer. . . . This is done. Then, while the husband is busy wrapping things up at his old job, taking care to maintain cordial relations, even advising the board on his successor, the essence of corporate life being volatility and no bridge ever being burned, the wife/mistress travels to the Pacific coast in order to familiarize herself with the lay of the land, find a new house in the right neighborhood, and so on.

The lover flies with her to the new city, chooses the house, the furnishings, everything down to the smallest detail. At this point in her mind she is so in thrall to him that everything they are doing seems entirely natural and normal.

She has come up with several photographs of the husband, from snapshots to formal corporate portraits. The lover flies to Budapest with the digitized photographs translated into holographic representation for a cooperative surgeon he knows from the old days and, without representing that he is still with the intelligence community, lets the surgeon think he is, so that the code of ultimate discretion will be in force. You are not that far apart, the doctor says, studying the holograph. And it's true, thinks the lover: After all, her attraction to me had to have been somewhat directed by our being more or less the same lean morph type, both of us having called up in her mind someone she loved as a child. I don't mean oedipal governance necessarily, all of us look for reprises of the pure attachments installed in us in our unconscious youth. There are transferences even then in those tender ages when model people imprint themselves as lifelong loves so deeply indelibly that you are heliotropic in their presence.

My nose will be broken and enlarged, the hairline brought down via transplants to a widow's peak, I will have to keep my hair close cut and grayed at the temples to add ten years or so. The jaw will be widened slightly with implants. I will have to gain about twelve to fifteen pounds, wear a shoe lift. . . .

But this cannot be a story about details. It cannot depend on a realistic presentation of thoughtfully worked out details to prop up its credibility. All of that can be passed over lightly in montage. The movie should operate in the abstract realm where practical matters give way to uncanny resonances with everyday truth. Because evil as it is most often committed comes of the given life, it takes not only its motivation but its form from the structure of existing circumstances, it is not usually a thing of such high-concept deviance and requiring such extensive planning to perform.

In fact the movie can be said to begin only with what in the lover's mind is the culminating scene, a work of performance art, in which an American business success, a man for whom he has no feelings whatsoever let alone dislike, will be dropped precipitously into material and psychic dereliction. He will come to a door he thinks is his own and not be recognized by his wife. She will deny that she knows him. A duplicate of himself will ask the police to take him away and charge him with stalking. Security guards will prevent him from entering his office. Hotels will not accept his credit cards. Old friends will back away from him in fear. Lawyers will not take his calls. His passport will be confiscated as a forgery. Disoriented, and only imperfectly understanding that something has been done to him, he will be left ranting and railing in a mad state of total self-displacement, a deportee from himself.

Perhaps, thinks the lover, he will go crazy. Perhaps he will attempt to kill me and end up in some hospital for the criminally insane. Another delicious bit of suspense is the measure of my control over her, calculable to the extent to which she can be trusted. If residual feelings of affection in the form of pity or terror will operate in her, perhaps to the point of revealing the truth to him, so that even at risk of criminal indictment to herself, she will bring down the whole beautiful work of art to a crashing conclusion.

What is most likely, of course—and how can I claim I did not suspect this of myself from the beginning—is that having brought about this crime of usurpation, I will discover that even this cannot stave off my profound, chronic lassitude, which can now be alleviated, if only for a moment, by abandoning the woman who has committed herself so obsessively, adoringly to me, so that all she has left for the life of her is the shattered husband whom she has betrayed.

And so we have the secular Enlightenment version of Amphitryon. And all of it from the lovely, self-assured young woman I sat next to at a dinner party. This is my laboratory, here, in my skull . . .

=

—Crows on the dock? So they're here now too. I have never heard of crows coming to saltwater. This is very bad. Look at them, three or four, hopping down from the piling to the dock, pecking away at the crab legs and clamshells left by the gulls. An advance party, a patrol. If they like what they find, the flocks will follow squawking and croaking in the waterside trees, raising hell like a goddamn motorcycle club. Jesus. I've got orioles here that flash in the blueberry, finches who like to balance on the tips of water reeds when the wind is up, I've got red-winged blackbirds, mockingbirds, cowbirds, cardinals, wrens, flickers, swifts, I've got skimmers, sandpipers, and bad-postured night herons like old ladies with hump necks. . . . Crows are smarter and bigger and noisier and they commune. They take over, they will drive out all the others, this is serious, I will have to watch them closely. You must go back to the suburban woods of Westchester, crows. You are inlanders, you flock in the big maples and come down to the street to eat the carcasses of squirrels. You don't look good against an open sky. Crows on the dock are a mixed metaphor.

—Let us consider for a moment those remarks of my teacher in the Luitpold Gymnasium: that in order to maintain his self-respect he required my attention, and that Jesus had been crucified by such as I. So there were the two elements now fused—the authoritarian and the militant Christian. And now I ask you to consider the possibility that the pious brainwork of Christian priests and kings that over centuries had demonized and racialized the Jewish people in Europe with the autos-da-fé, pogroms, economic proscriptions, legal encumbrances, deportations, and a culture of socially respectable anti-Semitism . . . had at this moment in my gymnasium classroom attained critical mass.

Let us imagine such small quiet resentments imploding in the ears of a thousand, a million children of my generation. And a moment later: the Holocaust. For you see what moves not as fast as light but fast enough, and with an accrued mass of such density as not to be borne, is the accelerating disaster of human history.

So what, to be logical, must we conclude? We must conclude that given the events in the twentieth century of European civilization, the traditional religious concept of God cannot any longer be seriously maintained. Well then, if I am a serious person, as I believe I am, I must seek God elsewhere than in the religious scriptures. I must try to understand certain irreducible laws of the universe as a transcendent behavior. In these laws, God, the Old One, will be manifest.

Now oddly enough, though these are cold, eternal, imageless verities, insofar as we are beginning to understand them, these great voiceless, vast habits of universal dimension, we may take comfort in their beauty. We may glory in our consciousness of them, that they are—incomprehensibly—comprehensible!

For, remember, there could in theory be alternatives to what is. For example, if gravity ceased to be a fundamental mechanism of the universe—let us do a thought experiment—what would result? Our solar system would fly apart, all the waters of the earth would spill out of their ocean basins and pour in crystals through black space as lumps of coal down a chute, the whole system of dark-mattered space and stars, sunlight, organic life, mitosis, one thing leading to another in an unfolding of necessary and sufficient conditions . . . would not be. Well, what would be? Perhaps after several trillions of years something organic would occur out of the vast eternal black shapelessness that did not depend on light or moisture in order to propagate—some formless ephemera nourished on nothing—and life, if it was life, would be defined in a way that cannot now be defined. Surely all of this is less an inducement to consciousness than what we have now, what we see now, what we try to understand now.

By way of calming our nerves, let us celebrate the constancy of the speed of light, let us praise gravity, that it is in action the curvature of space, and glory that even light is bent by its force, riding the curvatures of space toward celestial objects as a fine, shimmering red-golden net might drape over them. The subjection of light to gravity was proven by my colleague Millikan some years after my theory came

to me, when the light passing near the star X shifted by his measure-
ments to the red spectrum, indicating that it had bent. And there, my
dear friends, is a sacrament for us, is it not? A first sacrament, the
bending of starlight. Yes. The bending of starlight.

==

—Sarah Blumenthal's Conversation with Her Father
I was a runner. My job was to carry the news or the instructions from
the council to the families in their houses. Or messages from one
council member to another. Or to stand watch by the square, at the
entrance to the bridge, to let them know if the open car was coming
with the half-track filled with soldiers just behind it, which meant the
next bad thing was about to occur. I would run like the wind through
the back alleys and side streets to give warning. So I had responsibilities beyond my age. There were seven of us, seven boys, who were
runners. We wore special caps, like police caps, with a military brim.
And the stars sewn on our jackets, of course, so it was all very per-
verted, my military sense of myself. I felt privileged that the star
was not like all the other stars but some indication of rank, and the
military-style hat, and knowing what was going on almost before anyone else—all that made me feel special. Mr. Barbanel, the chief assistant to the community leader, Dr. Koenig—he said I was his best
runner. For the most important matters he chose me. So there it was,
I had a star on my tunic and a garrison cap, and I was the star runner,
that's the way I thought of myself.

I ask you to remember. I was only ten years old. At the same time
of living in this illusion, and of sometimes even secretly admiring the
uniforms of our enemies, I knew full well what was happening. How
could I not?

The overall duty of the council was to provide on a daily basis
worker brigades for the military factories in the city. If this was not
done, if the Germans thought we were not productive enough, that
would be the end of us. While the men and the younger women were
conscripted for labor, most women and the less able men were assigned to maintain the ghetto, to keep it functioning, the bakery, the
hospital, the laundry, and so on. So women as well had to be fit. Any

woman found to be pregnant was taken away and murdered. Or if the child was born, both mother and child were murdered. So pregnant mothers as well as old people, homeless children, and the physically incapacitated were kept illegally in houses all through the ghetto. When we knew a search was coming, each runner had a number of houses to cover. I would dash to my allotted houses and knock on the door a special way. This was the signal that people had to hide. It was all done quietly, efficiently, no screaming or shouting. Then, my route covered, either I would have time to get back to the safety of the council offices or I would hide myself somewhere, usually on the roof of some empty house, huddling against the chimney. These were the moments of the purest terror, when the illegals would be dispersed into all manner of hiding places, cupboards, empty potato bins, root cellars, attic closets, wells, underground crypts. And I would listen as inevitably some of these hiding places would be discovered. From different quarters I would hear the running feet of a squad of soldiers, or guttural shouts, then the screams of someone, or sometimes a pistol shot. The Germans brought Jewish ghetto policemen with them on these searches and tortured them on the spot to find out what they knew. People were found and dragged away, you could hear awful sounds from the different streets. Wherever I was, however safe myself, I would feel such rage—to the point where I would verge on a suicidal impulse to rush out and attack the soldiers, leap on their backs, claw at them, pound them. I felt this desire in my jawbone, my teeth.

When I was assigned to the square where the guards on post stopped and examined the work details crossing the bridge, my mission was to give the council warning of anything unusual. The guards were oafs, stupid men for the most part, they were the dregs of the German military, some clearly of middle age. In my runner's garrison cap I was virtually invisible to them. I could keep crisscrossing the square endlessly, even occasionally hunkering behind some pile of rubble in order to observe the goings-on. If for instance one of the workers was caught in the evening trying to smuggle in a loaf of bread or a few cigarettes, there would be a terrible row and the council would have to intervene in a hurry to try to negotiate the least possible punishment. Sometimes the soldiers would accost a woman worker and try to detain her in their guardhouse on some pretext or other, and that would have to be dealt with. In the middle of the day, when less went on, I stayed mostly in the side streets, though never out of sight or hearing of the square. I was a responsible child, but when things were too quiet and I could not resist the impulse I'd slip into one of the empty houses and climb out on the roof and maintain my watch there. Most of the ghetto houses were no more than cabins, but some were two stories, some were made of stone, there were barns with haylofts, stables, shops with flat roofs, a commercial building or two. The danger of watching from a roof, huddled in the crevice made by the chimney and warmed by the sun, was that I could find myself falling asleep and one of the open cars could come across the bridge and pass under me without my being aware. Usually, I was too hungry to fall asleep, though I did daydream. I could see the entire span of the bridge and the frontage streets of the city across the river that I had once called home. The veins of the city spread into the uplands and I could see the blocks of apartment houses and office buildings and, depending on where I was, I might even see the military factories against the hills where on windless days smoke from the tall stacks poured directly upward into the sky.

If I turned my head to the east, I could see where the terrain roughened into foothills and then mountains with canyons, all of it thickly forested with pine and birch trees. This terrain was magical to me because it was where the Jewish partisans were based who had guns and attacked Germans in military forays. I believed, quite unreasonably, that my parents were with the partisans, were themselves fighting heroes of the Jewish resistance. I believed this at the same time that I believed they were dead. I believed both simultaneously. I will explain this to you, because it also will show you how I became a runner in the first place.

Before the German invasion, before the eviction of the Jews, my father, your grandfather, had been an agrarian economist at the university. That meant matters of crops, farm production, and so on. That is why he was a secret consultant of the council. They had to figure out the distribution of foodstuffs allotted by the Germans. Of course there was never enough. It was my father who staked in two empty lots the plan for a community vegetable garden that the council brought to the Germans for their approval.

My mother had been a doctoral candidate in English language and literature at the same university. When we moved to the ghetto all of that was over. In the beginning my father went off every dawn with the labor details across the bridge to work on the assembly line in the airplane factory, and my mother was designated to teach in the ghetto school. But nothing stayed the same, restrictions followed one another, and more and more of the normal things of life were taken away. So one day the Germans shut down our schools, and after that my mother was assigned like my father to the labor brigades in the city.

I was warned to stay out of sight. I spent most of my time in our house. My mother had saved several books from confiscation and brought them home to me. The books were kept behind a loose wall board in my room. It was an attic room with a small window I could see from only if I got down on my knees. I studied those books avidly, French and English readers, math workbooks, and histories of European civilization. I relished books from the higher grades and liked to master them. My mama made up assignments from these books and even tests for me to take. I loved tests. I loved her voice as she read my work and graded it and I loved it when we bent over my workbook together in the evening after she made our supper.

Of course I had one or two friends. Joseph Liebner, who had been a year ahead of me in school and whose father was a baker in the ghetto bakery, and a boy named Nicoli, who shared with me his German-language cowboy novels, and the blond girl Sarah Levin, whose pretty mother, Miriam, taught music and who had told my mother that Sarah had an eye for me, a bit of news that I heard with feigned indifference. In fact every week on Tuesday I went down two blocks to Mrs. Levin's for my fiddle lesson. The fiddle was kept in her house, though it was mine. Naturally I could never practice. My lesson was also my practice for the lesson. It took place while the men in the carpentry shop next door were still working, so that the sound of the fiddle could not be heard over the noise. At such times Sarah Levin sat in the room, a thin child with pale hair and large eyes that watched me, which I told myself I hated, though of course it made me play smartly.

Still, most of the time I was alone. I waited for my parents, praying to God they would return from their day's labor in the city. As they'd come in the door, bringing the cold air with them, perhaps with a bit of smuggled food bartered from the Lithuanians, I would thank God for His beneficence.

It was in this period of my life I learned from observation of my mother and father what adult love was. That this could be maintained—a presumption of a father's male powers, a mother's beauty, her waiting upon him, her reception of him in their bed—when they lived stripped of their lives, enslaved, everything taken from them, I did not understand as something remarkable until years afterward. Now I only accumulated the evidence. The strong attraction between them had nothing to do with me. My mother could not stop looking at her husband. When he was in the room with us she was transfixed. I watched her bosom as she breathed. I noted the thickness of the curve of his forearm under the rolled shirtsleeve. I watched him stand out at the open door and look down the street each way before he permitted them to leave the house. When they readied themselves for work at dawn, he helped my mother with her coat and then she turned and raised the collar of his jacket. Upon each, front and back, was sewn the star of yellow cloth.

One night I was awakened by what I thought was the wind whistling through the cracks in the attic boards. But it wasn't the wind, it was screaming. Not from nearby, not from my house—I heard my parents in the room below, the urgent tones of their voices when they thought I couldn't hear them. I knelt at my window: The sky was alight. My street was quiet, the houses dark, but the sky beyond seemed to be flying upward. I saw the color of flame reflected on my nightshirt and called to my parents. Fire, fire! In moments my mother was with me, leading me back to bed. Shh, she said, it's all right, we are not on fire, you are safe, go back to sleep. I wrapped myself in the safety of my covers, I folded the pillow over my ears and hummed to myself so as not to hear those screams. It was a terrible sound, though distant, of many screaming voices. I watched the firelight fade on the inside of my eyelids. I fell asleep imagining the screams turning back into the wind, as if drawn up by God, rising to heaven.

In the morning the word came that the Germans had burned down the hospital. When I say the hospital, you must not imagine the sort of modern high-rise facility we have here. It was a cluster of houses that had been refashioned by opening walls and tying the buildings together with lumber so as to provide three wards of bunk beds, one for men, one for women, one for children, as well as some examining rooms, a small ill-equipped operating room, and a dispensary. The Germans surrounded the hospital, boarded up the doors and windows and, with over sixty-five people inside, including twenty-three children, set the place on fire. These are numbers indelible in my mind. Sixty-five. Twenty-three. Some of the patients had been ill with typhus and they feared the contagion, the decimation of the labor supply. So this was their solution, to burn everyone alive, including the staff. All the next day smoke rose over the town. The sky was overcast, the weather unnaturally warm. The smoke lingered like fog. My eyes smarted, I coughed to expel the smoke. I imagined I'd inhaled the smoke of the dead, and perhaps I had. At dawn, everyone had to go off to work as usual. In the evening, after the workers returned, though it was illegal to gather in numbers, several men slipped into the rabbi's house next door to say Kaddish for the murdered souls.

This was not the first of the so-called actions by the Germans. There were and would be others, sudden, unannounced sweeps of the houses, when they trucked people to the old fort on the river west of the city to be murdered. They had these bouts of efficiency. But with this particular horror, my father resigned from his role with the council. He had found his complicity in a life of helpless subjugation no longer endurable. There was a secret meeting of the council the next night after the fire, and when he came back, I was upstairs supposedly asleep but as awake and alert as I could be. A silence while my mother put the bread and soup before him. He pushed the dish away.

"Tomorrow is the monthly meeting with the Germans," he told her. "The council will make a formal protest. It would apply moral suasion to these ungovernable forces of terror." His voice was uncharacteristically leaden, toneless.

"What would you have it do?" my mother asked. She spoke softly. I could hardly hear her.

"Above and beyond the fact of our systematic slavery, they like to surprise us," my father said. His voice grew louder, angrier. "They like to amuse themselves. Schmitz, that jackal who runs things"—this was the chief S.S. officer—"how can the council bear to look at him, speak with him, as if he is human? This ritual pretense of a common humanity to which we have to subscribe if we hope to outlast them! As if we are the caretakers of madmen who must never be told they are mad. Schmitz and the others will be laughing to themselves while affecting civilized conversation. They will say it is wartime and things that are regrettable are nonetheless unavoidable. They will go on to discuss the flour and potato allocations as the next order of business."

"Ari, shah," my mother said. "You'll wake him."

"I can no longer endure this!"

That cry of despair I will never forget, not only for the clenching of my boy's heart that my father was, truly and in fact, without the resources to protect us, but for the piercing illumination it brought to me of my physical self as game for a predator. He went on about this effect of our history: that we had lived among them, the Christians, for generation upon generation, only to see ourselves bent and twisted to the shape of their hatred. We had been turned into Jews so that they could be Christians.

Now exactly what happened after this I cannot tell you. It was perhaps two or three months after the fire, emotions had become numb. The shock had worn off in the routine of work, secret meetings, secret prayers on the part of the religious. The return once more to the hope of outlasting them, to hanging on until liberation came. There had been rumors of the defeat of the Nazi armies in Africa. It was in this period that my parents failed to return home from their labor. To this day I don't know the circumstances. One morning at dawn, as usual, he helped her with her coat, she turned up his collar against the cold, they both kissed their son. They gave me the usual instructions for the day. And they opened the door into the dark morning and closed the door behind them and I never saw them again.

I do know that around this time a notice was posted in the ghetto—the Germans were calling for a hundred intelligentsia for special work as curators and catalogers in the city archives. Mama and Papa discussed this. She was against volunteering, arguing that the Germans could not be trusted. Papa's view was that it was a reasonable risk to take and that he should sign on. He believed if he had such a job he would see people he knew and could make contact with the Resistance. My mother said she wanted us to survive. My father said while any decision they made could be the last, of one thing he was certain, and that was how it would end for everyone who remained in the ghetto.

Well of course my mother was right, it was another of the Germans' murderous deceptions: The intelligentsia who had given their credentials for archival work were trucked out of the city to the old fort by the river and shot to death. But if my father was among them, what about my mother, who would not have volunteered? Or had she after all? But that would have been too reckless, both of them taking a chance with their lives and leaving a small boy behind. Perhaps if he had volunteered, she had been implicated in some way and taken off too before she could flee. Perhaps they had been murdered for other reasons having nothing to do with this question. I didn't know.

But there was another possibility—that they were still alive, that they had managed to escape and join the partisans. It was Rabbi Grynspan from next door who told me this on the very evening my parents didn't return. "Come quickly, you must not stay here," he said. "You are technically an orphan, though of course your parents are alive in the forest and will come back for you, may the Lord, Blessed be He, show them the way."

"They went with the Resistance?"

"Yes." This after a moment's hesitation.

"Well why couldn't they take me with them?"

"They thought you would be safer here. Quickly, no more talk. Unattended children the Nazis do not tolerate. You will be provided, never mind books, take your sweater, these shirts, wrap these things in your coat and come with me."

Thereafter, I lived knowing Mama and Papa were dead but at the same time waiting for them to come rescue me. I knew they were dead because they wouldn't have thought I'd be safer alone in the ghetto than with them. But I thought they were alive, because the rabbi had confirmed what my father had said, that he wanted to make contact with the Resistance. I lived in this irresolute state of mind for a considerable time, knowing in my heart they were dead, but always looking up from what I was doing to see if they had come for me. It was a long time before I stopped thinking of them altogether.

———

—If Albert is right, there is consolation to be derived from the planets. For example, that they're all spheroid, that none of them are shaped like dice or the cardboards laundered shirts come folded on. And thinking about their formation—how, from amorphous furious swirls of cosmic dust and gas, everything spins out and cools and organizes itself into a gravitationally operating solar system. . . . And that this has apparently happened elsewhere, that there are billions of galaxies with stars beyond number, so that even if a fraction of stars have orbiting planets with moons in orbit around them . . . a few planets, at least, may have the water necessary for the intelligent life that could be suffering the same metaphysical crisis that deranges us. So we have that to feel good about.

=

—Sarah Blumenthal's Conversation with Her Father

The rabbi took me to the council offices. Several children were there. Some were crying. I sat among them on the floor and leaned back against the wall and watched and listened. The council staff were begging everyone to be quiet. One man at a desk was typing. He had a typewriter because it was the council. I liked the clear, precise clack of the typewriter keys. I fell asleep for a while. When I awoke the other children were gone, the room was quiet, and a woman was kneeling before me. "You have a new name now," she said, smiling. "A nice name, too. Yehoshua. Go ahead, say it."

"Yehoshua."

"That's right. Yehoshua Mendelssohn. That is you from now on. It is the name you must answer to, and this is your registration that says you are now him that you will carry always in your pocket, all right? In case anyone asks? You live in Demokratu Street. I will take you there. It is pretty, it looks onto the vegetable garden."

The woman took my bundle and held my hand as if I were a baby and walked with me through the ghetto. Her palm was damp with fear, but she would not let go. She stopped in front of the door of a small house. "You have a grandfather," she told me, and then she knocked at the door.

The so-called grandfather was a tailor named Srebnitsky, a thin ill-tempered man, somewhat stooped, with gray hair curling from under his cap and with narrow shoulders over which a shirt and vest hung loosely. A musty smell came from him which I thought of as grandfather smell. He had pale blue eyes that glimmered with water. But the most powerful impression he made on me was that he was a stranger.

His house consisted of two rooms, a front and a back, and a small alcove that served for a kitchen. I was to sleep on a daybed in the front room, where the tailor maintained his business.

"So, I have a grandson," he said, not smiling. "Thus God in His wisdom provides. May I hope He will give me a daughter and son-in-law as well? And why not a wife as long as He's at it?" He spoke not to me but seemingly to the work in his hands, or perhaps to the hands themselves, which were long, smooth, and nimble and therefore fascinating, because they seemed so much younger than the rest of him. The needle flew through the cloth, in and out, and perfectly straight lines of stitches grew with amazing speed.

As the weeks passed I took on the duty of sweeping the floor of the bits of thread and shreds of rags that accumulated there. But nothing could be thrown out, everything went back in the rag bin. The garments brought to the tailor were threadbare coats, dresses, trousers that he would mend or tear down and reconstruct, somehow, with his bits of thread and rags from his rag bin, so that they could be worn again, at least for a little while. There was no money exchanged with the customers, there was scrip. More often there was barter. The Germans couldn't police that very well. A carpenter whose jacket he mended fixed a shutter so that it would close properly. A woman whose coat he lined left some soup.

The only book in the house was a Bible, so I took to reading it closely. I found some of it puzzling. Assuming the old man was pious, I began to ask questions of him. Gleams of triumph came to Srebnitsky's watery eyes. With relish he pointed out the contradictions and absurdities of the biblical text. "Look closely at what you're reading," he said. "The dates tell you. When this happened, when that happened. Samuel could not have written Samuel any more than Moses could have written Moses. How could they themselves know when they had died? Stories, nonsense, all of it. Pious fraud. And in the beginning? In the beginning—what? Who is talking, who is being addressed? Who was there? Where is the voucher? The people who made up these stories knew even less than we do. You want God? Don't look at Scripture, look everywhere, at the planets, the constellations, the universe. Look at a bug, a flea. Look at the manifold wonders of creation, including the Nazis. That's the kind of God you're dealing with."

I found myself oddly comforted by these remarks. I'd always had doubts myself about the biblical God, as I do to this day, as you well know and, I hope, forgive. Also, the old man's attitude reminded me of my father, who was a Zionist and a man of science, although he observed the Sabbath and the High Holy Days. But in addition there was a kind of hidden compliment in the regard the old man had to have had for me by talking to me as a person who was capable of using his own mind, thinking for himself and taking nothing on faith even though I was just a boy.

Most of the time, though, there was no conversation from Srebnitsky. Hour after hour he sat hunched at his worktable by the window, his beautiful hands playing a kind of nimble deaf-and-dumb speech in my mind. The concentration of his gaze on this small field of cloth, over which his hands spoke, I thought of as his defiance of all the lies of God and his obstinate refusal to succumb to the despair that swept through the ghetto in waves, like the fever.

His sewing machine had been taken from him, the loss of which he cursed every day. Their concession to his trade was to leave him his scissors and needles and boxes of notions and skeins of thread. Also his two human figures on wheeled stands, one male, one female, constructed in wire from the waist up. These tailor's dummies were often the objects of my contemplation. Though they could be seen through, I felt them as real presences in the room. I realized how little it took for something to appear human. Sometimes the dummies would get moved around and I would be startled coming upon them unexpectedly, mistaking them for real people. I fantasized their indifference, that nothing could hurt them. You could hang them, shoot them, you could hammer them into a shapeless clump, pull and twist them into one long strand of wire, and they wouldn't feel it, nor would they care. Being inanimate was an enviable, even transcendent, state in my thinking. Yet at the same time I had no difficulty imagining the dummies talking to each other. I liked to wheel them into a conversational position after the tailor had retired and just before I myself lay down to sleep: Well here it is evening, time to rest, the man would say to the woman. Yes, she would answer, and tomorrow the sun will surely come and shine its warmth upon us.

———

—Pem's Remarks to the Bishop's Examiners
The sensation of God in us is a total sensation given to the whole being, revelatory, inspired. That is the usual answer to the questioning intellect, which by itself cannot realize sacred truth. But is the intellect not subsumed? Does the whole being not include the intellect? Why wouldn't the glory of God shine through to the human mind?

I take the position that true faith is not a supersessional knowledge. It cannot discard the intellect. It cannot answer the intellect with a patronizing smile. I look for parity here. I will not claim that your access to the numinous is a delusion if you will not tell me my intellect is irrelevant . . .

The biblical stories, the Gospel stories, were the original understandings, they were science and religion, they were everything, they were all anyone had. But they didn't write themselves. We have to acknowledge the storytellers' work.

If not in all stories, certainly in all mystery stories, the writer works backward. The ending is known and the story is designed to arrive at the ending. If you know the people of the world speak many languages, that is the ending: The story of the Tower of Babel gets you there. The known ending of life is death: The story of Adam and Eve arrives at that ending. Why do we suffer, why must we die? Well, you see, there was this Garden . . .

The ending of the story implies that there might have been a different ending. That's the little ten-cent trick. You allow as how since things worked out this way, they could have worked out another way. You create conflict and suspense where there wasn't any. You've turned the human condition into a sequential narrative of how it came to be.

Well, the way I read it, God dealt from a stacked deck. Adam and Eve never had a chance. The story of the Fall is a parable of the glory and torment of human consciousness. But that's all it is . . .

Migod, there is no one more dangerous than the storyteller. No, I'll amend that, than the storyteller's editor. Augustine, who edits Genesis

2–4 into original sin. What a nifty little act of deconstruction—passing it on to the children, like HIV. As the doctrine of universal damnation, the Fall becomes an instrument of social control. God appoints his agents plenipotentiaries to dispense salvation or withhold it. I don't know about you, dear colleagues, but history has a way of turning a harsh light on my faith. We are bound to a theology hard-pressed to hold the line against incredulous common sense. So for instance new-born babies who die unbaptized as Catholics are condemned to the limboic upper reaches of hell? I mean . . . but in all its denominations, punitive fantasies of original sin have begotten and still beget genera-tions of terrorized children and haunted adults, and give those Calvin-ist graveyards in New England a particular poignancy as they call to mind the witch burnings, scourgings, and self-denials of the ordinary joy and wonder of life on earth to which the unindoctrinated mind is naturally heir . . .

How, given the mournful history of this nonsense, can we presume to exalt our religious vision over the ordinary pursuits of our rational minds?

The old tailor tended to deal with me as if I were an adult boarder who could take care of himself. Nevertheless, as I grew out of my clothes, he let them out or found me others. When I began limping because my shoes had become too tight, he bartered for a pair of wooden shoes. He cooked our potato soup or cut our bread and pointed to the table and we sat down to eat in silence. All of this I ac-cepted as the best that could be. In truth I was a boarder. The old man and I were not really related, and I never came to feel that this was anything but a temporary arrangement.

Living undercover, I could no longer see my friends from before or have my music lesson with Mrs. Levin or see that little Sarah, who was so crazy about me. From time to time the woman from the coun-cil who had given me my new name came to visit, to look around, to see that everything was all right. She would bring Srebnitsky a few cigarettes, or schnapps in a small jar. He accepted these things as his due. She would have for Yehoshua Mendelssohn a pocket comb or a pencil and notebook. But the best thing she ever brought, my most valued treasure, was an American funny paper, a sheet of color comics from an American newspaper used as inner wrapping in a package that had miraculously found its way to the ghetto. I smoothed out the wrinkled page and read it over and over, trying to work out the English words above the heads of the characters. One story was about a medieval knight in armor riding through the countryside on a white horse. Another showed a police detective in a yellow coat running along the top of a railroad car with a gun in his hand. It did not bother me that I could not take each story further than the six or eight panels in the paper, it was enough for me to know of these heroes and imagine for myself the kinds of adventures they had. Different periods of history were suggested, people were born into different times, each of which brought its own dangers. This was more or less the same thought delivered by a rabbi in a secret gathering of children for Chanukah. "The Holy One, blessed be His name, gave us the Torah, gave us compassion, humility, and the strength to stand up to all who would deny us our faith. And we are tested even as the Maccabees were tested, who recaptured the Temple from the wicked ones and lit the lamp that had just the oil for one day's burning but which, thanks to the Holy One, blessed be He, lasted for eight days. And we will break out of our chains and defeat the oppressors as the Maccabees did."

Each morning when I arose, I looked out across the street at the vegetable garden that my father had laid out for the community. Even in the cold, harsh weather, with the ground bare but for the dried-up stalks of plant stubble, I could see the furrows that outlined different sections and imagine his thoughts as he worked out what should be planted and where. In the afternoons I liked to walk there when it was dark enough. Nobody bothered me. Those soldiers posted to guard duty tended to be less vigilant, more concerned with keeping warm than guarding anything. But then the snows came like a burial shroud laid over the field. All the configurations of the ground were gone, there was just this mound of glaring cold whiteness. It was blinding, it wouldn't let me look, and for the first time since I had lost my parents I cried. There had come to me from that whiteness a terrible realization that my memory of them had begun to fade . . . their physical appearances, their voices.

Eventually, try as I might, all I could recover of them were flashes of their moral natures in the habits of my own thinking.

I came back one day from my wandering and found Srebnitsky at work cutting patterns from a thick bolt of luxurious material of a rich charcoal color and remarkable pliancy. Where had it come from? I would have asked had there not been in the tailor's attitude of concentration a demand for silence. His lips were moving as if he were talking to himself. He seemed angry. Yet he went about his work quickly and with precision. I sat to the side and watched his hands. Eventually they lifted the sections of cloth they had cut and tacked and slipped them over the wire male, who in that instant became an S.S. officer in the process of realization.

He stepped back to regard his work. "You see how famous your grandfather has become. News of his art has reached His Eminence S.S. Major Schmitz. Is it wrong of me to accept this honor?" he said, pointing at the dummy.

"You had to," I said with a youth's directness.

"Yes. I suppose so. I tell myself also that it is a hopeful sign, the first stirrings in their evolution that one of these thugs can actually be party to an ordinary business deal."

Here he uncovered a sewing machine with a treadle. "So I have it back now. So? Do I hear you saying something?" I shook my head, but he went on with his argument with himself as if I were disputing him. "If not for his skills, Srebnitsky would not be here. Just remember that. These hands you're always looking at with admiration—for I know that about you, although you are too high-and-mighty to become a tailor yourself—it's these old hands of his that have kept him alive. And if you don't think that's worth a damn, they've kept you alive too, Yehoshua Mendelssohn! Yehoshua Mendelssohn," he said again, muttering, as he turned to his work.

For of course, as I realized at this moment, just as he was a stranger to me, I was not his grandson. You understood that, didn't you, that I had been given the name of the tailor's dead grandson? He never told me what had happened, it was at the council later that I learned. Before there was a ghetto, when the war came to our city, the Russians pulled back to the east. Our Lithuanian neighbors took the opportunity to have themselves a little pogrom. Srebnitsky lived with his daughter and son-in-law and grandson Yehoshua in an apartment on

Vytauto Street. While he was at work in his shop in another part of town, a mob broke down the door of the apartment and rushed his family out into the street and clubbed them to death. All around, others were doing the same, killing Jewish people and looting their houses of furniture, rugs, dishes, radios, everything. Srebnitsky ran home and found the bodies of his daughter and her husband and son on the sidewalk. When the Germans occupied the city, they restored order by evicting all Jews and resettling them in the ramshackle slum on the other side of the river that became our ghetto. This was done not for our protection, of course, but to save us for forced labor in the war factories. I remembered that time myself, hiding in our own apartment, on a high floor, luckily, with the bureau lodged against the front door. And I remembered our own trek, with my parents pushing a cart of belongings and pieces of furniture we had been allowed to take with us across the bridge. Srebnitsky, bereft of all his living relations, had made the trip alone.

Of course the tailor's experience was not exceptional in any way, but years later, when I considered the act that brought about his death, I concluded that while anyone could be driven to the point of forswearing life, in cases like Srebnitsky's it was not the simple desire to die, it was the desire for self-transcendence which once realized brings one to the end of life. That is something different, not the same thing at all. And so the ordinary unendurable torments we all experienced were indeed exceptional in the way they were absorbed in each heart.

—

—Pem's Remarks to the Bishop's Examiners
Burkert, perhaps our pre-eminent scholar of ancient religions—do you know his work? He investigates the origins of the sacred, itself a heretical pursuit. He gives us the picture of the lizard who leaves his tail in the mouth of the predator. The fox who chews off his foot to escape the trap. You ask what that has to do with God. In that programmed biological response is the idea of the sacrifice. You give up a part to save the whole. Ancient myths abound in which human beings flee monsters and escape only by sacrificing pieces of themselves to divert or slow down the pursuit. Orestes gives up a finger,

and so does Odysseus. Finger sacrifice was very big in ancient Greece. But for the most part, over time the sacrifices have been ritualized, symbolized. You no longer mutilate yourself, you leave a ring on the altar in lieu of your finger. You slaughter a lamb. You leave a scapegoat in the desert. But when the fate of a community is involved, one man is chosen to jump into the abyss so that it will not swallow the community. One virgin is given to the bottomless lake. One person on the sled is thrown to the pursuing wolves. Jonah is thrown into the sea to save the ship and its crew. And just as the herd grazes in safety for a time after the lions cut one of them out and devour him, so does humanity feel safer from the nameless formless terrors if one of their number is sacrificed, if for the sake of all one must pay as the part for the whole, as the fox's foot is left in the trap.

Think about it. We are talking the intellectual's talk. We are finding the possible biological origin of the sacred, of what is most holy to us, our grand figuration of the incarnate God who dies over and over, from one Sunday to the next, so that the rest of us may find salvation.

Is all of this irrelevant? . . .

Pagels, working from the scrolls discovered at Nag Hammadi in Egypt in 1945, finds that the early Christians were profoundly divided between those who proposed a church according to apostolic succession based on a literal interpretation of Jesus' resurrection and those who rejected resurrection except as a spiritual metaphor for gnosis emotionally, mystically achieved, as knowledge beyond ordinary knowledge, a perception beneath or above the everyday truth. . . . So there was a power struggle. Gnostic and synoptic contested with competing gospels. The gnostics, who said no church was needed, no priest, no episcopate, were routed, inevitably, having no organization, given their views. While the institutionalist Christians were understandably concerned that their persecuted sect needed a network to survive, with rules of order and common strategies for survival, the concept of martyrdom, for example, being created to make something positive from their terrible persecution, it is also true that the struggle for Jesus was a struggle for power, that the idea of an actual resurrection, which the institutionalists put forth and the gnostics ridiculed, provided authority for church office, and that the struggle to define Jesus and canonize his words, or interpretations of his words by others, was pure politics, as passionate or worshipful as it may have been, and that with the desire to perpetuate the authority of Jesus continuing in the Reformation and the creation of Protestant sects, in which a kind of residual gnosis was being proposed in protest against the sacramental accumulations of a churchly bureaucracy, what is now Christianity, with all the resonance that it has as a belief and a rich and complex culture, is a political creation with a political history. It was a politically triumphant Jesus created from the conflicts of early Christianity, and it has been a political Jesus ever since, from the time of the emperor Constantine's conversion in the fourth century through the long history of European Christianity, as we consider the history of the Catholic Church, its Crusades, its Inquisition, its contests and/or alliances with kings and emperors, and with the rise of the Reformation, the history of Christianity's active participation, in all its forms, in the wars among states and the rule of populations. It is the story of power . . .

I'm sorry. You have questions for me and here I've been running on about these elemental things you well know. But I'm beginning to feel their weight. The higher criticism has gone on now for a hundred and fifty years. We must look again at what is staring us in the face. Our difference is in how we value these . . . distractions of the intellect. You regard them as irrelevant. I wish you saw them as a challenge. Our tradition has great latitude. What unifies us is the sacraments, but there is division among us when it comes to doctrinal issues and I think we must acknowledge that. All these miracles we affirm are a burden to me. Yet I think of myself as a good Christian. This is a profession of faith. I hope you will not use it to expunge from the ranks someone of my generation who you feel has brought the 1960s along with him. Thank you.

=

—The Midrash Jazz Quartet Plays the Standards

STAR DUST

Sometimes I wonder why
I spend the lonely night
dreaming of a song?

The melody haunts my reverie,
And I am once again with you
When our love was new,
and each kiss an inspiration,
But that was long ago: now my consolation
is in the stardust of a song.
Beside a garden wall, when stars are
    bright,
you are in my arms
The nightingale tells his fairy tale
of paradise, where roses grew.
Tho' I dream in vain
In my heart it will remain:
My stardust melody,
The memory of love's refrain.

The singer asks why he is wasting his nights
    longing for his lost love
Whom he dreams of as a song. Of course he knows why—
He is obsessed, he can't help himself
    he is in a mawkish self-pitying frame of mind.
She must have shone for him like a star
    if the song he hears is no more than its dust.
How peculiar to invoke in the name of lost love
    the cinderous products of a nuclear conflagration.
This is his problem, his metaphorical desperation.
One wonders at his sentimentality
—to have even pretended he was in paradise,
    the Garden of Eden
where everything lasted forever and the roses never
    stopped blooming
and his sweetheart sang duets in the evening
with a perching bird cherished by Chinese royalty—
As if no ancestor of his ever ate the fruit
    from the famous tree,
As if love were eternal, life death-free.

                          (*weak applause*)

If what you're singing to yourself
   is not a song
but the dream of what a song should be,
Of course it's all wrong,
The song breaks down as dreams do
And everything you thought you knew
   is gone
Each note a lamentation.
That's the real problem of the heart:
The mind's in disarray
and night and day
can't be told apart.
As if God in consternation
   has set the world back to its start.
And where the lover stands in all of this
   as dream, as song, it surely is no Garden.
There is lightning, there is rain,
celestial fires, worlds in collision
And the song of love's recision
is the music of the spheres.

                                         (*indifferent applause*)

What's worst of all is when he's alone in the night
   but she's there, she hasn't gone.
He recalls the time they were one
Which is the only paradise we can presume
   to try for
Though of short duration
lasting not as long as a rose in bloom.
So now they're not in the Garden anymore
Like he was the only boy in the world
   and she was the only girl
but sitting in opposite chairs in the living room
And maybe he's reading the paper or pretending to
and she has a book or a Bible
and between them they have nothing to say to each other

Except to try to coordinate their doctors'
   appointments.
If he took her in his arms now
She would flinch and pull away
Totally flustered by this bizarre behavior
And perhaps in his reverie he gazes out the window
And sees some lovely slender young girls passing by
and thinks in the words of the poet,
"Once I knew one lovelier than any of you."
Which is not much consolation.
No more than the sight
of the stars of night
which shine big and brightly enough
but are dying embers
in the ashes of his lethargy.

                                          (*very scattered applause*)

              We sing the blues,
                 Make up words
                 To imitate
                 The singing birds
           In the garden of Adding,
                 Live Even and Odd
                 She's not in his arms,
                 They're looking for God
           A nightful of stars,
                 Is turned to dust
                 And here I am,
                 In Paradise lost.

—The singer dreams up a song
—each note a lamentation
—as we sit in our living room chairs
—here in Paradise lost.

                Sometimes I wonder why
                I spend the lonely night
                dreaming of a song?

The melody haunts my reverie,
And I am once again with you
When our love was new,
and each kiss an inspiration . . .

(*grateful applause*)

===

—One morning in the winter, just minutes after Srebnitsky had sewn the military insignia on the shoulders and the piping on the lapels, a car pulled up by the front door and the S.S. officer who'd commissioned the work arrived. It was S.S. Major Schmitz, the commandant and executive of all terror. I ran into the back room and slipped out the door. This enterprise of the tailor's had bothered me from the beginning, because it violated the rule to remain anonymous as possible, to do nothing to stand out. If his skill with the needle had made him useful and kept him, and me, alive, it also raised the possibility of death. The logic of our wretched circumstances ensured that there was no simple proposition that did not contain its opposite.

I positioned myself by the vegetable garden fence some distance down the block. It was a cold, cloudy morning. In the drabness of winter and amid the shabby dwellings of this street, with wisps of smoke coming from the chimneys, the commandant's staff car stood out, the awesome luxury of another world. It was a black Mercedes sedan with a squarish cab and a long, low-slung engine hood with a chrome radiator grille for a prow. It had huge silver headlights. It shone brilliantly, apparently untouched by slush and snow and soot. The driver occupied himself by going around with a rag and rubbing away the most recent affronts. I knew from the way he glanced at me that I could come as close as I wished, so that I, a Jew boy, could see what German civilization was capable of, the glory of this machine, and the casual magnificence of its driver. He wore the enlisted man's S.S. uniform with a holstered pistol.

Of course what drew me to the car was not its luster but the heat rising from the engine. So I was to have an unobstructed view of what happened. When Major Schmitz came out he was wearing his new custom-made uniform, including a rakishly blocked garrison cap. He was a portly man with wide hips. Behind him was Srebnitsky, carrying the old uniform over his arm. The driver sprang forward to take this. He opened the rear door for his commandant and then the front door and was occupied in the next moments settling the uniform carefully over the front seat. Schmitz stood posing in his smart uniform and black boots with his hands on his hips and a contemptuous smile on his face. "But you won't pay?" Srebnitsky asked in a coy voice. The officer laughed. "Not one pfennig for Srebnitsky's beautiful work, even the sleeves lined, and all of it done in double stitching?" And he began to laugh as well. "Not even a cigarette for the old tailor who has worked so hard, the artist who has made this garment for the beautiful major of the Third Reich?" They were both laughing heartily at this joke, a Jew expecting to be paid. Srebnitsky suddenly frowned, his shoulders rounded as he peered closely at something on the new uniform. In his hand were his scissors. "Forgive me, Your Excellency, a bit of thread, one moment." And putting his hand to the chest of the commandant, who looked skyward to endure this final snip of perfection, he yanked at the lapel and slashed the scissors-point downward across the front, a gesture so sudden that from one moment to the next a big flap of the ruined tunic hung down to the officer's knee. "Sew it yourself then, thief!" the tailor shrieked. "Thief, that's what you are, that's all you are. All of you, thieves, thieves of our work, thieves of our lives!"

The major stood dumbfounded, I think he had even cried out in fear. But his driver leapt upon the old man and clubbed him to the ground with the butt of his pistol. Then he began kicking him. "You dare to attack a German officer?" he shouted. "You dare to lift your hand!" He then aimed his pistol at the stricken tailor and would have shot him then and there had the major not commanded him to stop. Holding his ripped tunic against his chest, Schmitz was like a woman covering her breasts. He looked around to see who had witnessed his humiliation, and thank God he did not see my face, for I had turned my back and was disappearing into the alley between two houses. From this vantage point in the shadows moments later, I saw the car flash by in the street. I listened to the fading sound of the motor and then I ran back to Srebnitsky, who lay in the snow where he had fallen. His head was bleeding, he was coughing and poking at his throat and trying to speak. I knelt down beside him. He began to shake his head and made an attempt to smile, and then he was coughing and cackling and coughing some more, and his eyes for a moment rolled up in his head. Then suddenly I was pulled to my feet by one of the neighbors. "Don't you know any better? He's finished, your old man. Move, run, get out of here!" And then he himself ran back to his house and slammed the door.

What he meant, that neighbor, was that when a head of family committed a crime or was otherwise designated for execution, it was the Germans' policy to kill his dependents as well. That is why when my parents had not come home I was quickly taken to the council office and given another name. It was to the council I ran now, by myself this time.

My arrival immediately stilled everyone in that busy place, the pale terrified face of a child a warning signal they knew all too well. What I had to say put them on the alert. Several boys were summoned and dispatched to spread the word among the houses and shops for people not known to the Germans to go into hiding. I sat there dumbly while these boys, whose ranks I was to join, ran off in all directions. In a matter of minutes, everyone in the ghetto knew what the tailor had done. After a while the news came back that he had been apprehended and taken to the Gestapo headquarters. The question now was how the Germans would adjudicate his crime. People began to gather in the street in front of the council office. Rumors were rife—the price for Srebnitsky's act would be thirty, fifty, a hundred Jewish dead. Several times Mr. Barbanel, the chief of staff, had to go outside and tell the crowd to disperse and go about their business.

In clear distinction to the public, who were becoming increasingly agitated, the council staff remained calm. The calmest of everyone, perhaps the source of the calm, was the council president, Dr. Sigmund Koenig, a handsome man in his sixties, a man of great dignity, a good six feet tall. Eventually he went outside and his mere appearance stilled the small crowd that was gathered. He told them he was awaiting a call from the ghetto commandant as to exactly what was to be done but that he doubted there was any immediate danger of a major action. He spoke almost in a whisper. Standing behind him in the doorway, I could barely hear what he said. He wore no coat or hat. The cold did not seem to bother him. He was neatly dressed in a gray double-breasted suit with a clean shirt and tie. I would come to understand this was his only suit. It was threadbare, I had a tailor's eye for such things now, and it hung in a way that suggested his own physical wear and tear. His shirt collar was loose around his neck. His black shoes were also well worn, and I'd noticed the right eyepiece of his spectacles was cracked, so that his eye itself seemed fractured. Nevertheless, everything about him was meticulous. He was clean-shaven and he had this fine silver hair that was combed back in a long wave that caught my attention as something poetic, the pennant of some medieval knight flowing above him as he cantered into battle. He walked back to his inner office and took no notice of me. I wouldn't have expected otherwise from a man of his eminence.

It was sometime in the afternoon that a German soldier on a motorcycle arrived with a written order that the council immediately provide carpenters to construct a gallows in the town square leading to the bridge. Shortly thereafter, Dr. Koenig was able to reach the commandant by phone. He was told all Jews were to be in the square at dawn to witness the hanging of the tailor Srebnitsky. To everyone but me, it seemed, that was a great relief. Now that my pretend grandfather was finished, the council staff considered calmly what to do with me. From a search through the records they determined that no family was then available with a dead child whose identity I could assume.

Mr. Barbanel, the second in charge, a man I would come to revere, walked over to where I sat on a bench and squatted in front of me. He must have been about thirty-five or so, which made him by far the youngest member of the council. He was a thickset man with a good honest face, a thatch of black hair, and dark eyes under thick black eyebrows and a wide mouth and a Slavic ski nose that looked as if it had been punched into shape. He could joke, Barbanel. He could talk to a child.

"So Yehoshua X, man of mystery, secret agent, are you ready for your next assignment?" He had in his hands a garrison cap of just the kind I had seen on the other boys. And with no further ceremony, he plopped the cap on my head and I was thereby placed under the wing of the council itself as a designated runner, known to all as Yehoshua, though with no last name, neither Mendelssohn nor my own family name, and with no identity card for my protection, but instead the runner's garrison cap with a yellow band that matched the yellow star on my jacket.

I suppose it was to keep me from brooding that I was quickly put on official runner business accompanying Micah, an older, gangly boy, on his rounds that evening as he informed his "customers," as he called them, that they must be at the square at dawn. After a while Micah encouraged me to deliver the message. I managed all right. The old man would be hanged and now I was going around telling everyone to be there to watch him hang. I felt weird, as dizzy as if I had been turned around in circles. I was no longer the tailor's pretend grandson but a pretend someone else—a nameless public charge? a council runner? I didn't know—but in any case a boy who knew how to hide when a person was in trouble, and who knew how to tell everyone to come see the trouble the person was in.

I spent my first night upstairs in the runners' dormitory above the council offices in the grip of a cold dread. How sickening to see an old man knocked down and then kicked. And then he had lain in the snow with his eyes rolled up in his head. It was at that moment I should have helped him instead of running away. I could have stayed with him for a little while anyway, even if only to get him back to his house.

In the night, in the darkness, is when you see the truth. I didn't exonerate myself because I was a child.

Now another thing is that I had never before this been close to the actual management of the ghetto, though I had of course heard my father speak critically of the council. And so as I lay awake through the dreadful night, I thought of what I had seen in the office and I had mixed feelings about it. I had been treated kindly enough, that wasn't what disturbed me. It was that everyone was so calm, it was uniform, the calmness of being on the inside, of seeing the whole picture. And it was undoubtedly necessary if they were to function. But in a sense, to my young eyes their calmness, the effect of it on me, was to propose that what was happening was routine, as if this terrible power of the Germans over us were normal.

This Dr. Koenig, so burdened with his responsibilities—it may have seemed to me that he functioned at the level of the Germans and was their equal. Given his unassailable dignity, the Germans may have had the same impression, and perhaps to deny to themselves that this was so, they had given him, as I was to learn, the derisive title "chief Jew," a ridicule which let him know where he stood. Of course he was no fool, the situation did not have to be described to him. He understood everything. Nor did he deny to himself or the other members of the council what they might have been tempted to think—that their roles were not morally ambivalent. For every extra ration they argued for, or relaxation of rule, they paid with a concession. It was a brutal calculus of bodies and work and food and fuel and health and sickness. I do not mean here to question his honor, his fortitude, his nobility, Dr. Koenig. He had been pressed into leadership by virtue of the high regard in which he was held by the community. He comported himself with courage under the most dangerous circumstances, which I came to understand in some detail later. But at this time he did nothing about the tailor who was at the center of the crisis. Not that he could have changed anything, of course. But in my ten-year-old heart, wretched with its own guilt, it seemed to me that he and everyone else was quite ready to accommodate the disaster that had overtaken Mr. Srebnitsky and let it run its course. I have thought about all of this a great deal. This calmness that so puzzled me as a child was first of all the characteristic of doctors, who are familiars of death and are composed in its presence. Sigmund Koenig was, after all, a physician. But beyond that it comes of a capacity to respond with pragmatic realism to experiences that are surreal, a capacity given to adults, though not usually to children. And this is where the ambiguity occurs.

Of course all of these niceties of thought were later to vanish as I myself was connected to the administration as a runner, and absorbed myself in the drama of my duties.

At dawn the Germans lit the square with their guardhouse floodlights and the headlights of their trucks. Enough of the citizenry were gathered, perhaps a thousand, perhaps fifteen hundred, to fill the square and satisfy the authorities. There was absolute silence but for the idling engines of the trucks. Prominently in attendance were Schmitz and his staff, officials of the Lithuanian police, the mayor of the city, assorted soldiers, and so on. Mr. Barbanel had suggested that it might be better for me to stay back in the dormitory until the whole thing was over, but I chose not to. In fact I worked my way through the crowd until I was off to the side quite near the scaffold.

When they brought out the tailor, he was draped over the shoulders of two Jewish ghetto policemen and already half dead. His feet were dragging. He could not walk, it looked to me as if his legs had been broken. They lifted him up the steps to the platform and held him propped under the arms while another policeman tied his hands behind him and slipped the noose over his head. His hands, those slender deft instruments I had admired, were mangled protuberances covered with dried blood. At the last moment before they kicked away the stand under his feet, Mr. Srebnitsky seemed to come out of his agonized stupor. He lifted his head and, of this I am sure, saw the scene before him clearly and, appreciating its magnitude, read his glory into it. You ask how I could know this: I had seen, we all had, the charred remains of the hospital victims, we knew the designated anonymity of the corpses machine-gunned en masse at the fort. I think now a mad triumphant light flashed from the tailor's eyes before the stand was kicked from under him and his frail body swung from the neck. There was no movement from him, no struggle, the life was gone from him almost instantly. The officials from the city got into their cars and drove off, the soldiers dispersed, the work details gathered in their ranks and passed through the gate and began their trek across the bridge. An S.S. man hung a crudely lettered sign around the corpse's neck: This Jew dared to raise his hand against a German officer.

The light began to appear at last in the sky. I lingered in the square. I had wanted Mr. Srebnitsky to see me, to see that I hadn't forgotten him. I sat down for a while with my back against the platform.

He'd had it in his power with his scissors to stab the commandant. For a moment I thought he'd done just that, so great was his rage. I have since concluded that he must have understood the disaster that would befall the ghetto were he to kill the man. So you see, what he accomplished was specifically self-sacrificial, a modulated act of defiance as deft and precise as his tailoring.

But after all these years, what lingers in my mind of this cantankerous old man, this iconoclast, this embittered soul, is that he let out my clothes as I outgrew them and saw to it that I got a new pair of shoes when the old ones no longer fit.

There is one more thing: The Germans had ordered that the body be left hanging on public display for twenty-four hours. An Orthodox rabbi found this an intolerable impiety. He came to the council office and demanded that something be done about it. Mr. Barbanel lost his temper. "An impiety!" he shouted. "Tell me, what isn't an impiety! To have murdered him, what was that—you have another word for that?" The rabbi turned on his heels and ran off. He went to the square along with another man, a helper who carried a white shroud. They climbed the platform and were in the act of cutting down the body when a German guard raised his carbine and shot them both dead.

===

—The planet earth is blessed with water, great slops of it, swaying tonnage of saline ocean and sea, clear blue lakes and fish tremblant rivers, streams, brooks, rills, and pulsing springs, mountain runoffs, rains, mists, fogs, and hurricanes. At our birth billions of years ago, an amorphous heap of buzzingly radiant star spinoff, we melted inward to a core of iron and nickel, molten at its edges, and formed on top of this a hot rock mantle, and mineral crust. We began immediately to cool, thus creating enormous clouds of vapor, which rained down into the great craters and basins of rock until the seas were filled. The rock dissolved into soil, granulated into seabed, and the seabed granules salinated and produced the first bubbling nitrogenized, oxygenized possibilities of blind, dumb life. Dead cellular matter flung up from the seas fertilized the rock soil. We are a blue oasis in black space, cocooned in our atmosphere of nutrient gases. We look peaceful but we are not. We are a planet of water and rock, sand and silt and soil. The tectonic plates under the earth's crust move and shift about, breaking the landmass into continents that float and change their shape over eons. The plates collide, ride one over another, crack, and great upheavals of the sea floor rise gasping into mountain ranges, enormous volcanoes in the seafloor create islands that bob up in the oceans, the earth's crust quakes, shivers us into different shapes, we buckle and cleave, storms assail our heavens, our mountains shake thunderous avalanches of snow down upon our valleys, our Arctic and Antarctic ice floes crack like the bones of God, our wind-worn dunes of desert pile up to bury us, maniac tornadoes fling us about and thump us against the ground like rag dolls, great floods of viscous burning lava bury our villages, and in all this fury of planetary self-fulfillment, we spin about an axis and roll around the sun, and our oceans are pulled and pushed by lunar tides, our oceans roll in waves which exist apart from the water they pass through, our atmospheres are shot through with electromagnetic frequencies, and we stand abroad our terrains totally magnetized by the iron core at our center, with our skies at night tumbling with asteroids and flashing with the inflamed boreal particles of solar winds that flare like the luminous eyes of saber-toothed tigers circling the darkness beyond our fire.

What a merry planet, everything said and done. For isn't it, after all, livable?

—belted kingfisher, a small diving bird with an overlarge, probably swelled, head and an absurd regal bearing conferred by the black band around his neck: he has beaked a baby bluefish and now whaps it several times on the piling. Whap whap. Kills it dead. Tosses it in the air and catches it on the vertical so that it slides down his gullet smoothly. Given his competence, the little kingfisher has a right to be self-important. Certainly not disposed to make invidious comparisons with diving birds five times his size, the osprey, for example, who can hover high up, wing-beating in place, and, seeing a shadow in the water, drop out of the sky like a stone.

—Of course there can be no secular Amphitryon. The credible impersonation of the husband can be possible only via a species of magic given to a mischievous, horny god like Zeus. To attribute such ambition to a man, even one as malign and talented as this fellow is, is to grind your way into a tank story clumsy, top-heavy with armament, and clanking forward on the treads of its plot. That's why it's a movie. It concludes something like this: Our seducer-usurper during the course of his life of covert adventure had spent some time with the Jivaro tribe of headhunters in the upper Amazon country near the Peruvian-Ecuadoran border. He had learned their ways from one of the elders. Now, with the unseated husband a constant annoyance, a vengeful fighter, unwilling to accept his defeat, having among other things found the means to buy a secondhand van to live in which he parks on the street in front of the dark-hearted couple's estate, and successfully representing himself in court as having that right as a citizen of parking on a public street in daylight hours, and having legally argued his further right to picket the house with placards and handbills explaining his unjust fate, and in all ways having managed to promote a continuation of the story, even to the point of getting a feature article written about himself as an interesting eccentric in the local suburban newspaper . . . he summons forth from the imposturing husband a degree of retribution inconceivable from someone who had not spent time off the edges of civilization.

The generous usurper invites the aggrieved and beggared CEO into the great house and without ceremony kills him. He decapitates the corpse and discards the body. Never mind the details of that. The details of what he does with the head are more interesting.

You don't want the skull, of course. You run your knife up the back of the neck to the crown and then you peel off the face and scalp, a time-consuming process when done right, because you don't want to pull the features out of shape. The skull, including teeth and eyes, discarded, you are left with your basic material.

You turn the face skin inside-out and sew up the eyelids. Then you stitch the lips together and, last, after turning the skin right-side-out, sew up the incision you made up the back of the head until you have a pouch about as big as the original head. You drop this into boiling water, to which some herbs I cannot name lest this become an instruction manual for some idiot . . . are added to keep the hair from falling out. After several hours the pouch is approximately one third its former size.

And in this shrunken manner the beggared CEO is presented on an outstretched palm as a trophy to his stolen and enslaved wife, who, just before committing suicide, calls the police to tell them her husband has murdered the derelict camped outside their house and that they will have all the evidence they need hanging from a string of beads around her neck. Ironically enough, the shrunken head now resembles the dark-hearted impostor as he was before his cosmetic surgery, more than the husband before his shrinking, so as if God is an épée of irony, this sharpest of points is delivered posthumously to the impostor, who, having been established as a missing person since his cosmetic crossover, is now brought to trial as the murderer of himself.

And what was proposed as a tale of subtle existential horror turns out after all to be a simple waxworks melodrama, wherein the author, like his villain, gets his just deserts. And if it is true that a sociopath can never show restraint but must go on and on in ever greater amplification of his evil until he is destroyed, so must an author honor the character of his idea and allow it to express itself in all its wretched insufficiency until it too reaches its miserable

end.

⸗

—1. I number my thoughts for the sake of clarity so that each thought rings clearly and in its own distinct pitch, like a bell.

1.01. In other words I propose to think only in facts. (This in itself is not a fact.)

2. I have the name Ludwig Wittgenstein.

3. Ludwig is a common German name.

4. I believe, however, I was named after Ludwig van Beethoven.

5. While the truth of (4.) cannot be verified, my belief that it is true is a fact.

5.01. My belief is a reasonable inference from the fact that my mother was a pianist and believed it a fact that music was essential to life . . .

5.11. . . . and that my older brother Paul became a concert pianist . . .

5.21. . . . and that my older and suicidal brother Hans was a musical prodigy . . .

5.31. . . . and that my sisters Hermine, Helene, and Margarete were all gifted or musically literate . . .

5.41. . . . and that Brahms and Mahler were friends of my parents and came to play music in our home.

5.51. Brahms, Mahler, my parents, and everyone I knew believed it to be a fact that Beethoven was the greatest of all musical geniuses.

5.61. I believed that in being named after a genius, I myself was a designated genius.

6. It is a fact that my parents and siblings did not share my belief.

6.01. They were led to their conclusion by the fact that I did not speak until I was four years old.

7. I was able to speak long before this but was so appalled by the world in which I found myself that I chose silence.

7.01. Ever since, in all the philosophy I have done, I have distinguished the truths that can be spoken from the truths that exist only in silence.

7.02. Ever since, in all the philosophy I have done, I have argued that the truths of silence, when spoken, are no longer true.

8. My first memory is of the grand staircase in my home in the Alleegasse, Vienna.

8.01. It rose on thirty-four marble steps ten feet wide.

8.02. It was carpeted in a luxurious red, green, and white nap—the colors of the Austro-Hungarian empire.

8.03. The carpet was held to the bottom of each riser by a shining brass rod.

8.1. Railings with alabaster balusters in the shape of slender vases lined each landing.

8.12. Side walls of pink Carrara marble provided reflections, to infinity, of a person ascending to the great foyer.

8.2. The ceilings were framed in carved and gilded cove moldings.

8.21. They were frescoed in patterns of Persian elements.

8.3. At the top of the staircase hung an immense tapestry of gentlemen in silk tights and ladies in broad-brimmed hats and hoop skirts and parasols posed before a woods, with thick pink clouds and a pale blue sky over them.

8.4. Before this, on a pedestal, stood a large Dresden urn with flowers that were changed every morning.

8.5. Crouched on the floor on either side of the urn was a Chinese brass dog.

9. The baroque splendor of that palatial home in the Alleegasse nauseated me then and nauseates me now to think of it.

9.01. Nausea catalogs the indigestible contents of the stomach that are to be brought up.

9.02. Memory that is nauseating catalogs the contents of the mind that can never be brought up.

9.03. After the peristaltic crisis, the feeling of illness or weakness is generalized through the system.

9.04. The memory of the grand staircase in the palatial home in the Alleegasse produces in me a generalized despair of the *fin de siècle* culture of my youth.

10. My parents gave over their lives to the climbing of such stairs.

10.01. Their grandparents were Jews who had converted to Catholicism.

10.02. At the technical school I was sent to, Adolf Hitler was a student two grades below mine.

11. When I came home from the Great War, I immediately signed over to my siblings the immense wealth of my inheritance.

12. I designed on the principle of the cube a severely simple, unadorned, unembellished, unornamented home in the Kundmanngasse for my sister for whose soul I feared.

13. I went off to live poor and work with my hands in the country.

13.01. I taught elementary school arithmetic to the children of peasants.

14. I was drawn to philosophy.

14.01. I realized that the language of Western philosophical thought was choked with pretentious baroque tchotchkes, like my ancestral home in the Alleegasse.

15. I bought a notebook with ruled lines.

16. I retired to a cabin on a Norwegian fjord and was more desolately alone than I could endure.

17. I wept in order to hear a human sound.

18. I looked into the endless Norwegian night and considered the new physics of Einstein.

19. I wrote in my notebook that even if all the possible scientific questions are answered, *our problem is still not touched at all.*

=

—At the Knickerbocker with Pem:
I've got the tape on, is that okay?
Whynot.

Has anything else happened?

Am I still in, you mean? Hanging by a thread. As far as they're concerned, how can they not show charity to one of their own, or their once own? And I won't quit, I'm afraid to quit. My office, however meaningless, I think of as staving off dereliction. This crucifix dangling from my neck protects me from myself.

Come on . . .

Don't laugh. Even when I had a family and lived on Park Avenue I was never that far. My vagrant nature shadows me. Always has. My real home is the city streets. I walk them. There is something in the streets for me, some secret, not necessarily in the interest of my well-being. . . . Another reason I won't quit is I still pray. I find myself still doing that. Do you pray?

No.

You should try it. As an act of self-dramatization, it can't be beat. You get a hum, a reverberant hum of the possibility of your own consequential voice. Like singing in the shower. [laughs] . . . I shouldn't talk this way. Why can't I have a feeling without crapping all over it? The truth is I still have hope for myself . . . the long shot that I'll convert myself to an associated conviction. Catholicism, say, or Lutheranism. Like the great Bishop Pike, who moved around, a Catholic, then a Protestant, a dabbler in spiritualism. . . . Ah well, maybe he's not the best example, being another good mind gone to ruin.

What about the big cross, Pem, the one from St. Tim's?

What about it?

Last time you hinted at another explanation. Something I missed in the Heist chapter.

Did I say that?

You did.

Well you may have it in there somewhere, you know, you just don't know it.

Come on, Pem, this is important.

[inaudible] . . . Let me pay for the dinner this time.

Why?

I'm not destitute. Besides, I can't be bought that cheaply. I'm worth more.

You think I'm taking advantage?

No, no, you know that's not it. We've had that out. I said I didn't want a royalty, and so on. All that is firm. But I get nervous. These are the substantive matters of my life.

Gentlemen?

What are we drinking?

Absolut on the rocks.

A Stoli Cristall for me . . .

So?

I may want to write my own book. [laughs] Look, he's turning pale.

No, why not, you should.

Not what you do. Nonfiction. Nonfiction about fiction. The opposite of what you do.

You think so? I'll give you my research.

[laughter]

I do like the attention, I'll admit that. If you do your job, I expect the demand on me to write my own story will be fierce. Horse's mouth kind of thing. Big publisher's advance. Oh boy.

Then we'd better get back to work. May we?

Stoli for you, Absolut . . .

L'chaim. . . . Point is, they may not have been the mindless creeps I thought they were who lifted the cross. And it may not have been anti-Semites, or Jewish ultras, who brought it to the roof of the EJ synagogue. Poor Joshua was beginning to think so too.

Then who? I don't understand. And anyway it was an affront whoever put it there.

Maybe, maybe not.

What else could it have been?

That is Sarah's view. She remains the superb rationalist.

Well I'm on her side. Don't you guys teach that Christianity is the successor religion? So where would Evolutionary Judaism evolve according to the belief of a militant Christian if not to the cross? And where was this errant little synagogue headed according to an ultra-Orthodox Jew if not to apostasy? Either way it was vicious.

I remind you that the later Wittgenstein says there is meaning after all in propositions that can't be verified.

Wittgenstein? How did he get into this?

You know, of course, Christianity was originally a Jewish sect. Everybody knows that.

So. What does that have to do—

Please. Am I or am I not your Divinity Detective?

Okay, okay.

Just bear with me. Paul—you know, Paul. Fellow had that stroke on the road to Damascus?

A stroke? [laughs]

Why not? I mean it knocked him out, and left him weak and wobbly. A vision stroke. We don't have those anymore. Strokes today, you just lose capacity. His turned him. He'd been fairly contemptuous of Jesus before that. You following this?

I am trying.

He was fervent, Paul, he'd found their Messiah. That's what he preached. Mostly they weren't buying it. Meanwhile there were these gentiles who were listening in the back. He got a better reception there. But the gentiles were scared of circumcision, as who could blame a grown man. So he told them they didn't have to be circumcised, they could still become Jews. Did you know that? That was it, right there.

That was what?

. . . [inaudible] . . . and out he went, bag and baggage. And the gentiles with him. I mean, there were circumstances working, in-history circumstances. You can have a revelation, fine, but then what? In this case, a new religion. In all cases. New visions spring from old, sects break away from churches and become churches, ideas of God bloom like viruses. Over and over . . . [inaudible] . . . react to the historicizing of God, saying, No that's not it, that's not it. Because God is not historical. God is ahistorical. In fact probably God and religion are incompatible propositions.

The God of the Bible operates in history.

Sure He does.

You deny the validity of all revelation?

All revelation is countermanded. Let me ask you one: Do you believe God gave Moses the Decalogue, the Ten Commandments on Mount Sinai?

Well it's a great story. I think I'm a judge of stories and that's a great story.

They're all great stories. The Decalogue structurally, generically, is modeled on the ancient Mesopotamian lord-and-vassal treaties. Did you know that?

No.

Do you believe Jesus was the son of God, resurrected? Do you know the predominant culture of his life and times was Greek? The predominant language was Greek, all through the Roman empire? So how many Greek mystery cults told of resurrections?

I have trouble remembering the Greek myths.

Dozens. The Gospelers were writers. What is it you said writers do? Make the composition? Put things in, leave things out. To a secular fellow like you this may not be news, or even bad news. But if you're a religious guy like me and you're not a fundamentalist, you've got trouble. Do you turn the truths of your faith into a kind of edifying poetry? Then you're a religious schizoid, your right brain believes, your left can only relish the sentiment of believing. And Jesus as the chosen son is no more valid than Jews as the chosen people. And what has happened to God in all this?

You think human thought was a different mode then?

It was brilliant then as it is now among the cosmologists. It was sophisticated, it was politically astute, it brought order. It deferred terror. Mode? I don't know. They used what they had. Visions. Hallucinations. Just as science is using what it has. So. There it is. I've told you everything. Let's have another. Miss? Could we have another round?

Wait a minute, Pem.

Well, everything you can buy.

You never knew any of this before?

I always knew all of it. We all do. Divinity students read Nietzsche for immunization. Fact is, most of us make a decision and stick to it. . . . But if you want to speak of modalities, I'll tell you what I've kept. What I know in my heart and in my brain is the closest I'll ever get to a revelation of my own. I am still happily, thankfully vulnerable to one aspect of the ancient apprehension. I can recognize a sign when I see one.

What does that mean?

Not a stop sign, my secular good buddy.

Uh-oh. You mean after all you've been saying—

I know it's hard.

. . . like it was the Jews for Jesus? Is that what you're telling me?

Everett, goddamnit, give me a break. . . . It's not the Jews for Jesus or any other forlorn fucking thing you can think of! Why did I bring this up! Talking about it is ruinous, it turns it to shit, like everything else.

Well I can't [inaudible] . . .

Listen: It doesn't matter what maniacs put it there or why they did, don't you understand that? A sign is a sign. And when you know it's a sign, that's enough. That's how you know it's a sign. It is not something whose meaning is instantaneous. It doesn't light up on Broadway. And it's not something you go looking for, it has to come to you. That's what signs do, they come to you. There is moment to this thing, where you know something . . . has finally happened. It is a thunderous silent thing. I made a mistake even mentioning it.

Shall I tell you about our specials?

Not now, dear, we have some drinking to do. . . . I shouldn't talk about it and neither should you. Let's forget the whole thing. . . .

Come on, Father.

Listen, I'll just say this one thing. You place a big brass cross down on a synagogue roof, what could you be doing? Well, you could be doing with one brilliant stroke everything I've been translating into language for you.

=

—Joel, he was the littlest runner . . . Isaiah, Dov, Micah, who went to work in the city eventually. When a boy grew too tall, you see, and his voice changed and he was clearly then fit for factory labor, another identity would be found for him and off he would go. Daniel, Solomon . . . Maybe in some cases these were their adopted names, as Yehoshua was mine. I don't know. But all were the hope of the Jewish parents who had left them orphans, this covey of kings and prophets waiting up in the loft for their assignments.

I will say that there was not a great spirit of camaraderie among us. We had each suffered great losses and were depleted in spirit. Also we were hungry most of the time. As growing boys we did not have enough to eat, and this made us lethargic. When we were not busy we tended to fall asleep. So there was never a problem of noise, none of the normally outlandish behavior of boys. We were quiet and kept our own counsel. And we were each privy to secret things we were taught to keep absolutely silent about, not even confiding in one another about where we went or what we had to do.

In these circumstances we grew stoic, with an unnatural patience for our age. And so even now, in my adult survival and the blessings I have amassed for myself, meaning your late dear mother and yourself, my great blessings and consolation, and even in the sacred bliss of walking as a free man down an American street, I have my constant companion, the shadow of my unlived past, the other-named boy of my lost history.

When my father's vegetable garden was again in flower, long lines of refugees began to appear, shuffling across the bridge with their bags and valises as the Germans strove to replenish the supply of slave labor for their war plants. The newcomers camped in the square while the S.S. examined them and passed them over to council staff to assign them their dwellings. The runners were employed in leading them first to the delousing station. Lice were a constant problem in the ghetto, I'd had them myself. The danger, of course, was that they carried diseases like typhus.

Every once in a while those who had been rejected for one reason or another would climb onto the bed of an open truck, and when it was full, the truck would be driven back across the bridge. I could not look at those people.

By the summer the ghetto population had swollen to six or seven thousand. Food rationing became more difficult to manage. Public sanitary measures took on a greater urgency. More people were recruited to work for the council, the German managerial bureaucracy increased. More and more often I had to run like the wind from my observation post in the square to let them know a staff car flying a Nazi pennon from its fender was crossing the bridge. And there were all the new people to be registered, under their own names or some other, and testimonies for Mr. Barbanel secretly to record. Many of these refugees brought news with them of the fate of other communities. Outside the city of Kovno, people had been taken into a field where pits had been dug, and they were herded into these pits and machine-gunned from the embankments, and then others were pushed in on top of them and machine-gunned, and in this way, to the screams of agony, with men and women and children murdered and bleeding and buried alive, ten thousand people perished in less than a day. Several sources attested to this number.

Whenever Mr. Barbanel received reports, he either wrote down verbatim what he was told or asked the person reporting to write a statement. He kept a diary in which he reported everything that happened, along with the relevant documentation, the latest regulations, the execution orders, the deaths, minutes of the council meetings, orders signed by the infamous Commandant Schmitz, proscriptions, dicta, identity papers for the work details—every imaginable item went into this history of his. I often saw him writing. He used whatever paper he had on hand—unused student exercise books, for example. Even now I can close my eyes and see Barbanel's handwriting, a neat Yiddish, like stitches sewn into the page, the characters very small, the words flying off his pen line after line in his passion to say what happened each day, each moment, of our lives as captives, that supple, deft determination to put it all down, record it indelibly, as something of immense human importance. As it was. As it always will be. Of course his doing this was illegal. The Germans were quite aware of their culpability and forbade unauthorized writings or photographs. They had confiscated all cameras. But as the chief aide to Dr. Koenig, Barbanel had always to be writing something, and it was relatively easy for him to enfold this within his formal duties.

Gradually, over time, sitting on the bench in his office while he interviewed a new arrival or seeing him stuff a week's past orders from the German command into his briefcase, I understood what he was doing and asked him one day if he was by profession a historian. Barbanel looked surprised for a moment and then smiled and shook his head. "You are one smart kid, Yehoshua," he said. "Yes, I'm a historian, by necessity. But you wouldn't tell anyone, would you." This was a statement, not a question. I swore I wouldn't and we shook hands on it.

Barbanel had been a dealer in lumber before the war. I suppose it was because he was a younger man that he generally took bolder positions than Dr. Koenig in council discussions. It was good morale for us boys that he poked fun at the enemy, made fun of their ways, as if it were not their power over us but their stupidity that characterized them. In the presence of the Germans he was not deferential but matter-of-fact. He made no effort to hide his contempt for them, yet for some reason they tolerated this.

Now that I knew about Barbanel's archive, I was brought further into his confidence. Every week or so he put in my hands a packet wrapped in oilcloth and tied with twine. "For Miss Margolin, and watch your step." I would slip the packet under my shirt and run with it to this nurse in the hospital, Greta Margolin, who was his friend and, as I realized only when I was older, his lover.

Miss Margolin was every bit as brave as he. Not only because she kept the diary for him, but because she was involved in the very dangerous business of smuggling women who were pregnant out of the ghetto, and in at least one case of a woman who had somehow escaped attention, delivering the baby and taking them both out, how and where, I didn't know. She was a real nurse, the only real nurse there. I suppose she was in her thirties. Of course I was in love with her. I looked forward to these runs though they were probably the most dangerous thing I did. This Greta, it was not so much her beauty, though she was quite good-looking, with prominent cheekbones, a good well-defined jaw, and straight straw-colored hair, which she tied behind her . . . but the way she smiled and her eyes lit up when she saw me. She had a lovely healing smile, it broke out, that smile, spontaneously and with such affection in it, as if in that moment no troubles could interfere with what was between us as dear human beings, the inviolable state of human love that was the true natural thing. "Yehoshua, my boyfriend, where have you been all this time?"

Mr. Barbanel, I could admire and trust and even revere, though without knowing it, but there was about him always a sense of urgency, the need to get things done or undone. With Greta Margolin, in her always sparkling clean white nurse's frock, I found a dignified bearing, a composure, that I remember now and that my boy's heart translated as her physical attraction. In my eyes she was the most beautiful woman I had ever seen. I watched her hands as she received the manuscript package from me, sometimes they touched mine. I would be flustered and, without ceremony, run off and hear her soft laugh behind me.

She stored Barbanel's manuscript somewhere, I didn't know where, but I understood her nurse's position was a factor in keeping it safe until she could smuggle it out of the ghetto, across the bridge, to a hiding place in the city or perhaps in the countryside.

Barbanel's diary, by the time I was aware of it, must have run into thousands of pages, volumes, a whole trunk full of material. And since neither he nor Greta Margolin was to survive the destruction of the ghetto, to this day those papers are hidden there in the earth of Eastern Europe, in its rubble, in the wreckage and ruination and dust of its Christian tradition.

I myself am not a writer and so I cannot convey to you the presence of this couple, their living presence, the immediacy of the breathing being of them, their greatness of life. My worshipful memory of them disguises the truth, that they were ordinary folks who in normal times would have lived out quite modest lives. They were resplendently nothing special, Josef Barbanel and Greta Margolin, no more than my own mother and father, no more than any of us.

I think now that though Dr. Koenig knew and approved of Barbanel's secret archive, he did not know, or pretended not to know, about Barbanel's shortwave radio, which was kept inside a wall in our attic dormitory over the council offices. Two or three nights a week, Barbanel would climb the ladder to our quarters and we would assist him as he pried open the wall board to expose the radio and plug it in to a socket affixed to our one light fixture. We had several training practices in closing the radio down quickly. And one boy always kept watch at the window and another stationed himself beside the door to listen for any sounds below.

There were immeasurable gains to our morale in having that secret radio, which I think Barbanel understood. He sat cross-legged on the floor, with his earphones on, and listened with his eyes closed to the late-night British news broadcast. We studied his face intently, trying to learn from his expression if the news was good or bad, watching him nod or shake his head or lift his fist in silence, sitting through fifteen minutes of this, totally rapt, fearless and, above all, connected in spirit to the rest of the world.

The radio was a battered German-made table model, a Grundig, with rounded edges and a cloth register over the speaker and a dial that raised or lowered a bar up and down an illuminated scale of shortwave frequencies. I felt I could see into the glowing radio as into the cosmos. I was moved to have philosophical thoughts. Why was the scale of numbers on the Nazi radio recognizable to me, a Jewish boy? Because numbers were immutable. Their order was fixed, universally true. Even Nazis had to comply with them. Well, if numbers were the same for everyone everywhere in the universe, didn't that mean they had to have been installed in our brains by God? And if so, why—except to teach everyone the nature of truth. It was true, for example, that two plus two of anything was four. No matter what you applied them to, numbers, being fixed and eternally what they were and nothing else, epitomized truth.

I wouldn't have wanted to mention my idea to my father or the tailor Srebnitsky. But in the darkness of our loft, I would stare into this illuminated cosmos of radio frequencies and nurture the idea that numbers were the imperishably true handiwork of God. (Not that the Nazis would ever know.) And that He had given us the power to perceive His imperishably true handiwork for a reason. The reason was so that we would be able to perceive the Messiah when he came, whose identity would be as self-evident as two and two equals four, and whose coming would bring the universally recognized, imperishable, and beneficent truth of God to everyone and everything in the world for all time to come. Such were a child's thoughts in the darkness of the illuminated frequencies of the Grundig radio.

$$=$$

—I mean, Sarah functions, she is raising their children, running that household. She resigned from Emanuel and works now only for what's left of their little congregation. But she's in a state deeper than mourning. I'll tell you something—could we have another round here, please!—I'll tell you something, this woman . . . Not that she is angelically inhumanly perfect . . . but there is such a gravity of soul there, such immense inherent, I don't know, decorum. This isn't ordinary piety I'm talking about, and certainly not sanctity, a word I hate, it's more as if she is naturally endowed with a modest urban grace—as if she's a New Yorker living here but also . . . in Tillich's country of ultimate concern. Am I being totally incoherent?

No, I think I understand.

You were right that I'm attracted to her. You got that right. I don't remember saying so in so many words. Christ, I'm in love with her, I want to be with her. I would convert, if that's what it took. But I make no move. I have the feeling this would trivialize me in her eyes, that, in a way she would immediately forgive, I would reveal a lack of understanding of her serious, smiling, irrevocable . . . widowhood.

And believe it or not I, too, mourn him. To deal with courage with the incredible assault on God, by modernity, by the century, and by the religious themselves. The quest for a believable God, Christ how I understand that. A thin, wiry little guy, Joshua, there was not an ounce of fat on him, a runner's build, he was really intelligent, but so genuinely modest, he had a characteristic frown—I don't know, of self-judgment?—he was a serious, gentle soul, neat, meticulous in his thinking, with a very natural serious precision of mind, and this is what she loved, what she found in him as the mate for her and a father for her children. I mean, I was transfixed by both of them. Isn't that rare? Where do you see that nowadays, people of Godliness whom you want to be anywhere near?

=

—By this time, a group of houses at the south end of the ghetto had been converted to a new small hospital of thirty or forty bunk beds, the same Germans who had burned the old hospital having decided that those with infectious diseases must after all continue to be isolated, identified, and then dealt with in a more precise and perhaps less wasteful way. Of course Dr. Koenig was resolved never again to hospitalize a patient with typhus or any other infectious disease. At great risk to himself, he treated that patient at home and wrote a false diagnosis on his chart. I have told you of his bravery, and this was one aspect of it. But that was not all. With the complicity of the one other Jewish doctor and Miss Margolin, Koenig would occasionally admit someone for a hospital stay who was not ill but in some way at risk of discovery and execution. Then there was the matter of illegal midwifing. For all these reasons, the hospital was an extremely vulnerable area and its security was constantly monitored by the council.

So now one morning I arrived at the little hospital with a packet of Mr. Barbanel's writings inside my shirt, and Miss Margolin was in the admitting office with a man who seemed to be annoying her. She glanced at me over his shoulder and shook her head with the slightest motion so that I knew this was not the time to conduct our business. I stood against the wall, near the door.

"You are not sick," she was saying to the man. "There is nothing wrong with you."

"How can you be so sure?" He turned around and looked at me with a big smile on his face but with eyes that sized me up, from my runner's cap to my toes. "How can nurse know I am not sick without she examines me?"

He was an ugly, horse-faced man, his teeth broken and discolored. He spoke this odd, not quite right Yiddish. He wore farm clothes and heavy boots caked in mud. A cap on his head which he did not remove though he was indoors in the presence of a woman.

"You must examine me if I say I am sick," he said to Miss Margolin.

"Your head is what needs to be examined," Miss Margolin said. "Go back to work, and if you come here again like this, I will report you."

She opened the door behind her, and glancing coldly at him, she withdrew. The door closed and I heard the bolt slide into place.

"You know my sickness!" he shouted. "A man who is sick with love for you!"

He turned to me, not smiling now. "What do you look at?" he said. He was brazen, he stepped behind the counter and peered at the papers there, the notices on the wall, and everything else that was none of his business. I didn't move. I felt the packet of papers against my skin. I was afraid of him, but also angry and protective of Greta Margolin. I should have gotten out of there, but I hoped that with someone, even a boy, watching him he would feel constrained to leave. A minute later, he whistled a kind of soft nonchalant whistle as he walked by me out the door, tilting my hat over my eyes for good measure.

In all the stories and films, spies are cunning and subtle and it takes the whole story to flush them out. In the ghetto there was nothing subtle about them. They gave off the smell even if they weren't German.

Perhaps that same evening, or maybe the next day, Mr. Barbanel sat me down in private and told me the archival material he had taken such pains to assemble and that Greta Margolin had been hiding for him was no longer safe in the ghetto. "It must be moved," he said. "From now on things must be done differently. Do you understand how important this is?" I nodded. I knew. And I knew immediately, without asking, why he was confiding in me, for after all, wasn't I his star runner?

My drab little mind was brought to life by the excitement, the danger of what I was now to do. It was a feverish feeling, quite unhealthy, it was a drug, an amphetamine, this danger to a boy who knew if he was caught he could be tortured and shot.

Yet, in fact, as you might suppose, knowing Barbanel, my expeditions were reasonably safe. The bulk of the archive, a footlocker's worth, had been transported over the bridge and to the city, how or by what subterfuge or bribery, I was not told. It remained for me to smuggle out the current material wrapped in oilcloth and held with precious strips of adhesive tape to my chest and back. I made perhaps seven, perhaps eight trips over that many weeks, from the late summer into the fall. As the weather grew colder I felt safer, because I had not only a shirt to cover my contraband but a sweater and a jacket over that.

Now, this may bring a smile, but as a boy your father had a thick head of hair. You'll just have to believe me. They trimmed it closely and, besides that, dyed it to a color not exactly blond but certainly lighter. This was one of the pains they took to make me as inconspicuous or non-Jewish as possible for the city. I was outfitted in clothing my own size and not too small for me, as my own clothes were. Of course I wore no star or garrison cap. And I was given a fairly decent pair of shoes. These shoes I carried tied by their laces hung from my neck as I made my way out of the ghetto through an abandoned viaduct, so antiquated that the Germans did not know about it. The access to this pipe, incidentally, was by means of the cistern inside a stone mill house. I was not entirely comfortable scurrying along in a crouch like one of the rats who lived down there, trying unsuccessfully to hold my breath because of the cold, rotten smell of iron viscera and earth and animal droppings. But it was not that far to go, really. The viaduct ended in a pile of boulders and rubble at the river's edge maybe a half-mile upstream of the barbed wire fencing around the ghetto. Here the river was quite shallow and filled with rocks, it was at a bend, so that it was possible to cross unseen behind the cover of trees and undergrowth on both banks.

I'm making it sound more arduous than it was. A simple walk down a lane brought me to a lightly populated residential district on the city's outskirts. I simply waited at a corner for a streetcar. I was equipped with money, a knapsack of schoolbooks, I knew the Lithuanian language, and I had a false identity card with yet another name. Not once on any of these trips was I ever close to being discovered. I was never the object of more than a glance from a policeman or a German soldier, although women of a motherly age, as I got into the heart of the city, sometimes regarded me with curiosity, or even a look of suspicion. I would smile at them brightly and even tip my cap and wish them good day.

So this was Yehoshua X, Secret Agent Mystery Boy, in action. My trips were designed to put me in the heart of the city in the late afternoon, when the streets were active. But a crushing revelation awaited me each time I arrived. True, it was a wartime occupied city, with troop carriers rushing through the streets, and Nazi flags flying from the city hall, and not exactly a profusion of goods and foodstuffs in the stores and shops, and not exactly a well-fed or happy populace to be seen going about their business . . . nevertheless, to see the urban expanse around me, to be assailed by the sights and sounds of the city I had been born in and had gone to school in, the streets of stone apartment houses with courtyards, electric power lines, street railways, overhead signs that suggested the vast extent of city environs, to be recalled to the assumption of a normal historically grounded modern civilization, as wretched and anti-Semitic as it had been . . . and to compare this inevitably to the pathetic impoverished little slave camp in which we lived, with our rural hovels, penned like animals, and isolated, displaced, and habituated to the terror of not knowing each day if we were to be allowed to live to the next . . . it was unfortunate for anyone, let alone a child, to have this acute instruction driven home. I mean, if I had not been assigned to make these trips with Barbanel's documents, I would not have so keenly felt the terrible loss that had been incurred, nor understood with a voluminous awareness the catastrophe that had happened and was still happening . . .

My destination was a small Catholic church in a working-class neighborhood not far from the railroad station, a stone church, with a small graveyard in the front. Unfortunately I cannot remember its name. It probably wasn't that big, nothing as grand as the cathedral in the central square, but it seemed formidable enough to me, and I have to say, the moment I entered through the oaken doors was always the uneasiest moment of my journey. It was dark in there, with banks of flickering candles, those votive candles that reminded me of the yahrzeit or memory candles that, when we had them, we lit in the ghetto for our dead. I couldn't understand why there were gates, like prison bars, to separate the altar from the people praying in the pews, sometimes a German soldier or two, but more usually women, elderly women with babushkas over their heads. The women and the candles seemed very Jewish to me, although this could only be a puzzling thought, what with the large, painted, and very realistic plaster Christ hanging on his crucifix in the apse behind the altar with blood dripping from his forehead and hands and feet.

The procedure in which I had been trained required me to kneel and cross myself and then repair to one of the confessionals off to the side, on an aisle. Here I would wait for a few minutes until, having seen that the coast was clear, a priest, Father Petrauskas was his name, opened the door and led me to his rectory.

He was a kind man, the father, he would nod and smile in genuine friendship when he greeted me. Some of his teeth were missing. His head was shaven, and his face was so wrinkled with grooves, folds, and crosshatches that it seemed made of parchment. His eyes were slitted in his cheeks. His black suit was tight on him and very shiny. After I had removed my shirt, he would unwind the adhesive tape, always taking care where it had to be peeled from my skin, and accept the packets of material, and when I was again buttoned up, he would give me something to eat, a piece of bread with jam, or some soup, and sit across the table from me and watch me eat. I do not mean to libel the Catholic Church, but it has occurred to me from time to time over the years that this father may have been a Jewish convert to Catholicism. I don't know why I have that feeling, I have no evidence this was the case. Somehow he was known to Barbanel as a trusted friend and had taken this risk for what, given the exigencies of the times, might have seemed an almost abstract cause, the cause of the historical record, the helpless cause of no redress but memory.

I would leave, usually as darkness was setting in, and retrace the route and take the streetcar back to the edges of town, getting off one stop before or after my corner, where I drifted down the lane to the river crossing. Here I would once more remove my Lithuanian boy's shoes and crawl back through the viaduct into the ghetto. I would arrive exhilarated and go looking for Mr. Barbanel to report my success, and then I would change into my clothes like an actor after his performance and set my runner's cap firmly on my head.

=

—You can go up to look at birds in the short summer of the Canadian Arctic, flying from Yellowknife low in a DC-3 over the startled herds of caribou to Bathurst. There you camp on top of the impregnable tundra and go out in outboard motors with the Inuit, the people who live up there. In the summer, the lower Arctic is a sea, and they take you out in their open boats to an island where they know one eagle lives, or a clutch of phalaropes, or a white gyrfalcon raising a nest of chicks. The numbers are small in the Arctic, whatever is alive is noticed. The genuine face of pleasure of our guide at the tiller pointing up as a yellow-billed loon beat past I thought of as a collegial satisfaction. Some of these little islands you stop at seem to be made of eggshells and feathers and guano. There is another kingdom of life that has nothing to do with us. The Inuit who've not gone to the cities, those who stay behind living the old way—modified, of course, they use snowmobiles for their wolf hunting in winter—the Inuit hunt and fish, and navigate these waters by taking their position from a distant mountain, which appears as a face looking at the sky. The face is Indian, the top of the mountain is the nose, and these Inuit are therefore known as the People of the Nose.

Spent a half a day waiting below the gyrfalcon's nest and finally saw her, the mother, pounding over the valley with a shockingly large prey in her talons, a gopher, which was deposited with a great hovering whir of wings in the nest she had built on a rock ledge. The sky was an icy blue. She was a broad-chested bird, not as tall as an eagle. The fledglings screeching, my companions clicking their cameras, and I adrenalized with joy to see this beautiful predatory creature that Yeats had seen and that made me wonder what other way to live than boating through the Arctic seas to look at birds.

===

—As the earth spins on its axis, its planetary sloppage of water rises in tidal swells continuously around its periphery, bulging like the cornea of a farsighted eye. At the same time, the earth's rotation sends the sea waters spinning in opposite directions, westward in the Northern Hemisphere, eastward in the Southern, so that if water could plait, the earth would twist into a long blue-green braid. If for some reason the planetary rotation decreased sufficiently, the waters of the earth would fly off and crystallize into an ice blue ring that would eventually attenuate and head into space, an enormous comet with all its plankton, crabs, fish, bivalves, whales, siphonophores, and shipwrecks flash-frozen for eternity. The planet's remaining core of rock and mineral and molten magma would glow for a moment like an ember, or like the section of a radiant creature's toothy jawbone, before it crashed into the moon, creating a big burning smoking mass of disintegrated ores that would be neatly sucked up into the sun like krill into the mouth of a gulper eel. So be thankful to God that this system of cosmic checks and balances, as eccentric as it is, seems to be working. And just as there are the Alps and the Himalayas and the Andes and the Rockies, so there are undersea mountain ranges even more vast. And just as we have our sunlit river-running canyons, so does the sea bottom have its deep trenches. And as we have our flatlands and deserts, so does the seabed stretch for endless miles of abyssal plain. And just as we have our mountain goats standing transfixedly faced into the wind on the unequal crags of our highest mountains, so does the lightless, airless ocean bottom, with its tons of pressure per square inch, have its living tube worms and anglerfish, sea spiders, whipnoses, and sea lilies undulating slimed in the soundless blackness, their mouths agape and tentacles upheld to catch the flocculent dead matter drifting like snow from the blue and green ocean above. Nameless creatures composed of tendrils with suckers on the end, stems with mouths, or jet-propelled worms with toxic stingers and ink-ejection mechanisms, receive as God's bounty a perpetual fall of death that keeps them alive as they squirt and wriggle about their business. This is all part of the Universal Plan. We are instructed that life does not require air or light or warmth. We are instructed that whatever condition God provides, some sort of creature will invent itself to live in it. There is no fixed morphology for living things. No necessary condition for life. Thousands of unknown plant and animal beings are living in the deepest canyons of the black, cold water and they have their own movies. Their biomass is far in excess of our own sunlit and air-breathing plant and animal life. At the very bottom of the sea are smoking vents of hydrogen sulfide gases in which bacteria are pleased to flourish. And feeding upon these are warty bivalves and viscous, gummy jellies and spiny eels with the amazing ability to fluoresce when they are attacked or need to illuminate their prey. God has a reason for all this. There is one fish, the hatchet, which skulks about in the deep darkness with protuberant eyes on the top of its horned head and the ability to electrically light its anus to blind predators sneaking up behind it. The electric anus, however, is not an innate feature. It comes from a colony of luminescent bacteria that house themselves symbiotically in the fish's asshole. And there is a Purpose in this as well which we haven't yet ascertained. But if you believe God's divine judgment and you countenance reincarnation, then it may be reasonably assumed that a certain bacterium living in the anus of a particularly ancient hatchet-fish at the bottom of the ocean is the recycled and fully sentient soul of Adolf Hitler glimmering miserably through the cloacal muck in which he is periodically bathed and nourished.

—

—Moviemaking everywhere in New York and now they're here filming a scene on my block. Had to happen. A hum of self-importance fills the air. Police stanchions holding off traffic. Cables, scaffolds, camera lifts, reflector screens. Stars hiding in their trailers. Crowds waiting upon the ponderous filmic decision to verify my street.

Now I remember. Coming back from my morning run, I ran into two men taking serious pictures of the block. This was months ago. I thought they were Europeans. Europeans love the narrow thorough-fares of Soho. The nineteenth-century paving stones. Tight passage for the horse troops.

One man shot, the other loaded the cameras and carried the bags. I felt proprietary. Would they photograph the ancient garage from which no car escapes? Would they catch my Chinese streetwalker? Would they love the two exhausted trees? Would they sense the urban grit in the souls of all of us who live here, even on the clearest spring morning with the spray rising in rainbows from the Department of Sanitation water trucks?

It was just past dawn, and the low angle of sunlight brought out the solid geometric volume of the industrial iron-fronts, their recessed doorways and deep-silled windows.

In the late afternoon the photographers were back. The look of the street is different then. Sunlight attaches to the particulate matter churned up by the day's traffic, so that it seems adrift, a floating fall of luminous dust coming down the narrow corridor of the opposed buildings, sifting through the bars of the fire escapes, opaquing the big loft windows, shining off the Belgian block pavement, and seem-ing to drain away with evening into the blackness of the ancient garage and the culverts at the corners.

So that's what they were. Film patrol. And now look, an army on bivouac. Caterer's van. Generators. Portosans. Everything needed by troops on the move. Self-sufficient in a country they don't live in but only occupy from time to time.

All at once the street is bright and clean. I realize it is washed in light. Ordinary-looking people are going about their business. A cab pulls up, a man jumps out and grabs the shoulder of a woman who is walking past a building entrance and turns her around to face him. It is a seriously aggressive gesture, though quite tame by film standards. They talk, and from four stories up, I see the resistance of the woman accosted, it is in her posture. All of this is the action, but then they walk away, casually, in different directions, as if nothing of what they've said has mattered, and I realize the scene ended before I knew it and now the lights go out, and the cab backs up the way it came.

Now men with walkie-talkies are all over the place. A team of work-ers is placing litter in the street. For miles around, the city not being filmed is oblivious of its unimportance.

Silence again, the lights come back on. A cab screeches to a stop, the door flies open, a man jumps out and grabs a woman by the shoulder.

Movies are using up the cities, the countrysides, the seas, and the mountains. Someday every inch of the world will be on film. The planet will have flattened into an enormous reel. The night sky will screen us. The film stock will play out and drift and undulate, twist and spiral Möbiusly through the galactic universe. Life will not be simultaneous, it will be sequential, one story after another, story after story, as if all the DNA of every living thing were extended, on one strand, one byte at a time, to infinity.

—movie version: guy gets back from his morning run, sees a film company setting up on his street. The scene they are doing, a woman coming out of his building, a cab pulling up, a man leaping out and confronting her, grabbing her by the shoulder, she pulling back, her defiance, his rage . . . looks very familiar to him, like a scene from his own life.

All morning the scene is shot and reshot. He watches from his window. It becomes clear to him that the scene being filmed is . . . accurate. There's no other way to put it. He had done that, found his wife leaving just as he got home. The actor playing him is taller, with a thicker head of hair, but generally of the same build and long, slung-jawed face. The actress is a dead ringer—blond, lovely, slender, supple-hipped.

He can't imagine what is going on, who is making the movie, what script they may be working from. Had she written it? But how? She lived out to the edges of her life, filled it all with her restless animal integrity. And with such fine contempt for reasonable self-interest. When had she written about him, about their connection, their failed connection? Why would she have bothered?

His loft, with its large, unshaded windows, was furnished effortlessly, by her unerring impulse. Even now, the careless perfection of it makes him reluctant to move a thing. That flung-about inevitability of the furnishings gives him the illusion of her presence, of the continuation of their life together. She had found the place, lived there alone, and then he had moved in. It was hers, and was still hers, the place, the street, the neighborhood, though she was gone.

He wonders why he has stayed, why he takes the chance.

The company downstairs finishes its work, packs up, and the street is deserted by the end of the afternoon. He thinks maybe he is overwrought and reading too much into the coincidence of that scene, but unable to get it out of his mind, he spends the next few days testing the proposition that it is his life, or their life together, that is being filmed. To his dismay he is able to track the company around town, guessing where they are by assuming to know the locations they must choose from. He finds them up at Columbia Journalism, where she got her master's, he sees them at the Italian restaurant on Ninth Avenue with the decor restored to the way it was before the ownership changed. They even have the right table, the one in the corner under the sconce with the charred shade.

His attempt to approach the filmmakers is easily thwarted by the A.D.'s with the walkie-talkies, the security guards. Not that he is anxious to make himself known. He catches glimpses of the actress, and it seems to him with each successive scene they do she is becoming more and more like his wife. He doesn't know what to do. There are location days at Kennedy Airport, at Lincoln Center, at Battery Park. Eventually, he stops tracking them and retires to the loft to wait. And just as he knew they would, they knock on his door early one morning and move in, cables, cameras, lights, reflectors. He makes no attempt to stop them. Chairs are set up for the director, the script girl, the actors. Everyone seems to know him as the leading man. He is made up and takes his place as the camera rolls: There is a knock at the door. He opens it to find two detectives. They identify themselves and want to ask him a few questions. Would he mind if they came in?

"You'll think this is crazy or perhaps that I'm crazy," he says later, on the set of the overnight lockup, where he sits with two actors playing small-time criminals waiting for their lawyers to spring them. He realizes he is talking compulsively, but he can't stop. "Maybe I am crazy, but I swear to you something is going on with movies *in a way even the people who make them don't understand.* I mean, something weird has happened, so that I'm convinced that the people who ostensibly make them are no more than instruments of the movies themselves, servers, factotums, and the whole process, from pitching an idea for one, and getting the financing and finding a star, I mean, the whole operation, while seeming to depend on the participation of directors, producers, distributors, and so on, and for all the animosities and struggles among them, the struggles for control, the interference of studio heads, and profound dicta of the critics, in fact the entire booming culture of movies—all of it is illusion, as the movie is supposed to be, a scripted reality, whereas it's the movies themselves that are in control, preordaining and self-generating, like a specie with its own DNA. The human agencies who realize them, are subsidiary, like garden bugs who come into being to pollinate flowers, or those birds who live to ride atop the backs of African rhinos and beak away their lice.

"There are more movies now than ever, you have to agree at least to that, they are in a population explosion, in theaters, on television, on cable, on tape, on discs, they're everywhere, you can't escape them, they are creatures, movies, incredibly astute, complex creatures who persuade us that they are manifestations of our own culture, with individual identities but participating in genres, just as we are individuals but within ethnic frameworks. You think I'm nuts but it is possible, I mean you just ought to consider that possibility, that movies are a malign life form that came to earth a hundred or so years ago and have gradually come to dominate not only our feelings but our thoughts, our intellects. They are feeding on us, having first forced us to invent them and provide them with the materiality of their existence, which is film or, latterly, tape. Maybe you would have a better idea of what I am saying by thinking of them as having the same desire to suck us up into themselves as a tapeworm in our guts, one planetary tapeworm living in the guts of the earth, using up the cities, the countryside, the seas, and the mountains.

"But I don't expect you to agree, I know what you're thinking, and not even if I invoke those pseudoscientific horror movies to you, wherein one person, a scientist perhaps, sees some great threat to humanity that he cannot persuade the world of until it is almost too late—a giant bug, or plague or alien specie from space, a King Kongism of disaster is what I'm describing—even knowing that convention and having seen versions of it over and over, you are not about to credit me with the scientist's perception—the awful knowledge given only to the lonely hero, and perhaps his loyal girlfriend, herself the daughter of an eminent scientist, who will die during the course of the film—*because you think I've been watching too many movies!*

"But I offer to you as evidence my own life, which has somehow attracted the attention of the movie creatures. as they apparently have you, and look at me sitting here on this set with you, and already you think I'm just an actor reading his lines, that's the role you're supposed to be playing, but whether I am or not, I can testify that I'm feeling myself losing dimension, losing moral substance, complexity, I'm going flat, I'm turning into a shadow, and it's a terrible feeling wherein even your most intimate passionate feelings are, you suspect, words on a page written for you to act out.

"And I can't even tell anymore if this is the first time I'm saying this or the second or the one hundredth. Can you tell? Am I the real person, or the film image? And you? I just don't know. And even when I finish this monologue and the director calls, 'Cut,' I still won't know, because he too may be nothing more than an image, a shadow, an arrangement of downloaded ones and zeroes."

Cut! a voice calls from the darkness. And he hears bravos and a scattering of applause from onlookers that may or may not be a sound track.

—The Midrash Jazz Quartet Plays the Standards

GOOD NIGHT SWEETHEART

Good night sweetheart,
Till we meet tomorrow,

(applause)

Good night sweetheart,
Sleep will banish sorrow,
Tears and parting may make us forlorn
But with the dawn, a new day is born.
So I'll say . . .
Good night sweetheart
Tho I'm not beside you
Good night sweetheart
Still my love will guide you

> *Dreams enfold you, in each one I'll hold*
>> *you*
> *Good night sweetheart, good night.*

Good night sweet thing, good night little lady
I can't believe you sleep alone whatever lies you're
   telling me
So good night too to whoever's beside you
Hope he don't dissuade you
   from the dream I want you to have of me
I expect we'll meet in the a.m. as the new day comes
   up roses
Each of us lying, posing our poses
I won't tell you what I did with you at night in my
   drunk dreaming
if you don't tell me what you didn't do in that
   breathy voice of yours, and your eyes beaming
   and your heart streaming with happiness.
So good night, miss,
Good night, hurt so sweet,
My heartbeat, good night.

                                          (*applause*)

Hey you're the one, you know, I've been around but this
is something new, holding off at night for the bright
of the day, and then suggesting it with all sorts of
wordplay, and the surroundings not a deep purple haze
But a white tile kitchen and toast and OJ . . . you are a
witty woman, sweetheart, and I love your games,
I love holding you with your hair still wet
and your terry robe half open and beads of the shower
   water on your breasts, I love your demands
that we be clean and rested to say nothing of sober
   when we make love
and that it be done only in the realm of this
   household.
Well then good night my dear fine funny face
I'll wake you from your dreams in the dawning day

and we'll have some clean and loving conversation
before we latch on to the day's obligation
to earn a little money each in our capable way
so we can pay the monthly cover for this place,
lay down a fresh new paint job
and make the bedroom over for a baby—
Oh Baby,
you know I just have to have another little sweetheart
   like you
     to say good night to,
     don't you, sweetheart?
     Good night!

                                              (*laughter, applause*)

I am on my knees to God, God is my sweetheart
But He's saying good night,
My sweetheart is leaving
He is telling me to sleep
He is putting me out to bleak pastures
Forlorn is hardly the word for the terror
   of my grieving
Weeping out of me, scalding my eyes.
Trouble in mind, God I'm blue
Must I be blue always?
Sun is rain, near is far, high is low,
   day is night
Nothing is right, nothing is right
Who is this sweet-talking God, what's He up to?
He knows sleep doesn't banish sorrow
but works it over, again and again,
   in the drowsing brain
   finding pictures for the pain.
And what happens when tomorrow dawns
with never nothing different in the next day's
   daylight?
Will Your love lead me, will Your dreams enfold me?
After You've gone and left me, God,
With only Your empty promises to guide me?

(*puzzled silence*)

She's gone. It's done.
　　You've got no one.
　　Tho dreams deceive
And sleep consoles you,
　At dawn you'll find
No one beside you.
　　She's gone, it's done,
You're all alone.
　　The sorrow's yours
　　She's gone. It's done.

(*grumbling*)

—Good night, hurt so sweet, heartbeat, good night.
—Good night, my dear fine funny face.
—Will Your love lead me, Your dreams enfold me?
—She's gone. It's done. You're all alone.

Good night sweetheart,
Till we meet tomorrow,
Good night sweetheart,
Sleep will banish sorrow . . .

(*audience leaving*)

—Pem has taken to wearing his hair in a ponytail. I go with him on Friday evenings to Eighty-ninth Street, where, in fact, Sarah Blumenthal conducts the services of the Synagogue of Evolutionary Judaism. There are usually no more than ten or twelve people in attendance, less than half of the number when Joshua Gruen was the presiding rabbi.

As a result of study and discussion among the congregants, the Sabbath services are being redesigned to the basic and unarguable essentials, consisting so far of the Shema, the declaration of the oneness of God, the principle of abstract monotheism . . . a Kaddish, or ritual prayer for the dead, because this gives comfort to mourners, and renews their memories and restores their gratitude . . . an acknowledgment of the idea of the Sabbath both in the fact of the timing of the services and as the occasion for reflection in a state of freedom . . . and, for the rest, a commitment to the study of the Torah in order to derive from it the imperatives that would complete the restructuring of the services and eventually provide the theoretical basis for the evolved faith.

Pem loves these evenings, and I am surprised myself to find them so fascinating. The members of the congregation include a professor of Comparative Religion at Columbia, a judge of the State Supreme Court, a young woman studying at the Actors Studio, a married couple, both of whom are physicians, a Barnard junior, and, most touchingly, an elderly white-haired man whose son carries him up the brownstone stairs and retrieves him at the end of the evening.

Given his own scholarship, Pem finds much that is familiar from his days as a divinity student. I am in the different position of learning things for the first time. Little by little, the first five books of the Bible, the Torah, have under the group's analysis become the collected texts of the different historical sources, J, E, P, and D. This doctoral candidate from Harvard one evening discussed the work of his eminent teacher J. L. Kugel, who has attended in detail to the distinction between the original texts and the interpretive commentary that sprang up in the three hundred years before and a hundred years into the Common Era that has created the Bible we read today under the illusion that we are reading the original Scriptures. The biblical texts from the beginning were seen as enigmatic, as why would they not be, having been written in a language without vowels or punctuation. And since they were supposed to be divine in their source, and therefore of a supernatural perfection, the scholars, priests, and sages of antiquity felt called upon to explain the contradictions, un-God-like sentiments, unsavory passages, and less than noble acts of noble personages of the stories as well as whatever else could not be countenanced in righteousness . . . by interpreting them metaphorically, symbolically, or allegorically, or changing their meaning by adding punctuation, or opportunistically applying syntactical emphases, or by otherwise reimagining whatever they felt needed improvement if it was to be truly theologically correct. I was happy that evening to recognize the venerable ancestry of hermeneutics. Beyond that, as a writer, I am only fascinated by the power of this hodgepodge of chronicles, verses, songs, relationships, laws of the universe, sins, and days of reckonings . . . this scissors-and-paste job that is in its original form so terse, inconsistent, defiant of common sense, and cryptically inattentive to the ordinary demands of narrative as to be attributed to a divine author.

Migod. What have I been doing wrong all these years?

But the Comp Religion guy from Columbia has this take on it: He says the interpreters knew what they were doing when they didn't try to erase the inconsistencies and neaten things up. The priests and the redactors left in the stuff of the earlier spinmeisters. You never come close to God, you only hope to achieve a refinement of your awareness. The very contradictions, the histories living side by side with their rewrites, manifest the same struggle described in the narratives—to apprehend and accept the awesome completeness and creative totality of the Unnameable.

After these sessions, Pem and I usually have dinner at a restaurant on Broadway, Amarillo. Less often, Sarah B. has joined us. It's not a matter of rabbinical decorum (kashruth is one of the inessentials)—she is as concerned about leaving Angelina alone with only the children to be with as she would be about leaving her children alone without Angelina. As if, dear thing, having lost her husband, what else is she going to lose?

But when Sarah consents to join us, I feel like a chaperon. Why should I feel this way except that something like a courtship is developing? In the candlelight and over the glasses of red wine, they regard each other with a degree of attention they are not even aware of. And when I have something to say, their shining attention to me in unison is clearly an effort of will. Yet they would not hear of my leaving them by themselves. They are afraid of that, both of them, Pem because he doesn't want to descend to importuning, and she because of the enduring presence in her mind of her husband, Joshua. Her mourning should last, formally, for one year, but this is another inessential according to EJ, on the theory that whatever it takes to remember and memorialize your dead must come naturally from the heart. These things must work out anyway with a psychological inevitability, is the idea. But Sarah may be wrong about this, insofar as such a custom may be more for the sake of the living than for the dead. A closure. That they may go on. She is in her second year of the loss of her husband now.

But I do see a drawing together, slow as it is. And since both she and Pem live a life committed to explicit moral seriousness—that is the most abstract construction I can put upon it—their convergence will have to be more than personal. Last Friday night's study service at EJ dealt with Exodus 19–24, the giving to Moses of the Decalogue. On this evening Sarah led the discussion with great animation, her voice was strong, the consideration of this key episode seemed to lift her spirits, she was not worrying her way through the passages with her customary mien of skepticism and respect but with an assurance, even a sexiness of assurance. She lifted her head, ran her fingers through her hair, and a beautiful smile transformed her face, like the light of the sun breaking, her eyes shone, she has one of those smiles of total vulnerability that can so ambiguously be the moment before the onrush of tears. I'm quoting her from memory: "My sense here, what comes through to me, is the understanding these writers possessed of the morally immense human life. Do you see that? They were proposing an ethical configuration for human existence. Who before had done that in quite the same way? These Commandments were devised by human scriptural genius. . . . We could make the case then for God's presence after all in the humanly written Bible. The Lord, blessed be His name, as my Orthodox colleagues say [she smiles] . . . being what impels us to struggle for historical and theological comprehension. The biblical minds who created the Ten Commandments that have structured civilization . . . provided the possibility of an ethically conceived life, an awareness that we live in states of moral consequence that, if not yet, must someday bring us closer to a union of understanding with the Creator. What a gift, what a great and profound gift . . . and how worthy of reverence!"

Alone with Pem at our dinner following, I said I thought the two of them were beginning to look like they belonged together. "Really?" he said. "Really? Tell me what you see, how you can tell!" His face became more florid than usual. I couldn't have said anything to make him happier. Then after another glass or two of wine, the gloom set in. "She'll never have me," he said. "The boys don't take to me."

"How do you know?"

"I bring them games, toys, I play with them, I get down on the floor. They see me for what I am—not their father."

"I didn't know things had gone so far."

"What is 'so far'? She had to take Angelina down to the INS about something. So I sat with them. What is 'so far'? You ever been cut by kids? Getting down on the floor like an idiot while they watch television as if you're not there? I thought I had lived through all the possible humiliations. I thought maybe delivering a sermon to three people was as low as it got."

———

—You asked about this and asked and asked all through the years of your growing up, and I never wanted to tell you, first because you were too young, and I always wanted you to have your own life, and for it not to be a haunted life, however foolish that father's desire might have been . . . and, second, in recent years for an entirely different reason, which is that I wanted to reclaim the diary, Mr. Barbanel's archive, I wanted to find it and let it speak for me.

But plans give way to life. And here I am saying what I can, after all. . . . There came a time when nothing in particular had changed but our spirits had inexplicably darkened and a foreboding of total disaster drifted through our ghetto. A weariness had come over us, a weakening of our belief that we would survive. Our creed—to outlast, to prevail—seemed somehow less tenable. The suspense of the Germans' impassive treachery was more acute, because they were now on their way to losing their war. I know that sounds paradoxical. But the eastern front was collapsing, moving back in our direction, and they no longer had license to do their murdering with impunity. Work details had been assigned to the fort. We were not supposed to know what was going on, but we learned that the graves were being dug up and the remains were being burned. Sometimes when the wind came from the west, I thought I could smell what was happening. And of course the workers assigned to the fort were never seen again.

The freedom we had been living for, surviving for, now itself seemed a dangerous prospect. If the dead were evidence of their criminality, were not the living?

Then, one night, we received a clandestine visit from a delegation of Jewish partisans. The meeting took place in a cabin used to store paint supplies, sand bins, carpentry tools, and so on. It was not even one block from the perimeter. Somehow I had learned of the meeting, and Barbanel thought it would be safer if I was present, as a way of using the solemnity of the occasion to seal my lips. We sat and waited and then finally in the stillness of early morning, after I had nodded off several times, there came the signal, the soft taps, once, and then again. A desk was moved, and from a trapdoor underneath they rose into the room, bringing the cold and the darkness they had come from: three of them, two men and a woman. It was like birth, I had seen a baby born some weeks before and it was like that, first the head, then the shoulders. But then the rifle.

They waved off any assistance, by turns hoisting themselves into sitting position on the floor and then standing and facing us. Their faces and hands were blackened with dirt. Their rifles were like the ones the guards on the bridge carried, and this was thrilling to me, because I knew each rifle had to have been taken from a German. At the same time, I was frightened. These were the people who looked for help from no one, who prayed to no one. Every gesture was disdainful. Their eyes were cold, impatient, even the woman's.

They were children, the partisans. If I could perceive that at all at my age, then possibly I saw our connection insofar as the woman was such a slight, slim creature, with eyes past all grief. When she caught sight of me, I read in her face the compassion of an older sister, a momentary betrayal of her hardened mien, perhaps the unwitting disclosure of worry for a child, in this place, under the direction of old men. For it was a generational matter after all, the two men with her couldn't have been more than twenty or twenty-one, adults in my eyes, men with height and strength and dark beards, though of the scraggly young man's type, and thick black hair, and the one, the leader, with round-rimmed glasses that gave him, incongruously, a yeshiva bocher's appearance, and the other with a broad Slavic face and wide shoulders, the sort of oaf I would have stayed away from in the old days at school.

Without precisely knowing why from my impression of them, they were not as I had expected, they were not like my parents, their spirit was of a different order, and as I watched and listened, I understood what I of course had always known, that my mother and father had never been among them.

Nobody knew these three except Dr. Koenig, whose practice before the war had taken him everywhere in the district. Possibly he had delivered at least one of them, the young man who spoke for them, Benno, on whose eyeglasses the candles shone when he averted his head and allowed the doctor to grasp his shoulders in greeting. "Look, how strong!" Dr. Koenig whispered, in the first and last of the amenities of the evening.

The other two had taken up positions by the windows, where they peeked through the drawn sack curtains before turning to face the room. The one called Benno sat on a table and, holding his rifle loosely across his knees, he addressed us in a hushed, fluent Yiddish, a sound to me like a brook running over rocks. The Russian army was within a hundred twenty miles. As the front moves west, he said, your ghetto will be dismantled and you with it, he said. You will dig the graves you will lie in. It is just a matter of time.

Perhaps that is so. But already they are trying to destroy evidence of their murders, Dr. Koenig said. They are frightened of criminal prosecution after the war.

You are deluding yourself. If they don't slaughter you here, they will move you somewhere else and slaughter you.

The partisans were proposing to take people out—as many who wanted to come. They could move thirty or forty a night, Benno said. Three partisan units, one Jewish, two Russian, held militarily secure areas behind German lines. His group consisted of a hundred and fifty armed Jewish men and women and another two hundred people whom they took care of.

The third council member who was present was Rabbi Pomeranz, a very thin, slight, middle-aged man who wore an old battered homburg and whose beard had turned white. He sat in a chair against the wall and held a siddur closed on his lap, but with his finger keeping the place. And he was silently davening while attending to the matters at hand, his head nodding and his lips moving as he uttered to himself the prayers he knew without the book, but his eyes on the partisan who spoke.

The rabbi said: Perhaps the partisans didn't know the German policy regarding escape—people were executed who were caught trying.

Well, Rabbi, Benno said, look at me, we're here talking to you, aren't we? Do you suppose we just might know what we're doing?

Benno's partisans camped in the forests. For food, they requisitioned livestock and produce from the farms. In the villages with German garrisons, they attacked and destroyed them and then paid the tradesmen for sugar, flour, and other necessities from the German cashboxes. They could move about freely in the countryside because of their reputation, which they had earned by taking revenge on those people who reported them to the Germans, coming back and executing them and burning down their homes and barns, so that now that didn't happen anymore. Their attack squads performed acts of sabotage, blowing up railroad tracks, cutting phone lines. They ambushed the military who came out to undo the damage.

All well and good and may God grant that your work continue, the rabbi said. But the winter was coming. Could older people stand that life, under such hardship, living in the open?

If they can't, they will at least die free, Benno said.

Dr. Koenig said he was concerned about what would happen to those who chose to remain—once the Germans began to miss their workers they would retaliate, in their fashion, by taking hostages and executing them.

Benno answered that they would do that anyway as the Jewish resistance moved closer to the city and the garrison here began to feel its sting.

This is not an easy decision, Koenig told them. Many of these people are from the city. They would not know what to do out there with you. Here they get their few calories and survive another day.

You think we're just giving you problems, don't you, Benno said. You've lived as slaves so long you don't know anything else.

Barbanel, who had not said a word before this, jumped up and grabbed the young man by the collar. That is contemptible, he said. Show some respect. We have fought as hard as you. You don't know shit about us.

Benno shook off his hand and signaled the others. Their message had been delivered. They prepared to leave.

Regardless of what you think, the young woman said to Barbanel, you have the moral duty to inform people that we will lead them out. You cannot choose for them. Even this boy here. We have children with us now who are capable of firing weapons. People must choose for themselves. But if you impose your authority in this matter, you are as bad as the Nazis.

Oh my Sarah, I remember these words as if they were uttered yesterday. They opened the trapdoor. The thickset one who had said nothing and the woman descended and disappeared. Before following them, Benno took Dr. Koenig aside and, I assume, instructed him on how to make further contact. And before lowering himself through the trapdoor he addressed Rabbi Pomeranz: Since your prayers are so effective and have already done so much good, you, I expect, will choose to remain and pray to the Lord your God to save your people.

When he had gone and the desk was back in place, the rabbi stood and set his battered homburg firmly on his head as he prepared to go out. That's not why I pray to the Lord, blessed be His name, he said to no one in particular. I pray to bring Him into being.

Of course once the council met in full, it decided it had no other choice than to inform people there was now a means of escape from the ghetto. But the news could be disseminated only in the most secure manner, not only because of the obvious danger of the Germans themselves, but because of the spies the Germans installed among us, pretend Jews, or simple betrayers, as some of the ghetto police had become. So the procedure was painstaking, one by one, beginning with the people the council members knew personally. It was characteristic. Perhaps if it had not been so painstaking, more people could have been freed. But I had this new assignment, the star runner in his garrison cap finding the selected people at the hours they were available and summoning them, in secrecy, to the council offices. And in due course the underground railroad, if I may call it that, was put into place. The partisans had very easily infiltrated the city. As that Benno fellow had said, they really knew what they were doing. It was surprisingly effective. I'm not sure how it was done, what the actual means of escape was. Perhaps it changed from night to night. I think as many as two hundred fifty people got out before it all ended.

The council had given priority to those most fit to endure the difficulties of living in the open. And when people left, their registration and work cards were bestowed upon people of the same age and gender who didn't have them. In this way, it hoped to keep the Germans from realizing that our numbers were decreasing.

Barbanel spoke one night to all of us boys in our dormitory. Neither I nor anyone else can tell you what to do, he said. To stay here or to go. We don't know which is better or which is worse. All I can tell you is to decide for yourself. Circumstances have turned you into adults while you are still children. You have the responsibility finally for your own life.

As it turned out, of the six boys only two chose to go to the forest with the partisans. I would assume they guessed right. For myself, I realized that on all my secret trips into the city, it had never once occurred to me not to return to the ghetto. I could probably have hidden away, perhaps with the help of that priest, found some family that would take me in and spare me the fate of a Jewish child. Never had I entertained this idea. I noted too that Dr. Koenig himself could not go, for obvious reasons. This was true of course for Barbanel as well. The council had to stay in place and keep the ghetto running. And just as they could not consider leaving, neither would Greta Margolin. She would not leave Barbanel, to say nothing of the little children. The really small ones, she could not trust to the partisan wilds. And I, ambitious as I was to learn to fire a rifle, to kill Germans, to be like the partisan heroes . . . would not leave the lingering sense of my dead mother's sweet nature, something like Miss Margolin's as well as I could remember, or the fleeting sensations of my dead father, who, I decided, had something of the rough, exuberant courage for life of Josef Barbanel.

And so that was my decision. And now each day life seemed more and more tenuous, with the Germans visibly agitated, fearful, and more and more dangerous as the front advanced toward us. One night in my cot I heard what I thought was distant thunder. I looked out the window and saw faint diffusions of light momentarily graying out the starry sky. In the morning Barbanel told me it was artillery I had heard, maybe as close as sixty or seventy miles away.

At this time the work details were suspended and people were no longer marched across the bridge into the city. Smoke no longer rose from the smokestacks of the military plants. Guards were put in place around the entire perimeter of the ghetto. And the escapes contrived by the partisans were no longer possible.

Of course under these conditions my courier runs through the old viaduct were out of the question. I was actually prepared to go one afternoon when, standing with Barbanel at the open cistern in the stone house, I heard distant German voices coming up from the bowels of the viaduct. "Well that is that," Barbanel said, and set the cistern cover back in place.

We all knew something dire was about to happen. And soon enough the day came. All at once truckloads of troops were coming across the bridge. I ran for all I was worth to tell them at the council. It was my last mission as a runner. And it didn't matter. The news was blaring out of their loudspeakers in that terrible bureaucratic language of theirs. We were given fifteen minutes to gather our belongings. Soldiers ran down the streets, burst into the houses, clubbing people who didn't move fast enough. Buildings were set afire. All this by the directive of Commandant Schmitz. I couldn't see as much as I could hear. People were screaming, crying out, there was shooting. We were herded into the square. Miss Margolin had two infants in her arms, holding them in wraps with their heads hidden. People were clutching at Dr. Koenig, asking him to do something. The poor man held his head high, his silvered hair lifted in the wind, and he stood there as helpless as the rest of us. Mr. Barbanel I couldn't see anywhere, and then I did see him, walking in the crowd with his arm around an elderly man.

In our entirety we were paraded across the bridge, through the city, to the railroad station. The Lithuanian citizenry watched us from the sidewalks. Some of them laughed, some jeered. Some just went about their business as if it were an ordinary day. In all the confusion and shouting, either in the street, avoiding the rifle butts of the soldiers, or in the railroad depot when I was climbing into the boxcar, I lost my runner's cap with the military brim. But I didn't realize it until the car doors were swung shut and the bolts were slammed into place and we were there in the blackness. I was furious that I could not lift my arms to see if the cap was still on my head, although I knew that it wasn't. I had seen some people I knew climb into the same car, but I didn't know where Mr. Barbanel was, whether he was in the car, too, or Greta Margolin or Dr. Koenig or any one of the other boys. The car lurched and began to move. People were wailing, calling out, Where are you? to one another in the darkness, demanding to know what was going on, what was the meaning of this outrage. But I knew the meaning. I was locked up in a boxcar in a long train of boxcars of the packed standing and swaying living dead. And I was the star runner no longer.

≡

—Pem hits Park Avenue and finds a new doorman. Young Hispanic who gravely goes to the house phone . . .

My home once. Ten rooms on a high floor which somehow never had any sunlight.

Hiya, poopsie.

I haven't much time, Pem. What is it you want?

My clothes.

Thank goodness.

Not everything, my blazer, some ties and shirts. A carry-on.

I'd like all your things out of here.

So, the monsieur with whom you are forging your fate? He is to arrive then?

That's none of your business.

Sincerely, Trish, he is a very lucky *homme.*

And of course you want some money.

If that is what is in your heart, my child.

She takes one of those long lady numbers from the cigarette box on the credenza. In truth she has added poundage, Trish. A bit hippy now, though still elegant. Holds the arm of the cigarette hand at the elbow. Pale blue strand of smoke rises past the Vlaminck flowers.

My father says you haven't answered his letter.

Going back to the bedrooms: I will, Trish. Really I will.

It must surely have been intimacy if I can't remember it.

≡

—What do we mean to say when we say . . . *even if all the possible scientific questions are answered, our problem is still not touched at all?* So that if Mr. Einstein himself were to come to the successful end of all his experiments, if all his brilliant physics were carried to the triumphant end and he was not destined like the Moses of science to die before reaching that Promised Land . . . we would still be left just where we started?

So, *bitte,* what is our problem? Not the nature of the universe, therefore, but . . . what? The mind in consideration of itself? The self that proposes the world is everything that is, but finds itself excluded from that proposition? The I or self that can theoretically ascertain everything about the world except who and what it itself is—as the subject of its own thinking? Where can it be found? Where is it located? No more can be said on its behalf than that it is merely a presumption of the faculty of language, a syntactical conceit. It is the grammatical observation of the state of affairs it calls the world. If it stops constructing propositions, if it ceases to map the factual relations of the world with language, in what way can it be known to exist? Yet at the same time there is no world apart from the I's discernment, is there? All of us, the multitudinous selves who are mere phantom presumptions of language, no more than that, nevertheless contain all the experience of the world. I look for an appropriate image: the mirrors of a giant fun house from which there is no exit? Utterances echoing one over another forever down a bottomless cistern? But these are insufficient, being spatial. Consciousness is not in space, it does not exist in space, nor when it thinks of itself is its depth dimensional to any number it can conceive. Yet everything that exists, exists through us in the formulations of our world-containing selves.

So that is the problem, the solipsistic consciousness without which there is no world yet which is itself filled to its limits with the world and therefore unable to step outside the world to see itself in it. By this paradox I propose a merger of the real world that exists apart from my perception of it and the world that cannot exist except for my mind's perception of it. And since I grant you too the rule of this solipsistic kingdom of everything that is the case, we then have the paradox in three dimensions of what might be called democratic solipsism, each of us exclusive total ruler of the world that depends on our mind for existence . . . and none of us able to discernibly exist except as subject of others' consciousness.

Admittedly, this is a strange and seemingly self-contradictory idea coming from the Wittgenstein who would strip from philosophy all its meaningless metaphysical nonsense.

Yet I know you Americans obsess about God. And by my language game I am trying to tell you something very simple: Perhaps the most poetic description of our tormented human consciousness that is of, yet not in, the world is found in the term *original sin*.

As I said in my *Tractatus Logico-Philosophicus* . . . speaking of the idea of the immortality of the human soul . . .

6.4312. *Is a riddle solved by the fact that I survive forever? Is this eternal life not as enigmatic as our present one? The solution of the riddle of life in space and time lies* outside *space and time* . . .

6.44. *Not* how *the world is, is the mystical but* that *it is* . . .

6.52. *We feel that even if* all possible *scientific questions be answered, the problems of life have still not been touched at all. Of course there is then no question left, and just this is the answer.*

Parenthetically, I ask you to remember please that this was a very young man's work, written mostly on the front lines with the Austrian army during World War I, where I had requested combat duty hoping for death. The pages on which I wrote were smeared with mud and the pencil shook in my fist. The light of Very flares and shellbursts let me see what I was writing. Under fire, I became terrified as an animal but in the midst of my trembling I defined courage as, and took it in, the conviction that one's true world-creating, world-created soul . . . is finally inviolable by circumstance.

—Author's Bio

Everett appears as a small boy child
In the lying-in hospital no bigger than a brownstone
on the corner of Mt. Eden Avenue and Morris Avenue
the borough of the Bronx, the city of New York
   in the year 19–.
I was a breech baby, the first of many difficulties
I gave my mother, Ruth, a resolute woman, a gifted
   pianist
who had at a much earlier age fallen in love with a
   dreamer
Her original experience of the difficult race of men,

an impetuous ensign-in-training at the Webb Naval
   Academy on the Harlem River
my father, Ben, who in the First World War would leap
   over the fence
and break into the army canteen where my mother was
   serving coffee and doughnuts
to the doughboys, and risk death in the wrong white
   uniform
to see to it that nobody interfered with her.
This was romance, though of a distracted kind
and to a pattern established earlier, when they were
   in high school together.
He would see her going out in the evening with some boy
to have some ice cream while the sky was still a sunlit
   blue over the darkened trees of Crotona Park
and come over to them, who had not asked her out
   himself,
and threaten the boy with chin-to-chin pugnacity
if he did not treat my mother Ruth with respect
thus ruining the date, casting a pall over her evening
with his impertinent proprietary attitude
There in the Bronx in the early part of the century
when the streets were wide and new and the trees were
   young in the parks
and the red brick granite-trimmed apartment houses
   with their small courtyards
   were clean and redemptive
for the immigrant families who had managed to escape
   the wretched tenements of the Lower East Side,
And such courtship as was waged by Ben my father
was not yet construed as the bio-behavioral imperative
   to distribute his genes
Though of course Ruth married him and he did,
To my brother, Ronald, appearing in 19–
And to me eight and a half years later
a year of the Great Depression when not that many
   children could be afforded
least of all to Ben and Ruth,

and, I think now, to another child somewhere between us
A child stillborn in the mid- or late twenties
perhaps another brother
or a sister, who would have watched over me in the park
in the solemn responsibility engendered by my mother
and held me up to the water fountain when I was thirsty
The girl, Ruth would say for years afterward even when
    I was grown,
whom she had always wanted, the daughter for her
    loneliness in her house of males.
I mention such personal matters
only to indicate my place and time, the slender
    authority
I have for speaking of this century,
An observer obscurely situated
Apart from all the huge historical terrors, though
    there's always time, isn't there.
But now I confess how hard it is imagining my father as
    a wild kid, daring, headstrong,
Childhood being something that belonged to me, or my
    brother, our property, not his
and remembering him by contrast
as a serious portly man sitting in a chair by the radio
Listening to the news of the Second World War
    while at the same time reading of the war
    in the evening paper he held out like a field
    tent.
My father has been dead for forty years as I write
And I confess, dispirited, that the longer he is dead
    the more mysterious he's become in my memory
The personality fading, or becoming more complex,
we are left with a confirmed but invisible fact
a spirit without fallible character though remembered
    as a fallible man
Who did some things right and some things wrong
But who exists now as pure soul that suffered life
    and finally was done in by it
Though I keep and cherish my images of him

against this sad truth of the characterless soul
that is to me a meager consolation
for the failure of brilliant life
to maintain forever its rich specificity.
He played tennis in white ducks, I have a photograph
taken with one of those foldable Leicas of the time
that extend their accordioned black boxes along two tracks
A smart forehand at the risen end of the swing,
the body pointed forward,
a white long-sleeved shirt, dark hair, a dark mustache
A figure on the far side of the net,
    most of the picture being of the ground
A public court of brown clay, with an anonymous back
    just passing the corner of the lens in close-up
Chasing the ball forever, forever unknown
The apartment houses of the Bronx in the background
Everything circa 1925 in sepia.
She played too, my mother,
They would go out and hit into the 1930s
while I stood outside the chicken-wire fence
and nagged them for my turn.
She is buried next to him
in the Beth-El cemetery in New Jersey
But having survived him by thirty-seven years
is a lingering personality in my mind.
During her last illness she celebrated her birthday
an Intensive Care patient, just off the respirator.
Congratulations, Mother, I said. You're ninety-five
    today.
One eyebrow rose, the eye opened, the slightest smile
    was called back from her fading life:
Ninety-four, she said.
It was our last conversation.
And I feel her death now, some years afterward,
    as an uncharacteristic silence,
    a silence from someone who should be telling us
    what she thinks of our taste, or our ways of doing
    things

While announcing that she does not give an opinion
    unless it's asked for.
The last technology that she didn't understand or trust
was the phone answering machine: "Call Mother,"
is all she'd allow herself to say
    to my recorded request for a name a number a
    message
Clearly, sensibly, speaking not to a human being but to
    a machine, and speaking machine-talk to it.
Call Mother is what I would expect to hear today
had we installed a telephone in her grave.

In 1917, my father's naval training completed
    he received his ensign's commission
and shortly thereafter sailed as a signal officer
    on a troopship to Europe
Still in the wrong-colored uniform
Among deckloads of backpacking, leg-putteed doughboys.
But then, mysteriously, or perhaps not all that
    mysteriously,
His rank having been conferred by an institution
    that wasn't Annapolis
He was assigned to land duty in the trenches
as a naval observer of ground-war communications.
It is true, communication was his specialty
as it has been the specialty of all men in my family
at least since my grandfather came to America in 1887
    and took up the printer's trade.
Of course he knew that light shutters and semaphoring
    depended on the open sea
but telegraphy and telephony, on which the army relied,
    were just as useless in the trenches
when the barrage that preceded every German attack
    blasted away in a couple of salvos
    the cables and wires
so painstakingly laid to battalion headquarters,
And when the telegraph lines strung on poles

along the supply roads, and railroad spurs,
   and past the ordnance dumps and field hospitals
from regiment back to division
needed only one pole of shaved and creosoted pine
   to rise in the air as if launched
by the thousand-pound shell of a heavy howitzer
   and as if it were a lance thrown by Achilles
   with streamers of wire like a comet's tail
to leave a general as ignorant of the truth of his
   battle
as some wretched infantryman crouching alone
   inside his uniform
and the protracted, continuous roar of a distant
   bombardment
the answer in impenetrable war code to his inquiries.
My observant father understood this at a glance,
It didn't take an Einstein he said to me with a
   laugh,
War was the emergent property of human thought,
As stolidity is the emergent property of molecules of
   oak.
Responding to the navy's deepest hopes for him
he cross-dressed, donning the khaki tunic and tinpot
   of the dead signal lieutenant who had been his
   host
And while the air whistled and concussed
   and the earth all around him rose and fell
   like the heaviest sea
he took command of the surviving soldiers of the
   signal company
still from their giant wooden spools unwinding
   new lines of communication as the old ones
   were blown to bits
Or lofting from their upraised hands the carrier
   pigeons
that returned magically as spiraling clumps of blooded
   feathers,

And re-created them a company of runners,
    dispatching two-man teams
    to carry the front's intelligence to headquarters
    and relay the staff commands to the front,
because runners were the only thing that worked,
although the news they brought
    might be an hour or more behind the action.
Now for the longest time the American general Pershing
had kept his fresh armies intact under his own command
But in 1917, with things getting worse for the Allies
Whose total dead, British and French, by then numbered
    something over four million men
most of them having died obedient, young, dumbfounded,
    and in the enlisted ranks,
elements of the American Second Army, to which
    my father had been attached as naval observer,
were deployed under French command
along the southern reaches of the broad battleground
that stretched from the Belgian coast on the North Sea
southeasterly in a great crescent of devastation
    to the Swiss border at Bernevesin.
So I picture my father in the state of war
    a state neither French nor German nor American
    but founded to contest all sense and meaning.
Very flares lighted the night sky a radiant mustard
Shells blew in sizzling flashes, like ground lightning
And in the acrid white fog of the following sunlit
    morning
when the German infantry was understood to be finally
    advancing
behind the forward-creeping bursts of mortars and
    field pieces
that were the footfalls of approaching Death
    to the young men in the trenches
he found himself the last surviving runner
    of the signal company he had come to observe
    but had passionately adopted

The man beside him having flung out his arms
   and dropped to his knees for a final prayer
in their open-field run back to the trenches.
Now I have no proof of this, but in the years I was his
   son at home,
his older son Ronald away at his world war
my father liked to take us to the Sunday games
   of the New York football Giants.
They played in the old Polo Grounds at Coogan's Bluff.
We sat in the sun, I ate a bag of peanuts, he smoked
   his cigar.
And he would be knowledgeably silent amid the noisy
   expertise of the men around us.
I loved the green grass field with the white stripes
   and the sound of the punt that would boom
   through the stadium
a long moment after the ball was kicked. I rooted
   for the Giants, always, but he liked close games
and plays that outsmarted the opponent, no matter by
   whom.
He loved the runners of the game, for instance,
   in the post-war, "Crazy Legs" Hirsch of the
   L.A. Rams
who brought a crowd to its feet with his quick cuts
   and feints and spins
and who, with his leaps over tacklers, his high-
stepping, heart-stopping evasions of sudden arrest,
   all suggestive of a comic intelligence,
could make a run, no matter how short,
last longer than anyone had a right to expect.
And I have no proof of this, but I think my father
   remembered his own runs under fire
   as an inexplicable survival
and sought to soothe his terrible remembrances
   with the aesthetic abstraction of football
a military game with lines and rules and no great
   or lasting consequences.

In any event, he had brought the orders to retreat
    but found them anticipated.
The ranks were falling back the way he had come.
In the trenches dead men were slumped in small heaps
    as if consoling one another in their grief
    for the damage they'd sustained
Or they stood, bayonets fixed, floridly alert
    poised and awaiting the attack
their internal organs having ruptured
in the concussed vacuum of a shell burst.
He made his way transversely through the zigzagged
    trenches
looking for someone to whom he could report
but finding only rats cavorting in the shit and mud
    among the stores of biscuit and torn limbs,
Rats trajecting like small shells in every direction
    as he approached.
He stumbled over a young soldier lying
    with the muzzle of his own rifle in his mouth
    and his head resting in an amalgam
    of brain and mud.
My father stopped and hunkered down and,
    for the first time since coming to France,
    felt close enough to someone to mourn him.
This boy had been unable to endure
    the hours and hours of cannonade
that my father had barely heard
    as he took upon himself the urgencies of battle.
But now it opened up on him, as if he were this fellow's
    heir,
The terrible din, mechanical yet voiced as human,
    a thunderous chest-beating boast of colossal,
    spittingly cruel, brutish, and vindictive fury
which he imagined as the primordial conversation,
when a tank loomed above him, the muddied treads
    rampaging in air,
and in a great grinding spankling roar

spanned the trench and brought a rain of oil
    in the darkness upon him.
Now friends I know this is Ancient History
    as ancient as our grade school teachers
whom we hold in our memories with the same
    condescension.
I know that. I know the bones of the First World War
    are impressed in the continent's tectonic plates
under the weight of the bones buried over them.
That Europe's beaches are adrift with sanded bone
That her farmers in their fields plow up loops
    of chained vertebrae
Her rivers at night are luminous with the risen
    free radicals of calcification
And the archaeologists of her classical cities
    find skulls in tiers under the streets.
But listen for a moment. All history has contrived
    to pour this beer into your glass,
it has brought the sad, jeaned lady at the bar's end
    her Marlboros,
given the mirror behind those bottles its
    particular tarnish
and, not incidentally, lit us in this neon-blue light
    of illusory freedom.
How old was my father, twenty-four, twenty-five?
Here he was, a sailor, a lover of the sea,
    steeped in the earth's muck,
a young man defending a country not his own,
a runner run to ground,
everything he'd made of himself negated somehow
    in the wholehearted bestowal of his youth
and with an army of Huns hurdling over his prostrate
    form.
Not that he was a political innocent—
He'd learned from his father, my grandfather Isaac,
    the printer,
the sweet values of the civil religion, socialism.

He knew the German boys who would kill him if he moved
    were closer to him in what they had
      to gain or lose
than they were to the generals, and the regal families
    who directed them.
He knew that society was structured vertically not
    laterally
and that for a moment before the war had flared
    across Europe
not just the artists and intellectuals in the cafés
    of Paris and Vienna and Berlin
who wrote their aesthetic manifestos on cloth napkins
    and held their smoking Gauloises and Navy Cuts
    between their thumbs and forefingers,
but the people working in the factories and digging in
    the coal mines for their pittances
and the schoolteachers, shop assistants, and streetcar
    conductors,
proposed that they were not French or German or Italian
    but members of the universal working class
    that spanned all borders
    and was universally enslaved to capitalism
    and its monarchical appurtenances
    and its nationalist ideologies that were pure
    bullshit.
Ah the twenty-eighth of June, a bitter chill it was
    when a Serbian, Princip, blew away
    the Hapsburg archduke Franz Ferdinand,
    but more disastrously the Austrian Socialist party,
    whose betrayed members were soon enlisting
    alongside everyone else.
But my father's thoughts at this time, I will venture,
    were as follows:
his mother, his father, his sweetheart Ruth,
his sister Sophie, his sister Mollie and,
    not to make him less human than he was,
the French girl in the coastal town of Villedieu
    who had come to draw water from the well

in the square where he sat with his mates
    under the awning of the Café Terrasse de la Gare
    drinking white wine and eating bread and cheese.
But what exactly do you think when you think of
    someone?
You don't think in photographs, you don't think in
    flashbacks, as the movies claim
    (what else can they do?)
You may see a gesture that fades before it appears
    leaving only a sense of its fidelity
If you hear a voice it is a sample, barely realized
    more like the sound of a moral nature.
The thought of someone is a not quite visualized
    and almost inaudible
    presence in your mind
    —perhaps not even in your mind—
of your own assembled affections
an order of sensations very much your own,
like a wordless song you sing to yourself
or a fervent prayer you do not bring to speech
in praise of the unutterable specificity of character.
The thought of his mother, Ben felt as his own
    irrepressible adoration of her
His little Mama, whom he loved to tease and dance
    around the kitchen
till whatever wrong thing he had done
    was washed away in her laughter.
His quiet Papa, slender and straight, with a head of
    fine white hair
    and the cheekbones of the Siberian steppes
was his own intellectual formation
    the assumptions he wasn't aware of as assumptions
    that proposed the questions he was likely to ask.
His sweetheart Ruth was his longing for life
    the form of his aching loneliness
The American beauty
    who stood like the Statue of Liberty in his mind
Steadfast, loyal, Manhattan-born, like himself,

configured as the promise of the new world,
and supersedent of the historical disaster
   that was Europe
that his immigrant parents had despaired of
and where he lay pressed against the near trench wall
with an army of Huns hurdling over his prostrate form.
This should have been the final moment of our family's
   European connection
when, the advance having gone past him, supporting
   enemy troops
came scuttling down the trenches looking for living
   Allies they could kill
Food, boots, ammunition they could salvage,
and my father, hearing them in the adjoining angle
   of the zigzagged trench
summoned up a last remembrance of the old world
   Yiddish
he'd heard in his childhood on Stanton Street—
a Germanic dialect to hush and soften and make melodic
that language of expectorated shrapnel—
And shouted from cupped hands, re-Prussianed, he hoped,
   an order to the approaching soldiers
   to stop their goddamn malingering
and move out before he had their asses court-martialed,
   or words to that effect,
Which they did to his astonishment. And then he lay
against the other trench wall as a few minutes later
   the Huns leapt over in retreat,
a counterattack having been mounted which would
   by midnight leave everything as it had been before
except of course for the thousands of fresh
   corpses,
a fact my father understood when, roused up
   by the Limeys and the Frogs,
he climbed over the top and ran forward, bayonet poised
   into the littered sulfurous hell
   of No-Man's-Land
a maniac animal scream issuing from him

while his mind quietly assured him that the true soul
is finally left inviolable by circumstance.

———

—Perhaps the first songs were lullabies. Perhaps mothers were the
first singers. Perhaps they learned to soothe their squirming simian
babes by imitating the sounds of moving water, the gurgles, cascades,
plashes, puddlings, flows, floods, spurts, spills, gushes, laps, and sucks.
Perhaps they knew their babies were born from water. And rhythm
was the gentle rock of the water hammock slung between the pelvic
trees. And melody was the sound the water made when the baby
stirred its limbs.

There is the endless delight we take in new beings . . . and there is
the antediluvian rage they evoke by their blind, screaming, shitting,
and pissing helplessness. So the songs for them are two-faced, lulling
in the gentle maternal voice but viciously surrealistic in the words.
Rock a bye, baby, in the treetop, when the wind blows the cradle will
rock, when the bough breaks the cradle will fall, down will come baby,
cradle and all. . . . Imagine falling through a tree, your legs locked and
your arms tightly bound to your sides. Imagine falling down into the
world with your little head bongoing against the boughs and the
twigs, and branches whipping across your ears as if you were a xylo-
phone. Imagine being born. Lullabies urge us to go to sleep at the
same time they enact for us the terror of waking. In this way we learn
for our own sake the immanence in all feelings of their opposite. The
Bible, too, speaks of this as the Fall.

—**Things Noah Would Have to Have Two Of:** Dung beetles. Absolutely essential. Let's see . . . forty days and nights of rain plus a
hundred and fifty of swollen waters . . . all together about six and a
third months on board living with camels, horses, lions, jackals, wild
asses, goats, sheep, hedgehogs, boars, meerkats, caracals, wolves,
warthogs, jerboas . . . hmmm. You would know better than to shovel
that stuff overboard, when the waters receded you would need top-
soil. Still, that's lots of work for just two dung beetles, even in their
generations. Better make it four.

—

—And, Jesus Christ, the desert! the sun so hot, all that sucking swamp of after-flood, great placental slides of steaming slime, quagmires, concaving basins bubbling at their drain, lakes turning sodden with all their suffocating, swimming creatures flipping and flailing to fossilized death, schools of dead fish carpeting the earth, the soil drying, caking, cracking, the footage firming, and all that after-flood baking away into a merciless desert strewn with boulders, channeled with wadis, and with multitudes of bacterial creatures self-inventing in the ferment of rotting fish scale: this is the native terrain of all of us, the spiritual source, not on the white Arctic wastes of ice did the genius for religion assert itself, but here, on the plains of worn-to-microcrystal quartz blowing about under the sun into pebbly dustdevils and sandstorms that blackened the sky, all of it dictating a culture of nomadic herding, cloaks, and veiled head clothing. Forty days for Jesus in the desert— what is it about the number forty?—Moses and Elias too had been out there for their forty, and all of them, bag and baggage, the Habirus wandering around for forty years, the hot Saharan sand in their mouths, the sun of the Negev, the red rock, with the sandstone cliffs scoured into discs and altar stones, pinnacles and fluted columns, and the pathetic little water holes oased from the rocks, every one of God's company coming down to drink and eat of the dates . . . our spiritual home, each rock an oven to bake bread, a terrain covering more of the earth than Europe, a geological mirror of the dark breathless bottom of the briny sea, with its own stock of adaptables, naturally . . . its brine shrimp whose eggs could live dormant in the clay for years be- tween rains, its sandmites and toads, its darling beetles and jewel wasps, scorpions and locusts, beady-eyed snakes and horned toads and frilled lizards, its desert rats, sandfish, skinks and moles and fennec foxes. And every one of these brainless adaptors knowing to stay out of the midday sun, burrow in the sand, nest at the root of the cactus, and wait for evening to hunt for food, trap their prey or crunch it in their mandibles or sting it to death, or for the early morning to let the dew roll down their crustaceous backs into their scummy mouths, lots of company for Christ in the desert with maybe the owl at night hoot- ing from the highest transom of the mountain cave with a brown spiny mouse trembling in its talons.

—I was squeezed tight against the sealed door, inhaling the historic odors in the wood of hay, of hide, and with my lips pressed to a thin plane of slatted air of the ordinary, indifferent earth outside.

The plane of air was heated by light, cooled by the darkness, and so I was able to count off the days and nights. I detected the first light of dawn by a changing sensation on my tongue. I could occasionally hear something as well, such as the lowing of a cow at dusk, distant and almost indistinct amid the moans and prayers of the people around me.

Since the catastrophe was ours alone, it did not impinge on the traditional practices of railroad transport. Periodically the train was shunted to a sidetrack and left to sit there hour after hour, deaf to all our importunings and cries of despair, or it would creep forward, but then drift backward to stop in the silence of the impassive night, only to be suddenly on its way, creaking and shuddering through the switches, back on track, where it would clump along like some dumb and dogged beast of the Mitteleuropa peasantry.

We were one boxcar of a long train of boxcars of the packed standing and swaying, living and dying and stiffened dead. Each car was the traditional, standard carriage for freight, seven-point-one meters in length, three and three-quarter meters wide, with a battened roof slightly saddled for runoff, and set on a steel chassis with four flanged Krupp Steelwork wheels at European track gauge, and with coupling mechanisms front and back. A common sight, absurdly homely, top-heavy things, their wooden sides painted rust or olive green, weathered links of them waiting in every train yard of the continent, or grinding and rattling through the countryside, through villages at three in the morning under a cold moon, shivering, banging away in the sweeps of wind coming off the wide valleys, these commonest transports for the businesses of nations arousing the lean, visibly ribbed dogs of the villages to run alongside, and yelp and leap into the air and snap their jaws at the stench in their nostrils.

After the first or second day I began to gnaw on the slot in the siding through which I breathed the outside air or, as I thought, the wide expanse, as far as the horizon, beyond it, infinitely extending, of destinies not of this train. I had no purpose in mind, it merely seemed reasonable to mouth the hard wood hour after hour without stopping, except of course when I passed out and slept. When I was fortunate enough to have an actual splinter come away in my mouth, I chewed it for food. For water I had one night the wind-driven rain, like cold needles on the tip of my tongue. As I worked away, I found myself listening to the clacking wheels, applying rhythms to them, making up songs in my head to go with the rhythms, but somehow these songs were in my mother's voice, or my father's, and the voices were really more in the nature of evanescent images of my mother and father, and the images more like fleeting sensations of their beings, momentary apperceptions of their moral natures, which caused me to call out, as if they could be brought to resolution as my whole real mother and father. For my trouble I found myself returned to the mindless incessant clacking of the train wheels. I reasoned that if I could gnaw an opening large enough to climb through, they would be happy to greet me, these flange wheels that would flip me along one to the other and end my life sharply and cleanly.

But then someone directly at my back, a girl who had wept and wept the first day so that my shirt was wet by her tears, but had since then only whimpered in a high pitch almost like a cat, and, among the shifting stiffened bodies, had come to hold her arms around my waist, with her cheek pressed between my shoulder blades—this girl, with no warning sound, died, and, the train rocketing around a curve, her legs sank under her, and her arms slid over my hips and down around my knees so that I was pulled by her weight down a few inches to where I found myself looking through the slot through which I had breathed the air outside.

A blur, brush, a woods so close to the railroad embankment that leaves slapped against the siding, a dense woods so thick as to create shadows dark as night. Then suddenly a broad sunlit vista of a green field with a house and barn in the distance. "A farm!" I called. "Now a road. A horse and wagon." And so I broadcast the news of the world to those who would listen. Birch trees. A brook. Women, children culling potatoes. A river. A stationmaster lighting his pipe.

Among the people in my car whom I had seen climbing into it before me were some I knew. When I sensed from the smell of soot and the appearance of a track yard that the journey was coming to its end, it seemed to me important to recall who they were: Mr. and Mrs.

Liebner and their son, Joseph, who had been a year ahead of me in school, the twin old-maid sisters Chana and Deborah Diamond, the baker Mr. Licht, a Dr. Hornfeld, recently arrived, who had gone to work with Dr. Koenig in the little hospital, my friend Nicoli who shared with me his German-language cowboy novels, and the blond girl Sarah Levin with her pretty mother, Miriam, the music teacher, who had told my mother that Sarah had an eye for me. I could not see them now. They might have been there with me, but they were of the past. Even had I been able to turn and look behind me, what of them would I have recognized at this time of their degradation, when like myself they had been sundered from their names, when their beings were undone, when whatever they had been was in process of industrial transfiguration, when all together we were no more than a suspension of disjunctive torments of the living dying and stiffened dead of that boxcar?

—We arranged to meet for lunch at the Luxembourg, on West Seventieth Street. Fortunately it was not crowded this particular afternoon—it tends to be noisy with its art deco banquettes, mirrored and tiled walls—but the usual attractive clientele were there, on the youngish side, but commanding attention as people whom you might not know but who nevertheless looked familiar, as if you ought to have known who they were. The point is, she fit right in, she was wearing a smart gray suit, a black blouse, her neck was unadorned, her smartly cut hair was combed back to show her ears, which are quite small, and she was vibrant and alive to the place, leaning forward for our exchanges, holding her knife and fork above her plate as she spoke, and the chardonnay having brought a flush to her cheeks.

"You don't know what a luxury this is, lunch out."

"Liberation."

"Now that the boys are in school all day. But still, it's usually a sandwich at my desk, or a working lunch with papers all over the place."

She has a melodic alto voice, a lovely laugh. This was really the first time I'd seen her without Pem. I had given her the ghetto material to read and she was to tell me what she thought. There's a softness about her not quite up to aerobic fashion, but it's very attractive, it's her, Sarah, unapologetically, a suggestion of fullness under the chin, thin line or two around the neck, maternal bosom. And when her face was in repose or she became thoughtful, it was, God help me, sexy as hell. This had to be part of Pem's feeling for her, that she is a woman unmoved by the profane but urgently available in a holy union. Certainly there is no diffidence about her. She is direct, forthright, though oddly her small gold-rimmed eyeglasses make her seem even more youthful than she is—I would say she is nearing forty—and perhaps overly solemnized by Pem's description of her grief, I am repeatedly startled by her charm and the astonishing blue of her eyes and the infectious smile that breaks out and, for an instant, ambiguously suggests itself as prelude to tears. I think now she is, after all, the Sarah Blumenthal of the Heist section.

I wanted to ask what a woman like her was doing in a place like the rabbinate.

"Yes?" She waited.

"Never mind," I said.

"No, what were you going to say?"

"Stupid question."

"Go ahead, Everett." She smiled. "I'm asked it every day, usually by older men."

"What," I said, trying to recover, "if you like Frank Sinatra?"

Laughing. "Sinatra? Where did he come from? That wasn't—"

"Sure it was. And I know the answer. You listened to rock. Your generation tried to bury Sinatra."

"No, he was okay, just sort of irrelevant."

"Who'd you listen to?"

"The Dead. Creedence. Dylan, of course. But a few years ago Joshua brought home some of the early recordings with Tommy Dorsey, and I was ready to listen. . . . You know, I really don't mind answering your question."

"It's sexist. On the other hand I didn't have a sense about Pem either, at first, that he was an ecclesiastic."

"How would you characterize us as a class?"

"Well, as having a certain self-assurance, a knowledge mastered, a self-positioning for the life instruction of others. And often being hard to talk to naturally, as I seem to be able to talk with both of you."

"Rabbis are not priests or ministers. We can run a service, bury the dead and, among the Orthodox, rule on law. But essentially a rabbi is only someone who's done the reading."

"Which you have."

"It never stops . . ."

"But you didn't grow up religious."

"No, my family was nonobservant. I mean, maybe we would go to someone else's seder for Passover. That was about the most my father could tolerate. Every once in a while my mom grew wistful about it, but she knew better than to bring it up."

"So what happened?"

Sarah cleared her throat. "Well, she died. My mother died. It was sudden. I was in high school at the time. We were living in Chicago— my father had gotten a job teaching Comp Lit at Northwestern—and in the months after her death, I went to an institute in the city that taught Yiddish language and literature. She's American-born, but when I was a little girl I heard her speak Yiddish with her mother. . . . I think that was the beginning, wanting to speak Yiddish as my mother did, wanting to speak words she spoke with her mother."

"Do you have any brothers or sisters?"

She shook her head. "After I learned the language, I turned political and helped raise money to get Russian Jews out of the Soviet Union. Then as a junior at Harvard I changed my major to Judaic studies. Then the decision to go to Hebrew Union College in Cincinnati. One thing led to another, it was incremental, unplanned. Only looking back can I see that all together it was inevitable. One continuous stubborn . . . assertion."

"Directed even to your father."

"Without question. But it was after I met Joshua and we began talking that I realized that ethnicity, incorporating the tradition in yourself, is not enough. That one can do the reading and . . . not even have begun."

And then she was quiet, thoughtful, and so that I would not keep staring at her, I turned to the food on my plate. Only after the silence went on did it occur to me that she was composing herself to talk about my pages.

I said: "Did you—?"

"I did. I'm very impressed."

"Really? I was so—"

"No, it's terribly moving. Of course," she said, "anyone familiar with the literature will recognize that this is the Kovno ghetto you're talking about, from the Abraham Tory diary?"

"Yes, I relied heavily on it."

"But the Kovno ghetto was larger than you represent."

"Yes, I made it not much more than a village. But I wanted that geography. The bridge across to the city. The fort."

"And my father was not from Kovno, of course. He was from a village closer to Poland. The Jewish resistance in Poland was more developed than in Lithuania. Those could be Polish Jews you're talking about, their attitude, that Benno and so on."

"Yes."

"And I have to say, you must be careful not to oversimplify the way things were. Certainly in the Kovno ghetto they had clandestine military training, for example. They were doing all sorts of rebellious things."

"Yes," I said, my heart beginning to sink.

"And there was a black market in vodka. The heavy drinkers among the Jews were a danger to the whole community. And you say nothing about soap. My father told me they obsessed on soap—they had none, they risked their lives to smuggle it in, it was as crucial as food."

She saw my dismay. "But I was very moved," she said. "It may be inaccurate, but it's quite true. I don't know how, but you caught my father's voice." She laid her fork down, folded her hands, and stared at the tablecloth. "He was not appointed a runner, like your little Yehoshua. It was more happenstance than that, because even before he was orphaned, he made himself useful. He was a little fellow and he could dart about. And they came to depend on him. And then, when he was given his official runner's cap—that was toward the end. And it did save his life. In more ways than one."

"How is he managing these days?"

"He's in a good, well-run home and they try to keep him occupied."

"This is in Chicago?"

"Yes. He no longer speaks. Of course dementia is never pretty. But when I think of that prodigious intellect I grew up with . . . And he saw it coming before anyone. He detected the signs in himself and re-signed from the faculty."

"I'm sorry."

"No, listen, in one sense it's a blessing. It would have been too ter-rible for him to know of Joshua's death." Her eyes lowered, she took a sip of wine. "He never asked Josh to do that, to go over there, to find the diary. But that wouldn't have made any difference. He could never go back himself, it was just something he could not bring himself to do. He loved my husband. And he was proud of us, our calling, as only a parent can be whose children subscribe to a belief . . . that in his view cannot be seriously held."

"That's very Jewish."

"Isn't it?" Her smile broke out.

"Pem was enormously fond of your husband. I can understand why they hit it off."

"Yes." She opened her shoulder bag on the banquette beside her and began to root about. "Entirely different personalities, but Pem doesn't fit the mold either—of his tradition, I mean. He somehow lets you know in everything he says that his expectations of the world, or of God, haven't been satisfied."

She withdrew a letter. "At the same time, he seems to be appealing to some court or other not to pass sentence just yet. *Gottdrunkener mensch* is the phrase that comes to mind, how would you translate it?"

"God-bombed."

"That'll do. He can be exhausting to be with, the father."

"I'll say."

We laughed at that. "In fact he has gone and done something en-tirely uncalled-for, if not presumptuous. But he's a dear, good friend," she said, and unfolded Pem's letter and read it to me.

His search for the ghetto diary had taken him to Moscow.

=

—When St. Tim's was deconsecrated, Pem was left unassigned while the See wondered what to do with him. His first response was to as-sign himself to a hospice on Roosevelt Island, where he did a lot of the dirty work for the indigent dying as a kind of self-imposed penance, though without entirely understanding what he should feel penitent about. Perhaps that he was not himself dying. Yet death there had a kind of normality to it, it was reliably routine, some patients were weeks away, some days, some just hours, and everything was processional in the manner of life's other marked events such as christenings or college graduations. He noticed of the regular nurses and nurses' aides that they came to work as cheerfully as anyone else, as if the ready availability of dying people for their ministrations were the evidence of a healthy economy.

Pem had chosen the hospice across the East River as an appropriate dead end for his professional life. He was already working around in his thinking to a meaningful transition, to what he did not yet know, but he felt himself changing, and if he had any faith left, it was his conviction that when the brass cross of St. Tim's appeared on the roof of the Synagogue of Evolutionary Judaism, something momentous was announced. This was not a proposition he was prepared to argue with anyone—he had regretted mentioning it to me because, on the one hand, it belonged to a mode of thought characteristic of the ancient prophetic communications which he could no longer countenance and, on the other, because he felt, with the stunning power of superstition, that to discuss it, to speak of it, was for it to lose its light. He did not think of the sign as necessarily unearthly but as so cryptic as to render the motives of the human beings who had arranged it entirely beside the point.

Betrayable in speech, and positioned on the edge of unreason, his given sign was a challenge to his behavior. He must keep his own counsel, even as far as Sarah Blumenthal was concerned. His sign was ambiguous, he had recognized it for what it was but not for what it was instructing him to do. He felt that when he should confide in her he would know it without question, but in the meantime he had to be patient and attentive and alive to his life, the person on whom nothing is lost. He could hope that a revelation was evolving, that it was a slow process, and it might be manifest even in the moans of the dying. From the very beginning, even before the cross had been stolen, the events at St. Tim's had turned him into a detective of sorts, and that's what he'd decided his life must seriously become, a truly humble, dogged act of detection.

After hearing Pem's letter to Sarah, I wonder if revelation comes not like light to the eye but as an imposed ordering of that part of the self so deeply interior that it is anonymous.

=

—I've a pretty good idea of the father's walking routes now, today I begin at Union Square Park, I see the rat-poison skull-and-crossbones warnings planted in the grass . . . and on its west side, down the steps, is the truer park, the farmers' market, with its banks of potted flowers, office trees, truck farm produce from New Jersey . . . brilliant color fields of pears and apples, spinach, kale, carrots in the sunlight . . . anything organic in Manhattan draws crowds . . . the brisk, unsentimental exchanges between buyer and seller rehashing the first act of civilization . . . and west along Fourteenth, the venue for cheap clothes hanging from pipe racks on the sidewalk, big hand-crayoned sale signs in the windows, tables with hats and gloves for the coming winter, the ceilings of the stores strung with luggage . . . the traffic crawling by, big fumy buses, the smells of pizza, sidewalk incense free for the breathing . . . down Seventh past the double-parked parameds of St. Vincent's, with distant sirens on their way tolling the truth of eternal emergency . . . and, slanting eastward along Greenwich Avenue, Mexican and Indian restaurants, coffee ritual places . . . long-gray-haired man with little dog on a leash, three black kids, their voluminous jeans falling off their hips, thin blond young woman kneeling to tend to baby in stroller, stopped-in-traffic truck driver looking down at her, his arm dangling over his cab door . . . across the street one of the paranoidally fenced community gardens behind which soars the towered Romanesque strawberry-red Jefferson Market Courthouse, recalling the last century, when, given the great identity problem of the new world, every conceivable architecture rose from the sidewalks of New York, Romanesque, Gothic, Moorish, Belle Epoque, and Tenement . . . and across arterial Sixth Avenue along miserable, wretched Eighth Street once the glory of bohemian intellect, with the best bookstore in New York, now the venue of shoes and phony antique clothing, the boomboxed hatchbacks from New Jersey zooming up to the curb . . . south on sedate lower Fifth to Washington Square, with its competing performers, a limber black comedian in the center ring, he's brought his own sound system and, at the edges, sideshows of various strumming adenoidally voiced Dylan clones, each with his loyal group around him . . . and so in and out of the city's lightness and darkness, each neighborhood its own truth, with another kind of life to give you . . . and finally up Second, typically wide avenue of the East Side, past the Ukrainian hall and restaurant, I turn right down this sunless East Village street to have a look at what's become of St. Timothy's, Episcopal. A piously aspiring brownstone steeple that was probably the tallest thing in the neighborhood when it was built. Recessed behind its tiny churchyard and all jammed in now between the tenements, the street at each end colored up with the signs of rent-payers—cleaners, bodega, bar, checks cashed . . . the few gravestones in the patchy grass have sagged over the years like shoulders bowed in grief . . . and all of it, including the graves, now a theater company.

Gothic lettering over the doors, Theater of St. Tim's. They're playing Chekhov's *The Seagull*.

"Well, after all," I remember Pem saying, "wasn't drama born from religion? Exit gods, enter ordinary Greeks. Not to scant the polytheists of the mystery cults, they knew a thing or two, among which was how to put on a good show, with lots of music to go with the fucking and drinking. But over the long haul, we've probably done better with Sophocles."

———

—B. the film director in New York to get me to write a screenplay for him. We went to dinner and this was the story he wanted me to write—it was, he said, a story from "life," in fact his life, which is why he felt it had such authority: A couple of years before, he'd cast an actress in a movie in which she was to be badly mutilated by a sociopath who ranged through the neighborhood climbing fire escapes and opening windows to prey on beautiful unattached young women. Women who'd come to the big city to find a job and make a life—sad, winsome girls leaving a small town of grief behind them, having perhaps lost a soldier boyfriend to a war, or a pair of parents on a small farm . . . but anyway in the city now, the film being an homage to the forties film noir. B. wanted that forties deep-shadow black and white that told you how dark and inhospitable the world was.

And this actress, a lissome, long-legged, almost pretty girl, a little vague in a sexy way, with a good head of hair, she tested well and was cheap, she was just out of one of the New York acting programs, and this was her first movie and he gave her the role of the woman who lives to tell the tale, becoming romantically involved with the detective on the case who visits her in the hospital, and so on. B. cast this actress from some instinct having nothing to do with practicality, she felt right to him for this part in a way he didn't bother to analyze. He is not analytical in any event. And, well, they shoot the scene, the sociopath climbs up the fire escape and into the window of her boardinghouse room, because this is a past-tense movie, you see, when there were boardinghouses and poor neat clean girls took rooms in them . . . and the guy looms over her bed and she screams in terror and he doesn't rape her because that's not what the sex is in these movies, the sex is the horror, and he bends over her and begins to chew up her face with his big sharpened teeth and . . . a couple of takes and it's a wrap, it's gone so well and they don't have any budget to speak of, B. shoots the film in eight weeks. When it opens the critics notice her, though not crazy about B.'s work, he has done some respectable things, they tax him for wasting his time.

The actress pins everything on her good notices in this bad film, she can go to New York and do some Off Broadway thing, but her agent tells her to stick it out, there's work out here, film, TV. . . . So she stays, she's dating this one or that one, getting her name in a column every once in a while, but she misses out on one thing after another, not much happens, her agent not able to land her jobs . . . and one night she comes home just a little tipsy, she's got an apartment in West Hollywood, and a maniac is inside waiting for her, a real one. He pins her down on the floor and bites off her nose.

"I mean, this is no movie," B. tells me, "this is what actually happens! She screams, someone hears her, they get the guy, pull him off her, but the poor kid never recovers her sanity, she is today living with her prosthetic nose in a state asylum!" For a while it was a private sanitarium, but then the studio decided they'd done all they could, an in-house lawyer figured they are not finally responsible if some creep sees her mutilated in a film and decides this is her karma. But, B. tells me, and this is important, that it was never established that the maniac had seen the film! "Knowing what I know now," he says, "I'll guarantee that he didn't see the film! I mean, are these crazies capable of sitting still for two hours to watch a movie? I send the kid flowers every week, I worry about her, that it's not over yet. For all I know the guy's in the same institution, male psycho division, separated from her only by a dormitory fence. For all I know he's biding his time till he can get to her again."

So, B. asks me, what was the instinct that told him to cast the girl in the role—some specific vulnerability she flashed, a genome of her own doom, what? What did he see in her without even thinking about it—that's what bothers him. Earlier in his career he'd cast an actor to die of a heart attack who'd gone and done just that, and once, for a western, an Indian war thing, an actor he cast as a cavalry officer skewered by an Indian spear impaled himself on an iron fence-post in front of his apartment house after he fell drunk out of his third-floor window.

"I must foresee things," B. tells me with that Hollywood gift for effortless self-anointment. "I must have foreseen the fate of that poor girl." He shakes his head, stares at the tablecloth. "But how? What is my moral scorecard here? What do I know and when do I know it?"

"So, let's see if I have this right," I say. "You want to make a movie about a man who makes a movie with an actress whose fate in the movie is repeated in her real life, except that her real life is a movie that you are making with another actress about how your movies foretell real life—is that the idea?"

"It is positively occult, isn't it. A genuine occult mystery. Like it's screening right here in my own soul. I can't tell you how strange this is. It's the biggest picture of my career."

"Well, it could be something, all right, but—"

"I came right to you. With your philosophical bent, how could I think of anyone else?"

"I'm sorry, I don't want anything to do with it."

"Why not?"

"And put another nose in harm's way?"

"Oh. Oh . . ." Ruminating. "I see what you're saying. Not to worry. I'll find someone who isn't right for the part: I'll cast against type."

"That's only what you'll think you're doing," I tell him.

———

—Back to my waterside village on the Sound, the light of late September coming in at a slant, a golden beneficent light, placid, unrustled by wind, but like a ripening, with clear intimations of the year now harvested, the sere winter coming. A sad season, the Canadian geese thinking of flying south, flocking in their serious squadrons but circling indecisively, a honking false prophet among them wheeling them back down to skid-land on the coves. When they are fed by well-meaning people, they stay beyond their time and freeze to death.

Over by the ocean beach innumerable swallows darken the sky, swirling about like dust storms, but do they feed as they fly, actually vacuum the air of the insect legions, as swifts do? They are small as sparrows, white-breasted, blue-feathered, with swept-back forked tails and pointed wing-tips. Space is the dimension of their lives, it's what they live in, like bird galaxies, though not, like swifts, for months, years, at a time without landing. They have a weakness for telephone wires, they can't resist the linear communal perch as now, with a gingerly first touch down, a few suggest to the rest a break in their migration, until they clear out of the sky over the long stretch of sanded road just behind the dunes and settle shoulder to shoulder on the cursive telephone cable, pole to pole to pole, breasting the ocean wind, head feathers ruffling, these little fuckers know how to live, they are arrayed now for some celestial concert only they can hear.

———

—I was aware as I did my philosophy in my own way, standing in front of the students in states of abstraction while they waited to write down what I said . . . I was aware that to the degree they were awed was the extent they would make fun of me behind my back. Professor

Ludwig Wienerschnitzel. Arguing with himself, lapsing into his German, hearing what he had just said aloud as if someone else had said it, and then disagreeing vehemently. Coming up with one startling brilliant assertion after another, and erasing each one with a wave of his hand, a grimace of self-disgust. Demonstrating the physical exertion of real thought. Hours of this . . . performance. Finally sinking into a chair exhausted, his hair matted with perspiration. But always, I say now here as a confession, always with no purpose but to make things as simple as the world is in its hereness and nowness, baring everything as far as possible to its simple naked *given*. The world as . . . everything that is so, everything that is the case. So I did that hard work, and it proved infernally difficult. So difficult as to drive me to serious considerations of suicide. But when once achieved, all the difficulty is over, is that not so? It should have been easy now for everyone, and yet . . . I was not understood! I numbered my thoughts and put them in developmental order, as a student makes outlines of his reading. The easier to understand. I did all that could be done. But the simpler I made the practice of philosophy, the more difficult it became for everyone else. Not just people, not just students, but my colleagues, my fellow philosophers! The very men who had taught me!

God knows, I did not look for gratitude. Only for someone in this world who would say to me, "Ludwig, you are not alone." But all I heard from everyone was, Please explain this, say it so that I can understand it. You see? They didn't realize that to explain it was to negate it. I had reached the point of apparentness which is inexplicability. The point of all my work is to find only what can be said. And there is not much of that! I wrote to them, "Whereof one cannot speak, one must be silent." I said to them, If you would understand what I have written, read what I have not written and perhaps then you will understand. But this only puzzled them further.

Migod. I would tell this or that young Englishman with whom I walked or went to the movies after an exhausting lecture: If you would live in the true spirit of philosophy, don't be a philosopher. Well what about you, Professor? I have left philosophy before, I tell them, and I will leave it again before it kills me, it was a mistake for me to come back, I tell them. If you are a philosopher by training, abandon philosophy and work with your hands. Become a carpenter, a nurse, a hod carrier. Something simple and real in the real world, something that corresponds with the world as it is. If you are in love, I would tell this or that young Englishman, and, let me say here and now, there were never such enchanting young men as the English turned out, their skin coloring, their reticence, their capacity for self-subjugation, my goodness, what an enticement they were, what a constant, even agonizing enticement . . . But if you are in love, I would say to them, the one or two who genuinely did love me, we must separate, because love can exist only in separation, only in denial of the flesh is the love affirmed for what it is or otherwise it cannot be trusted as unconditional. And if it is not unconditional it is not love. That is the truth I practice when I have the strength to do so. All of civilization as it has developed is designed to sully our souls. All the values of society must be forsworn if you would live as a man. Wealth is a deadly condition. If you are wealthy, as I was—I was immensely rich—impoverish yourself, as I did. If you love, cherish your love by abandoning your lover, as I did. If you are an academic philosopher, leave it and live humbly, as I did. And if your obsession is language and thought, go to the movies as I do and let yourself bathe in the images, the lights and shadows, the places and sweet faces, let the pictograms flicker over you that are the opposite of language, that do not have to create analogs of the world in grammatical propositions, as language does, that do not have to map the world with sentences but are already there, simply and without effort, in it and of it.

I love movies. They make themselves out of the actual materials of the world, you see. They lift the world's appearances from the world as you would lift with your knife tip the iridescent blue-green coloration of the rainbow from the rainbow trout . . . leaving the substance of the world unchanged but rendered in exact homologous equivalence of itself. With movies you sit in darkness and learn that the world is everything that is the case. And that when they have reached their conclusion and the lights go on, what has not been shown cannot be spoken of, that there is a silence beyond them appropriate to the ineffability of that which cannot be expressed. And at this point you leave. From the darkness of the theater to the darkness.

But where was I?

—The Midrash Jazz Quartet Plays the Standards

DANCING IN THE DARK

(*applause*)

> *till the tune ends,*
> *We're dancing in the dark*
> *And it soon ends;*
> *We're waltzing in a wonder*
>   *of why we're here.*
> *Time hurries by, we're here and gone.*
>
> *Looking for the light*
> *of a new love*
> *to brighten up the night,*
> *I have you, love,*
> *And we can face the music together*
> *Dancing in the dark.*

I mean, no candlelight, no firelight, not one lumen,
This is definitely the dark we're dancing in,
As we ponder the meaning of our existence here—
Let me ask the equally imponderable question:
   Where is here? . . .
Of course we are lucky to have something under our feet
   on which to do our dancing.
   That's something.
On the other hand who are the we I speak of?
I'm holding on to you and you dance well enough,
   but I can't see you and you haven't said a word.
Are you in fact there?
If you are, you know as well as I do
   life is short and as time goes by
   we don't go with it.
We're both looking for enlightenment, am I right?
Like a love at first sight?
And when this luminous love arrives
   bringing us out
   of the darkness of where and who we are

We'll know what we're about,
   we'll see everything clear
including the person we're dancing with,
yes, babe, the person we're dancing in the light with,
   though obviously it won't be either of us.
Until that happens, if it ever does,
I am holding on to you and you are holding on to me
   which I suppose is some consolation.
All in all, this not very promising situation
   suggests
That, arm in arm, we'll be left facing the music
Though how music can be faced when it's all around you
   in the darkness
    is anyone's guess . . .

                                      (*applause*)

I can't let that go unanswered—
My colleague here is so into his own mind
No wonder he's in the dark
No wonder he doesn't see anything.
Lighting up the twists and turns of his brain
With all the voltage of a neutrino
He's dancing with his shadow
Dancing in the darkness of his mind.
I don't see a woman there
How could any woman dance to that beat?
I know what a woman can dance to
I know what it feels like to hold a dancing woman
Alive in her exertion, lithe, powerful in her being
   though she is narrow in the shoulders
   slender-waisted and light on her feet
I smell the sweet cleanness of her hair
She rests her temple on my cheek.
I feel the pulse in her wrist,
I feel her trust as she follows my lead
   and leans the small of her back into my hand
We sway and pirouette and match our steps
   our intimacy hums like another voice of the music

it flows through us as an uncanny harmony
And that is all the conversation I need from her
Dancing in the dark with her.
This is a blessed darkness we're dancing in
lending to us for the time of our dance
our centrality in the world, the magnitude of our
    romance
For as long as our song goes on.

                                         (*applause*)

Whereas I see this as a scene in a nightclub.
Tables lit with small shaded lamps surround
    the dance floor,
A dim white gleam on each tablecloth
A wirey glow on the rims of the wine glasses . . .
This is a nightclub I have never had the good fortune
    to play in,
Terraced, with curved walls and lots of space
    between tables,
A supper club, in fact, where darkness is visible
And the sidemen sitting up on the stand
Are led by a non-playing leader with a baton
As he smiles with his back to them and looks
    benevolently upon the two dancers.
They're all smiling on the bandstand, they're getting
    paid
This is a Hollywood nightclub, you see
All fake, a soundstage for a movie nightclub
And the two dancers are the stars of the movie
And this is the scene where they discover they love
    each other
They dance staring into each other's eyes
While I and the rest of the band play on for them
    with big stupid smiles on our faces
Because the gig pays.
And the extras sitting at the nightclub tables
    in their black ties and evening gowns
They're getting paid too.

We're all extras in the lives of these star dancers
Dancing in the carefully lit dark
   with the dim spotlight on each tablecloth
   and the wirey glow on the rims of the wine
   glasses.
Now here's why we're here:
It happens to be a really bad time outside the
   nightclub,
The country is broke, no one is working,
Men stand in the cold streets on the breadlines
Duststorms sand the paint off jalopies
   abandoned in the desert
Worms eat into the cheekbones of the hungry
   children in the mountains
There are no brothers who can spare a dime
Certainly not in the street in front of the club
   where the cops slap their billies in their palms
and keep the beggars at bay
   behind the police stanchions.
The beggars are waiting for the two stars to finish
   their dark dancing
And take their fur wrap and lambswool coat from the
   hatcheck
And come out to the street to hail a taxi
And toss a few dimes their way.
But this won't happen. The two star dancers
   will go on dancing
He in his black clawtail coat and slicked-down hair
She in her silver sequined gown with her
   clenching ass-halves clearly delineated.
These dancers of the silver screen
waltzing round and around
pretending their song will soon be over
are in fact the appointed collectors of the dimes.
Prying our hands open, uncovering our thin ten-cent
   hoard
They are hauling in the precious dimes of
The beggars in the street, the extras in the scene

We beggars and extras come to sit in the dark,
   on one side of the dance or another
So that the dancers may lighten all our nights
   until our time ends,
And we're gone.

                     (*smattering of applause*)

         Our life in the dark
           Is short as a song
           A chorus or two
           Our time is gone
         You and your lover's
           Waltz is over.
           Darkness has won.
      The music goes on
           Your dance is done
           The music goes on.

                     (*applause*)

—I mean, no candlelight, no firelight, not one lumen,
—This is an enlightened darkness we're dancing in
—With the wirey glow on the rims of the wine glasses.
—The dance is our life. We are given the dark
      to dance our life in . . .

        Dancing in the dark
        till the tune ends,
        We're dancing in the dark
        And it soon ends . . .

                     (*acclamation*)

              =

—Pem's bishop not as I imagined. A small man, almost tiny, fragile-looking, with prematurely white hair. Not a bad sort, generous enough with his time, direct, clerically dogged. Made a point of telling me he was wary of writers, reporters especially. I told him I was too. I assured him that while I was undeniably a writer, I had never sunk as low as reporting. "I'm relieved to hear that. Reporters look for conflict, from wars to divorces, they home in on internecine struggle, the bloodier the better. And where there is empathy, it will be portrayed as its opposite. . . . Father Pemberton, however embattled he may feel, is the object only of our deep concern and collegial regard. You should know that. It is no small matter what he is going through, and his suffering is mournfully acknowledged in my prayers. On the other hand I have to say it is largely self-inflicted. I love him as a dear friend, we were at Yale at the same time, but—and I have said this to his face—he has never quite shaken the sixties. His absolutism is so clearly of the generation that came of age then. I'm a few years older and managed not to contract that . . . habit of militancy. But Pem leapt to the barricades and there he has remained. The issues have changed, but the inflexibility, the all-or-nothing nature of what he wants, what he demands? That hasn't changed."

The bishop smiled. "There is something in the father that is downright evangelical, don't you think? God's little joke."

A woman had entered with a tea service and set it out on the bishop's desk. Some moments passed while he fussed with the teapot.

"Where is Pem now, by the way, do you happen to know why he doesn't return phone calls?"

"He's gone to Europe."

"Ah-ha: I'm glad to hear that. A change of scenery."

"Actually, I think he's trying to track down a Jewish ghetto archive hidden during the war."

"I see. Will you join me? There's lemon here, or milk and sugar."

"Thank you, this is fine."

"Although on reflection," he said, "it doesn't surprise me that Pem would find something like that to do, given his obsession with the Holocaust. He is critical of postwar Christian theology. Dismissive, in fact. Whereas our struggle is heartfelt and apparent to anyone who would care to see it. Some of us resent his attitude—that he would pre-empt a moral position that we all share." He frowned. "This is never hot enough. I'm sorry."

"No, it's fine. Really."

"Tom Pemberton may speak of the Holocaust, but it's Vietnam that's in his soul. You know who his father was, of course."

"Also a member of the clergy . . ."

"You might say. R. R. John Pemberton, Suffragan Bishop of Virginia. Very High Church, a stern guardian of the faith. A priest who wanted no role on the national stage. But by way of self-sacrifice, he signed on to the heresy charges against another bishop of that day, James Pike, of California. And that is how he is remembered, of course. You'll find Pike in the first paragraph of his obituary."

"Pem has spoken of Bishop Pike."

"He would. . . . You know, the See understands the value of secular therapies. I've urged Pem to avail himself of a psychologist. He may have one father too many."

"I don't understand."

"Pike was a destructive influence. Standing in the pulpit, he cast doubt on Immaculate Conception, the Trinity . . . it was as if the wretched counterculture had seeped through church walls. But he impressed some seminarians. It's not impossible that Pem has internalized them—his natural father, John, of the historic church, and the maverick adopted father, Jim Pike—and set them against each other. There is your story, there is the conflict if you're looking for one. Or does it sound to you like cheap psychologizing?"

"Just a bit."

"I assure you it's not. You would think, given our creedal affront to his reason, Pem would have left the church by now. On the other hand, given his dissident nature, why did he come into it in the first place? And if it is not that . . . if that is not the struggle, we have to begin speaking of evil."

The bishop rose and looked out of his bay window. "I don't want that, I don't want to admit I suspect Pem's naïveté. Because he has got to be smarter than that, and so it would be a quite calculated naïveté. Wouldn't he have to know that reason and faith, rather than being incompatible, are complementary? Reason no less than faith sanctifies the ethical life. Both would liberate man from himself. The same mind that conceives the mathematical theorem loves the order of a world under God. Reason and the imagination are parallel paths to God. They need not intersect. One can call on perspective to imagine them as merging in the human experience . . . if in the distance.

"In the meantime, what is abhorrent is pride, this is the sin that is so disastrous, this is where the evil arises, in human self-aggrandizement that forgets how Jesus the Christ came down to us and in our form was broken on the cross."

—Okay, so what I've got: A preppie to begin with, on the hockey team at St. Paul's—a big-shouldered kid—then four years at Trinity in Connecticut. The sixties going full blast, teach-ins, sit-ins, marches, ritual draft card burnings, and Pem spends a summer in Mississippi registering black voters, has his head cracked open and, fully accredited, joins the Yippies around the Pentagon. And what happens then is that he opts for seminary. The bishop wonders why. But as the son of a stalwart churchman, raised in rectories from Seattle to the Upper East Side, what else would Pem go up against if not his house?

I will write of him that as vague and inherited as it may have been, the young man had faith. He may have been confused, but began to see in all that roiling madness of Vietnam and the agonies of the civil rights movement that the church was an institution of truth and sanity. There were clerics around—not just Bishop Pike—antiwar clerics, liberation theologians, models of principled civil disobedience getting themselves manhandled and thrown in jail. Martin Luther King, the Berrigans . . . what gave them such strength? What carried them? Faith was the redoubt. And raising hell was a matter of faith. So here was a reasonable program for a child of the sixties: He would take the Gospels for what they were, a manual for revolution.

Every degree of religious belief from zero to three hundred and sixty, his needle wildly swinging—this is the truth of my friend Father Pem.

—Also true that, after a year off for work in the Peace Corps, about which I will have more to say, he comes back to Yale to finish his degree and he meets the young woman he will marry, Trish vanden Meer. Smart-looking, poised, out of finishing schools in Switzerland. A major in political science. Dots her *i*'s with a circle. Kind of preppie woman he's always avoided, so they fall in love.

Trish likes his raspy baritone, the broad face with a shock of hair always over his forehead, his sexy mouth. He is not even six feet but appears larger, the size of a strong presence, a divinity student with a good name and no money to speak of, and manly as hell. This thing of his not appreciating how appealing he is, like a big shaggy dog. The heavy black-rimmed glasses he wears that tend to slip from the bridge of his nose and that he is forever pushing back up, which somehow to her typifies a certain disorder in his life. He will need taking care of. And this thing of his vulnerability, how a mere idea can take hold of him and shake him up, how concerned he is to share his thoughts with her, though she feels it is more that he relies on her to listen while he gives his brain a workout. She is fascinated that any man could live this hard.

And her attraction for him? She is coolly sexual, a slim, athletic blonde, plays a good game of tennis, is fluent in French and Italian, makes Phi Bete in her junior year, and her father is a big deal in the Johnson administration Tom Pemberton detests.

———

—Dear Pemby,

I had to smile as I took up my pen and thought of the likely expression on your face when you found a letter from your faux pop in the mail. So you see you've already given me a good moment. These days they happen rarely, though I can usually rely on a few during a day's sail, when the wind cooperates and I ratchet up a close tack and haven't to do much more than hold the tiller and taste the spray on my face. I've gone back to the old wood Hereschoff, you remember her? Gaff rigged? I don't know why. She's a bit beamy, not terribly fast, but pretty enough and without airs, like a good first wife. I can work up the momentary illusion of peace. I hear that hiss and quiet slap of boat-going, the sibilance of the elements, as if the wind and light and water are the gods in quiet conversation, just as if the old pagan polytheists had it right in the first place, begging your pardon. I seldom go out farther than a mile or two, and keep to a shorewise course, I don't know why, except that I feel a strong urge to do otherwise. Or maybe it's this odd oceanic disgrace, if you want to know, that there seems to me more floating garbage, more oil slick and unnameable waste the farther out you go. And I am a prissy sort.

I haven't come promptly to the point, have I? Not like me. But I'll assure you of one thing. I am not writing with the intent of getting you back together with your estranged wife. First of all I don't think it's possible, knowing both of you as I do, and second of all I see you in a new appealing light now that we are no longer faux son and faux pop. Frankly I can't imagine what either of you saw in the other to begin with—the peculiar institution that was your marriage is something worth scholarly attention someday, though not by me. I have more demanding priorities. Priorities. Yes, you would be surprised at how even such aged p's like me are still in this thing, very seriously in this thing.

What new appealing light? you ask, fixing immediately on what interests you most. Well first of all, that for all the difficulties of your life, one of which has actually hit the papers, you dwell in innocence. These are such sweetly normal things, a broken family, a lost crucifix, people on line for their dollop of mashed potatoes or whatever else it is that fills your busy days. I'll grant you it's a kind of tortured innocence, and I don't mean to patronize your well-nursed angst, but troublewise, I would change places in an instant. It is such an enviable employment, God's. Not that I've not always known that, but I do see it in this new light. Given that you're obligated to tell us what we already know and don't want to hear, consigning yourself to a role in life both ineffective and tiresome, I have come to see you as the unwitting, perfect surrogate for every righteous gentleperson who has ever stood up in an audience and demanded an apology of me, or written me a tear-stained letter about the brother, son, or husband whose death I was responsible for, or spammed my E-mail with every manner of vile imprecation, or booed me at a book-and-author luncheon, or stood and turned his back as I was given an honorary degree. You are their prophet, Father Pemberton. For your entire generation of cowardly, namby-pamby, self-involved, gutless unregenerate hippies who enjoy the good life of the American hegemony without wanting to shoulder the burdens of it.

My reasoning is thus: If I learn how to communicate with you, perhaps I can actually reach the others. Much the way an anthropologist in the field, or jungle, studiously learns the language and mores of the natives in order to gain their trust. What do you say? I am thinking, of course, of my country. Will you as well, finally, think of your country? If so, here is our first problem:

A legless longhaired man in a wheelchair has taken to picketing my house here in Alexandria. Each morning he arrives in one of those disabled-people transport vans and is deposited at my gate, where he simply sits staring up at the house. At noon, he is carted away for lunch, I presume, but is back in the early afternoon, and does not leave until darkness falls. I have watched from an upstairs window through my binoculars: the person who deposits him and takes him away is a young woman, a daughter or a wife, and very obviously devoted to him she is. He himself appears to be in exceptionally good health, strong, broad-shouldered, his chest, biceps, and triceps well displayed in a tight T-shirt with the sleeves rolled to the shoulders. Lower-class macho, or should I say machee. Probably has a good disability entitlement, too, which is perhaps what he celebrates with the small American flag pennoned on the frame of his wheelchair. I have after a couple of weeks of this called the police. But when they tell him to move along, he does, rolling himself for a walk along the winding tree-shaded streets with the same legal standing as a person with legs. When they leave, he of course comes back to his station. I have thought of sending out lemonade, but that could be read as a kind of mockery, couldn't it? I have thought of inviting him in, risky though that may be and in any event a stratagem to be saved until the press takes notice, as it undoubtedly will, and itself begins to appear at my gate. I have thought of leaving, I can always go abroad, but expect that would be seen as running. But whatever I do the game is his, Father. How would you handle this? What counsel do you offer me, a man not without his own medals and somewhat poorer for having given his postwar services for small pay year after year in the interest of his country's welfare? Shall I picket him? Shall I order a wheelchair of my own and roll down the driveway with a lance at the ready?

Hoping to hear from you, and with warmest personal regards,

As ever,

Your Faux Pop

⸗

—Author's Bio
You remember how my father, Ben,
   a young naval officer out of his element
survived one awful night of the Great War
by shouting out orders in Yiddish,
   a language created in the teeth of European
   history,
to the German soldiers pouring through the trenches.
This was a gutsy, ironic, purely American expedient,
   was it not? It saved his life.
At war's end, he sailed home with Pershing's
   troops,
left the navy, and married his sweetheart Ruth
   in Rockaway Beach, Long Island, New York,
and went into the record player business,
   as a distributor of soundboxes.
The soundbox for the wind-up record player of that day
was a shallow open-faced cylinder
   the diameter of a silver dollar
threaded to the end of the playing arm
and with a screw holding the steel needle
that wobbled along in the grooves of the 78 RPM record
   delivering the impulses to the resonating
   oil paper membrane inside the soundbox
that produced the tinny voices of Rudy Vallee and
   Russ Columbo
for the American people to dance to.
In 1922 my brother Ronald was born
and in 1926 he was held aloft on a windowsill
of my father's office in the Flatiron Building
so he could see the Lindbergh parade passing by
   on Broadway.
The cheers of the crowd below resounding
   through the hail of ticker tape
My four-year-old brother swayed and would have swan-
   dived into the maelstrom

except that my laughing father's sure hands
   gripped him and pulled him back inside
where my mother, Ruth, not one to make light of life,
   turned pale and nearly fainted.
In 193- I was born
and the family achieved its finished composition
Mother, father, and two sons
Bronx apartment dwellers through the Great
   Depression.
I won't go into that except to say,
by 1941 my father, Ben, who had managed until then
to support us with a radio and record store
   that he had opened with a partner,
     finally went under and became a salesman
     working for other people.
By 1943 the young ensign of World War One
was my worried portly father sitting in an armchair
   by the radio
listening to the news of World War Two
   while at the same time reading of the war
   in the evening paper he held out like a tent
because his older son, my brother, Ronald,
   was in England somewhere
flying with the Army Air Corps as a radioman,
My family being disposed to communication
and my brother being disposed since the age of four
   to diving through the air.
So, not to put too fine a point on it,
the family was back in Europe helping out again.
My brother toured the skies of Europe
   at the radio table of a B-17
the so-called Flying Fortress
because it lumbered along with its load of bombs
   turret gunners in its tail and nose
   and a third gunner in the dorsal position
   above and behind the pilot.
With all that armament, by today's standards
   it was a not very large plane

though large enough in the sights of the anti-aircraft
   guns or the attacking Messerschmitts
   flying circles around it.
Later, the B-17s were flown at night,
There being no deeper darkness than Europe's
   at war.
They were lit underneath by the fires of their own
   bombs
ten thousand feet below them, and drew tracer fire
   as a magnet draws nails
And though there was the terror of going down in
   darkness
the crews felt the odds were better flying in it
   than in daylight,
a view only partly shaken by the heavy losses
   they were taking.
At particularly bad moments, flak exploding
   the aircraft seeming to jump with fright,
or a new wheezing sound from the engines,
   smoke pouring through the cabin.
My brother dearly loved the equipment in his charge
   the numbered dials, the needle gauges
   and, through the seams of the black metal
   cabinetry, the reliable glow of the
   radio tubes.
With bombs away the plane seemed to drop upward
   and the chatter on the intercom
homeward bound, of these boys, the oldest of them maybe
   twenty-five,
was feisty, verged on braggadocio, till at dawn
they saw their landing field and grew quiet,
having come back alive for one more day.
After a dozen missions, my brother was given
   a leave
a weekend pass, actually, which he spent—
by invitation tendered through his squadron HQ
which meant it was more or less an order—
at a small English castle in the Cotswolds.

His host was a general, Lord Something
   or Other
who lived there with his widowed daughter
and a small staff of very slow moving ancients.
My brother offering his credentials
primary among them his father's service in the First
   World War,
The general, a frail blue-eyed man of Great War
   vintage,
responded in kind by conducting his guest
   on a tour through his ancestral portrait gallery
   breezily dismissive of what he was so proud of,
the generations of mustachioed mutton-chopped
   bearded bemedaled officers from whom he was bred.
The general sported a dab of dried egg yolk on his tie,
His morning shave had missed a chin spot of stubble.
What class, my brother thought, and was about
   to write off the weekend
when the general's daughter made her entrance,
   a fair-complected tall outdoorsy woman
   the young widow of a British tank commander
   killed in battle against Rommel's forces
   in North Africa.
As he told me about her, my brother called her Miss
   Manderleigh:
Her widespread eyes were large, her full lips red.
She wore her dark hair in the pageboy style,
   a modest blouse and skirt and low-heeled shoes.
Her hand which she placed in his was soft and warm,
and her smiling easy hello made it clear
   in not so many words
   she understood his plight.
He had some time alone to walk about.
He didn't understand how these people
could live in this crenellated manor of yellow
   Cotswold stone,
apparently unaware that it was going to ruin
   inside and out.

It stood unattached to the acreage, not rooted
  to the land
but set down upon it, with no trees, but dead bushes
  in urns
and an indolent stone animal or two
  to express its distinction.
Out back, a walled half-acre was given over
  to a Victory garden,
And beyond this was a long slow-rising upland
    to which Miss Manderleigh pointed as she brought
    out a picnic basket, and a heavy portable radio
Like a hostess determined to see
  to the fun of her guest.
He still had no idea, he hadn't even thought of it,
except perhaps as his own fantasy, though
it was just the two of them, my brother told me
Trudging up the long hill road that was like a church
  aisle
between the hedgerows bowing like deferential
  courtiers
  in the sharply rising wind.
Oh dear, Miss Manderleigh said
The sky a weird green vault, the first drops falling,
And then this rainy blow was upon them,
a very un-English rainstorm
And by the time they reached the shelter of a barn
  they were soaked to the skin.
Birds had been barnthwacked by the wind.
Two or three of them in the tall whipped grass flapped
  in circles around their broken wings.
Inside, in the darkness, the portable radio my brother
  held like luggage
had somehow switched itself on and suddenly
They were listening to a shortwave speech of Hitler's
Sounding like the spillage from an upended toolbox of
  nails and nuts and bolts,
The crisis of the world war rudely denying
  any pastoral exception

and probably accelerating the two young people's
instinct to make love while it still was makeable.
She turned the radio off, he lit a lantern
and warmed himself in the sight of Miss Manderleigh
her wetted pastel picnic outfit, all the over-
   and undergarments pressed like a single sheer wrap
   against her newly apparent person.
Amused to be so flummoxed, Look at this, she seemed to say
With her lips pressed together dimpling her cheeks
   in comic self-denigration, her eyebrows raised,
   the lantern light shining from her eyes
This surprising strapping girl with fleshy pink
   shoulders
the upper back rounding as she crossed her arms
over her breasts, a curious glance at her raised foot
   in his hand
As if the undressing were being performed on someone
   else.
Not that my brother reported the details
—he is given to reticence in all matters sexual—
But I embellish his account
with horse blankets to burrow under
a bottle of wine from the basket,
the cork popping, the wine in two glasses
the cucumber sandwiches and deviled eggs neglected
the wind whistling through the siding
a couple of farm horses in their stalls
   seemingly glad for the company
their shudders and snorts modified in his mind
   to a kind of animal approval.
That evening at dinner the general in dress uniform
   presided from the end of the table,
Miss Manderleigh and my brother on either side.
They dined on the garden's produce
   and game birds from the fields.
You knew in this country at war where everything
   came from.

When the general was ready to call it a night
he muttered his hopes for my brother's well-being
 and shook his hand.
His man helped him up the winding stairs.
Ronald and Miss Manderleigh drank brandy and soda,
 and played cribbage by the fire
And when she was satisfied the house was quiet
 she led him to her room.
He told me he'd become quite drunk but did remember
 her bed, the four posts carved like chess bishops.
I like to think how they must have swayed in parallel,
 rhomboiding east, rhomboiding west,
until the pale dawn crept under the hems of the wartime
 window drapes.
I like to think how this weekend of pragmatic
 English sport
was by this time an achieved hallucination in his mind.
How he'd imagine them shuttling to the matins bells
 of the cathedral a Cotswold away,
with monks in their cells yawning as they scourged
 themselves,
and the latinate syllables rising like unnerved
 barnswallows into the dark European morning.
And not much later it was Good-bye First Sergeant
First Sergeant it was in that way of patriotic
 flings with doomed Allied airmen,
And everything wet in the gray light,
 the stained quarry stone of the castellated
  manor.
 The old bedewed high-polished black Bentley
 the browned gravel under his feet.
He looked off to the barn a rolling hill away
 so oddly placed to kill the wind-blown birds.
The chastened hedgerows still now, the morning cold and
 calm.
He stood there not knowing what to say, they had not
 exchanged addresses.

He felt from her no lingering intimacy.
She was one of that English race that did what had to
    be done.
They were threadbare now, on their uppers, but they
    still did what needed to be done.
As an American soldier he was new to that,
There was so much they would not speak of
Anything they did was a form of mourning.
Miss Manderleigh exhausted, and badly in need of sleep,
Her smile was a terrible struggle on her swollen lips
and her hair too hastily combed this morning
for the illusory farewell of a sweet and lasting
    friendship.
And he would never forget the genderless sad soul
    that stared from her eyes,
erasing from his memory their color, as he said
    good-bye.
    Good-bye Miss Manderleigh, good-bye.

Twenty-four hours later all the crews of my brother's
    wing
were put on alert, and at dawn the next morning
the Flying Fortresses, each carrying five thousand
    pounds of bombs
lumbered down the runway into the mists over Suffolk.
Group joined group circling in the sky
    over East Anglia
until the rendezvous of all 140 B-17s
    and their P-47 fighter escort was made.
The bombs of this particular mission
    were intended for the ball-bearing factories
    in Schweinfurt, deep inside Germany
Or perhaps Regensburg where the Germans made
    their fighter planes
Or was it Regensfurt or maybe Schweinburg
I'll have to remember to check that with my brother
He is as reticent about his war experiences
    as about his romances as a young man

A modest family hero, now in his seventies
    playing tennis every day
And proud of his three grown sons with whom
    he likes to fish,
And devoted to his first wife of forty-odd years
    and to a martini before dinner
And to the rituals of the High Holy Days.
In any event the mission would prove a disaster
Although the Fortresses were fitted out
    with long-range fuel tanks,
the P-47s had only fuel to fly them
over Holland as far as the German border and back
But it was over Germany that the Huns appeared,
their squadrons of yellow-nosed Messerschmitt 109s
diving from the rear upon the stolid
    straight-flying bombers
    maintaining their formations
as they were raked by the fighters' wing cannon
    Punctured, stippled, set on fire
their own .50-caliber twin-muzzle turret guns
    kerchunking away at the infuriating stings
of the curling diving here-and-gone 109s.
The intercom was filled with shouts, commands,
    and someone moaning.
The cabinetry of gauges and lights and glowing tubes
    at Ronald's station
Seemed all at once to fall in upon itself
    like a sandcastle
The lights went out, the intercom went dead
He found a glowing piece of shrapnel
    burning through his glove
The fuselage wall in front of him was like an eye
    of blue, the color of his mother's eyes
Smoke suddenly filled the shuddering Fortress
    and almost as suddenly dissipated.
He disentangled himself and ran forward
for the reason that the craft was tilted
    in that direction.

He found the co-pilot slumped on his stick, the pilot
   gesturing.
Ronald pulled the dead boy back from his chair
   —his head was almost severed from his body—
gently cradled him to the floor of the cabin
   and took his place.
He removed his own flight jacket using the fleece
   lining
to wipe the blood out of the co-pilot's
   oxygen mask,
and put the mask on.
He wiped the blood spatter from the windows.
A calibrated row of lights marked the
   path of German rounds through the fuselage.
The 17's nose having been brought up level,
he was ordered to hold the controls
   while the pilot, whose face was smeared with blood
   attempted to clear it from his eyes.
So there was Ronald maintaining his new station,
Ahead the sky was filled with broken
   formations of Fortresses
Pairs of Focke-Wulfs now taking over from the 109s
   curling out of the sun
   diving upon the 17s,
Flying right through their groups,
   machine guns spitting
and soaring off insolently for another run.
It didn't seem to matter that one or another Hun
   would explode or tail off in a plume of smoke,
They were suicidally joyous.
The bombers burst into flame,
   or spun like falling leaves
   or wheeled over themselves on their wing-tips
   or dove straight-arrowed into the ground.
Contrails and tracers crisscrossed the sky
   indecipherable messages
   punctuated with bursts of black flak
Bodies flew past, parachutists caught in the slipstream

pieces of wing, engine cowlings, hatches
  a bare foot, a head in its leather helmet,
  instrument panels, a propeller idly turning
All the debris of machines and men
  Sky crap now to be flown through.
How long it lasted he couldn't tell
  there seemed to be no other possible life
  until finally the Focke-Wulfs were outdistanced
and what remained of the squadrons
  perhaps sixty planes,
  came within sight of their target.
With only a vicious covering flak to fly through
  the crews were ready to go to work.
Bomb bays were opened, the Fortresses turned
  made their approach
  and went in for their runs.
The city below seemed to puff out all at once
There was a new sound under the engine drone,
the wumphing of delayed explosions of the ground,
  accompanied by cradle sways of the aircraft
His plane suddenly rising, Ronald heard the bombardier
  shout, Bombs away
He imputed an anthropomorphic sense of triumph
  to his plane
that had delivered its stern message to the Germans.
Now let's get the fuck out of here, the pilot said.
Only then realizing no response from the stick.
  Whatever he did, nothing happened.
The flight plan called for avoiding the Luftwaffe
  that had tormented them on the way in
by continuing on, heading south over the Italian Alps
  to airfields in North Africa.
But the run had pointed them westward over Germany.
He could not coax the plane to turn or bank, or climb
  or do anything except go forward.
It felt to him as they droned onward
  that the cables were stripped,
  hanging by a thread

And that any minute everything might come off in his
   hands.
Oh shit don't do this to me, Ronald heard him say.
Gradually they decreased altitude
   by temporarily slowing the ground speed
   and feathering two of the engines
Until they were flying soundly enough
   in order to avoid detection
   just five hundred feet
above perversely neat fields lined with hedgerows.
Small herds of cows moved to a sluggish gallop
   as they passed
An old man pointing, a woman was at her clothesline
   a railroad station porter shaking his fist
A long freight train on a siding, guards raising
   their rifles,
Ronald felt all of Germany was now alerted
   to this wounded American beast lumbering
   over the countryside.
Yet on they went, just three or four crewmen left alive
   in their freezing pungently burnt-out plane
   alone, without radio contact,
And the wind whistling through a thousand
   tears in the fuselage
and dead comrades slumped in their shattered
   gun turrets . . .

Friends, brothers and sisters
How can we see to it that our stories
   don't falter like old veterans parading?
The experience of experience is untransmittable,
The children shrug what's done is done,
   and history instructs them finally
not to be in the wrong place at the wrong time,
As some thirty million were in World War Two,
   each a packet of terminal agony
   for at least one unendurable moment

and all the loving structures of consciousness
   satanically compressed as the world
   came to an end.
I ask how many times the world may come to an end
   before the world comes to an end?
Sitting in the rubble of the pilot's cabin
   the green fields below grayed in the dried blood
   on the window screen,
Perhaps my brother Ronald had intimation
   beyond the circumstance in which he found himself
Of a Europe so historically steeped in fantasy,
   fantasy of king, fantasy of priest,
as to be instantly enlistable to the causes of
   murderous storytelling
From the mouths of its most monstrous twentieth-century
   impresarios,
the loudspeaking sociopaths who always knew
   whom to blame.
Or perhaps he ruminated on the difference between
   war and peace
as a matter of organization, the deaths of peace
being comparatively haphazard, slapdash, local
   or attenuated by such means as poverty
compared to the surefire concerted mass
   mobilization of war death.
More likely, as he sat freezing in his shirt
   and then, no more comfortably,
   in his flight jacket whose fleece lining
   was hung with small stalactites
   of the dead airman's blood,
he thought of his mother and father, Ruth and Ben,
   while not quite able to visualize them
but feeling them as prevailing moral presences
   conferring strength merely from their existence
   as his mother and father.
And he thought of his kid brother, Everett,
   who so seriously took instruction

in the throwing and catching of a baseball,
and he felt that Everett's protected innocence
was strength-conferring.
He checked his watch: in the States
their day was in full swing.
He swore he would someday rejoin
their modest life of work and school and home
and never forget to thank God for the blessing
of this coherent family.
Meanwhile the sky had grown dark, bad weather
loomed.
Slowly, the pilot gained needed altitude
not knowing at what moment of his urging
the craft would no longer fly.
The British called their airplanes machines
a locution too quaint for a Flying Fortress
in my brother's opinion
But with every tremor of the wings
every sputtering choke of the engines
the accuracy of it came home to him.
Now I don't know when or exactly how it happened
that Ronald was ordered to bail out.
The sky was black by then, the storm had hit,
Perhaps lightning shorted the instrument panel.
They were flying blind, the compass spinning,

The turbulence was fierce, knocking them about,
And I think he said the far starboard engine was on
fire.
In the light of the flames he saw the wing
beginning to pull away.
The pilot shouting at whoever was alive to get out,
the plane yawing, bouncing, cracking up,
Ronald staggering aft and finding his chute,
A door was open, the rain hitting their faces,
men tumbling out ahead of him
And with one glance back at the pilot

rising from his chair
   giving the plane up to its dive
Ronald leapt into the raging thundering darkness.

Bartender, another beer for these brothers and sisters
   gone dry in the mouth, and for me.
Immunity to murderous loudspoken storytelling is
   storytelling, isn't that so?
A story on the page is like a printed circuit
   for our lives to flow through,
A story told invokes our dim capacity
   to be alive in bodies not our own.
You would want the whole planet in voice
and the totality of intimate human narrations
composing a hymn to enlightenment
   if that were possible.
In any event, here is this young airman,
   age twenty-two
falling to earth in the harness of a parachute
His arms wrenched and shoulders about to desocket
as he bumps up on the crests and drops in the sloughs
   of the turbulent storm of black air.
He descends through cloud undergoing momentary
   silent fullnesses of illumination
before going black in vituperous thunder.
He is not able to hear his plane crash.
In this great resounding sea of lightning-lit
   darkness,
Deeper than any darkness he has known
And with a continent of bone wrack rising to meet him
He can remember nothing of Miss Manderleigh
Not her words, not her cries, not her intimate bodily
   facts
not her shape or size or form or smile or touch
But only the genderless soul staring from her
   love-dulled eyes
erasing from his memory their color, as

he shouts into the sky
Good-bye, Miss Manderleigh, good-bye!
He really thought it was the end of him.
But the parachutist who meets neither land nor water
    invokes a realm of mythic prophecy
As when impossibly the woods of Dunsinane
    begin to stir though there is no wind,
    uproot, grow feet, and move out
to take the measure of that poor dumb bastard
    Macbeth.
My brother thought first he had come down on seashells.
    because of the jarring crackle under his boots,
But dragged some distance, twisting and rolling
    until he spilled the wind out of his chute,
he was whacked and pummeled with what seemed to be
    staffs or rake handles.
He thought it was some peasant reception committee
    showing their patriotism.
Only when he came to rest, one ankle twisted
    under an immovable bough,
did the xylophonic sound track of the action
    play in his ears
And in the ensuing silence he realized
    he held in one hand an ulna
    a tibia in the other.
He'd arrived in a field of the war before,
    reopened by an errant shell of this war.
It was the improvised graveyard of ancient bones
    and skulls
still helmeted in the stylish French couture
    and phallic German,
the skeletal warriors of his father Ben's generation
    hastily shoveled under as the Great War moved on.
He had reason to hope he was in France
    But at first too stunned to move
    and then in too much pain
he lay there in that boneyard all the night.

He learned that bones of a certain age
   are hollow, weightless, and rise with the breeze
   like flutes of straw or bamboo.
They play, they ripple, they gently bongo
   among themselves,
They clack like train tracks, shiver and shir
   like cards being shuffled,
They clink like wind chimes, hoot soft as owls.
He imagined a badinage of ghosts
   past protest, past outrage, gibbering.
But in the morning a real French peasant found him.
He was hidden in a farmhouse,
   nursed, bone set, and brought back to health.
During this time he put together some working radios
   for the local Resistance
and achieved the affection of an entire family
   this intrepid American boy from the Bronx
   with a shock of hair fallen over his forehead
and a taste for fresh unpasteurized milk
   still warm in the pail.
They embraced him, bid him good-bye and he rode
   hidden in haywagons, carts, and trucks
From one safe house to another for weeks until
   a fishing boat smuggled him across the Channel.
He'd been the only one of his crew to survive.
But soon enough was back in the air again,
   at war in the fire-cracked nights of Europe
Unable at times to know if the machine he rode
was flying level or diving toward the earth
If the screaming he heard was the engine's
   or his own.
And that's how I choose to leave him—
In the war after the war . . . before the war
Before his tour was over and he came home.

—The rabbi has faxed me her father's file. Not much there. His letters to the Justice Department. Their bureaucratic replies. Two 1977 articles from the *Times*: deportation hearing, a finding. Blurry head shot, bald fellow with sickly thin face. Three people testify man in question is the ghetto commandant, Schmitz, but his lawyer shoots down their testimony. They were elderly, easily befuddled. Defendant testifies he is Helmut Preissen, an ex-corporal who only did guard duty in the ghetto for three months before he was shipped to fight on the Russian front. This is same ID he presented to the immigration authorities after the war. The judge finds in his favor. . . . Letters to and from the Simon Wiesenthal Center, the functionary there agreeing with Sarah's father that Preissen is almost certainly Schmitz, but short of convincing documentation, the ID cannot be made that will justify reopening the case, although their file is being kept open.

Less agreement from the Department of Justice, the lawyer there somewhat defensive about his handling of the case.

—a nest of three peregrine falcon chicks, on the ledge of an iron-front window, top floor across the street. Whoever lives there is sensitive to the brood and keeps his shades down. What a great privilege to have them in my binoculars. I can tell when the mother is returning, they are quiet balls of fur. Then all of a sudden, and she may be blocks away, they start squawking, their beaks opening like post diggers, their gullets aimed at the sky. And a moment later there she is winging down the canyon, she's got a city bird in her talons, a rock dove. Hovering, alights, wing stretched to a fluster of infant demands, holds the prey with one foot, a hail of breast feathers and then she is pecking it apart methodically, pulling off red hanks of flesh and dropping them in those gullets.

—Suppose this guy works for the *Times,* a middling career, never gets as high on the ladder as he feels he deserves, you can see it in the set of

his mouth. Others are given the plum foreign assignments, top editor-
ships, and with the passing of years his nagging sense of having been
badly used sinks into the hunch of his shoulders. Now an ordinary-
looking gray-haired man in his late fifties, he has gotten no further
than deputy editing one of the lesser sections.

What finally becomes intolerable is the nature of the corporate
judgment, that he will never be a top-grade newspaperman: in unas-
suageable bitterness, he takes early retirement.

For the first month or so he is in deep funk, missing the routine, his
secret sense of possessiveness of the newspaper, that it was his, and
missing too the affronts to his sense of himself, the welter of gossip,
the daily ups and downs of small triumphs and defeats. Above all, he
misses the feeling of being on the inside.

But at the same time, the outside perspective reduces everything to
reasonable proportion. The paper is not the world, it is a simulacrum
of the life of the world, its wars, famines, business, weather, politics,
crime, sports, arts, science categorized and worked into stories flattened on folded newsprint. And what he has now if he will only seize it
is all of that—but raw, unformed, and unwritten! He is released into
the dimensions of unmediated reality.

So now in the suspense of having done what in his years as a wage
slave he has dreamt of, detaching from the institution he has lived by
to confront himself in freedom, this man who has never gotten so
much as a traffic ticket undertakes the practice of bold, uncharacteristic behavior. He stops shaving, lets his hair grow, pretends to be mad
in the street, watching with pleasure as people get out of his way. He
remarks rudely on the businessmen climbing out of their limos at the
Park Avenue hotels, is boorish in stores and scornful in art galleries.
Wandering the West Side piers at night, the dark streets under the sections of elevated railway that have not been torn down, he goes with
the tight-skirt whores into the taxi garages, or screws them in fleabag
rooms on West Street. He does everything he can think of to break
down the unacknowledged presumptions of sixty years of living by the
rules.

But these acts of will do not transform him. Hating himself, he still
aches for assignments, servitude, for the small triumph of the Friday
paycheck, the camaraderie of the saloon. In desperation he begins a
novel but abandons it after a few thousand words. He cannot bring

himself to call his still working friends. He stares at his phone waiting for it to ring, knowing it won't. Mentally they've written his obit and set it in type, the actual day of death being no more than the signal to run it.

It is only when he finds himself considering the idea of phoning his ex-wife that he realizes his life hangs in the balance. He begins seriously to think. And his thought discovers a plan of action for himself the mere contemplation of which is enough to make him feel alive again.

Newspapers, he decides, tell stories that, with few exceptions, are never completed. There is no end to the stock market story or the story of the power struggle among nations. These stories are unending, bull and bear cycles, war and peace cycles. Elections may be held, someone wins or loses, and parties increase their majorities or lose their majorities, and all of it is in flux, quite temporary, and the lasting effects of legislation are weakened in time by administrations that ignore the law or flout it or revamp it. Games won or lost are succeeded by other games, championship seasons dissolved in free agency and last-place seasons, the cosmologists of the science pages define and redefine the nature of the universe, its size, its dynamics, geologists periodically increase the age of the earth, businesses are bought and sold, looted and resold, merged, spun off bankrupted, renamed, restored. Human enterprise goes on, pulsing with ambitions that can never be satisfied.

It is true that trials are held and defendants are found guilty or innocent. And of course there is the swan song of an obituary. On the other hand, there are major obits, King Leopold's, Hitler's or Stalin's or Pol Pot's, for example, that do not provide closure simply because the subjects died before they could be put on trial. Simple death is not retribution in such cases. It is not closure when such men die of natural causes without sentence passed upon them that would enact the sacraments of universal moral law. The fact of their death is incidental when their crimes have not been charged to them in the awesome voice of a God-inspired civilization.

Still, the law could hardly come up with commensurate punishment for such creatures. I myself would send them to the lowest circle of hell and install them at its icy core, where they would be embraced by the scaly arms of Satan, who, over billions of years, would roar his foul excoriating breath into their faces and vomit his foul waste alive with squirmy larvae and dung beetles over them while, languidly, cell by freezing, exquisitely outraged cell, absorbing them into his hideous being . . .

Ex-*Times* guy decides that the occupational cynicism of reporters has to do exactly with the incompleteness of stories, especially as justice fails again and again to catch up in time to effect just endings.

He decides the desire to end a story is powerful within him. His obscure years of work have conferred a moral endowment. His years as a journalist have instructed him in all the delusions, and rationalizations, including righteousness, for doing evil or for covering it up. He has all along been his paper's curator of the stories that could have been completed but never were. And for what purpose other than the obvious one of this new and thrilling assignment? He will be the closure man.

In a state of solemn joy and fervent resolve, he calls upon his old colleagues, who, unable to detect in his manner anything different from the colorless drab they have always known, grant him the professional courtesy of access to the clips. In less than a day he has chosen the stories he will complete.

The first is the story of the former S.S. sergeant living in Cincinnati.

＝

—When Sarah and Pem arrived in Vilnius, Joshua Gruen was still alive, skull fractured, both arms and several ribs broken. One lung was collapsed, and he'd developed pneumonia. The American chargé d'affaires met them at the airport and rushed them to the hospital. Sarah immediately questioned the adequacy of medical care but had to agree finally that Joshua's condition made it too dangerous to fly him out. He was in a coma. Permission was asked to trepan him to relieve pressure on the brain. Pem sat with Sarah Blumenthal in the corridor outside the operating room. He said she did not cry or speak but simply stared at the floor. They had flown from Kennedy to Frankfurt, waited two hours for the connecting flight, and had come straight from the Vilnius airport to the hospital. He supposed exhaustion served her as a kind of sedative. He said he closed his eyes and prayed silently for Joshua to pull through but thought that Sarah had probably not prayed.

They were put up that night in the ambassador's residence. The ambassador and his wife couldn't have been kinder. They took care of all the arrangements for shipping the body home. Sarah's grief was such that a doctor was called in to minister to her. She was sedated for twenty-four hours. In that time Pem went to the hotel where Joshua had been staying and packed his few things. He told me the rabbi had been reading Gershom Scholem's *Kabbalah*, Emil Fackenheim's *Encounters between Judaism and Modern Philosophy*, and *Trent's Last Case*, the 1930s English country-house mystery by E. C. Bentley. He said he supposed Joshua had gone back to it as to a classic.

Also in the hotel room was the rabbi's notebook in which he had written a careful account of everyone he had spoken to about the ghetto diary. The church where it had been hidden no longer existed—a modern apartment house stood in its place. There were two or three additional names and addresses—presumably people he had not had the opportunity to contact before he was assaulted on the doorstep of the ancient synagogue which stood boarded up on Vokieciu Street, there being no congregants, only visitors, as to a graveyard.

———

—Reichsmarschall, I have the honor to report on the status of the work gone forward according to the directive of the Reichsleiter by which the Institute for the Exploration of the Jewish Question is to establish and maintain a museum for the acquisition, inventory, and ultimate exhibition of items of Judaic historic or anthropologic interest such as libraries, religious artifacts, productions of folk art, and all personal property of intrinsic value.

1. The crating and dispatch via military transport of all such property is simultaneous with the removal of the Jewish source populations from each of the 153 villages, townships, and ghetto districts of the

Protectorate (Directives 1051, 1052). This assures the accurate attribution of inventory according to region and province of each and every item from which exhibition items will be chosen, heretofore a particularly complex undertaking given the increasing volume, on a daily basis, of received materials.

2. Appended is a manifest of collections by category. Numbers of items of each are not supplied, being provisional:

Torah (Pentateuch) parchment scrolls handwritten, Torah scroll mantles silk, Torah scroll mantles velvet, Torah scroll vestments hammered and engraved silver, Torah scroll crowns engraved chased silver with semiprecious stones, Torah scroll valances silk, Torah scroll valances silk velvet, Torah text pointers silver, Torah text pointers wood, Torah text pointers silver or wood in the shape of small hands with index finger extended, Torah finials engraved silver, Torah finials gilt leaf, Torah binders silk, Torah binders linen, Torah curtains silk, Torah curtains silk velvet, Torah curtains velvet, prayer shawls silk, prayer shawls linen, prayer shawls silk gold embroidered, prayer shawls silk silver embroidered, prayer books daily, prayer books holiday, books midrash (theology), candelabra silver, candelabra brass, mezuzot (door amulets) carved wood, mezuzot leather, Chanukah (holiday) lamps silver, Chanukah lamps pewter, Chanukah lamps brass, dreidlach (children's spinning tops) wood, dreidlach cast lead, keys synagogue, "eternal" lights pewter, "eternal" lights brass, readers' desks oak, readers' desks pine, lecterns oak, lecterns pine, combs burial society, pitchers burial society, shroud cloths burial society, uniforms burial society, banners trade guild, flags trade guild, synagogue ark lions rampant carved wood, synagogue ark lions rampant carved wood painted, alms boxes wood, alms boxes copper, alms boxes silver plated, skullcaps velvet, skullcaps silk, wedding rings gold, engagement rings silver and diamond, ceremonial wedding dishes silver, ceremonial tankards silver, salvers silver, place settings china, place settings silver, serving bowls, cups, saucers crockery, cooking pots iron, cooking pots enameled, kettles iron, skillets iron, cutlery steel, tools carpentry, implements farm, portraits men oil on canvas, portraits women oil on canvas, portraits children oil on canvas, country scenes oil on canvas, country scenes watercolor on paper, hand-colored photographs bride and groom, hand-colored photographs children, hand-colored photo-

graphs family groups, cameras, typewriters, book sets uniform binding, books individual, books reference, books art, sheet music bound,
sheet music unbound, music instruments stringed, music instruments
woodwind, music instruments brass, music instruments percussion,
surgical instruments steel, surgical instruments chrome steel, bedsteads
wood, bedsteads brass, mattresses horsehair, quilts, duvets, pillows
down, pillows cotton, washbasins ceramic, washbasins pewter, evening
clothes men, evening clothes women, top hats men, coats men, coats
women, suits men, dresses women, wallets leather, purses leather,
purses beaded, school uniforms boys, school uniforms girls, combs,
cosmetics, hairpins, barrettes, notions, pipes, cigarette cases, cigar
cutters, shoes men, shoes women, shoes children, binoculars, opera
glasses, eyeglasses, watches wrist, watches pocket, hearing trumpets,
inkstands, pens nibbed, pens fountain, stationery plain, stationery
embossed, umbrellas, walking sticks wood, walking sticks wood and
silver, chessmen ivory, chessmen wood, pull-toys children, dolls children, board games children, wagons children, snow sleds children,
paint sets children, composition books children, pencil boxes with
pencils children.

===

—I will say, posthumously, that Europe is the world's sore affliction,
that you in America who have taken the best that Europe has to offer
while hoping to avoid the worst are, in your indigenously American
phrase, "whistling Dixie." All your God-drenched thinking replicates
the religious structures built out of the hallucinatory life of the ancient
Near East by European clericists, all your social frictions are the inheritance of colonialist slave-making economies of European businessmen, all your metaphysical conundrums were concocted for you by
European intellectuals, and you have now come across the ocean into
two world wars conceived by European politicians and so have installed in your republic just the militarist mind-state that has kept our
cities burning since the days of Hadrian.

Why do I tell you this? My own genius as a twentieth-century
philosopher of language, insofar as it has been recognized by those in
your country who are capable of understanding me, could be said, like

Ludwig van Beethoven's, to be redemptive. Europeans or not, a few of us have done some good. I have tried to save language and thought from the aphasic minds of our philosophers. I have for example distinguished *things,* which inertly exist or just lie there, from *facts,* which are the propositions of things in relationship, in much the same spirit that Flaubert (who, though a Frenchman, is worthy of our respect) discovered how things were brought to life in his fiction by having them interact with other things. A wheel is a thing, not a fact, and a paving stone is a thing, not a fact, but if the wheel rolls over the paving stone, they both come to life as a fact. Even if it is a fact solely in his own mind. *Sun* is just a noun and *window* is just a noun, but if the sun shines through the window, together they are jolted into propositional life.

So to distinguish things from facts . . . may not seem like much at first glance. However, by similar techniques of analysis, I've reclaimed language for what it can reasonably do, and thereby defined everything beyond its limits as responsive only to our dumb awe. What this means is that I have liberated your thought from the heavy chains of European culture. The nonsensical idealism of Kant, Hegel? Done, *kaput*! The metaphysical gibberish of everyone from Plotinus to Descartes? Swept away as so much clutter in the house. My achievement in the interest of the given nature of the world is equivalent to Einstein's. We are both revolutionaries, he in having overthrown the false cosmology of Newton, I in having upended Plato and all his descendants.

Of course I am interested only in truth, not glory. I leave glory to others. But I do have to wonder why, having returned to the mind of modern man the serenity of the carpenter at his bench, the composure of the farmer in his field, I am not recognized by clerks in the bookstores. I do not begrudge Einstein his stardom, it was to be expected given the naive respect for the scientific mode of thought in our century. But, to tell you the truth, the old walrus is not all that profound in his thinking.

In fact let me tell you something about the theoretical physics of not only Einstein but those other Europeans you Americans have elevated to a celebrity far beyond my own—Planck, Rutherford, Fermi, deBroglie, Bohr, and so on. . . . They have a method, no doubt of that, a righteous empiricism that is in great repute. But their proprietorship of the universe offends me. They have no more use for the old philosophers than I have, but only because they presume to take their place. I ask you—what could be more basic to meaning than the proposition that a thing cannot be both itself and not itself? Is that not the beginning of all logic, does it not in fact express the fundamental structure of the human mind? Yet here they do one experiment proving that light is composed of a stream of light packets or particles or quanta . . . and follow this with another experiment proving that these quanta have the properties not of particles but of waves. Depending how, in the submicroscopic realm, you choose to observe or measure light, so will it respond as one or the other: Light partakes of mutually exclusive states of being!

Oh these European scientists, migod, my mind caves at the thought, the thought—they insist this is the fact—that not only light but all matter, in its submicroscopic essence, all the stolid carpentry of the earth, is similarly indeterminate. The thickest most inert oaken log, for example, is vulnerable to the electron chaos within its oakenness and, given enough time, could be penetrated by the slight pressure of your finger!

Is this magic? you ask, and I reply with a cry of despair that it is worse, it is science.

You who study the star clusters, the galaxies, the planets and their moons, you who tread the earth and date its rocks, you who sift the sands of the desert and plumb the depths of the ocean for the blind creatures living there . . . I invite you, I challenge you, to come with me, as Dante went with Virgil, I am your guide to the infernal shambles of human reason, the shattered, unassembleable fractions of consciousness . . . the dreck of the real, our wrecked romance with God. This new hell is where our inquiry begins.

＝

—Hesitate to intrude on Sarah's privacy. Perhaps it's that seeing her without Pem around I feel just a bit shifty, double-dealing. I have to admit I find her attractive, a not entirely professional feeling, there's a little of Pem in me as far as my half wanting, or deluding myself to expect, something that is hardly likely to happen. So that's part of it.

I'll be glad when he gets back. Having latched on to the St. Tim's heist as a story and having befriended the good father, I now find myself at the mercy of his life. What Pem does, and when he chooses to tell me about it, makes me his literary dependent. If I dropped the whole idea, he'd probably be relieved at first, but then resentful for having been abandoned. He likes the attention, even as he worries that I'm stealing something from him—his mind's life, his being.

It's possible.

But there's nothing improper in going to the Friday night services at the EJ. This last time, discussion had to do with the concept of the survival of the soul. It was the elderly man, the man whose son carried him up the stairs for the services and came and carried him away at the end, who raised the subject. The rabbi came over to where he sat and sat down next to him and took his palsied hand in her two hands. She said, "The Orthodox believe that there is a soul and that it transcends death and that there will be a time, 'the end of days,' when it will be reunited with the resurrected body." She looked into his eyes and smiled as he nodded solemnly and then she rose and went back to the front of the room.

"The word *soul* is a beautiful word, isn't it?" she said. "It carries so much, it expresses, really, longing for union with God, for the final resolution of all our questioning, the arrival, the profound blessed peace of the radiant answer."

"Is it only a word?" someone said.

Sarah folded her arms. "It's an idea. Probably as a religious proposition first made by Philo of Alexandria, a Greek Jew who lived at the same time as Jesus. But in his hands it may be more a Greek idea, a Platonic idea, than a Jewish idea. The Christian tradition really goes to town with it, distinctly separating it from the body, the body turning to dust, the soul rising to heaven, and one lives a good righteous life for that reward of the soul's union with God. The Jewish tradition is less driven by rewards, one lives the righteous life for its own sake, it is an intrinsic good unencumbered by ulterior motives. And we are not generally, so . . . pictorial."

Sarah directed a commiserating glance at the old man to soften what she had to say. "Probably because it is an unanswerable theological question, it is something we cannot know, the nature of the soul, it's a poetical idea that produces much emotion but no knowledge. . . . Reform teaching, for instance, is that yes there is a soul, but it is nothing as literal as the Orthodox believe. And finally the Reconstruction idea dismisses any likelihood that what we might call the individual personality persists in some other form.

"We've spoken of Reconstructionism before. Rabbi Mordecai Kaplan devised it as a way out of the theological, doctrinal disputes of such matters on the grounds that they were beyond our knowing. Reconstruction is like linguistic philosophy, it wants to use language only as far as it can make sense. So the theology, ideas of the soul and so on, is considered to be tentative, all dictates as to God and God's nature are in the suspension of our progressive knowledge, and what we hold to in the meantime is the tradition itself, its folkways, its proven means for structuring life in moral terms and providing beauty and consolation."

A young woman, it was the Barnard student, raised her hand. "But what do you think, Rabbi?"

Sarah stood behind the reader's desk at the front of the room. The EJ Torah rolled on its spindles lay before her, valanced in a simple prayer shawl, or tallith. I had seen it scrolled open, its edges charred, it was one of those recovered from the Holocaust. She brushed the silken tallith with her fingers as she answered, never once looking up.

"My husband, Rabbi Gruen, said to me once, 'Reconstruction is only a start.' He meant that by its means we can presume to examine every element of the tradition without bias and decide what to dispense with and what to keep. But not merely for the sake of making linguistic sense, not for the cherishing of beauty, or consolation, not for preserving our cultural identity for its own sake, because that finally is insufficient, a theology in neutral, idling. No, you subject the tradition to your irreverence to get back to where it began, only that, back down to the ground level of simple . . . unmediated awe. It is there, which is necessarily the state of reverence, the sharp perception of God's presence in the fact of our consciousness . . . and therefore everywhere and in everyone and everything—it is that constancy of awe we hope for, a pre-Scriptural state as alive to us as the contemporary moment, and which, of course, comes with absolutely no guarantees. That is where we begin . . ."

—Ex-*Times* guy flies to Cincinnati with an open-ended return. Checks in at a hotel, the Something Arms, on one of the residential streets in the hills above the downtown. Rents a car, cruises around to get the feel of the place. Whole city smells like beer. Lots of red brick, white granite steps, sun bronzing off the Ohio River down below. He remembers from accounts of the Eichmann kidnapping that the major problem was identification. That they would have the right guy. Took a while. The suspected Eichmann worked under an assumed name. Wore heavy black-rimmed glasses, looked unprepossessing, came home to a not very nice neighborhood, a cubelike flat-roofed cinder-block house in the middle of an empty lot outside Buenos Aires. Hardly befitting a man of his achievement. On the other hand, with its small windows on all four sides, it could not be sneaked up on. He could enfilade the entire lot. They rented cars, vans, kept changing them, for the surveillance. Suspect came home the same time every evening. During the day they wore work clothes, and once knocked on the front door, spoke to a younger man, a son. Such pride of family. Drew from him the virtual assurance that the family name was assumed and hid a great glory. So they decided to make the move. The actual kidnap not that difficult, it was dusk, they grabbed Eichmann as he walked home from the tram stop, wrestled him into a car, and laid him in the back with their feet on him. It was not neat, even close to being bungled, but he offered no resistance. Strangely acquiescent, Eichmann. Cooperated fully as they gave him a shot of something, dressed him as an El Al pilot, and walked him catatonic through Argentine customs along with the rest of the crew.

But thinking this over, ex-*Times* guy realizes he comes from the other culture. Reporting the fact, getting the story. That culture. Getting the spelling right. It is like a ball and chain, it drags on him. A heavy weight to pull, it is one thing to have the resolve to end a story, another to make the muscles actually do it. Actually make something happen in the world. All his life he has looked on. Civilization paid people like him for doing nothing. For living subsidized, the way a farmer is paid for not planting crops.

Knows in his heart that what was most difficult for the Israelis is easy for him, and sadly he concludes all the necessary detective work by looking in the hotel phone book and finding the assumed name and the address. So now the time has come. He must pass over to the other side. He must break through the inertia of his soul. Something akin to transfiguration. His excitement vanished, he is only mournful as he drives aimlessly around Cincinnati avoiding his destination, feeling like a fool. Feeling hapless. Has absolutely no idea of how to proceed. Notes the styles of the residential gardens, the shrubbery pruned and sculpted obdeltoid, napiform, cuneate, even pandurate. Odd to see these big, well-cared-for houses standing in green gardens filled with the smell of beer.

He drives past the S.S. man's address a couple of times, the house the same as the others on this hill street, though slightly more modest. Decides he can accomplish nothing from a car, he can't see anything just driving past and it is too dangerous to pull up, no cars are parked on the street, everyone who lives here has a driveway, a garage. Keeps going, drives down the terraces into the lower city, and in a riverside neighborhood of porched cottages and clapboard houses sees a yard sale going on and, without knowing why, stops and takes a look. Among the peeling painted kitchen chairs and the used books and the couch with sprung springs and the other crap, sees a bike, a three-speed 28-inch wheel, only the third speed works and the rear tire is soft, but he buys it for twenty dollars. Goes to a garage, gets air for the tire, and has himself a working surveillance bike. Beginning to feel at home in Cincinnati. He goes back up the hills, parks in a shopping mall, takes the bike out of the car, takes off his jacket, tie, rolls his sleeves up, his trousers, and he's on his way. He is a graying, over-weight, middle-aged man getting in his workout, puffing up the hills, cruising down, waving at the kids in the yards. He figures he does this a few days the same time every day, nobody will notice him anymore. Begins to think about buying a gun. Something to fit in his pocket. That will be tricky. Probably do better to go across the river to Kentucky. Still, there are laws, the gun shops keep records. A knife, then? Some sort of hunting knife from a sporting goods store. Or one of those underwater harpoons that the divers use to spear fish. Carry it in a case. Walk right up to the door. And so he is thinking imaginatively and not without pleasure and is feeling better about himself and coasting down a hill now in the right neighborhood . . . but somehow loses his bearings, the bike wobbles and he is able to right himself only by bouncing up on the sidewalk but at the same time going faster than he should . . . and a man appears, coming down the path from his house and turns onto the sidewalk, unhearing, unseeing, a heavyset elderly man with a cane . . . and later the ex-*Times* guy can't remember if he shouted Look out or just shouted, unable to understand how someone, even someone that old, could be so unseeing, so unhearing . . . but he does remember the catastrophic impact, and the fedora, the man was wearing a hat that flew up, and the white hair rising the body already falling but turned now facing him, the black-rimmed glasses askew over his chin, the terrified milky eyes, and a good clear complexion for such an old man, jowly, florid, healthy . . . but simultaneously the back of the head hitting the brick retaining wall of the man's own lawn with a thwack, a burlesque konk, the comic human body always looking for the opportunity of expression, and there was this unwanted sudden intimacy as he fell on top of the man together with him on the sidewalk, smelling his onion breath, hearing the hiss from his throat, feeling the nap of his cashmere jacket, and finding the man's plaid muffler in his own mouth . . . his nausea rising, the nausea of shock but also disgust, using the man's body to push himself upright, pressing the man's shoulders against the sidewalk, and rising, feeling the disgust of death before he knew that it was death, because now here was his bike upturned, with the front wheel spinning in the air and the handlebars lopsided, and the palms of his hands were scraped raw, Jesus Christ, the old fool! and now realizing a certain stillness at his feet, an absence of response from the pole of pain to the pole of laughter, a vacuum in the world's vitality in the exact shape of the still hump lying before him . . . because the man was dead, suddenly unequivocally dead, as if there hadn't been that much life left to him in the first place, it was all instantaneous, no rattle in the throat, no blood, no mute imploring eyes, just a suddenly achieved openmouthed cadaverousness . . . outraged now at this calamitous idiot, didn't you see me? didn't you hear me shout? shouting now at the dead form, outraged, insulted, shaking with umbrage, righting his bike, jerking at the unaligned handlebars . . . and around him the street is empty and quiet . . . and as if to punish the old fool for doing this, for making such a mess of his transfigured intent, he mounts his bike and rides off wobblingly down the hill, the rear wheel scraping with every rotation against the bike frame.

That's the scene. Ex-*Times* guy makes it to the mall a few blocks away, throws the bike into a dumpster behind the A&P, and drives back to his hotel. He should have called for help, seen to the old man—but how could he explain himself, or what had brought him to this place? Sickened, pulse racing, he lies down, fearful of a heart attack. Instead he dozes off. Wakes hours later disgusted with himself and determined to forget the whole thing. He checks out and goes to the airport to wait for a flight back to New York. Picks up an evening paper and sits at the bar. Reads that a hit-and-run bike killer is at large. Some kid saw the whole thing from his window. Imprecise description of biker, a heavyset white man. The victim an elderly refugee, age eighty-one, of such and such a number on such and such a street, who had some years ago been accused of gaining entry to the United States by hiding his wartime role as a machine-gun platoon sergeant in charge of mass executions of Jews from the Kovno, Lithuania, ghetto, a charge that was later dismissed for lack of evidence. Neighbors say . . . he was a good kind man . . . who lived alone since the death of his wife . . . had something of an old world elegance about him . . . tipped his hat to women in the street . . . came to his porch on Halloween with handfuls of candy for the trick-or-treaters.

$$=$$

—Of great songs, standards, composers will tell you the basic principle of their composition: Keep it simple. The simpler, the better. You want untrained voices to handle it in the shower, in the kitchen. Try to keep the tune in one octave. Stick with the four basic chords and avoid tricky rhythms. These composers may not know that this is the aesthetic of the church hymn. They may not know that hymns were the first hits. But they know that hymns and their realm of discourse ennoble or idealize life, express its pieties, and are in themselves totally proper and appropriate for all ears. And so most popular ballads are, in their characteristic romanticism, secularized hymns.

The principle of keeping it simple suggests why many standards sound alike. One might even say a song can't become a standard unless it is reminiscent of existing standards. Maybe this is why we feel a new good song has the characteristic of seeming, on first hearing, always to have existed. In a sense it has. Just as we in our own minds seem to have always existed regardless of the date of our birth, a standard suggests itself as having been around all along, God-given, and waiting only for the proper historical moment in which to make itself available for our singing.

===

—Finding the ghetto archive seems to have transformed Pem. Eastern Europe has slimmed him down, he is still substantial, but his bulk seems more contained if not exactly muscled, he moves more fluidly and looks put together, washed and groomed, perhaps because he's cut his hair, rid himself of the ponytail, and now that his stomach is somewhat flattened his trousers don't droop over his shoe tops. Is there renewed vitality, mimetic elation moving through him? I'm persuaded that setting off on a quest, a self-appointed mission, and succeeding can surprise a fellow out of his usual humors. That he's actually done something! I won't mention this to either of them, but there is a literary template here, call it Christian knighthood, and the fact that his lady is Sarah Blumenthal, a rabbi, a widow who lives with her two children on the Upper West Side, is what makes it possible.

Also, something darker here, something he wouldn't allow himself to feel, a successful competition with a dead man.

He had only the names in Joshua Gruen's notebook. Vilnius, once Vilna, is a heavily rebuilt city, given World War II and the Soviet taste for high-rises. A picturesque river with grassy banks winding through it. The Neris. Same river my little runner Yehoshua speaks of.

What did it feel like to be in this town of history architecturally erased, but still there in the buried bones, and in the brains of the children, their ethnic resolve booming like the football they kicked through the schoolyard? He took the streetcar that stopped outside his hotel door, and the bell rang and the car swung around corners and the pantograph flashed like lightning and Pem felt the menace lurking under the town's modernity, the old historic demons with their sharpened pitchforks riding around in the latest-model cars and taking their business lunches in the fine restaurants.

He hunted down every name listed in Joshua's notebook—people

Joshua had seen and not yet seen—and made no headway. The church had long since disappeared in which the priest Father Petrauskas had agreed to hide the ghetto diary. The father himself was no longer alive. The site of the church was now given over to a six-story apartment house with terraces.

The chargé d'affaires at the American embassy remembered Pem and arranged an appointment for him with a priest at the office of the Vilna diocese, but that too yielded nothing. The Russians had torn up the city and its German defenders in 1944 and not much was left after that but rubble.

One afternoon—he didn't know what it could possibly accomplish—Pem took a cab to that little burned-out synagogue in the poor part of town in front of whose doors Sarah's husband was fatally beaten. The synagogue was being preserved by the city as a ruin. Pem talked to the caretaker, an elderly Lithuanian woman, who spoke a broken English, and he paid twelve litas to stand inside the doors and see the remnants of dark wood reading desks and pews arranged in a square around a central table. A wrought-iron frame with sconces hung over the room. Sunlight pouring through the fallen-in roof lit up the dust suspended there, motionless, as if set in place permanently by the conflagration of years before.

The old woman remembered the incident of the American who was beaten. It was dark, she was in her cottage behind the synagogue, and she heard shouts and screams. It was she who found Joshua bleeding in front of the doors. She called the police.

Before that she had heard someone knocking on the synagogue doors, and if the knocking had continued she would with some irritation have gone out and around to the front of the museum—that is what she called the synagogue, the Jewish museum—and told whoever it was that it was closed. But then she heard the shouts.

Pem realized at this point that Joshua had never talked to the old woman, that he hadn't had the chance. He now said to her that the American who'd been beaten was a rabbi and had come to Vilna to seek journals from the ghetto that had been held for safekeeping by a priest in Vilna. Yes, the woman said immediately, that would have been Father Petrauskas, my own priest from the Church of St. Theresa on Kaunas Street, and she crossed herself. We all knew what he had done, she said. And that wasn't the only thing. Not at all. Sometimes he hid people. Oh yes, he was a Jew lover. He thought the business with the Jews was not right, he said it was not right what was being done to them. Nobody told on him, he was a good man and meant well, he was a better priest than most. The father lived through the war, but the war destroyed his church and he was never the same. I used to cook him a meal now and then when he lived in the home they have for them and Josip would bring it to him.

Who is Josip, Pem asked.

He is my son, he is my only surviving child, my youngest, the others were all killed in the war. He was too young. He was an altar boy for the father.

Where is Josip now, Pem asked.

Where would you think at this hour, at his business, he is a tile setter, if you want to know, the best in Vilna.

And so Pem tracked down this Josip, a man in his fifties, who told him that the Russians had come to loot Father Petrauskas's church and discovered a battered wooden chest that the father kept in the closet of his own room in the rectory, where he slept. The chest was padlocked, Josip said, it was sealed with tape and wrapped around with thick rope. The soldiers, with their arms full of candlesticks and silver, called for an officer. When the officer arrived he was unlike the men, he seemed very civilized. He smoked a cigarette with a holder and his uniform was quite clean. Josip was afraid the father would be taken away, but the officer questioned the father politely and the father told the truth—that what was in the chest were writings of Jews. The officer, with a black crayon, wrote a description of the contents in Russian, then signed his name and serial number right there on the top of the chest and then ordered the soldiers to remove it without disturbing the seal and that was the end of the matter.

"My training as the Divinity Detective stood me in good stead," Pem told me. "Clearly that had been an intelligence officer questioning the father. The Russians swept up anything that might conceivably be of importance, even though ninety-nine times out of a hundred they would never look at it again. Moscow is a really interesting place right now. The vaults of the KGB are like a flea market. It took some time, but they'll sell you anything if the price is right."

—The chest is impounded at JFK until, at Pem's request, he can get in touch with the Justice Department and have one of their attorneys present when it is cracked open, as customs has insisted it must be. If the archive includes documentary proof of the identity of the ghetto commander, S.S. Major Schmitz, it will have to resist a challenge in court, and so the circumstances of the unsealing of the material have to be irreproachable.

And now, the arrangements having taken the better part of two weeks, the day has come. Pem and Sarah ride out to JFK in a taxi. It is a late weekday morning, it is raining. They do not speak. Sarah uses her cell phone to remind her helper, Angelina, that the boys have half a day of school because of a teachers' conference and will have to be picked up at lunchtime. Sarah's raincoat has fallen open, she is wearing a suit, and Pem notices how well shaped her pantleg is above the knee. The observation directs him to an intent reading through the rain streaks of the color-coded directions along the airport highway.

Pem's new triumphalist self-regard is on this morning absent. Rising behind his eyes is the old familiar bleakness. It is not that Sarah isn't tremendously impressed by what he's done. On the contrary, she seems to have awakened to him in some way, she seems to have moved with him into an acceptance of their growing intimacy. But he wonders about his own motives—if he is incapable of an act that does not contain its own corruption. Could this have been at heart no more than a seductive stunt? He had flown into Moscow, he had made calls, spoken as a priest to the fathers, a diplomat to the attachés, a con man to the hustlers, he had flashed his roll, laid on a lot of attitude, and fearlessly penetrated the KGB. Of course they were all like beggars with their hands out, but he didn't know that, did he?

Certainly, as an act of contrition, it hardly qualified. It was an adventurer's act of contrition.

In his gloom, the curves and forks and ramps of the airport road system, and the various terminals on the horizon, seem to constitute another kind of city, a city of unearthly scale whose denizens are huge flying machines, one of which suddenly emerges from the overcast and roars over them, its landing gear like talons.

Minutes later in a small office in the International Arrivals Building, Sarah, Pem, a young woman from the U.S. Attorney's office in New York, and various customs people watch as an inspector takes up a hammer and chisel and goes to work. The chest sits on a steel table. It is larger than Sarah understood from Pem's description, she had imagined it as the size of a footlocker, but it is larger, deeper. It looks homemade, it is hammered together with big heavy nails and metallic corner pieces. It was painted white, but where the paint has flaked off there is raw lumber.

She sits in one of the bridge chairs lining the wall. The customs man has found the rusted locks impervious and asks now if he can pry off the hasps, which, he warns, will splinter the wood. Without quite realizing the proprietorship she has been granted, Sarah nods her approval. Yet the sound of the splitting wood makes her wince—as if her father's history is seeping into the room.

The hasps are pried off and the thick rope is cut. The attorney takes a small camera out of her bag and snaps three, four pictures of the Russian writing across the top of the chest. Then the inspectors move forward. They carefully lift out packages of various sizes wrapped in oilskin. There is in addition an oilskin lining against the inner sides of the chest, the fierce preservation of these materials is unmistakable and, to Sarah, itself an urgent message that brings a sob to her throat. The inspectors unwrap the packages to find sheaves of paper bound in twine, booklets, manuals, folders, rolled-up blueprints, diagrams, stapled documents, envelopes of various sizes, each labeled in a small, neat Yiddish script. They open every packet, every envelope. Then, having run their hands along the inner walls of the chest, they agree among themselves that there is nothing here of interest to them. They replace everything, more or less as they found it, and excuse themselves.

Pem and the attorney dive in. In notebooks, students' bluebooks, and unbound pages, a diary in one increasingly familiar hand covering a period of three years, 1941 to the date in 1944 when the ghetto is dismantled and the survivors are marched to the railroad station. And reams of documentation, rules and regulations issued by the Germans, innumerable orders, with the signature of Commandant Schmitz, confiscating all domestic animals, then all wagons and, subsequently, all books, typewriters, cameras, candelabra, jewelry. It is forbidden for Jews to be seen on the street after seven P.M., it is forbidden for Jews to possess farm tools, for Jews to assemble more than three together, and so on, everything taken away, little by little, until there is only life left to take away. And then testimonies of witnesses about the ways in which that was done. Sarah reads some of these and provides stunned summary translations. In a separately wrapped packet is a complete dossier on Commandant Schmitz—a c.v. with date and place of birth, names of his parents (mother's maiden name Preissen, apparently the source of the name Helmut Preissen claims as an American citizen), schooling, date of joining the Nazi party, date of entry to the S.S., commission as an officer, and finally a quite clear black-and-white photo of the man in full Nazi regalia, standing plump and righteous before a scaffold with the dangling body of a hanged Jew miscreant behind him. But there is material, too, on other S.S. men and Lithuanian policemen and known Gestapo spies and the attorney wants all of it and asks permission to have the entire archive removed for photocopying before Sarah takes possession of it. The attorney is trying very hard to be businesslike but has trouble finding her voice. She will also want to FedEx certain of the originals to the war-crimes office of the Department of Justice. She is sure the deportation case against this Preissen/Schmitz will be reopened, but there are several hundred open cases on file of suspected Nazi criminals living in the United States and perhaps some of these other materials on individuals will be relevant as well.

The attorney goes out to make her arrangements and now Pem and Sarah are alone in this bare fluorescent-lit room . . . the big white chest sits open on the table with all its materials spilled about, and unexpectedly it appears to Pem to have the texture of a museum installation, the diary entries in their tiny Yiddish script on paper as pliant as the folds of white mourning shrouds, the open wood chest standing broken open as the repository of a sacred scripture. The entire composition is in shades of white, everything white on white, including the gray-white walls of the room. There is no Christ in the picture, but in Pem's breast is the same instinct to pray once evoked in him by the painted Crucifixions of Cimabue and Grunewald. The uncanny feeling comes over him, like the dizzying blood drift of an illness, that this bare unadorned room of industrial windows and terrible harsh light is what a new church must aspire to, though where the thought of a new church has come from he doesn't know.

I claim he realizes in the next instant that if he opens his mouth and confides in Sarah, she will turn and flash upon him the implacable judgment from her anguished blue eyes that he is beyond redemption. Suspecting this may very well be the case, he takes the chair next to her and is quiet.

Sarah has in her hands typed lists of those who have died in the ghetto and also those who were taken from the ghetto and never again seen. Each name has a date and place of birth next to it. Not infrequently, the names of entire families are listed. There is no time or distance in Sarah's apprehension of these pages, they are not historical but, in their simple exact notation, a curve of the universe's light flashing through her, lasing her consciousness into these leaves of paper, letter by letter, as if the newly dead are being written down as she reads, with the thunderings of jets and the drone of passing traffic in her ears.

And now Pem hands her an envelope of forbidden little black-and-white photos . . . a line of men and women marching to work behind barbed wire . . . a husband and wife and their child on a bench having their picture taken, the cloth stars sewn to their coats . . . simple pictures, calm, expressionless faces . . . a woman on her knees in the vegetable garden . . . the members of the council posing in business suits with stars . . . a body in a business suit hanging from a gallows, the head, awry, staring heavenward . . . winter, snow on the ground . . . and here, seven little boys in front of a wood cabin, they are standing at their idea of attention on the steps of this wood cabin . . . they wear military-school caps and stars on their breasts that might possibly be imagined as insignia of their office as runners for the council . . . unsmiling little boys, one with shoulders hunched up in the instinctive posture of self-protection . . . or perhaps he is cold . . . they are all underdressed, with short pants and sweaters and jackets they have outgrown . . . but each of them at attention, feet together, arms pressed against his sides . . . and they are looking into the camera in the full knowledge of death. Sarah finds her father in the first row.

—After my talk with Pem's bishop, I had looked into the matter of the notorious James Pike, bishop of California. It was true, Pike was pure sixties. Said all the evidence as well as theological common sense suggested Joseph was the biological father of Jesus. Said he could not accept the doctrine of the Trinity, that it verged on tritheism. Said he had trouble with the Second Coming, too. Said none of this made him a bad priest or weakened his faith. Episcopalians are interesting.

But when I brought the subject up with Pem he grew irritable. Yeah, I know, that's my bishop's read on me—Pemby, son of Pike. You don't buy that, do you? I mean, true, the man was gutsy, liberal as hell, a breath of fresh air. But he was also a bit of a lightweight. When his son died of an overdose, Pike went to a medium who summoned up the son for a chat. Did you know that?

No.

That was a tragic thing, his losing his son—but being conned by a spiritualist? Arthur Ford, that was the guy's name, he was a studious medium, he did his homework, he kept files on people, including a thick file on the Pike family. Spiritualism is the dementia of the religious mind. And you know how Pike died, don't you?

In Israel.

In Israel. Went off to the desert looking for the historical Jesus. With a bottle of Coca-Cola in his hand.

You seem a bit on edge.

I am not on edge. You're the one who's pissed off.

I?

Because we didn't call you to come to the airport with us.

No, I'm over that. I can work from things I hear about secondhand. No big deal.

This is a delicate time for Sarah. And for me too.

You don't have to apologize.

I'm not. But when you come back to me with my bishop's bull-shitting—

I thought I might see what he looked like, that's all. I don't usually run into bishops in my line of work.

Did you tell him where I was? What I was doing? What did you tell him?

Nothing!

Come on—

Well, nothing important . . . Just that you'd gone to the desert to look for the historical Jesus with a bottle of Coca-Cola in your hand.

That's funny. . . . So I'm being paranoid?

Only a little.

He'd just gotten married, too, Pike. A new young wife. His third.

Miss? Can we have another?

They had a car, they'd rented a car. A way out, the car broke down, they started walking. Apparently this was not much of a road, no more than a dirt track, but they thought they'd been driving to Bethlehem. So what would you do, you start walking?

Keep going in the same direction.

That's right. What any sane person out in the goddamn desert— keep to the road. Just walk on down the road to Bethlehem. But the story is they're wandering around for hours in the rocks, the canyons, totally lost. How did that happen? The road petered out? I don't know. They'd come away without a map. What was the matter with these people?

So eventually he can't go on, man is in his fifties, not terribly fit. They didn't know from fitness back then. So they agree she will go on, try to get help. And, what I suppose, he finds some ledge with a bit of shade, they say good-bye, and she strikes out alone. He sits there in the desert after she's gone, it is very hot, he has placed himself in the home of his soul, this mountainous red desert, he can see the caves of the Scrolls, he can smell the peculiar wryness of the Dead Sea, that saltine air . . . the light shimmers in his eyes in waves, the red rock gives intimation of the stony ground of his religion. Off his left ear some sort of hirsute spider slowly climbs the cracks of the abutment he's leaning against, the salt is so thick in the distant sea as to be insoluble, the sea is a drying agent, he sits in its influence, its aura, and feels it deliquesce the sweat on his brow, on his back, he watches it fade the color of the cola in his bottle, he lifts the bottle to his lips, but before he can drink the level of colorless liquid sinks and leaves to his transfixed gaze a crust of dry sugar at the green bottom, a waxy residue of gum. And then the green bottle turns white . . .

To my astonishment, Pem's eyes were tearing.

Listen, Father, I'm concerned for you.

This is my problem, Everett, not yours. Just remember that. Trouble with you writers, you don't keep your distance.

He takes out his handkerchief, wipes his eyes. Clears his throat.

I loved Pike because he knew the accumulated doctrine was simply not credible. Fantasy. Historically accumulated bullshit. But he adored Jesus the man. He wanted to find the real Jesus. He quit the church, you know, he never lacked for guts, he unfrocked himself and took the trip to the Holy Land.

Is that what you're going to do? I mean now that you're an experienced traveler? Quit, and then really go to the Holy Land, like Pike, wander out there and die of heat prostration?

Maybe. It cheers me to talk with you, Everett. You ready for another round?

I just ordered one.

This going back to where it started. To where it went wrong. That point. Before the history. That's what he was doing. Oh migod, what a longing there is. So dangerous. It can kill you.

=

—Follow the Bouncing Ball

Young scientist Louis Slotin was testing the bouncing ball by halves, using simple screwdrivers to nudge its two cored hemispheres toward each other on a steel rod. At a certain point he must not go beyond, the spherical closure of the hemispheres would give indication of being about to happen. This was the moment of synapse, the precise critical measurement he was looking for. He was a daring fellow, as well as a brilliant biophysicist, he'd flown for the RAF in the Second World War.

He was hunched over the apparatus, peering at the minute incremental lines of measurement on the steel rod, when one of the screwdrivers seemed to jump with a will of its own. For that one bobbled instant it sprang up and knocked the hemispheres together.

In his hospital bed, Louis Slotin would remember through his searing agony the intense blue light that had flooded his eyes. He thought in that moment a clamping of the hemispheres should make a hard sound. Instead, there was a terrible hiss of transfiguration. With his bare hands, he grabbed the bouncing ball and rent it in half. And all at once the quiet room filled with normal daylight.

Out in the desert, near the village of Oscuro, or Darkness, the scaffold was built to hold the Bouncing Ball. Louis Slotin's colleagues, wearing black armbands, drove out to the desert near the village of Oscuro where the two halves of the Bouncing Ball, primed now in their casing, were attached to a pulley and slowly hoisted to position on the scaffold.

At a discreet distance, Louis Slotin's colleagues hunkered down in their trenches awaiting the dawn.

———

—Oh, Lord, our Narrator, who made a text from nothing, once more I dare to speak to You and of You and inevitably from You in one of Your own inventions, one of Your intonative systems of clicks and grunts and glottal stops and trills. But truly how can this be different from the macaw's cry, from the broad-leafed fronds ticking with green snakes, or from the sun splotches on the riverbank appearing as swift, elusive jaguars.

I remember the village people with their laughter, how they refilled my gourd with more of the fermented manioc. They were familiar with my scholarly circumspection, my prudery, the importance of my notebooks, but gently led me to the thatched hut where she waited, childishly singing, where she waited to be made serious and attentive to herself. And around the camp now they danced, with their innovative system of clicks and grunts and glottal stops and trills, it was a glorious language, speech that was sung, speech that was danced and drumbeaten, powerfully evocative of You, my Lord, plashing and eddying like the swift river while I untied the nuptial skirt, unfolded it to a squared marriage cloth of the finest weave washed for generations in the flood tide of the surging rivergod, upon which she lay back in the ritual fashion, all limbs reaching outward to the four points of her lateral heaven, and when I touched the insides of her thighs the soft skin prickled, her feet arched and pointed, her fingers curled, and when I smelled her skin it was the smell of the sweet tubers and roast plantain, the cocoa of the earthen riverbank washed in the water of the fresh rainbowed fish. And her hands lighting on my shoulders were of the infinite wife's understanding, she was blind to me in all but her hands, I was blind to her in all but my lips upon her lips, the village spins with the dance, we rise on the singing system of grunts and trills, we whirl about, the great trees bend, all life flies off the broad fronds sparking through the black celestial universe, the jaguared stars, the star elephant, the hanging monkey of the lit heavens, falling endlessly outward, voluminizing the vault of the universe forever . . . yet absolutely fixed, silent, peaceful, and motionless.

You will understand my impertinence, Lord. I beg this because we are so ritualized in our faiths: You are a special concern, and we think to address ourselves to You only in special ways, at prescribed times in architecturally induced states of mind. Usually we wear our best clothes. We sing our hymns of desperate expectation. We appoint one of us to petition You without embarrassment, on behalf of all of us. I have petitioned You from my office: Speaking to You from a pulpit is deemed appropriate, whereas speaking to You unhoused, unshaven, at an ill-chosen time, everyone rushing by on business, is a piteous form of madness. We must have a title, a pulpit, a day, to speak aloud, my Lord, to You.

And months later the community gathered to help her love me. She had turned inward, lost her vitality, as if my love for her were a slow poison. She sat about, she could not stir herself. Her mother came to sit with her, her father, her aunts and uncles. She is possessed by a demon, they counseled. Do not put her from you, it is an illness, it is not her true soul speaking. I will not put her from me, I assured them. In fact I wanted to confess to them my aching adoration of her moment-by-moment existence, that I adored everything about her, that her being was in every moment of its life appropriate and to be worshipped. She was thoughtful, withdrawn, and I loved her for that too. I imagined the purity of her thought, I knew it was incapable of anger or guile, this was the season of the rains and I knew her thought was as truthful as the rain. I would stand in her thought as I stood in rain. But the affronted husband does not say such things. The affronted husband folds his arms across his chest.

She could not love me, she tried but was dry for me, she was so small, she wept, but her pale brown body was intransigent, with a will of its own, and you cannot in love force into her, not in love, and I loved her, she was my completion in this life on the wide river, she was of my ultimate concern, excluding from my mind everyone not living on the wide river in the shade of the tree vaults with families of monkeys passing by like puffs of wind in the leaves, passing like clouds, like rain showers, and the tree snakes embracing the tree trunks, and the birds of primary colors inquiring, always inquiring, step by step, each branch a proposition to be tested, a doubt, till they dropped, clawed to my hand.

She had such dark eyes, rounded to the brim with their brown blackness, ripe as fruit waiting to be bitten, to be tasted, but the shadows curved under them and set them back in her broad, troubled brow, her hair hung lank, she did not wash her hair in the river until her mother led her there, she preferred to go every day where the children were and sit with them and play and sing their songs. I think I missed most her laughter, she laughed with a deeply melodious helplessness, her voice breaking like water on rocks in a New England brook.

By this time I had mysteriously received a letter from one of my teachers at Yale, how our letters make their way, smeared, torn, crumpled, lost, found, and then quantum-delivered eight thousand miles, the final mile by the hand of someone who does not read. Come home, all is forgiven, a gentle ecclesiastical joke. But the community had been busy. In my sorrow I was called to ceremony. She was there. She removed her girdle cloth and danced around me, she was high-breasted, unchilded, long-waisted, round-calved, and where the parts of her joined, as where the buttocks met the backs of the thighs, the junction was uncreased. Oh my, oh my. I have seen bodies like this only in the Hermitage, on the three dancing Graces sculpted in white marble by Canova, with their arms entwined, their lovely looped arms, and their slender hands arched from the wrists. . . . Her straight black hair swung out behind her, her arms led the way, the fingers swimming ahead into the night, it was a raucous dance, a nightclub hooch of a dance, I found myself laughing, I knew more of her now, if she was not just my incredibly beautiful native child bride but funny, there was a moral adulthood I hadn't perceived, I was learning, my heart like the drum beating and the whole town chanting her to health. And all of it was prelude to the removal of my shoes and kneesocks, my walking shorts, my underdrawers, my shirt, neckerchief, my hat, and, going around me dancing, the manioc sweet fermented milk of the jungly mother flowing from the gourds and drowning my blushing protests. The stars came out over the wide river, the light of our fire lit the sides of the great trees, the fibrous vines ran up, ran down, and piece by piece she donned my clothing, strutting around with greater and greater assurance, until finally, galumphing in my shoes to the great merriment of us all, she was me, a cartooned white prudish would-be missionary American Peace Corpser with anthropological pretensions, every gesture perfect, excoriating, and when she imperiously removed from my face my precious spectacles and placed them upon her nose, the lenses resting on her nostrils, her head lifted and the corners of her mouth turned down under my stained and lanyarded sun hat, and she stroked her imaginary red beard, great drunken waves of revelation came over me, blowing up the flames of the fire, and she fell on me and kissed me on the lips and we were laughing through our kisses, she was so relieved, so happy, that I knew her at last, and we sat naked side by side and ate with our fingers the roast wild boar and sweet yam paste, drank the jungle milk liquor and sang their song of deliverance. And then the shaman raised his arm in blessing and declared her soul no longer possessed, and wished everyone a good night, and everyone wished him a good night, and repaired to their huts for a great bout of communal lovemaking like the chattering monkeys of the forest, like the uhn-huhnking green hyenas and the snake ticking slithers of your forest, Lord. And she, when I slid lubriciously into her, took my demon and bit my lips and swallowed my blood, I became her heaving screaming demon, we clashed like warriors in their armor, I killed her and she killed me. We were never again who we were on that night, neither my missionary love, unlettered, not the future Reverend Pemberton, B.D.

. . . oh, Tommy, telling these dirty stories, confessing life's momentous fucks. Augustine doesn't go into details, but he had that girlfriend of the lower class, his *consuetudo,* Latin for habit, who was bad for his career. The sex is in the disparity, from the fourth-century olive-eyed slave dancer of the dusk to the little bought Victorian girls of the working class thrown across the madam's bed eeyowing to have their hymens torn with the shirttailed gentlemen's shilling clutched in their moist hands. Lord, we cannot begin to account Your injustices. The numbers are exponential, we examine them one by one and they crush us in waves, and if we let them hurl us over ourselves crashing and turning with their incredible breathtaking multiplicative fury we find only one at a time available to our comprehension quietly sitting there like a gravestone. The quantum of the unjust dead of the earth is given to our study. Can it all be as simple a mechanical law as we have in our depth of need attributed to You—our best, most famous, never to be duplicated one and only original sin?

. . . now she really is possessed, this story has a moral of sorts. I have in front of me on my desk her packet of letters going back years, some with color photographs. I did not attend her ordination. Here she is in her whites before the island altar, the silver cross upon her bosom, the collar around her neck, the hair cut short for propriety, the black shining hair. The lovely tan face, heavier than I remember. Serene, blissful. She wears rimless glasses, eight-sided, very fashionable. The church wall behind her is the curved, corrugated steel of a Quonset hut. She holds the staff aloft with Jesus crucified, my native wench, who took everything I had to give, the Reverend Tonna mBakita, missionary plenipotentiary to the disfigured, lymphomaed Tobokovo Islanders of the A-test range. She writes me every Christmas in my own language: Father Pem, she calls me. Dearest colleague, Father Pem. I look at her handwriting and think of letters addressed to country-music stars asking for the meaning of life.

——

—Movies began in silence. The early filmmaker learned to convey meaning without language. The title card that was dropped into the sequence only nailed down the intelligence given to the audience nonverbally. (Young couple on porch swing at night. He removes a ring from his vest pocket. He gazes into her eyes. Title card: "Milly, will you be my wife?") That is true also of sound film today, where the dialogue is like the old cards—needed only for the final touch of specificity. When sound came in, talkies were more talky. Screenplays derived heavily from theater and books, and so films of the thirties and forties, even action films, swashbucklers, noirs, are more talkative, endlessly so, than they are now. Now films work off previous films, they are genre-referential, and, with the possible exception of comedies, talk less. After the set is lit, the camera is positioned, the actors have taken their place, costumed, their hair dressed to indicate economic class, education, age, social status, virtue or the lack of it—ninety-five percent of the meaning of a scene is established before anyone says a word.

Thus the term *film language* is an oxymoron. The literary experience extends impression into discourse. It flowers to thought with nouns, verbs, objects. It thinks. Film implodes discourse, it deliterates thought, it shrinks it to the compacted meaning of the preverbal impression or intuition or understanding. You receive what you see, you don't have to think it out. You see that lit and dressed scene, hear the music, see the facial expressions, bodily movements, and attitudes of the costumed and hairdressed actors—and you understand. Moviegoing is an act of inference. In the profoundest sense, films are illiterate events. This may be why some of the most fanciful prose written today is written by film critics, who assiduously address themselves to films that are hardly worth the attention. Why? It may be the dreariest, stupidest of movies—it doesn't matter. You get from the critic a full and cogently articulated reaction. However unconsciously, the critic is defending verbal culture, subjecting the preliterate or postliterate filmgoing experience to the extensions of syntactical thought.

Fiction goes everywhere, inside, outside, it stops, it goes, its action can be mental. Nor is it time-driven. Film is time-driven, it never ruminates, it shows the outside of life, it shows behavior. It tends to the simplest moral reasoning. Films out of Hollywood are linear. The narrative simplification of complex morally consequential reality is always the drift of a film inspired by a book. Novels can do anything in the dark horrors of consciousness. Films do close-ups, car drive-ups, places, chases, and explosions.

=

—In today's E-mail:

Everett: The desert is where Pike went wrong. It's here in Metro-Diaspora. Whatever it is, it's in this bloody, noisy, rat-ridden, sewered, and tunneled stone and glass religioplex. Isn't that what the sign says?

But therefore visible only to the unhoused derelict mind. So I'm quitting the church.

> God bless
> Pem

=

—You say all history has contrived
   to pour this beer into my glass
and given the mirror behind those bottles its
   particular tarnish,
But I notice your war stories are secondhand
   your father's bio, your brother's, but not yours.
You're one of the lucky bastards who seem
   to have slipped the formation
that has marched quick-time to this moment.
Hey, good buddy, you see this chair?
Let me roll back a moment from the table—
   you see it now?
I come here because of the dark blue light,
   morning or noon it's permanent night in here.
The regulars, they know what I look like,
   they don't stare
I'm just another rummy with his reasons.
The bartender, he's used to me
Not many people come in off the street to stop
   and make me feel pitiful
I rev myself up with booze and attitude
And the sad, jeaned lady at the bar's end smoking
   her Marlboros,
She don't care, she gives me a smile,
There's times if she is feeling
   sorry enough for herself
she will get down from her bar stool
   and wheel me to that room in back
   and kneel before me

and perform her sacramental deference
    in the way of women from time immemorial.
And for a few moments there is no goddamn history,
    which if you think about it
is an infinite series of befores and afters,
    as in before, when I had legs, and after,
Or when I still had a spleen and then didn't,
Before I was gut-shot and lay rotting in my own shit
    in the elephant grass in the sun,
    and after,
And so on, including when I still had an asshole
    and now don't.
But this last time that she was kind to me
    I thought of the little whores of Saigon
    who laughed as if they really liked whoring
    and who fucked as if they liked fucking
And who we thought of as meat, who were meat
    War meat, like us.
And now I don't know if it will work anymore
    this good lady's back-room act of grace
Any more than morphine when you can't do without it.
I mean my history may finally have found me out here
    hiding in the blue bar of my illusory
    freedom.
Oh man you want a war story . . . I don't know.
I don't know how to tell stories
I can try to tell you how we lived over there
    but if I speak of it in words and sentences
    I will be lying.
    I should speak in tongues
So that it will be God recounting what I have done
    and have had done to me.
Maybe He can make a story of it, maybe He can make it
    His story.
All suffering is distinctive
It does not cross, there is no synapse firing
    soul to soul,

Christ or no Christ,
And the best we can come up with is compassion.
Fuck compassion.
I know the Second World War was no picnic
But the G.I.'s, the worst off,
   who've spent their lives in V.A. hospitals
Maybe they've found solace, justification,
   having fought for a cause, having won,
Which gives them a means of forgiveness
   for the state they're in,
And that by this time no one gives a shit.
As a grunt I can't find that in myself.
Not my honor, but my sanity,
   what's left of my mind,
depends on my not forgiving.
I think I hate the ones who now apologize
   for sending me in there
Almost as much as I hate the righteous ones
   who won't apologize
   for their realpolitikal fantasies
   that sent me in there.
It is wrong to think we fought a war.
That was no war, it did not begin as wars begin
   it did not end as wars end
Everything that made military sense was
   irrelevant
Who lived, who died, who won or lost the day
   changed nothing,
It did not matter, there were no conclusions
   to be drawn
No victories that stayed victories
No advances that were met with retreats
   that weren't advances.
The worst inflictions of overpowering armaments
Left a temporary stillness in the dunned hills
   some phosphorescing blue and green bird feathers
   rising on the smoke

No it was no war, no organized animosity
   of the social states
It was just some of us dropping in
   travelers condescending
to the satanic realm of the earth
Where the trees were armed,
and the runners of the colonies of ants
   drummed the ground
and the naked children crawled under the
   dazed water buffalo
to drink the blood dripping from their teats.
We shot the monkeys down from their green canopies
   and like panthers
Crawled slung between our hunched shoulders
   through their tunnels
to catch them and kill their pretty faces.
Meanwhile parts of me were being shot away
   and no sooner was a piece of my flesh
   plopped in the grass
than some hairy rat had clamped on its bloody morsel.
Sometimes the earth heaved up and rained
   green salads of forest flora
   bats and cricket crisps and mantis heads.
Spumes of yellow rice shot up like fireworks,
Radios crackled with unintelligible speech
I heard the cries and bleats and shrieks
   and cockadoodle doos
Of predators and prey fulfilling their
   genetic destinies
Beetles and wasps alighted on blood
   turned viscous under the sun
   and stuck to it
Bird-size butterflies trembling to lift off
   the blackening blood pools of dying men
Flights of yellow jackets driven to frenzy
   with the smell of rich-blooded human compost
And oh the leeches how shrewdly they snuck
   into ears and urethras of the exhausted

sleeping their watch through the blessed night
   beside the river,
   there to expand.
One man took a machete to his cock
Another living host I shot at his request.
I was no angel, good buddy,
I'd kill whoever needed to be killed
I was an executioner, I lived in satanic bliss,
I could break their skinny backs with my boot
I could heave their tidy beings from the chopper
   a thousand feet in the blue sky
This was not war, this was life as it is
   and was and always will be
As God gave it to us
   as he gave us
   the violin spider
   chief arachnid of the satanic kingdom
   of the earth.
You know about the violin spider, of course.
The pure thin high-pitched tone it emits
during the spinning out from itself of its web
   of a particularly thick calibration
   akin to the gut strings of the violin.
This web is woven between tree trunk and forest floor
where it is meant to trap not flying insects
   but large crawling pests and small animals.
A man who unwittingly walks into the web
   of the violin spider
finds that it folds to his weight
   as would a hammock.
And then the spider itself is upon him,
   a furred creature with serrated legs
   who spins around him with incredible speed
   a tightly woven binding over which
   it simultaneously spreads a gluey impasto
   that conveys a burning sensation to the skin.
In seconds the man, try as he might, cannot release
   himself,

He is still holding his weapon
   but finds he cannot
   pull the trigger
He cannot wield the knife in his hand
He must struggle helplessly as the creature
wanders over him, his hands and wrists, his face
   his neck
Doing a bit of intelligent military reconnoitering
   before it chooses the tenderest place
   to bite into with its mandibles
   and begins to suck through its proboscis
     the blood, its food.
What's that you say? It sounds like no spider
   you've ever seen?
Explain then the browned desanguinated bodies
   I found
   lying flat, like bladders, on the forest floor.
Will there be a monument to the victims
   of the violin spider of Vietnam?
How can there be—monuments are for wars
And this was not a war, though we Americans
   thought it was
But life objective, impartial,
   giving itself to everything that demands it,
   from woolly mammoths to the sulfide worm
crawling on the fulminating stacks
   at the bottom of the deepest sea.
When we consider the varieties of life on this
   Satanic planet,
   in what assorted shapes and colors, of what skills
   and blunt intentions to survive,
   we can hardly congratulate ourselves for being
   one of them,
Can we, good buddy?

—How does it work, I said.

The question amused him: Well, Everett, it's as you'd expect, they do it at dawn in the courtyard, you're standing at attention, the drums roll, and in front of the priestly ranks the bishop steps forward, he yanks off your crucifix, tears off your collar, and bends your fingers back.

I thought as much.

It's just an exchange of letters. You tell them what's in your heart. They decertify you.

Will I see those letters?

I don't know. Maybe. Why not? Not all that much to see.

So what did you say?

That they all know what I know, none of it holds up, the difference being the value to them of the symbolism and the church built around it—it's there, it has a historical constituency, it's a system that works for people. And as far as I'm concerned that's no longer enough.

So that's that.

There's a committee supposed to try to talk you out of it. I told them not to bother. They were grateful. . . . I know what you're thinking, Everett.

You do?

You're feeling superior. Someone who read his Diderot in college and consigns these issues to the seventeenth century.

I never read Diderot in college.

Didn't he say religion is the ignorance of causes reduced to a system?

He said that?

Someone said it. . . . The truth is I didn't think life as an ordinary citizen would be this . . . enigmatic.

Citizen Pemberton.

Yes, it takes getting used to. There are odd little moments, peculiar problems.

Like what?

What to do with the vestments. Throw them in the garbage? Burn them? Leave them hanging in the closet? Pack them? Give them away? Nothing is quite right. And the books. The dear old texts. Makes me nervous to see them lined up on the shelves just where they've always been. But they're books, for Chrissake, what am I afraid of? So it's all that . . . My stuff.

Your life.

The stuff of my life. Thirty or so years of it. I'm having these sudden deferential dips of the intellect. As in . . . What have I done? Because there were certain advantages I think I will miss.

Like what?

Well, it's a credential. The cross is society giving you permission to express concern for another human being. You wear the collar and people accept that you hang out in a cancer hospice. You can do that and not arouse suspicion you're some sort of fetishist of suffering.

Come on, Pem—

Really. If you're a priest, a rabbi, a nun, people know you've dropped out of the material culture. They accept it, they may not believe what you have to say, or care that much, but they listen to you, sometimes they talk. And of course there are the few who do believe in what you have to say—those are the ones I wouldn't want to see me now.

Why not?

Well it's like someone who wears glasses all the time, he takes them off, and what? the ears stick out, white circles under the eyes, he looks naked. And of course blinking, half-blind. That's me as a secularist. And this poor child of God at death's door, he realizes your promises weren't worth diddly-squat.

Poor child of God?

I'm guess I'm still attached to some of the words.

It's natural.

Not that I regret anything, I'm only talking about having to adjust. That takes a while. Especially for someone who's never been able to come to a decision without replaying it a thousand times. But you know I have to wonder about all those years I put in. What could I have been thinking? Solemn processions, colors and collars and little charms. . . . Was I a broad-church Anglican—or an animist? I pick up my old paperback Augustine. *City of God*. Every page almost totally underlined.

Well now, wait a minute, he's a hell of a writer, Augie.

You would like him, wouldn't you? With his writer's bag of tricks. All those doctrinal notions treated as if they exist, like characters in a

Henry James novel. God's Grace is my favorite. And that impassioned rhetoric . . . To know God, you must long for God. But then, what about Faith and does it come with, before, or after Longing, and so on. The voice makes it. Didn't you once tell me it all comes of the voice?

I did. It does.

You trust this voice . . . speaking whereof it knows. You're suckered right in. Even you, Everett.

Well he loses me when he says babies are born damned to hell unless someone sprinkles water on them. He loses me there.

All right then.

But *City of God,* that's a good title. I like the image, don't you?

It does have a certain something you don't get from green pastures.

You can go for a walk, for one thing.

Pick up the paper and a coffee at the Korean.

Catch an afternoon flick.

I guess I'll keep this book.

Why not keep all of them?

Why the hell not. My collection in history of religion. After all, I haven't given up God. Just the Trinity.

========

—The Midrash Jazz Quartet Plays the Standards

THE SONG IS YOU

I hear music when I look at you
A beautiful theme of everything I ever knew
Down deep in my heart I hear it play
I feel it start and melt away . . .

Why can't I let you know
The song my heart would sing
What beautiful rhapsody of love and youth and
    spring
The music is sweet
the words are true
The song is you!

—

THE MIDRASHIM ARE HONORED TONIGHT . . . TO HAVE
IN THE AUDIENCE A LEGEND OF THE BUSINESS . . . IN
FACT THE GREATEST OF THEM ALL . . . NOW THAT CAN
MEAN ONLY ONE PERSON . . . AND IF YOU GIVE HIM A BIG
ENOUGH WELCOME, MAYBE HE'LL COME UP HERE AND
DO A LITTLE VERBALIZMUS OF HIS OWN!

(prolonged heavy applause)

Thank you, well why not, I'll give it a try . . .

Man here claims he looks at the broad and hears music. Says love is
a song in his heart. What you'd expect of someone makes his living
as a songwriter.

(laughter)

Little plug for the trade. Would a general say I hear war when I look at
you? More like it. And he alone can hear this song of her? Why's that?
What can that mean other than he loves her even though she wears
thick glasses and has a fat ass?

(whistles, laughter)

And to top everything he's got this problem he can't let her know
how he feels: What—he's shy? Shy! Tell me who in this goddamn
world is shy? Young, old, the lame and halt. Clobber you over the
head with what they feel.

Oh man I wish just once in my long fucked-up life someone had
come up to me who was too shy to tell me what they thought of
me . . .

(happy, knowing applause)

Like Fanny, the mother of all broads: You what? You want to be a
singer with the band? An open-hand left across the ear. Like this Miss
Pretty on the wall? Lookatim with his pipe and mascara'd eyes—this is
what you want? Ma, I cry, that's Bing! A right now follows, my both
ears ringing, I am ducking, covering up, my arms taking the blows.
A boy with the band? Like some cheap cunt standing up to sing her
chorus? Whores her days through the saxophone section? Genderless,

my ma. Ripping my hero off the wall, tearing him into shreds. Finding the 78s one by one, snapping them in half like hardtack.

Or my father: I never learn to read, he says. You know what it's like? (I can read, Pa, he doesn't hear me.) Like you're blind, you come to the corner a stranger takes your elbow. Everything, I'm the last to know. Is that what you want for yourself? (I can read, Pa!) You're not listen you fuckn kid, come back here, I beat the shit out of you!

The tough culture of my life in the house, in the street, it's a broadcast you can't turn off. Priests are the loudest, a church that doesn't know the meaning of restraint, the word pealing over the neighborhood bong-abong-abong, the word abonging. Okay for the old ladies in black, in their minds they're still walking to mass down the dirt roads of the olive trees, the widows crossing themselves in the votive darkness, dropping to their swollen knees, the knuckles of their hands like wood knots. But not for me such smells and bells, you put your money in the poor box and you're out of there. Bullshit the father on the church stoop. Wonder what possessed him.

I'm talking before the war, before the war after the war, a Jersey waterfront town. The streets sinkholing into the swamps they were built on. Slack-wired telephone poles leaning every way but up. Horizons of refinery pipes, navy airships disappearing in the yellow clouds. Sky lit at night by the chemical fires of the Meadowlands. And the people we were, breathing all this. Made who we were in our slums of assimilation. Shopping in our dark little stores, the lights turned off to save money. Snapping open the change purses to lift out the pennies one by one.

Oh, I remember, my friends, and no thanks for the memory.

But this kid, he's making the Depression all his own, my thick skull the only strong bone of me, portable studio of my sound, resonant chamber of the voice. Secret of my success, my thick skull. My father shouting, We don't want you here no more. My mother shouting, You fucking no-good bum. I was always running out slamming the door. When it was really bad, heading for the docks. A nickel ride, the streetcar banging around the corners, streets so narrow you could lean out the windows and touch the two-family houses on either side. Flat-roofed houses of wood. Kids staring from the porch. Up and down the hill streets, the river appearing and disappearing as you pointed up and dipped down, the spires of the alabaster city across the river rising and sinking like the band stage at the Paramount, letting you know you were noplace, that you were no one living in noplace, that the true life was over there, the other side. Last stop everyone off at the birdshit docks by the stinking river, coupla black men with fishing poles hoping for an oily perch for dinner, and you. Kid with no hips. So skinny had to belt his trousers up at the diaphragm. Sits on the splintered stinking river wharf and looks across the river at the city of white stone. The beautiful city. I'm sitting among the splotches of duck shit, the pecked-out crab shells, a kid without consolation. Chest of a begging bowl. Bones as thin as crate wood, the wired crates for oranges and grapefruit that you could twist in your hands and split lengthwise, that's what his bones were like. What is he, fourteen, fifteen? Staring across the water at the city burning off in the sunlight. Hearing the back-and-forth nail clicks in the sky, guard dogs of the Depression.

So now you know who the you of the song is?

Man wants to write my biography what do I tell him? Can I tell him how when I shoveled the ashes from the furnace I only filled the tip of the shovel because I couldn't lift any more than that? What's takinim so long, Fanny's dulcet tones down the cellar steps: You fuckin die down there? Taste of ashes in the basement, the things in your life you don't remember till it's time to die. Goddamn stuff on my tongue. Oilcloth with knife scratches, pattern of tiny yellow flowers over the kitchen table. Round-finned motor humming on top of the icebox, grease gummed with dust. And such historic layers of off-white paint jobs in the rooms, the walls were not plumb, the corners not squared, closet doors wouldn't close. Pointless, pointless stuff.

But other things you knew you'd never forget, indelible secret things that didn't grow up with you but keep to this moment in the original feeling. Fanny in her nurse's uniform, the big-mouthed mother of all women, midwifing slick newborns out of them, taking them in when they got beat up, giving them the operation for the unmarried, yes, the auxiliary doyenne of St. Francis doing this because she was not only my mother but the mother of all this world of women in my house.

So early on yours truly knows what a girl is, I seen one through the keyhole undressing, the school uniform falling in folds over the wooden chair, a silken sound, and this ordinary girl in all her breath-taking sweet springing tautness climbing up on that kitchen table of little yellow flowers of the oilcloth . . . and she waits, and weeps, so lovely from the soles of her small feet, every soft-built inch of her making such sense, like God is giving me a look and I'm saying, Of course, of course, as if once seen it is not an introduction but a remembrance, of course, of course, there could have been nothing else but this as I've always known, they are calved and thighed, curved-assed and cunted. And as she lies back the high breasts broadening on the chest tremble as, staring at the ceiling light and knuckling her teeth, she cries so scared she doesn't make a sound. What I don't recall now is her name, that girl, she was from the neighborhood, I'd seen her with the others in her school uniform, an older girl, in a higher grade than me, familiar-looking in the dark green skirt, the white blouse, the kneesocks, all of it hiding in ordinariness the wondrous revelation of legs opening on command, the knees rising, till through the keyhole the broad nurse-white back of Fanny and the sheet she flings out save me from disaster.

Not a song in the heart, you wimp, a roar in the loins, a screech in the brain, a blinding glimpse of God's work, and that is it for you for-ever, you're theirs.

But fighting it, making that mistake of all stupid kids that this is what you can do to girls, this is how you handle them, the way of the world. Really knowing but not knowing how it is by leaving himself out, the longing going out of him as out of nothing, the awful draw-ing need unattached to him but like a weather, all around him, color-ing the sky.

Every one of my pals just as stupid. Why the jokes were told, why the cigarette in the corner of the mouth, why the two-handed crotch adjust, the raised-eyebrow sneer, the raucous applause at the bur-lesque, but swallowing on a dry mouth and feeling the heart in the crate wood chest banging in time with the drum vamp.

The Fools of Song. That was the name we gave ourselves. In certain ears it was faintly Chinese. Like Tin Pan. Tin Pan say love is pop song in heart.

What were the chances for any of us, what odds would you have given? Me, flexing my arm, show you my number-six-linguine bicep, or Vinnie who we call Slapsy because his brain works as if he's been decked once too often, or maybe the stolid Mario who is called Brick or Shithouse because he is built like a brick shithouse, or Aaron aka Jewish, an alien from outside the neighborhood who hangs out with us because he likes our raucous Italian ways. I mean, the wit here is not of the playing fields of Eton. We filled our snowballs with rocks. We sang the hits on the corner in front of the candy store.

Jewish, whose father runs numbers, has the scratch for our trips to the Union City matinees, he is in training for the rackets, Jewish, a sometime substitute bagman practicing his padrone-ship, though deficient in the crucial gift of self-importance, a terrible lack that means he will never make it in the wiseguy world. Besides, he has a touch of palsy it must be, one foot the toe drags, the heel doesn't quite meet the ground. Gives him an unbalanced stride, like someone about to lift off. Threadbare corduroys and sneakers winter and summer and shirttails flying as he went down his runway. A sweet goony kid, an eager expression, mouth a perpetual smile, big front teeth. And to top everything, this silly high-pitched bray verging on the maniacal, and it was an embarrassment there in the cavernous theater of dreams, so loud and piercing that the stripper twirling her tasseled tits and bumping and grinding her ass to the drumbeat would actually stop what she was doing under the lights and glare in our direction.

Once a week, the bus to Union City. A woman of a late childbearing age marching around a stage under a pink light. Jewish braying, Mario punching my arm at a particularly exquisite moment of the choreography, Slapsy muttering holy shit over and over again in a display of his powers of articulation, and I sink down in my seat suffering a complex and not remotely pleasurable excitement. I actually worry that she will see me watching, the stripper. There is such female contempt coming off that stage. And swinging her ass so expertly, ba-da boom, ba-da boom—well it was of a vulgarity, believe me, that in all my years of saloon life, and the indulgence of women, I have never seen topped. This was a low-down dirty use of pulchritude, confirmed by the cretin in the checked suit and floppy shoes and derby who staggers from the wings with a three-foot pink rubber prong sticking out of his pants. At the same time of my case of nauseatingly aching balls, I am angry at the fat dancing slut's representation of the abilities of women. I didn't want it to be that way.

Another one who got to me, a vapid skinny stripper as slender and titless as a boy, who drifted across the stage in such a drug-induced torpor not even Buddy Rich could have kept time.

How did I get onto this? Why am I thinking of this? Maybe—and I am after the fact by some seventy years—maybe I believed what went on in a theater should be different from the street. I don't pretend the boy I was could think it through. This nothing kid, who would not finish two years of high school, tries to harmonize with the other Fools on the street corner—he decides performance is another realm? What the fuck did I know about show business to think it should give you something you couldn't find outside? But by Christ I swear that is exactly the conviction that came to me, like I was a student of the performing arts, poo-poo pa-doop, and where it came from I will never know.

So in the same custom we have of thanking this one or that one in the awards ceremonies, I thank Jewish for helping me perceive, by way of its negating sleaze, my own way out. His way out, incidentally, I won't go into here, except that it was abrupt and premature, my poor Achilles-tendoned pal.

But in the meantime I am trying, right? Always, no matter how confused, navigating by my sight of the alabaster city. How much better for me if I was shy like in the song, if I only shyly imagined kissing Angela Morelli under the boardwalk in Asbury Park. Slipping my hand under her wool bathing suit. I can't be your girlfriend anymore, she says. It's not that I don't like you, I do, but I can't take the chance something happens and that's my life. I want to do something with my life. Dark eyes shining, a wonderful serious girl. She pushes my hand away: You got no prospects. No job. You quit school. Don't you want to make something of yourself? It's like you got no self-respect, hanging out on the corner singing stupid songs with those others have nothing better to do. So what are you crying, Angela, if I'm the one with no self-respect—and what else does your mother say? It's not just my mother says that, I got eyes that see for myself you don't do nothing. I got ears that don't hear about no ambitions of yours.

No ambitions, Angela, no ambitions? I had the ambition to fuck you, shouldn't that have been enough? I had the ambition to fuck you and the world with you!

So, now you think you know who's the song?

He smokes three-for-a-penny cigarettes, works on his pompadour in the bathroom and, like the little girl said, leads the Fools in the latest hits in front of the candy store: *I wanna be loved by you, just you, and nobody else but you. I wanna be loved by you a-lone, poo-poo pa-doop.*

First career move, an act of self-distinction, to go solo. Brick, my man, you got a tin ear, why don't you give up, go punch a door or something. And you, Slapsy, you can't even remember the fuckin words. Words are the song, asshole, they are the meaning of the notes, they are what the fuckin song is about. Riding them like that, killing their joy, which was to croak the tunes of our culture on the street corner, stick it to the old world cockers upstairs: Here we are do me something. Killing all that, killing the Fools of Song forever. Whatayou the director all of a sudden? You think you know everything, who made you the leader. You guys are shit, you don't know how to sing. Maybe not but I can bust your fuckin face. So I throw myself at Shithouse, the only way, hoping they pull us apart before he snaps me in two.

So that's the end of that, I'm alone, only Slapsy hangs in there, follows me around, does things for me, cops a Philco radio and gives it to me, that kind of thing. And he's been with me since, all these years, not too much upstairs, but loyal unto death. What I like. We have grown up together, my life an epic of change, his always the same, narrowly fixed on me, my personality, my career, I fill his mind. A very narrow bandwidth, old Slaps. If he were a wife, I would have dumped him long ago. He got out of there, though, didn't he, on my coattails, but out is out and who will say he could have any other way? Peculiar way to live, though. When anything good comes along, an honor, an album makes platinum, medal from the president, whatever, Slapsy likes to think it's happened to both of us. This calls for a drink, boss, we deserve it, we are the best!

But don't take it too hard, Slaps—you know I love you.

Paul Whiteman is who I hear on the Philco, tuned in low late at night with my ear to the cloth, and Rudy Vallee, and Russ Columbo and Jack Leonard. Picked up stations as far away as Pittsburgh, Billy Wynne and his orchestra playing the Pocono Room at the Three Rivers Hotel. It was not just music, it was class. *Here is the Drag, See how it goes; Down on the heels, Up on the toes. That's the way to do the Varsity Drag.* Rudy Vallee a Yale man which he somehow always let you know. Jolson, a good voice but he oversold everything he sang. He was not it, Jolson. Cantor, beneath contempt, a clown, no music in him at all. I didn't like comedians who also sang. I wanted singers who were serious about what they did. I wanted performers to be purely who they were and nothing else. Style was what I listened for, elegance, a good lyric connoting taste and showing wit. You understand, by such homemade discriminations this punk of nothingness from New Jersey was instructing himself. I copied down the Gershwin songs, the brother's lyrics, kept a notebook, he was the pinnacle for me, George, high style, sophistication, no idea he came out of the Lower East Side, a little Hebe kid no more to the manor born than I.

My serious singing was alone on the dock, bringing the voice through the nasal passage, testing it, hearing it, finding it, all the while looking at the city across the river, singing to it with the resonance I could hear in my skull, my thick skull. I wanted to hang my voice on the city of white stone, weave my voice line by line up and down back and forth, wrap the whole fucking city inside my voice. And now you know it, don't you? The song is you, big town, you were always my song across the oily wide river, the gulls riding the wind, dropping the crab shells at my feet, the black men fishing with eternal patience off the end of the dock for a decent meal.

Another year before I would actually get on the ferry a block away and make it across. Paying for it with a messenger-boy day job in Newark. And the island of Manhattan rising up before me as a human place, coming into focus: liners at the piers, smoke from stacks, smells of the West Side stockyards. Down the ramp and into the life. Horns, lights, streetcars, buses, trucks, police whistles, the flow of mayhem. Who had organized it, how did they make it work? How people knew which door to enter. How they found themselves at home in buildings forty floors off the ground. I walked the streets wanting to hug the lampposts. Sopped up the noise, the important noise of the city. Studying the way people walked, the figures that caught my eye, male and female, their clothes. People of all walks pooling at the lights. Horses still clopping along then. Like a scientist, experiment, take a cab, tell him where you want to go, pay the fare and the right tip, without giving it away what a rube you are. Take a look at some of those hotels where the bands played. Get the confidence to walk in of an evening, sit at the bar with your cigarettes, and look old enough.

Watch the band, picking up on the sense among them of their control of the room, their inner circle of performing knowingness.

All of that, without its being mine. I am still this punk kid staring in the store windows. But I swore somehow I would bring it down, seduce it, conquer it. How? With the lyrics of romance! I would use the common coin, the pop tune. Can you beat it? All the enfranchisement in the world, the education, the genius, the power and politics and money, and—what?—this kid like that story of the juggler, I would sing my heart out if I would ever learn to sing, and the Blessed Virgin herself would come down in full color from her marble pedestal and wipe my sweaty brow with the hem of her robe. Did I know there was enough longing in the world to make it work? Callow, I was a callow kid, so insular in my dreamt Manhattan while the world was blowing apart, Nazis goose-stepping, tearing Jews from their homes, Stalin icing millions in the gulags, the Japs practicing beheading techniques on Chinese coolies, the Burmese with their loaded carts jamming the roads out of Rangoon, Italians dive-bombing the Ethiopes waving their spears at the sky, whole fucking world showing its true humanity, screaming baby on the railroad track, blood pouring down the mountains, irrigating the deserts, reddening the seas, the world a big bloody circus of human mutilation, with a degree of murderous, insane rage to blast the planet off its axis . . . and here I am crooning in bel canto:

> *Why can't I let her know the song my heart would*
>   *sing*
> *What beautiful rhapsody of love and youth and*
>   *spring*
> *The music is sweet, the words are true . . .*
> *The song is you!*
>
>   *(tearful shouting loving standing ovation)*

———

—Ex-*Times* guy, now a self-certified killer, is holding his head up a bit more these days. Less slouchy, doesn't look at the ground as he walks, shoulders not so rounded. You can tell if a man's been defeated in this world by the way he walks in the streets of the city. There are a thousand walks of defeat, each one tailored to a specific morphology, but all very clearly what they are. Ex-*Times* guy now elevated out of the shuffling class of the disgruntled, unappreciated, betrayed, embittered, or catatonic. It's not that he has forgotten the accident factor in his closure of the S.S. sergeant's story, but he has worked it out to his credit: He thinks now he had seen the old Nazi killer from the corner of his eye and recognized him before he lost control of his bicycle and bounced up on the sidewalk and ran him over. He thinks now his body took control of his mind, there was a conflict resolved by the reversal of control systems wherein not his conscious thought was the directing intelligence but the electric buildup of intent in his skeletal and musculature systems. He had crossed over, gone right through the transom of his freedom, how beautiful that the moment could be so explicit.

Ex-*Times* guy feels now there's nothing he can't do, nothing too bold, too outrageous for his contemplation. Has his hair trimmed short, works out in the gym, buys some new, well-tailored outfits. This shlumperer of the past sixty years is now, if not elegant, at least sartorially passable. Finds himself a woman to treat with manly inconsideration. She is a publisher's copy editor in her forties, a thin little blond woman with whom he has in common prescriptive views of grammatical usage and loyalty to the old Second Edition of Webster's Unabridged. But beyond that she exhibits a disappointing gullibility when he fantasizes over dinner now and then and alludes to mysterious professional affiliations.

The former Guatemalan death squad commander who is next on the list owns a restaurant in a mall in Queens, just off the Long Island Expressway. Presumably this is a story whose closure is more conveniently accomplished, involving a short cab ride from the F train at Queens Plaza. But ex-*Times* guy is alarmed in spirit by the sociological complexity of a mall restaurant in Queens. He stands in front of the restaurant looking out on the thousands of parked and parking cars, the shopping hordes, the chain megastores, he hears the shouts of mothers, observes the bitter staring ahead of children gripping the chrome railings of their strollers. The air vibrates with the continuous whine of unending traffic going in opposed directions on the adjoining

L.I.E., suggesting to him a mindless mimicry of purposiveness. Masses of terraced red-brick tenements filling the sky, filthy fluttering pigeons homing in on scraps of junk food, children darting on their in-line skates between the parked cars, cruising packs of fashionable teenagers with their floppy jeans, unlaced Air Jordans, and reversed baseball caps . . . could any clear moral distinctions be drawn, or principles acted upon, in this bedlam of free people? This was not an appropriate venue for high seriousness, nothing ethically important could happen here.

But when he steps inside the restaurant itself, his spirits immediately revive. The room is lit in permanent evening. Haciendic decor, with latticed alcoves behind each banquette. The tables are covered in starched white cloth and at each setting is a crystal water glass. The waiters wear bolero jackets. A pleasing unlocatable sound of falling water erases any errant sound of the out-of-doors. It is the lunch hour and perhaps two or three tables are occupied by men in suits—no women or children anywhere. Sitting at the bar talking to the underworked bartender, a man in a blue blazer turns to look at him as he enters: Ex-*Times* guy's heart kicks in, it is the Guatemalan colonel of the clips, a trimly built man with a good tan, a hairline beginning well back on the crown, and a thick black mustache. Not recognizing the patron, he leaves the welcoming ritual to a waiter and turns back to the cigarette in his ashtray.

Ex-*Times* guy, his gorge rising, sees in that glance the same ranking arrogance that presumed to decimate the intellectual class of a country for the country's sake while managing to murder villagefuls of peasants in the bargain.

But this is just a surveillance visit. Twice more he will come for lunch by himself, and each time his death-squad restaurateur is there, at the bar, and each time he offers no more than an impassive glance before he turns his back to the room.

Third time ex-*Times* guy is seated at what is now his table. In his breast pocket is a ten-inch Carborundum steel carving knife purchased from the Hammacher Schlemmer store on Fifty-seventh Street. Two young men in dark suits and rep ties join him. Neat young fellows with short, crop-eared haircuts. No trace of accents as they speak to him, ask him if he's from around here, working here or living here. That's none of your business, says ex-*Times* guy. And who the fuck are you? I don't recall asking you to sit down. We have credentials, one of

them says. Let's see your fucking credentials. In due time, the other
one says.

The room is otherwise empty of diners and the waiters have disappeared. Owner at the bar crushes his cigarette, stands, saunters over,
and sits down on the opposite side of the table. I am Guillermo your
host, he says, smiling, a bright, blinding smile of capped teeth. And I
am the avenging angel, ex-*Times* guy says. He is feeling bold, suicidal.
The two young government men without appearing hurried are in an
instant standing behind him, at either shoulder. Guillermo is laughing, tilting his chair back on its rear legs. You are not the first to make
this claim, he says but certainly, of those, the least prepossessing. He is
now even more amused by his own wit, genuine laughter cascades
from his mouth of white teeth. Ex-*Times* guy can actually see the pink
palate and the fleshy flap of the uvula. He cannot grab the knife in his
breast pocket, because the two young men are pinning his shoulders
to his chair. In a mindless rage he strains at their grip, half rises, lunges,
and spits in the notorious death squad commander's face. Who in-
stinctively jerks backward. This carries him over, and for an instant
ex-*Times* guy sees the new unscored leather soles of his shoes. Ca-
cophonous chair splinterings, shouts. Lungfuls of breath basso-
belched from a body. But the sound of a skull cracking against a mall
restaurant floor of wood-grained plastic affixed to a concrete base, he
would later reflect, is less resonant than the sound made by a skull
cracking against a brick lawn-retaining wall. They are different sounds,
of different pitch. Of course the quality of skull bone may have something to do with it. But whereas he knew immediately the old man in
Cincinnati was dead, he did not know, running through the mall parking lot toward the L.I.E., that he had spit the Guatemalan colonel to
death. It wasn't until he read his *Times* the next morning that he
learned he'd struck again.

=

—We were lining up Pem's books, taking them out of the cartons and
putting them in the shelves of the newly finished top-floor library of
the EJ synagogue. Most of the volumes had been in storage since his
departure from St. Tim's.

Everett, he said, try not to read each book before you shelve it, okay?

Some good stuff here. How do I get a library card?

He laughed, he is happier these days, but I meant it. I put aside a small stack of his guys I have to read: Tillich, Barth, Teilhard, Heschel.

That's about right, he said after glancing at my choices. But as you will see, all these brilliant theologians end up affirming the traditions they were born into. Even the great Kierkegaard. What do you make of that? I mean, when your rigorous search for God just happens to direct you back to your christening, your bris . . .

=

—Up on the stage of the grand ballroom of the Waldorf, one actor after another extolling the evening's lifetime-honoree film director. How he taught them, brought out the best in them, changed their lives, and so on. All to be expected. Directors hand out the jobs.

But then two or three writers on the program come up to extol the evening's lifetime-honoree film director, telling of the superior artistry with which he wrought movie magic from their humble books and screenplays. Not quite the same mechanism working here as with the dependent actors, because how many times can any author expect to sell movie rights to a particular director? No, this is something else, call it the denigration of the literary. A sacrament of the movie culture, the denigration of the literary is most satisfying when performed by the literary folks themselves.

The ballroom, softly lit, chandeliered, all aglitter. A big-time black-tie evening. I am fortunate enough to attract the wine waiter just before the lights go down for the showing of the famous scenes . . .

When movies began they were shown in storefronts, dumps, you paid a nickel and sat down on a bench. They were silents, of course, one-reelers, and everyone made them, they were cheap to make, people made them about their own lives. They told the stories of their lives, how they lived in hovels, tenements, how they worked for pittances, how they were fired from their jobs by bosses in suits and ties, how when they were old they were fired, how when they spoke up they were fired. They showed themselves at street corners talking to one another, going to one another's houses, they showed themselves in public meetings electing from among themselves their union leaders, they showed themselves going on strike, marching in the streets, carrying placards, getting run down and trampled by mounted police. Blacks showed themselves getting lynched, women showed themselves molested and pushed down on the floors of their kitchens, girls showed themselves giving birth in alleyways, drunks showed themselves dying with the delirium tremens, babies showed themselves dying of starvation, old people showed themselves being stuffed into pine boxes and dropped into graves. They all loved these movies about themselves and the truth of their lives. Sometimes a pianist played to go along with the action. But the audiences talked back to the films, stood to give advice, screamed warnings at the dangerous moments, cheered at the triumphs over villainy, cried when the lovers stood before the altar, and in all ways carried on to the extent that some poets in the audiences thought if they could only record the audiences talking back to the films, new films could be made about audiences watching themselves in films and talking back to them. And then films about those films, and so on into infinity. Obviously, some ontological order had to be established and this came about naturally as the competition among films created a demand for longer, more complex films. That meant filmmakers could no longer afford the cost of their films and so they went to banks and insurance companies for the money. This money was duly tendered, thus making banks and insurance companies the solemn judges of just what films were to be made. These judgments were made and a business class of professional filmmakers arose to effect them. The banks and insurance companies liked films showing peace between the unequal races, and happy workers and smiling shop foremen and well-dressed well-fed children and monogamous husbands and wives and hyperfunctional families as smoothly running as if on ball bearings going to church and being greeted and blessed by kindly gray-haired pastors. These films showed people driving in their motorcars, marveling at the heroism of cowboys, they showed villains as rough-hewn sociopaths standing apart from normal God-fearing human beings, and they showed love as the driving force of all life. They found loose-limbed, acrobatic little fellows to take pratfalls and show the comedy of life, and they showed pompous fat ladies getting their comeuppance, and self-impressed fat men getting taken down a peg or two, and they showed cross-eyed cops falling over each other in their efforts to apprehend kids with peashooters and they showed darling children with chocolate cake smeared over their faces and comedy teams pushing pies into one another's faces, and gradually evolved a system of social archetypes into which they fitted physically appropriate persons they renamed as actors and found a place in the California sun to generate on an orderly industrial basis these corporate movies, which, whatever their period, contemporary or historical or futuristic, demonstrated to the audience watching them, now sitting in dark, palatial theaters built just for the purpose, that movies were a form of life to which life must aspire, as it has now shown every sign of doing.

—This past Sunday, Pem and Sarah and Sarah's boys walk over to Central Park to meet me and a new friend of mine, Miss Warren, at the specified tree near the western edge of the Sheep Meadow.

Miss Warren is a freelance magazine writer born and raised in New Orleans. In certain journalistic circles she is something of a celebrity. I met her at a publishing party and have known her for a week and I can't imagine what beautifully maladept instinct of mine has persuaded me to bring her here.

All New York is out this afternoon. We stroll around, watch some softball, find a grassy spot for ourselves, unwrap the deli heros, uncork the Snapples, and prepare to have one of those balmy, ritually relaxing Sundays when the sense of loss is in every heart and a nonspecific melancholy seems to permeate the air.

Pem points out to Sarah's boys how they can track the movement of the sun as it flashes in the windows of the residential towers of Fifth Avenue. They respond politely, but they are wearing their baseball mitts and, having seen the big guys, are ready for action. Pem rolls up his sleeves. Okay, he says, let's hustle. The boys run out to their imaginary positions. Pem keeps up the palaver, each successful catch or throw draws his praise, each dropped ball his encouragement. Sarah watches. The older boy, Jake, now nine, has filled out since I last saw him, his hair is his mother's light brown, and he has her fair skin and wide-set blue eyes. He's reached the age when he can pick the ball out of the air with his glove hand and whip it back to Pem on a line in a somberly casual exhibit of skill. Pem, catching the softball without a glove, is hard-pressed to keep smiling. The younger kid, Davey, about five, is dark-haired, wiry, a dead ringer for his father. His tosses sometimes arc backward and land in the grass behind him, and on the catch his outstretched glove doesn't quite meet the ball as it arrives. He is undeterred in his ineptitude, then suddenly angry, slamming his glove down and going to sit sulkingly in Sarah's cross-legged lap for consolation.

Now, through all of this, Miss Warren is talking away in what seems to me an attempt to establish her sisterhood with a woman scholar of her own generation, though she is not naturally curious as a journalist is supposed to be. This is not a conversation of questions and answers but more like a monologue: *The New Yorker* has just accepted her piece about the Muslim extremists in Afghanistan. She will use the money to pay off part of her debt to a divorce lawyer, who has not done all that well by her. The divorce lawyer actually offered to let her pay off her bill with sex? Her ex-husband, and what a mistake that was, is a famous philologist who teaches at Princeton, one of those obsessively neat and tight-assed, basically fag types, who expected her to be the perfect little academic wife. "Doesn't that beat all?" she says.

"Davey," Sarah says gently, lifting her son to his feet, "they're calling you. Go on back and play, you'll get the hang of it if you keep trying."

Miss Warren, with numerous tendrils of her red-blond pile of hair escaped from her comb, wears her one and only outfit, day and night and for all continents, her khaki multipocketed bush jacket, soft shirt, fatigue trousers, lace-up boots. Around her neck, a blue railroad man's kerchief, carelessly tied. She chain-smokes long, thin cigarettes. She is tall and blowzy and sits hunched over with her legs in the full lotus, her jacket pockets bulging with her cell phone, beeper, cigarettes, pads, Palm III organizer, and, for all I know, a couple of grenades.

In Peru to write about the Shining Path guerrillas, Miss Warren fell in love with one of their leaders? He was killed in a skirmish and the Nationalistas cut off his dick and sent it to her in a box at the school in Lima where she had gone to lecture. . . . In Sicily, to do a piece on the culture of poverty there, she lost her way and was picked up by three farmhands, who dragged her into a barn and took turns fucking her.

She somehow got away? She found a village and told an old woman what happened, who told the local mafia chief, who invited Miss Warren to watch the men being executed the next morning in the town square. Which she did?

Every once in a while, Sarah Blumenthal glances at me with what I read as the inevitable question: Is this woman really the mythomaniac I think she is? I have to admit Miss Warren's tales of adventure are a touch exotic for a Sunday in Central Park. But having heard them before, I am of the opinion they may really have happened. Part of the trouble is in the style of narration, the diction of the locker room and the breeziness of tone together suggesting the utter inconsequence of the horrific events being reported. So the truth or falsity of these tales really isn't the point, Miss Warren sets off alarms in either case.

She is saying now the superintendent of her building in Soho is a fat old slob of a lecher who likes to walk into her loft unannounced hoping to see her in her underwear. As soon as her application for a gun license comes through, she will take out the piece and scare the shit out of him, and if that doesn't work she'll shoot the fucker.

Sarah's eyes are lowered and I imagine that she's thinking no longer of the woman I have brought this afternoon to the park but of what possibly could have possessed me to do so. It is a good question. Pem and the boys are engaged in the game of running bases, lots of shouting and laughing as he huffs back and forth between the two of them to avoid being tagged. . . . In this shining arcadian New York scene Sarah has to be coming to terms with the fact that I have a life beyond following Pem around, and that it is likely to include a weakness for the profane mysteries. I feel a distinct hollowing spasm in the solar plexus. I am not serious about Miss Warren, though she is quite an armful, and her appetite is honorably congruent with her sexual self-advertising. But in what is left of the afternoon, I will make a point of showing my pleasure in her company, especially in view of the ambiguous politeness she will have inspired in these clerical folk. In fact I am grateful to her. She has served to establish me in some new and distinctive filial relationship with Thomas Pemberton and Sarah Blumenthal . . . as if they are the long-married couple and I am the younger sibling or son who has brought his date around. Though they have not said anything to me, I am anticipating that they will soon marry. Pem said some time ago that I should keep my distance. And that is what by these self-revealing, self-degrading means I am apparently intent on doing.

=

—We know of the Earthly City and the City of God, but there is a third city, the City of Birds, at Valdemingomez, an enormous garbage dump north of Madrid. After you do the Prado, do Valdemingomez, it is a great urban aviary, its population of storks, hawks, egrets, linnets, kites, jackdaws, ravens, condors, and turkey buzzards, when aroused, can circle Valdemingomez and, with a boost from the trade winds, wing-whiff its miasma of sulfurous gases as far east as Rome. The birds of Valdemingomez don't migrate, why would they? Summer and winter, here they stay, over a hundred thirty species of them, even a few accidentals from the tropics—the albatross, the blue-footed booby—have come to look things over. Eggs are laid in old Big Mac containers, nests are lined with cassette tape, the songbirds flitter in and out of rusty cans, grackles huddle in TV cabinets, gulls bomb old sofas with the clamshells of paella, and when flocks of rock doves go cooing and pecking over fields of chicken bones, the bones clack like train tracks, clink like wind chimes, shiver and shirr like shuffled cards, bongo and bop, and chickuh-chick-chick like a hot marimba band. Special rates for ornithologists.

=

—Of the Sunday in Central Park, I remember too that the boys found a brown ant population in a patch of dirt under a tree and I hunkered down with them to watch these infinitesimal creatures, each not an eighth of an inch long, go about their business building an underground city. Two or three different trails of them radiated from the mound, and ants coming and going got in each other's way, sometimes bumping. They waved their antennae about as if they'd never seen another one such as themselves before, though that was clearly not the case, the case being that some sort of chemical messages were being synapsed back and forth before each continued on its way or, sometimes, reversed itself and went back the way it had come. Ants don't look for that much out of life. They may be brainless, but nothing alive is more purposive, disciplined, and with a stronger work ethic, their lives are all work, even the queen's, perhaps especially, down there under the mound where we couldn't see her. Lacking brains, ants make do with genetically programmed little nervous sympathies that allow them to contribute to the general welfare. Whatever their role in the society, as egg tenders, warriors, guards, food gatherers, they are all working for the queen, preserving and protecting her as an egg-laying monarch whose fecundity determines the future of the society. Yet any given ant in its life probably never sees the queen, or more than its immediate confreres, although if it circulates more widely than that, certainly with no memory of having met any specific fellow ant before. Yet ant by ant, body by body, and without any visible central decision-making mechanism, they seem to take instruction from one another, antenna to antenna, and are unified in their responses . . . almost like parallel processors, or in fact our own cortical structure of neurons. They each comprise one cell of a group brain, unlike our own in being unlocatable, somewhere above and around them, an invisible organ of thought that is beyond the capacity of any one of them to understand.

And these are the simplest, most modest kinds of ants, as I explained to the kids, these are domesticated Central Park ants, the house sparrows of the ant species. There are others in the jungles and rain forests and veldts of the world, big ones, that build leaf bridges in trees, cultivate crops, float across rivers on rafts of their own devising, march, make war, eat meat, bite like hell. They are ants that have a patriotic sense of their anthood, if not a degree of self-esteem.

And then everything was all right again, the adults having come over to see what we were looking at, and enjoying the rap.

But now I speculate re the ants' invisible organ of aggregate thought . . . if, in a city park of broad reaches, winding paths, roadways, and lakes, you can imagine seeing on a warm and sunny Sunday afternoon the random and unpredictable movement of great numbers of human beings in the same way . . . if you watch one person, one couple, one family, a child, you can assure yourself of the integrity of the individual will and not be able to divine what the next moment will bring. But when the masses are celebrating a beautiful day in the park in a prescribed circulation of activities, the wider lens of thought reveals nothing errant, nothing inconstant or unnatural to the occasion. And if someone acts in a mutant un-park manner, alarms go off, the unpredictable element, a purse snatcher, a gun wielder, is isolated, surrounded, ejected, carried off as waste. So that while we are individually and privately dyssynchronous, moving in different ways, for different purposes, in different directions, we may at the same time comprise, however blindly, the pulsing communicating cells of an urban over-brain. The intent of this organ is to enjoy an afternoon in the park, as each of us street-grimy urbanites loves to do. In the backs of our minds when we gather for such days, do we know this? How much of our desire to use the park depends on the desires of others to do the same? How much of the idea of a park is in the genetic invitation on nice days to reflect our massive neuromorphology? There is no central control mechanism telling us when and how to use the park. That is up to us. But when we do, our behavior there is reflective, we can see more of who we are because of the open space accorded to us, and it is possible that it takes such open space to realize in simple form the ordinary identity we have as one multicellular culture of thought that is always there, even when, in the comparative blindness of our personal selfhood, we are flowing through the streets at night or riding under them, simultaneously, as synaptic impulses in the metropolitan brain.

Is this a stretch? But think of the contingent human mind, how fast it snaps onto the given subject, how easily it is introduced to an idea, an image that it had not dreamt of thinking of a millisecond before. . . . Think of how the first line of a story yokes the mind into a place, a time, in the time it takes to read it. How you can turn on the radio and suddenly be in the news, and hear it and know it as your own mind's possession in the moment's firing of a neuron. How when you hear a familiar song your mind adopts its attitudinal response to life before the end of the first bar. How the opening credits of a movie provide the parameters of your emotional life for its ensuing two hours. . . . How all experience is instantaneous and instantaneously felt, in the nature of ordinary mind-filling revelation. The permeable mind, contingently disposed for invasion, can be totally overrun and occupied by all the characteristics of the world, by everything that is the case, and by the thoughts and propositions of all other minds considering everything that is the case . . . as instantly and involuntarily as the eye fills with the objects that pass into its line of vision.

So we, too, are subjected to a kind of quantum weirdness, defined in our indeterminacy by how we are measured . . .

≡

—Sunday

In my new vestments, blue blazer, charcoal slacks, and a gray turtle-neck, I launch from the cement dock and high-wire it over the river on the Roosevelt Island Tramway. Windy day, rocks a bit. Are you up here, Lord?

Nobody in the crowded car notices that I am no longer a priest.

East River estuary, heavily tidal, inviting, aglitter with sunlight.

Why am I doing this? Apparently Sunday is still subject to the old urges, the residual feelings. But mostly I wanted to see that one dying lunger, name of McIlvaine.

Not that it was easy, deciding to come out as a layperson.

The hospice, run by the city for indigent terminals, a low yellow-brick building on the south end of the island.

Gulls in a line on the bulwark breasting the wind. The surging currents look unswimmable, suggestive of exile. Confirmed by the view across the river of the immense risen wall of Manhattan. At its foot, the FDR Drive traffic crawls along ant-file. And from this vantage the Fifty-ninth Street underbridge throws a broad shadow across the river as it soars past on its way to Queens.

In the lobby people wave, nod, as they always have. "Cool threads, Father," says a security guard. One of the aides asks if I have a heavy date.

Not to worry, right, Lord? They think we're still talking.

I climb the stairs to the men's floor, the third. Sound of my new loafers, bought too large, clopping on the stair treads. That and my loud breathing.

You walk into a ward and are met by the generic blank stares of the pre-dead. People dying retreat into themselves. Everything of interest in life seems foolish and pointless to them now. Everything vital—the sun in the window, the sympathetic visitor, the nurses who suppose a continuing daily life—is a matter of deep, painkilling indifference.

Old McIlvaine, dying, was not of the pre-dead. Nor was he among the pious few who came out of themselves to pray with the father, grip his hand.

Not this old man.

Bed after bed. Some new faces, some old faces, some rasping away with noses pointed in the air, their mouths open. Lord, don't have taken him, let him still be here.

His anticlericalism was gentle. If I wanted to pray, he told me, go right ahead, if I wanted to read a psalm, he would listen with a smile. Made these concessions, as if in some instinctive understanding of the trouble I was in. "That's very pretty, Father. . . . If you say so, Father. . . . I wouldn't want to disillusion you, Father."

A newspaperman, a city reporter all his working life, moving on every time a paper closed under him. *World-Telegram, Journal-American, Herald-Tribune, Daily Mirror,* God knows what others as the papers hyphenated themselves out of existence. He attributed the closings to himself: *"I am become death, the shatterer of newsrooms. Waiting that hour that ripens to their doom."*

He is not where I last saw him, do they move people around, why would they do that? . . . and then I hear the unmistakable cough of the lunger, it seems to come up from the city sewer system, cavernous and gurgly, gravel-spewing.

Here he is, next bed to the end, still alive, though more emaciated than ever, the nose even bonier, the eyes and cheeks like sinkholes, the incongruously full head of gray hair in a wilted pompadour on the pillow.

"Mr. McIlvaine!"

The skeletal hand rises in greeting, he puts a finger to his lips. "We're doing our hymns," he says in his juicy whisper.

Only now do I register the nun sitting beside McIlvaine's bed, a young sister in an attractive contemporary habit. She is strumming a guitar and in a thin, lovely soprano she sings

> *Oh, shine on, shine on harvest moon, up in the sky.*
> *I ain't had no lovin' since January, February, June*
> *or July . . .*

I'm bewildered, so intently in my own mind, I hadn't seen or heard her. McIlvaine's voice has summoned up an actual pitch, he stares at the ceiling and growls along in his fashion, his eyes shining. On the last line and without missing a beat, they swing into

> *The bells are ringing for me and my gal*
> *the parson's waiting for me and my gal . . .*

which melds into

> *There's a somebody I'm longing to see.*
> *I hope that he*
> *turns out to be*
> *Someone who'll watch over me . . .*

Clearly they've done this before. The nun sings with her eyes closed. She has to be Hail Marying in her mind. McIlvaine presses on. A fierce humor is carried on his sepulchral voice. The duo is now into "Sentimental Journey."

I look around the ward and see from the heads on the pillows an uncharacteristic alertness, something other than the generic blank stares of the pre-deads . . . here a gaze back at me, there something like a smile, and in one bed, a living cadaver, completely still and staring upward without expression, but his hand, raised barely above the bedclothes, waving in time to the music . . .

Lord, what have you done to me?

Now McIlvaine's motioning for me to sing: "Follow the bouncing ball," he says, and because this is the man I have chosen to hear my confession, I do, adding my baritone to the soprano and the growl, one golden oldie after another, and feeling the same love for You, tears welling hot in my throat, as when in the pulpit, with my congregation, I belted out, *A mighty fortress is our God . . .*

=

—Background on the EJ synagogue: there are no social services provided, no day care, Hebrew school, and so forth, and for the time being, in what Joshua Gruen described as its first phase, the effort of instruction is directed toward adults. Congregants with children are encouraged to enroll them in Reform synagogue classes for their religious instruction, though Sarah is happy to integrate the bar mitzvah or bat mitzvah service into the Saturday morning meeting.

The essence of the EJ approach is to take the various aspects of Jewish teaching and practice, consider their historic sources or origins and their theological rationale and, insofar as possible, hold them up to modern scholarship and begin to separate what appears to be inessential, or intellectually untenable, or simply, blindly, customary . . . from what is truly crucial and defining.

Insofar as possible this method is incorporated into the weekly Sabbath service on Friday evening, with the Saturday morning service more or less a replay. With the coming around of the various holidays there is an additional opportunity to maintain the inquiry on a topical basis. Every service has a traditional liturgical beginning and ending (in English of course) but an extended effort of examination as its middle. This is not in the form of a sermon by the rabbi but of a rabbinically directed seminar discussion. I have found most interesting so far the several weeks given over to the documentary hypothesis of biblical authorship. There are of course reading lists provided by the rabbi, and there is a small but growing library for the use of the congregants, and so the radical EJ, is, ironically, a kind of continuing-ed yeshiva.

Pem and Sarah agreed that his preconversion studies should be conducted by a rabbi other than her—he meets weekly with a former colleague of hers at Temple Emanuel. My friend is profoundly grateful to have been circumcised as an infant. "Jesus," he said to me, "that would be one hell of a test of the faith." There is another conversion ritual less assiduously held to by the Reformed—a ritual bath or immersion in a mikvah—but he wants to do that. "In front of three witnessing rabbis you duck yourself naked in the pool, and when you come up you're reborn as a son of Abraham. As a dissolving Christian I find that comforting," he says. "Has a nice Baptist quality."

"Pem, tell me truly, how much does your converting have to do with wanting to marry Sarah?"

"How can I answer that? She has everything to do with it. And nothing. I don't like the question."

"I had to ask."

"Trouble with the secular mind. Always looking for the percentages. Scale of values, one to ten. This is a reason I became a religious in the first place, you know. The possibility of an indivisible good, something with no parts. Sarah is my conversion, my conversion is Sarah. We will have a holy marriage, but this is all a continuation for me of my sadness that the followers of Jesus led us down the wrong path. A two-thousand-year detour. I don't mean the beauty of the ethics, of the man. I mean the theology. I mean when they stepped him up in rank from prophet. Gave him familial ties. Does that answer your question?"

"Pretty well."

"You don't have your tape recorder today."

"I gave it up."

"You know, it may have been Isaiah who left them the opening. He should have made it clear, the messianic idea as a longing, a navigating principle, redemptive not on arrival but in never quite getting here. He didn't make that clear, old Isaiah. . . . I'm giving you gold, Everett."

"I'll remember."

"With Sarah, we're getting back to it. Though I'm not sure she realizes how far back it'll be. I've been doing my homework. The Jews did a lot of maundering themselves. We've got a long trek back through a thorny wood. But at least it's to the one God."

$$=$$

—Last night, Friday, the Synagogue of EJ was jammed, must have been thirty people in the room, I arrived late, found a seat in the bay window.

Sarah was in rabbinical black, the robe open over her street clothes. The Torah still in its simple vestment lay on the table before her. I looked for Pem and saw him sitting up in the first row.

They were doing their seminar. Tonight the codes of conduct, the mitzvoth, of which there are some six hundred thirteen, were the subject of discussion. A well-dressed middle-aged woman whom I did not remember having seen before was saying that though Reform Judaism had once discarded many of these ritual obligations, now it appeared as if such things as wearing a yarmulke, observing the dietary laws, and the liturgy in Hebrew were to be restored. Was the rabbi aware of this?

"Oh yes," Sarah said. "It was big news."

"So who are we to pursue this radicalism?" the woman said, addressing the congregation as if it were a jury, "when even the Reform rabbis are going back to the traditional ways." She sat down and waited for the rabbi's reply.

"Well, we have the same right of inquiry assumed by the generations before ours, including the Reformed, wouldn't you say? To accept, to reject? Or to change our minds, just as they have? The glory of Judaism is its intellectual democracy, though some would try to deny this . . ."

"The Orthodox," a man said.

"Not to name names," Sarah said, smiling.

With the increasing attendance at the EJ, there was a reiterative quality to the discussions, as Sarah was called upon by the newcomers to locate the EJ idea vis-à-vis the established branches. This was a growing problem for which the rabbi had not yet found a solution. She had printed up material outlining the synagogue's approach, but not everyone who came in picked it up and read it or, in reading it, was ready to accept it without question. She welcomed all newcomers, but the rising numbers were making the seminar model less workable than it had been in the days of the founding families.

The woman who had asked the question was somewhat heavily dressed, clearly used to a more formal Friday night worship, and probably a migrant from the Reformed persuasion she had just cited. People had to be satisfied that they were doing the right thing when they came up the stone steps to this unusual synagogue.

"These codes of conduct," Sarah said, "and the commentaries on the codes, and the rabbinical commentaries on the commentaries, all this is the group voice trying to enunciate over time what it means to be a civilized human being . . . but the key to all of this is 'over time.' So, here's my question: Has time stopped?"

Sarah held her hands out as if expecting an answer. She was really good. She was patient and smart and beautiful in a nonsexy rabbinical way, and she was in control.

"Today it is not just rabbis who are literate," she said. "That's point one. Point two, this is no longer the Bronze Age. I don't know about you, but I can't take seriously the sacred obligation regarding the ritual sacrifice of animals to appease or honor God. . . . Another instance: I don't think it is required of me in this century to wear a prayer shawl with fringes knotted at the corners as specified in Numbers so that I won't forget the Ten Commandments. I think I can be trusted not only to remember them but to live by them."

"Perhaps the rabbi knows better," another man piped up. "But what happens to the tradition, where do you draw the line—when there is nothing left?"

This again was not one of the regulars. I heard some murmurs of disapproval. But I now added to the code a six hundred fourteenth mitzvah, the ritual obligation to work the rabbi over before you deigned to join her congregation. The questions had been asked before, the answers had been given before, the debate was as sacramental as reading from the Torah, not just among the three branches but within congregations and within congregants. What observant Jew did not decide personally among the sacred obligations which were to be followed and which dispensed with?

"There is a line you draw and it's this: God is not honored by a mechanical adherence to each and every regulation but by going to the heart of them all, the ethics, and observing those as if your life is at stake, as it may well be, I mean, your moral life, your life of consequence as a good, reflective, just, and compassionate human being. Isn't that what Hillel meant? 'What is hateful to you, do not do to your neighbor. That is the whole Torah,' he said. 'The rest is commentary upon it.' "

The man spoke: "I for one observe the ritual Sabbath blessings of the bread and the candles. This is not a matter of ethics. This is what we do. This is the tradition."

I watched a beautiful flush rise from Sarah Blumenthal's throat to her cheeks. Her eyes shone. She folded her arms and thought about what she would say. I looked around at the expectant faces: Most of the congregation, if that is what we were, hoped our rabbi would comport herself brilliantly. I wondered if Pem understood what was going on. Every time a question was asked, he turned in his chair and glared at the person.

"I too say the blessing when I light the candles," Sarah said. "If a ritual takes us out of the ordinary range of feelings and directs our minds to the consideration of who we are and hope to be, it is ethically meaningful and there is no conflict. But let me ask you, what do we mean by tradition? We mean the devotions that have served historically to identify us to one another and to others. But the word *tradition* characterizes us, not God. Our longing, our obsessing. Our poetry, the epic of our people, but not—"

An elderly man stood up from his chair. "Excuse me, Rabbi," he said. "I am mostly on your side. But epic? Epic is for the Greeks!"

This brought laughter, and a couple of people applauded. The startled old man looked around with a grin and, emboldened, held the floor. "You know, I saw this was a synagogue on my walk a few months ago. I dropped in, I liked what I found, a modern young rabbi not afraid to ask questions, intellectual discussion of this and that, and a nice little service, though some things it takes some getting used to. Like I wasn't so happy with a co-ed minyan, but let that pass. This is a small congregation, nothing fancy, nobody putting on airs. And nobody hitting me up for the building fund. So if you new people are interested, fine, I can recommend this place. . . . But please, Rabbi," he said turning back to Sarah, "am I wrong that there are some things we must not question? For instance that the Torah was given by the Creator, blessed be His name. That we accept the yoke of the Kingdom of Heaven. Without this, never mind no tradition—it's no religion. Nothing."

I saw Pem slump in his chair and hold his hands to his head. It was that moment—he knew it well—when rationalism hits the wall.

The little man was receiving the appreciative remarks of the people sitting near him. Was I wrong, or did I see in Sarah Blumenthal's eyes at this moment a longing for her husband's resurrection? I had to wonder, not without some anger at myself, if she had depended on Joshua for her theology, if she was capable of carrying his ideas forward.

But now a heavyset man arose, an act that, given his size, was necessarily disruptive, with his chair scraping and nearly tipping over, and the people on either side of him leaning out of the way. He said to the rabbi: "Orthodox devotions that do not let in the light of modern knowledge are no more than a form of ancestor worship." The room went silent.

"You are saying"—turning to the little man—"that the ancients were in closer communication with the Creator than we ourselves. That they knew more, that they worked out everything that had to be worked out. And now it's all fixed and immutable. Doesn't that mean we are reverencing something or someone between us and God?"

The man was magisterial, with a large head of thick gray-black hair and startlingly rude features—the eyebrows bushy, the eyes heavy-lidded and bagged, deep lines descending from the corners of the prominent nose, and gate mouth, sagging cheeks. The voice was deep. "In the Shinto religion of Japan, ancestor worship is piety. In the synagogue, I should have thought, it is the opposite."

His words had brought Pem to his feet, or rather to turn and, with one knee on his chair, half raise himself to see who this was. When I had first come in the man had caught my attention, a broad-backed figure hunched over like Rodin's thinker, although less reflective than impatient. He had looked familiar, but I couldn't place him. Now, as he spoke, all at once it came to me.

"It was not a large world, ancient Israel," he was saying to no one in particular. "The Hebrews conceived of a cosmic God, a magnificent single God of the universe, but naturally in terms of their land and its crops and its tribal wars, and His up-and-down relationship with them. So He was localized to a great degree, the Creator, the applicable honorifics being Lord or King. All very understandable."

The speaker raised his head and addressed himself to the room. "But if you take the trouble to think of what we know today about the universe . . . how it is roughly fifteen billion years old, and how it suddenly inflated and has been expanding since, how space is ineluctably time, and time is ineluctably space, how gravity can bend it, how another force in space countermands gravity so that the universe doesn't collapse into itself . . . and how the universe in its perhaps ever increasing rate of expansion accommodates not just galaxies, which contain millions of stars, but multiple clusters of galaxies that are themselves strung out in clusters of clusters . . . and with all of this a dark matter we are yet to understand . . . well, it would seem to me that the Creator who originated the universe, or what may possibly be a number of universes of which this is the only one we are capable of perceiving . . . the Creator, blessed be His name, who can make solid reality, or what we perceive as reality, out of indeterminate, unpredictable wave/particle functions . . . or perhaps make everything our senses can note or our minds deduce . . . out of what finally may be the vibration of cosmic-string frequencies . . . that all this is from Himself, or Herself or Itself, who is by definition vaster and greater than all this . . . and has given living things evolving forms and the human species a slowly evolving consciousness that is barely beginning to appreciate the magnitude of what is being revealed. . . . Well, I am forced to ask the traditionalists among us if our Creator, of blessed name, is perhaps not insufficiently praised by our usage of the honorifics Lord and King, let alone Father and Shepherd. . . ."

The man sat. A long silence. The rabbi cleared her throat. "I think, now, perhaps it's time for the Kaddish?"

=

—"Everett, who was that!"

"It has to be Seligman. Bigger, heavier, and he combs his hair now. But it's Seligman, all right. Christ. Am I glad he didn't see me."

"Why? What's the matter with him?"

"Seligman was a shlub, he landed on people. Never had enough lunch money. Never paid attention in class. I had to tell him the plot of *Macbeth*."

"When was this?"

"At Science. He'd plop down next to me in study hall to copy my algebra homework."

"Where?"

"Bronx Science. That was my high school. The Bronx High School of Science."

"Wait a minute. . . . you don't mean Murray Seligman!"

"He never tied his shoelaces. His teeth were green."

"*The* Murray Seligman—the Nobelist in physics?"

"That too."

Pem peering into my eyes. A smile, slowly widening. "My oh my . . ."

"What, my oh my?"

"Who told him about the EJ? He just walk in?"

"How should I know? Ask Sarah."

"She probably won't know either. It doesn't matter anyway."

He leans across the table, puts his hand on the back of my neck, and kisses me on the forehead. "Ways of God. You'll just have to take my word for it. This is the Divinity Detective you're talking to."

"Pem—"

"What happened this evening was signal."

"Oh right. Murray the jerk who nearly blew up the chem lab. He was such a slob they wouldn't let him do the experiments. Don't give me that!"

"Give you what? What am I giving you? I'm not attributing anything to the slob. I'm attributing to the occasion. I'll tell you something, Everett. As a secularist, you don't understand—if there is a religious agency in our lives, it has to appear in the manner of our times. Not from on high, but a revelation that hides itself in our culture, it will be ground-level, on the street, it'll be coming down the avenue in the traffic, hard to tell apart from anything else. It will be cryptic, discerned over time, piecemeal, to be communally understood at the end like a law of science."

"Yeah, they'll put it on a silicon chip."

"For shame! These are democratic times, Everett. We're living in a postmodern democracy. You think God doesn't know that?"

"I need a drink."

"Waiter, another round! . . . What are you so upset about?"

"I don't know."

"You're upset because you're implicated."

"Give me a break."

Pem begins to laugh, a great chesty, robust baritone laugh. "You're upset because it's coming through you! As the cross arriving on the roof of the synagogue, as I have fallen in love with Sarah Blumenthal, as the great Nobel Prize–winning physicist who showed up this evening is the jerk who copied your homework at Bronx Science . . . and as you have erroneously, gloriously assumed you could write a book about it!"

—Sarah Blumenthal's Address to the Conference of American Studies in Religion, Washington, D.C.

In the twentieth century about to end, the great civilizer on earth seems to have been doubt. Doubt, the constantly debated and flexible inner condition of theological uncertainty, the wish to believe in balance with rueful or nervous or grieving skepticism, seems to have held people in thrall to ethical behavior, while the true believers, of whatever stamp, religious or religious-statist, have done the murdering. The impulse to excommunicate, to satanize, to eradicate, to ethnically cleanse, is a religious impulse. In the practice and politics of religion, God has always been a license to kill. But to hold in abeyance and irresolution any firm convictions of God, or of an afterlife with Him, warrants walking in His spirit, somehow. And among the doctrinaire religious, I find I trust those who gravitate toward symbolic comfort rather than those who reaffirm historic guarantees. It is just those uneasy promulgators of traditional established religion who are not in lockstep with its customs and practices, or who are chafing under doctrinal pronouncements, or losing their congregations to charismatics and stadium-filling conversion performers, who are the professional religious I trust. The faithful who read Scripture in the way Coleridge defined the act of reading poetry or fiction, i.e., with a "willing suspension of disbelief."

Yet they must be true to themselves and understand theirs is a compromised faith. Something more is required of them. Something more . . .

I ask the question: Is it possible that the behavioral commandments of religion, its precipitate ethics or positive social values, can be maintained without reference to the authority of God? In my undergraduate seminar in metaphysics at Harvard, the professor said there can be no *ought*, no categorical imperative in Kantian terms, no action from an irresistible conscience, without a supreme authority. But that does not quite address the point. I ask if after the exclusionary, the sacramental, the ritualistic, and simply fantastic elements of religion are abandoned, can a universalist ethics be maintained—*in its numinousness*? To a certain extent, in advanced industrial democracies, such behavior is already codified with reference to no higher authority than civil law. If our Constitution not only separated church and state but adapted as the basis of civil law something of the best essence of the

Judeo-Christian ethical system, was there not only a separation but an appropriation, which largely goes unremarked by our more passionate preachers?

Suppose then that in the context of a hallowed secularism, the idea of God could be recognized as Something Evolving, as civilization has evolved—that God can be redefined, and recast, as the human race trains itself to a greater degree of metaphysical and scientific sophistication. With the understanding, in other words, that human history does show a pattern at least of progressively sophisticated metaphors. So that we pursue a teleology thus far that, in the universe as vast as the perceivable cosmos, and as infinitesimal as a subatomic particle, has given us only the one substantive indication of itself—that we, as human beings, live in moral consequence.

In this view the supreme authority is not God, who is sacramentalized, prayed to, pleaded with, portrayed, textualized, or given voice, choir, or temple walls, but God who is imperceptible, ineffable, except . . . for our evolved moral sense of ourselves.

Constitutional scholars are accustomed to speak of the American civil religion. But perhaps two hundred or so years ago something happened, in terms not of national history but of human history, that has yet to be realized. To understand what that is may be the task of the moment for our theologians. But it involves the expansion of ethical obligation democratically to be directed all three hundred and sixty degrees around, not just upon one's co-religionists, a daily indiscriminate and matter-of-fact reverence of human rights unself-conscious as a handshake. Dare we hope the theologians might emancipate themselves, so as to articulate or perceive another possibility for us in our quest for the sacred? Not just a new chapter but a new story?

There may not be much time. If the demographers are right, ten billion people will inhabit the earth by the middle of the coming century. Huge megacities of people all over the planet fighting for its resources. And perhaps with only the time-tested politics of God on their side to see them through. Under those circumstances, the prayers of mankind will sound to heaven as shrieks. And such abuses, shocks, to our hope for what life can be, as to make the twentieth century a paradise lost.

Thank you.

═══

—Songbirds: Skylark . . . Red Red Robin . . . Bluebird of Happiness . . .

═══

—Of course movies today no longer require film. They are recorded and held in digital suspension as ones and zeroes. And so at the moment the last remaining piece of the world is lit and shot for a movie, there will be another Big Bang . . . and the multitudes of ones and zeroes will be strewn through the universe as particles that act like waves . . . until, shaken by borealic winds or ignited by solar flares or otherwise galvanized by this or that heavenly signal, they compose themselves into brilliant constellations that shine in full color across the night sky of a remote planet . . . where a reverent, unrecognizable form of life will look up from its rooftops at the faces of Randolph Scott, Gail Russell, George Brent, Linda Darnell . . . to name just a few of the stars.

═══

—I anticipate not being invited to the wedding. From remarks Pem has made, I think it will be a simple five-minute event down at city hall. Flowers from the peddler at the curb. Echoing catacomb-like corridors of marble. ID and marriage license in one hand, divorce papers in the other. Ministry of the Civil Service: windowless room with stained-glass insets.

They used to do this feature regularly in the papers, lovers forging their fate with civic blessing. Picture of the line of couples and their chosen witnesses, handsome West Indians, scared and pale eighteen-year-olds from Queens, sturdy young Latinos in tropical colors, stylish, lots of laughter, ready to break out dancing, a quiet older couple holding hands. Pem and Sarah. This is their principled decision—the municipal sacrament.

Maybe Seligman will be their witness.

Now I am thinking of the marriage night. It is unpleasant imagining any two people you know making love, but I have no trouble here, this is such a pure thing, such plighted troth, there is nothing pornographic about it, Pem lowers his clumsy adoring being on Sarah, her hands wander over his back like the learning fingers of a sightless person, he is practically weeping for joy, he tucks a strand of her hair behind her ear just the way she does when she's bent over the Torah, he touches her mouth, and when they kiss there is nothing at work in his mind, no running commentary, the indissoluble self is dissolved. I say it is dark, it is late, the boys are asleep on the floor below, but the dimmest light from the street seems to gravitate to her eyes which shine dark as plums. I can't imagine what it is like for her, but as she guides him, holds him, he sinks into total recognition, as if they have always made love, as if they have been man and wife for a practiced time. There is no sense of discovery, of a new knowledge, and whatever her particularities of flesh and bone, they are transformed instantly into the only shape and structure that it is possible for a woman to have . . .

Pem hasn't completed his conversion studies, but I don't think they will wait to marry, Sarah in her progressivism coming out to meet him halfway, as it were. He said to me last night that he has never felt as completely, wholly Christian in his life as he does now, studying to be a Jew.

Pem, I told him, maybe you better not say that to anyone else.

Why? It's true.

Are you sure you've got the right perspective on this?

Well, I admit, part of my thinking is in the nature of making spiritual reparations, so to speak. Maybe that's where it began. But it's more than that now. I feel liberated, restored to my mind, my intellect is being admitted into my faith. Everything is coming together, it's all so logical. I have never felt as honest, as without misgivings in my belief in the Creator. It is unattached to mythology. It is nonpictorial. Admittedly there's a lot of pseudohistorical clutter in Judaism too, but that's what Sarah and Joshua founded EJ for, to get back to the crucial first things. And that's what we will do. For me, now, Judaism is Christianity without Christ, and I have a glad heart.

A glad heart. I like that.

It's more than a fucking phrase, Everett. It's a real feeling-state.

Okay.

Migod, there is something about the secular disdain that is really awful.

I don't have the secular disdain.

You would do better with a glad heart than the secular disdain.

I do all right. I like birds, I like women, I like language. These foolish things gladden the heart.

Do you know, Everett, what the anthropic principle is? It is quite simple: that our universe, having exploded into existence at an inflationary rate, and spent billions of years swathed in an opacity of gases before photons brought light into space and everything cooled—

Wait a minute, what are we on to now?

Seligman told me this—after photons lit things up enough to create the furnaces of stars in their galaxies and stellar dust and dark matter . . . well, from all this perturbation just those elements were created that allowed for the appearance of human life. That is the anthropic principle. Whatever the universe is composed of seems to have made us possible.

Seligman told you that?

It's an idea kicking around among the cosmologists.

Is that the best they can come up with? The self-evident anthropic principle?

Well why it's useful to them, it smooths out some of their problems. They are in less of a bind if it turns out that there are other universes besides this one that may not have the necessary components for human consciousness.

Like what?

Like hydrogen and carbon and space and time and such.

I see.

But ours has these things that allow us to be having this conversation. I'm telling you just so you know there are some secularists who do not have the secular disdain.

—A little thought experiment: If we were to build a rocket ship and send it off into space, and this rocket ship were equipped to feel like home, with roads and houses, lawn chairs, VCRs, Kmarts, football fields, and wars . . . the space traveler, upon awakening, would not be able to tell if he was on earth in the usual orbit or drifting forever, irrevocably and without remediation, through the anthropic universe. You see how simple it is?

—And so it's done, they were married downtown in the middle of the week, and I was right in not expecting to be best man, there was no best man, there was a best woman, Joshua Gruen's sister. I understand that, I understand why Sarah would make that choice, the thoughtfulness of it, the acknowledgment, in the midst of her joy, of her loss, the loss to both of them. A large, meaningful choice enacting the impeccable ethics of Sarah.

The sister's name is Judy, she's a psychiatric social worker, midthirties, small dark-haired woman wearing a corsage, trim little figure, quite nice, just a little tearful as we sit talking in the Senate Room of the Jefferson residential hotel on East Seventy-second Street on this Sunday afternoon.

"I'm happy for Sarah," Judy says. "She's a wonderful person. She and my brother were a marriage made in heaven. But after everything she's been through, she deserves some happiness. I think this is good for the kids, too."

Judy's husband, Al Something, teaches English at some community college in New Jersey—he is not that convinced. Pepper-and-salt beard, which he strokes as he watches Pem, who at the moment is dancing and chatting away with an elderly white-haired lady.

"I don't believe in conversion," Al says. "I don't think it's possible. What do you call a Christian Marrano?" he says to me.

Around the small dance floor are several tables with white cloths at which the guests sit nibbling on the hot and cold hors d'oeuvres. A bar to one side, the bartender not overworked, it's a sherry and soft-drink crowd. I go over, and when I ask for a double vodka on the rocks, his face lights up.

Maybe fifty, sixty people, most of whom I don't know, the extended relationships of Pem and Sarah. It will take me a while, but I will come to understand that on one side sit the Pems and on the other the Sarahs, not a combination conducive to partying, no horas on the dance floor, the combo plays dance music, slow-swinging, gentle—piano, sax, guitar, bass. They're not bad. But in this crowd, when someone gets up to dance everyone watches.

On these occasions it's always a strain connecting the principals, your friends, to the relatives and friends from their past. Another world. You have the feeling that the wedding guests are just those people whom the bride and groom have spent their lives trying to escape. I am surprised on two counts, one that there is any wedding reception at all, and two that it is here at this stuffy hotel. But this is the residence of Sarah's dowager aunt, the late mother's older sister, Myrna Fein. Seeing her instruct one of the waiters, I understand this is her show.

As I think about it, I don't know how Sarah has been able to keep her establishment going. How much Joshua could have left her in insurance, whether there was money in his family, or if there's a mortgage on their synagogue. . . . Money doesn't seem to be a problem. I know Pem is broke, but I don't have the feeling she is. Yet her father as a lifelong academic could never have been that well-heeled. And nursing homes are expensive. How can anyone write a proper novel without talking about money?

Judy and her husband get up to dance. They greet Pem and Sarah, who are now together on the dance floor. The two couples fox-trot in a kind of open half-embrace as they talk. Pem gesticulates with his free hand. They all laugh, even sister Judy's skeptical husband.

Sarah is wearing an ivory suit with a bronze silk blouse that picks up the lights in her hair. Her hair is longer now and tied simply behind her neck, in the style of an American revolutionary. Her ears are unadorned. I see she is not wearing her specs for the occasion, for a moment she looks past the others straight at me, but I realize she is too nearsighted, too beautifully, radiantly nearsighted, to actually see me.

And here is Myrna Fein, the hostess, bearing down on the guest who sits alone. Settles in the chair beside mine. A stout woman, a round pretty face, heavily made up. Huffs and puffs to catch her breath, staring at me all the while.

"So you're the writer . . ."

"I am."

"Are you married? I don't see a wife here."

"No."

"Are you divorced?"

"I'm a confirmed bachelor."

"That's nothing to be proud of. My eyes tell me you're approaching the age when you'd better find a woman to take care of you. You wait too long, what woman will want the job?"

"Thank you for your very good advice, Myrna."

"You're patronizing me. When my husband died ten years ago, I took over his business. A parts supplier to General Motors. I sold it last year for forty-five million dollars. And I'm telling you, you don't want to be the perennial extra man at my Sarah's table."

Whammo.

"I know all about you," she says. "I've got eyes, I'm not as stupid as you think."

Across the room, I find the little bishop. He looks older and smaller in civvies. He is relieved to see me. "I'm not sure just how to proceed," he says. "Do you happen to know if anyone is going to give a benediction?"

I glance at Pem on the dance floor. He has a glass in his hand. His arm is around Sarah's waist and he is swaying to the music as he talks to two young women, who look oddly familiar.

"I think Pem will eventually say something."

"I'll wait then. Frankly I don't know what is appropriate. He is so full of surprises, I've been watching this man for thirty years now and he still surprises me. But she is a handsome woman, his bride. Striking-looking, in fact." He smiles. "Rabbis aren't usually that good-looking."

I see Pem waving at me. I go over and he introduces me to the two young women. They're his daughters, Kimberly and Pamela. Kim and Pam. Now I see the resemblance: Both have the Pemberton jaw, the large head, they are what the department stores call plus-sized, Kim is the blonde, Pam is the brunette. They are smiling broadly, two sets of bright white teeth. Little children come running up between us, one belonging to Kim, one to Pam, they pull away and scatter before they can be introduced, and everyone is laughing, the mothers shaking their heads in mock resignation. Pem puts his arm around my shoulders. "This is the man who is writing my spiritual biography. He's going to make me famous," he tells them. "Your father will be on all the talk shows."

"Oh, Daddy, don't exaggerate."

"I'll make you proud of me yet."

"Oh, Daddy, we're already proud of you," the blonde says, looking suddenly quite unhappy.

When his girls are gone, Pem takes me by the arm and walks me to the side of the room. "We found out yesterday the son of a bitch died two months ago."

"What son of a bitch?"

"Schmid, Schmitz, whatever the fuck his name was. The Nazi who ran the ghetto. Died in his sleep. A home in Yonkers. We had him good and nailed, too. Damn!"

"Well he's dead, anyway."

"He never had to stand up in court and let the world take a look at him for what he was."

"Yes, well that's why Dante invented hell."

"Dante didn't invent hell. He furnished it. Your glass is empty, come with me. And then, properly armed, you will meet some of my Virginia meshpochehs."

My friend the bartender fixes me up, but Pem is gone when I turn around. A small pack of children and some gawky preteen girls, unaccustomed to dresses and hose, have gathered around a table on which the wedding gifts have been collected. Every gift is beautifully wrapped and unopened, but just the idea of presents is enough to have attracted these children. They stare and whisper to one another. I see among them Sarah's two sons, Jake and Davey, and their attention to this pile of shiny white boxes with white ribbons is more proprietary than curious. They don't want the others to touch anything.

When I appear they all scatter. On the table among the gifts are elaborate baskets of flowers. I check the cards: One from a Rabbi and Mrs. So and So, one from nurses at the hospice on Roosevelt Island, another from Trish vanden Meer ("Congratulations to both of you," her message from the heart). The largest display of all, a great elaborate horseshoe of flowers with a pennant printed with the words *God Bless Pops and Mrs. Pops* and is signed "From all your friends at the Church of the Sweet Vision."

I am feeling hot, the hotel is overheated, I go to a window but it won't open. Frost is on the windowpanes, winter is icumen in. As soon as I've finished my drink I will leave. I find myself resentful that Pem and Sarah all this time have had lives and relationships other than their life and relationship with me. I wonder if I'm losing the ability to hold my liquor.

But moments later everything is all right once again, Sarah has taken my arm and led me to the dance floor. The combo is playing "My Blue Heaven" in a lively tempo, I have never before touched this woman except to shake her hand, I am holding her now, my hand is in the small of her back, I am connected to her animacy of being, I hold her ringed hand in my other hand, I can feel her heat, she is flushed with her happiness, there is a clean herbal scent coming off her hair, she is laughing at my solemnized slow-time dance step to the fast-time beat, but I mean it, I mean my solemnity, she understands and puts her cheek against mine, and my knees nearly buckle. "You will always be our friend, Everett," she says in my ear, and I am about to declare something spectacularly foolish when, fortunately, her wretched older boy, Jake, taps me on the elbow to cut in. I bow to him. And Sarah dances away with her son in his starched white shirt and red tie and unusually well combed hair, her arms outstretched, and looking down on his solemnity of concentration in the healing pleasure of her serene love.

—I'm trying to remember everything that Pem said when he got up and grasped the cordless microphone. The band stopped playing and he stood there swaying slightly while the room went silent. His double-breasted blazer hung open, his tie was loosened, his forehead triumphantly cowlicked.

"Friends," he said, "I will not speak of my happiness, of my prayerful thanks to the Lord, may His name be blessed, that my dear love Sarah Blumenthal has found me worthy of her attention. You can believe that I will passionately live what's left of my life to earn what she has given me. I will soon be a Jew. I will find the joy of a hallowed life by her side in observance of the Commandments and the enactment of the simple rituals that were devised by the ancients to incite our humility and urge us to a perception of the holy. I am trying to say this without using the word *communion*," he said, smiling shyly, and a few people laughed.

"Yet since I'm technically still a Christian, I suppose that for the moment I stand with one foot in each tradition—although traditions are not loci, are they. One foot in each camp? That's not right either, camps, opposing sides, furthest thing from my ecumenically correct mind . . ."

He paused, lost in thought. People were stirring, looking wary. Not Sarah, she was fascinated, gazing at Pem with her two boys leaning back in her arms as she sat at the table with her first husband's relatives.

"In any event the Jew that I almost am tells me that once my conversion is affirmed by the rabbinate, I need no longer be burdened by the idea of the millennium, which is the calendrical construct of the Christian tradition—I mean as some significant event in history, some turning point, some symbolic means, at least, of looking back, or up, and of taking stock. I will have tapped into a different set of numbers entirely, a number set just as arbitrary, of course, but somehow less mythologically loaded and media-attended.

"So the fact that my dear Sarah and I happen to have married at the very end of this last century of the Christian millennium may have no significance at all, except insofar as it causes us to reflect and to remember that our coming together, as blessed as that is, and as morally resonant, even to the point, perhaps, of proceeding from a mysterious imperative . . . I say we cannot help but reflect that our union has depended on the continuing catastrophe of our generations, the crisis of the time of our own lives and the lives of our parents and grandparents, and that it could not have occurred except in the wake of death, the death of her father's childhood, the death of her dear, intrepid, brilliant rabbinical partner, Joshua, father of her sons Jacob and David . . . and, not impossibly, the death of redemption, of hope, for the entire species.

"So with this in mind a prayer of lingering numerical awareness may not, after all, be inappropriate. I want to say this prayer or petition as my final act as a Christian and an ex–Christian priest. You need not bow your heads . . .

"Dear Lord, blessed be Your name, I speak to you in one of our intonative systems of clicks and grunts, glottal stops and trills. There have been monstrously evil mortifiers of humanity in the historic generations of every adult in this room, in our own lives and the lives of our mothers and fathers, grandmothers and grandfathers. . . . Evil debasers of human life have been responsible collectively for the enslavement and horrible death of many tens of millions of human beings. An exponential murder of souls has gone on, a torture and agony of demolishment, in wars, in genocides, with the masses of the violently dead in our century consigned by their very numbers to the lists of anonymous oblivion. And they are not resurrectable, they cannot and will not resurrect even in the imagination of your Christian faithful.

"I am not going to get into the question of how a supposedly omniscient God such as Yourself would allow these human catastrophes to occur, though your record even before this century has not been all that commendable, but I will tell you . . . the relentless and unimaginable genocidal cruelties shuddering across the world in our age have brought You into disrepute, and the uninhibited degradation of the idea of life has thrown some of us into the despair of cursing Your name and impugning Your existence.

"Even among those of us clinging to a love of You and an irrepressible longing for Your love . . . there is a risen suspicion, that You are part of the problem. Men use You at will for their most hideous purposes. You do not seem to resist—anyone who wants You, and for whatever foul, murderous reason, can have You. You are bought and embraced like the lowest, most pathetic streetwalker. And the world You have created, or that has used You to create itself, suffers not only the headline killers of our century, the contemptuous rulers of tribes and nations, but the miserable, wretched numbers of the rest of us, who inhabit the back pages and work in symbolic emulation of their spirit, living fervently to enrich ourselves at the expense of others, so that even in our most advanced industrial democracies life is adversarial, and the social contract breaks down continually, as if we were not meant to be justly governed nations but confederacies of murderous gluttons.

"And so as I consider the headline killers of the century . . . the dictators, despots, homicidal tribalists, generals, colonels, and ministers of righteousness, carelessly murdering kings and revolutionists who have taken our lives and assassinated our souls . . . I know in my own sinful heart and from the depths of my craven being that they are cast in history from the human die, they are my kind . . . stamped out of my genetic code . . . and with a family resemblance so unmistakable as to set me to weeping in terror and despair.

"Do you not find this a grave challenge to your existence, Lord, that we do these things to one another? That for all our theological excuse making, and despite the moral struggles and the intellectual and technical advances of human history, we live enraged—quietly or explosively, but always greedily enraged? Do you not find it an unforgivable lapse of Yours that after these thousands of years we can no more explain ourselves than we can explain You?"

Here a pause, and in the silence, Pem turned and picked up a glass from the table behind him and drank—what? Water? Vodka? I couldn't tell. But he had all the time in the world, this was an audience riven, after all he had spoken from pulpits for years and knew what he was doing. But I had never heard him deliver a sermon and I was as astounded as everyone else. I did manage to glance over at the bishop, who had turned pale and was sitting in his chair as if roped to it.

"Lord, if You were to give evidence of a real hell," Pem said, "not the invention of our inflamed imaginations, but a real one, with the right people in it, I would have some hope for You as You have been traditionally conceived. . . . If you were to cause the odious monstrous being of Satan to flourish in the nether depths of the superstring universe as we once believed he flourished in the depths of our own geology, and devise him of such mass, so huge and cold and of such gravity that nothing could ever escape from him that is drawn into him as into one of the black holes of the universe . . . and if you were to let him be anguishedly made of physical self-contradiction, ice and flame, peculiarly crustaceous but pulpy skin and, say"—here he sent a glance over to the group of children at the side of the room—"with multiple eyes cataracted with congealed blood and with slimy claws and tendrils to reach his every extremity, all of him stinking and loathsome . . . and if you were to show us the headline killers of our century, the murderous rulers of tribes and nations, agglutinated in his embrace while over billions of years he roared his sickening excoriating breath into their faces, and vomited his foul waste alive with squirmy larvae and dung beetles over them while languidly absorbing them into his hideous being . . . and if you were to make him particularly solicitous of that gibbering, bug-eyed, teeth-gnashing asshole of the German national religion, and that steely slit-eyed peasant shit-brain of the Russian revolutionary religion, and that little colonialist bastard exterminator-king of the civilized Belgians, and that stone-faced rouge-cheeked killer cretin of the South Asian jungles . . . as well as all the torturers of the banana republics, island tyrants of the Caribbean and Pacific seas, tribal thugs of Africa, and ethnic-cleansing goons of the Balkans—and if for good measure you were to throw in all their bankers and arms suppliers, and their loyal legions of rapers, impalers, beheaders, bludgeoners, bayoneters, machine gunners, machete wielders, death squad kidnappers, crematoria designers, and slave camp administrators . . . and let their own foul pollutions of being act as stings and allergens to so torment Satan that he would attempt with his fiery foul breath to melt the agonizing ice of which he is composed and wash them from him . . . who in their turn would cling more perversely to his suppurating skin and suffer ever more agonizedly and in ever increasing torments of consciousness as slowly . . . over thousands of millennia they were absorbed into his icy guts, cell by exquisitely tormented cell . . . until they were one with him, alive and screaming in the hell of his black icy being, forever and ever . . . well then, well then, Lord, I think I could remain your priest . . ."

Pem took out a handkerchief and mopped his brow. He said now almost in a whisper: "But as it is, I think we must remake You. If we are to remake ourselves, we must remake You, Lord. We need a place to stand. We are weak, and puny, and totter here in our civilization. . . . We have only our love for each other for our footing, our marriages, the children we hold in our arms, it is only this wavery sensation, flowing and ebbing, that justifies our consciousness and keeps us from plunging out of the universe. Not enough. It's not enough. We need a place to stand.

"I ask for reason to hope that this travail of our souls will find its resolution in You, Lord, You of Blessed Name. For the sake of all of us on this little planet of Yours I ask this. Amen."

Pem returned the microphone to the bandleader. Sarah rose from her chair and came across the floor and hugged Pem, and kissed him, and as he held her around the waist, she leaned back in his arms and brushed the hair from his forehead.

—In a gallery on lower Broadway, the artist has put down a model railroad track with a train going round and round, the engine of which is welded to the visored headpiece of a suit of medieval armor. So an expressionless iron face mask is leading the train round and round. Trouble is, the train keeps running off the track and the lovely young woman in charge has to get down on her knees and, with her high heels flopping and her tight-skirted and quite shapely ass presenting itself to the onlooker, she must set the train wheels back on the track . . . and as this happens three or four times while I'm trying to look at the other quirky installations in the gallery, I have to wonder if she too isn't part of the artist's intention. I hope so.

A few of the artists are doing wonderfully insouciant and blunderingly lovely things amidst all the ordinary art in our time. I like this fellow who goes around the world wrapping whatever he can get his hands on . . . the Reichstag in Berlin looking like an unusually large package delivered by UPS . . . or, in a Swiss park, the grove of trees bagged in polyester . . . or the Pont-Neuf done in saffron silk, all these rippling shimmering scrims through which light can pass, outlines revealed. . . . He ran miles of open umbrellas along the California coast and wants to come to Central Park and staple it with rows of steel gates flying nylon flaps of gold. Let him come, Mayor. Let him come, Commissioners. I like the idea of out-of-scale art as world occupation, planetary embrace, I like the inverse relations of such projects, the coolness of the years of planning, the huge amounts of money . . . for the capricious result, the abruptly reconformed and freshly wild appropriated public space. I like the outrage of making ephemeral art of the city, the land.

Another haunting artist has been going through the cities of Europe projecting ghostly photographs of the dead on the same buildings in the same windows and on the same sidewalks where they once lived. In a doorway in Berlin, an old Jewish scholar stands with his books, on another street a family posing in front of the apartment building from which they will be deported, in Amsterdam a company of marching German troops shines down from a window . . . all these spectral images coming on at night for cars to drive past, passersby to walk through, hurry away from, shudder at, as the past conflates with the present and time and space compress to a point.

Bring him to New York, this artist, let him do us! Bring art out of the closet, into the street, bring back the artists who have themselves spray-painted and hung inside picture frames, let the artist who likes to tie himself in a canvas bag and lie down in front of traffic tie himself in a canvas bag and lie down in front of the traffic. . . . And where is John Cage when we need him, or is he still here, with his uncopyrighted music of the world's sounds, every whirring motor, every birdcall, every heartbeat . . . and with each moment of apparent silence the realized art of his consciousness?

I call for cabaret to be spoken in tongues . . . for one giant symphony to be made of all the Irving Berlin songs . . . and let there be an upbeat animated Disney production of Wittgenstein's *Tractatus Logico-Philosophicus*. We need all this, I think it must happen, we need for this to happen here in the city.

≡

—Every city has a museum, a park, a church with a steeple, a public school system, and a ball team. Every city has a bank. Every city has a courthouse and a jail. Every city has a hospital. The larger cities have these things in multiples. The larger cities have highways running through them. They have rivers with bridges over the rivers and tunnels under the rivers. They have subways, els, and streetcars, downtown skyscrapers, theaters and opera houses, and neighborhoods of fashionable, less fashionable, and unfashionable addresses. They have outlying districts of warehouses and factories and freight yards, airports, electric power stations, waterworks, and sewage treatment plants. They have slums. They have systems of invisible conduction—radio waves, television signals, cellular phone networks—to link their populations and transact their business.

It has taken time and the blundering wisdom and anarchic greed of our ancestry to construct the modern city of consolidated institutions. It is a great historically amassed communal creation. If you fly above it at night, it is a jeweled wonder of the universe, floating like a giant liner on the sea of darkness. It is smart, accomplished, sophisticated, and breathtakingly beautiful. And it glimmers and sparkles as all things breakable glimmer and sparkle. You wonder how much God had to do with this, how much of the splendor and insolence of the modern city creatively built from the disparate intentions of generations of men comes of the inspiration of God. Because it is the city of the unremarked God, the sometime-thing God, the God of history.

—The movie from this: And now more and more people are born into it. The wretched of the earth stream into it. All at once it passes its point of self-containment. Its economy is insufficient. It becomes less able to employ, to house and feed the crowds that hunker about in its streets. As the smog thickens and the rising global temperatures bring on intolerable heat waves, droughts, hurricanes, and monumental snowfalls, the sustaining rituals of the society break down and ideas of normal daily life erode. The city begins to lose its shape, its outlines blur as its precincts expand, and the class distinctions of its neighborhoods are no longer discernible. Crimes against property increase. The food supply is erratic, power blackouts come with greater and greater frequency, the water arrives contaminated, the police forces are armed like soldiers, and inflation makes money useless. Prophets arise in their clerical robes to speak of evil, to speak of irreverence and blasphemy. They announce that the wrath of God has come down on the city of unnatural pride, the earthly city. They call upon the pious to destroy the city. And the unremarked God, the sometime-thing God, is alive once again, resurrected in all His fury.

Politicians arise who decide the city is adaptable to any political abstraction impressed upon it. Strange diseases appear for which the doctors have no cure. Schools are closed. They become neighborhood armories. Plagues break out, hospital corridors become morgues, the elected leaders declare martial law, troops are everywhere, and the befouled shantytowns that have sprung up on the metropolitan outskirts are routinely swept by machine-gun fire. When the God-soaked impoverished mobs rush upon the city, they are massacred. The military mount a coup, the elected leaders who called them in are jailed, a governing junta closes down all television and radio stations, home computers are declared illegal, and around the beleaguered enclaves of the wealthy, high walls are built with periodically spaced guard towers.

It becomes a political commonplace resisted not even by theorists of the democratic left that totalitarian management, enforced sterilization procedures, parentage grants issued to the genetically approved, and an ethos of rational triage are the only hope for the future of civilization.

At this point we are introduced to the hero and heroine of the movie, a vitally religious couple who run a small progressive synagogue on the Upper West Side.

ABOUT THE AUTHOR

E. L. Doctorow's work is published in thirty
languages. His novels include *Welcome to
Hard Times*, *The Book of Daniel*, *Ragtime*,
Loon Lake, *Lives of the Poets*, *World's Fair*,
Billy Bathgate, and *The Waterworks*. Among
his honors are the National Book Award,
two National Book Critics Circle awards, the
PEN/Faulkner Award, the Edith Wharton
Citation for Fiction, the William Dean How-
ells Medal of the American Academy of Arts
and Letters, and the presidentially conferred
National Humanities Medal. He lives and
works in New York.

ABOUT THE TYPE

This book was set in Galliard, a typeface designed by Matthew Carter for the Merganthaler Linotype Company in 1978. Galliard is based on the sixteenth-century typefaces of Robert Granjon.